PRAISE FOR

Chosen Ones

"With *Chosen Ones*, Veronica Roth keeps you guessing: playing with perception, multiverse theory, and the struggles that go along with being 'chosen' to save the world . . . She's created a universe that you never want to leave."

—Amber Benson, author of *The Witches of Echo Park*

"A hugely imagined, twisty, turning tale that leads through the labyrinths of magic and war to the center of the heart."

—Diana Gabaldon, author of *Go Tell the Bees That I Am Gone* from the *New York Times* best-selling Outlander series

"*Chosen Ones* by Veronica Roth is the cure for all those humdrum 'one true savior' narratives. This dark, complex novel rocked my heart and left me with a renewed sense that saving the world is a job that never ends. Roth's version of magic is as flawed and fascinating as her characters, and her story keeps you guessing until the wild conclusion. You'll never look at fantasy heroes the same way again."

—Charlie Jane Anders, Hugo and Nebula Award–winning author of *The City in the Middle of the Night*

"With *Chosen Ones*, Veronica Roth has pulled off a virtuoso performance, conjuring a stunning thriller/fantasy/sci-fi chimera like nothing I've read before, a story of ex-heroes struggling with the trauma of their past, what it means to have once saved the world, and the dark side of destiny."

—Blake Crouch, *New York Times* best-selling author of *Recursion*

"Roth somehow manages to make universe building look easy. She sets it all up—world, characters, premise—so smoothly that you hardly notice until you're a hundred pages in and hurtling down the tracks. An insightful exploration of desire and ambition that also touches on broader societal topics, including celebrity, social media, trauma, and recovery. A thought-provoking novel with ample emotion and a sense of playfulness with form. And one more thing: when the inevitable adaptation of *Chosen Ones* hits the screen someday, I just hope it captures Roth's fascinating and original theory of magic."

—Charles Yu, author of *Interior Chinatown*

"Roth (*The End and Other Beginnings: Stories from the Future,* etc.) made her name by writing best-selling YA action/adventure novels like the Divergent series, so it makes sense that she can so expertly deconstruct those tropes for adult audiences. There's a lot of magic and action to make for a propulsive plot, but much more impressive are the character studies as Roth takes recognizable and beloved teen-hero types and explores what might happen to them as adults. Roth makes a bold entrance to adult fantasy."

—*Kirkus Reviews,* starred review

"Roth's first novel for adults (after the wildly popular Divergent series for teens) is driven by Sloane, a stubbornly unlikable heroine who wears her troubles on her sleeve but doesn't truly understand her full power until the shocking ending. Those who like twisty power plays and very detailed worldbuilding will appreciate this . . . The many fans of Roth's YA series will be clamoring for her adult debut, which features magic, lots of sarcasm, and a hint of romance."

—*Booklist*

Chosen Ones

CHOSEN ONES

VERONICA ROTH

A JOHN JOSEPH ADAMS BOOK

Mariner Books | Houghton Mifflin Harcourt

Boston   New York

First Mariner Books edition 2021

Copyright © 2020 by Veronica Roth

Reading Group Guide © 2021 by Houghton Mifflin Harcourt Publishing Company

hmhbooks.com

Library of Congress Cataloging-in-Publication Data
Names: Roth, Veronica, author.
Title: Chosen ones / Veronica Roth.
Description: Boston : Houghton Mifflin Harcourt, 2020. |
"A John Joseph Adams book."
Identifiers: LCCN 2019033899 (print) | LCCN 2019033900 (ebook) |
ISBN 9780358164081 (hardcover) | ISBN 9780358434696 (hardcover) |
ISBN 9780358434702 (hardcover) | ISBN 9780358274995 (hardcover) |
ISBN 9780358168478 (ebook) | ISBN 9780358375425 (int. edition) |
ISBN 9780358451174 (trade paper)
Classification: LCC PS3618.O8633 C49 2020 (print) | LCC PS3618.O8633 (ebook) |
DDC 813/.6—dc23
LC record available at https://lccn.loc.gov/2019033899
LC ebook record available at https://lccn.loc.gov/2019033900

Book design by Emily Snyder

Printed in the United States of America
DOC 10 9 8 7 6 5 4 3 2 1

Image of Chicago skyline on title page from beboy/Shutterstock
Chicago map by David Lindroth, Inc., page 3
Cordus map by Virginia Allyn, page 125

To Chicago,
the city that endures

PART ONE

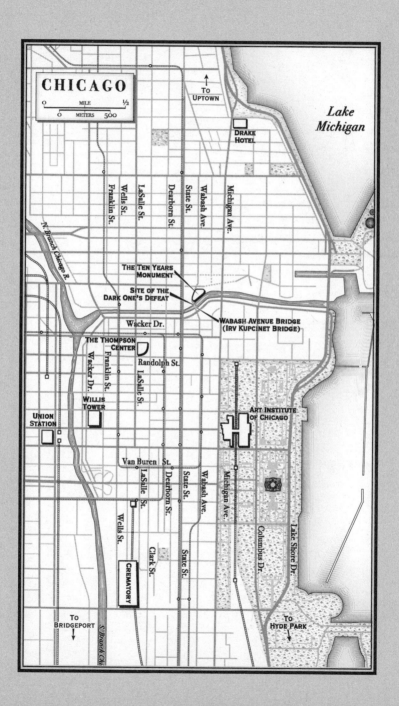

EXCERPT FROM
Comedian Jessica Krys's standup routine
Laugh Factory, Chicago, March 20, 2011

I've got a question for you: How the fuck did we end up with the name "Dark One" anyway? This guy shows up out of nowhere in a cloud of fucking smoke or whatever, literally rips people limb from limb—apparently using only the power of his mind—recruits an army of minions, levels whole cities, brings about a degree of destruction heretofore unknown to humankind . . . and "Dark One" is the best we can do? We might as well have named him after the creepy guy in your building who looks at you a couple seconds too long in the elevator. You know, the one with the really moist, soft hands? Tim. His name is Tim.

Personally, I would have gone with something like "Portent of Doom in the Form of a Man" or "Terrifying Fucking Killing Machine," but unfortunately, nobody asked me.

The Dark One and the Emergence of Modern Magic

by Professor Stanley Wiśniewski

There are, of course, some who would argue that the little understood force we informally refer to as "magic" has always existed on Earth in some form. Legends of supernatural incidents date back to the beginning of human history, from Herodotus's *mágoi,* who commanded the wind, to Djedi of ancient Egypt, who made a show of decapitating and then restoring birds such as geese and pelicans, as recorded in the Westcar Papyrus. Arguably, it is an integral part of nearly every major religion, from Jesus Christ turning water to wine, to Haitian Vodou practices, to reports of Theravada Buddhists levitating in the Dīrgha-āgama — though, notably, these acts are not referred to as "magic" by practitioners.

These stories, great and small, appear in all cultures across all regions in all of time. Formerly, scholars might have said that it's simply human nature to devise imaginative stories to explain things we don't understand or to aggrandize those we perceive to be higher or greater than ourselves. But then the Dark One came and, with him, the Drains — those infamous catastrophic events that could not be explained despite valiant attempts by scientists to do so. Perhaps there is no truth to the ancient legends at all. But perhaps there has always been a supranormal force, a little understood energy, that intrudes upon our world.

Whichever theory we posit, one thing is certain: no "magic" was ever as plain or as powerful as the Drains the Dark One wielded against humanity. It is the purpose of this paper to explore various hypotheses for why this may be. In other words, why now? What were the circumstances leading up to his arrival? What goal was he working toward before he was thwarted by our five Chosen Ones? What effect has he had on the planet since his death?

SLOANE ANDREWS DOESN'T CARE (NO, REALLY)

by Rick Lane

Trilby magazine, January 24, 2020

I don't like Sloane Andrews. But I might want to sleep with her.

I meet her at her neighborhood coffee shop, one of her usual haunts—or so she says. The barista doesn't seem to recognize her as either a customer or one of the five teenagers who took down the Dark One almost a decade ago. Which, to be honest, seems remarkable, because world-famous face aside, Sloane Andrews is that wholesome, clean brand of gorgeous that makes you want to get it dirty. If she's wearing makeup, I can't see it; she's all clear skin and big blue eyes, a walking, talking cosmetics ad. She's wearing a Cubs hat when she comes in with her long brown hair pulled through the back, a gray T-shirt that's tight in all the right places, ripped jeans that show off long, shapely legs, and a pair of sneakers. They're the kind of clothes that say she doesn't give a fuck about clothes or even about the long, lean body that fills them.

And that's the thing about Sloane: I believe it. I believe she doesn't give a fuck about anything, least of all meeting me. She didn't even want to do the interview. She only agreed, she said, because her boyfriend, Matthew Weekes, fellow Chosen One, asked her to support the release of his new book, *Still Choosing* (out February 3).

In our preliminary exchanges about this interview, she didn't have many ideas for where I might meet her. Even though everyone in Chicago already knows where Sloane lives—in the North Side neighborhood of Uptown, just blocks from Lake Shore Drive— she flat-out refused to let me see her apartment. *I don't go anywhere,* she wrote. *I get accosted when I do. So unless you want to try to keep up with me on a run, it's Java Jam or nowhere.*

I'm not sure I could take notes and jog at the same time, so Java Jam it is.

Her coffee secured, she takes off the baseball cap, and her hair falls to her shoulders like she was just tumbling around on a mattress. But something about her face—maybe it's her slightly too-close-together eyes or the way she cocks her head sharply when she doesn't like what you just said— makes her look like a bird of prey. With a single glance, she's turned the tables, and I'm the one on guard, not her. I fumble around for my first question, and where most people might smile, try to get me to like them, Sloane just stares.

"The ten-year anniversary of your victory over the Dark One is coming up," I say. "How does it feel?"

"It feels like survival," she says. Her voice is flinty and sharp. It makes a shiver go down my spine, and I can't figure out if that's a good thing or not.

"Not triumph?" I ask, and she rolls her eyes.

"Next question," she replies, and she takes her first sip of coffee.

That's when I realize it: I don't like her. This woman saved thousands—no, millions—of lives. Hell, she probably saved *my* life in one way or another. At thirteen, she was named by prophecy, along with four others, as someone who would defeat an all-powerful being of pure malice. She survived a handful of battles with the Dark One—including a brief kidnapping, the details of which she has never shared—and came out of it unscathed and beautiful, more famous than anyone in the history of being famous. And to top it off, she's in a long-term relationship with Matthew Weekes, golden boy, the Chosen One among Chosen Ones, and quite possibly the kindest person alive. But I still don't like her.

And she couldn't care less.

Which is why I want to sleep with her. It's as if, by getting her naked and in my bed, I could force her into some kind of warmth or emotion. She turns me into an alpha male, a hunter, hell-bent on taking down the most elusive prey on the planet and putting its head on my living-room wall as a trophy. Maybe that's why she gets accosted when she goes anywhere—not because people love her but because they *want* to love her, want to make her lovable.

When she sets down her mug, I see the scar on the back of her right hand. It's wide, stretching all the way across, and jagged and knotted. She's never told anyone what it's from, and I'm sure she won't tell me, but I have to ask anyway.

"Paper cut," she says.

I'm pretty sure it's supposed to be a joke, so I laugh. I ask her if she's going to the dedication of the Ten Years Monument, an installation artwork erected on the site of the Dark One's defeat, and she tells me, "It's part of the gig," like this is a desk job she applied for instead of a literal destiny.

"It sounds like you don't enjoy it," I say.

"What gave me away?" She smirks.

In the lead-up to the interview, I asked a few friends what they thought of her to get a sense of how the average Joe perceives Sloane Andrews. One of them remarked that he had never actually seen her smile, and as I sit across from her, I find myself wondering if she ever does. I even wonder it out loud—I'm curious to know how she'll respond.

Not well, as it turns out.

"If I were a dude," she says, "would you ask me that question?"

I steer us away from that topic as quickly as possible. This is less a conversation and more a game of Minesweeper, with me getting more and more tense with every box I click, every one increasing the odds I'll set off one of those mines. I click once more, inquiring about whether this time of year brings back memories for her. "I try not to think about it," she says. "If I did, my life would turn into a goddamn Advent calendar. For every day, there's another Dark One chocolate in a different shape, and they all taste like shit." I click again, asking if there are any good memories to choose from. "We were all friends, you know? We always will be. We speak almost entirely in inside jokes when we're together." Phew. I guess it's safe to ask her about the other four Chosen: Esther Park, Albert Summers, Ines Mejia, and, of course, Matthew Weekes.

It's there that we finally get into a groove. The so-called Chosen Ones bonded quickly after they met, with Matt as the natural leader. "That's just the way he is," she says, and it almost sounds like she's annoyed by it. "Always taking charge, taking responsibil-

ity. Reminding us to argue about ethics. That sort of thing." Surprisingly, it wasn't Matt with whom she had an immediate connection, but Albie. "He was quiet," she says, and it's a compliment. "All of our brothers and fathers had died—that was part of the prophecy—but my brother had died the most recently. I needed the quiet. Plus—the Midwest, Alberta, they're similar places."

Albert and Ines live together—platonically, since Ines identifies as a lesbian—in Chicago, and Esther went home to Glendale, California, to take care of her ailing mother just last year. The distance has been hard for all of them, Sloane says, but luckily they can all keep up with Esther on her active (and popular) Insta! page, where she documents the minutiae of her life.

"What do you think about the All Chosen movement that's popped up in the last few years?" I ask. The All Chosen movement is a small but vocal group that advocates for emphasizing the role the other four Chosen Ones played in the defeat of the Dark One rather than attributing the victory primarily to Matthew Weekes.

Sloane doesn't mince words. "I think it's racist."

"Some of them say that elevating Matt over the rest of you is sexist," I point out.

"What's sexist is ignoring what I

say and claiming I just don't know any better," she replies. "I think Matt's the real Chosen One. I've said so multiple times. Don't pretend you're doing me a favor by knocking him down."

I then move the conversation from the Chosen Ones to the Dark One, and that's when everything goes awry. I ask Sloane why the Dark One seemed to take a special interest in her. She keeps her eyes on mine as she sips the last of her coffee, and when she sets the cup down, her hand is shaking. Then she puts her Cubs hat right over that glorious just-fucked hair and says, "We're done here."

And I guess if she says we're done, we're done, because Sloane is out of there. I throw a ten down on the table and run after her, not willing to give up

that easily. Did I mention Sloane Andrews turns me into a hunter?

"I had one off-limits topic," she snaps at me. "Do you remember what it was?" She's flushed and furious and radiant, part dominatrix and part sly, spitting street cat. Why did I wait this long to really piss her off? I could have been staring at this the entire time.

The off-limits topic was, of course, anything specific about her relationship to the Dark One. Surely she didn't expect me to abide by that, I remark. It's the most interesting thing about her.

She looks at me like I'm the soggy piece of paper in an alley puddle, tells me to go fuck myself, and jaywalks into traffic to get away from me. This time, I let her go.

I

THE DRAIN LOOKED the same every time, with all the people screaming as they ran away from the giant dark cloud of chaos but never running fast enough. Getting swept up, their skin pulling away from bone while they were still alive to feel it, blood bursting from them like swatted mosquitoes, *oh God*.

Sloane was up and panting. *Quiet,* she told herself. Her toes curled under; the ground was cold here, in the Dark One's house, and he had taken her boots. She had to find something heavy or something sharp—both was too much to ask for, obviously; she had never been that lucky.

She yanked open drawers, finding spoons, forks, spatulas. A handful of rubber bands. Chip clips. Why had he taken her boots? What did a mass murderer have to fear from a girl's Doc Martens?

Hello, Sloane, he whispered in her ear, and she choked on a sob. Yanked open another drawer and found a line of handles, the blades buried in a plastic knife block. She was just pulling out the butcher knife when she heard something creak behind her, the pressure of a footstep.

Sloane spun around, her feet tacky on the linoleum, and swiped with the knife.

"Holy shit!" Matt caught her by the wrist, and for a moment they just stared at each other over their arms, over the knife.

Sloane gasped as reality trickled back in. She was not in the Dark One's house, not in the past, not anywhere but in the apartment she shared with Matthew Weekes.

"Oh God." Sloane's hand went lax on the handle, and the knife clattered to the floor, bouncing between their feet. Matt put his hands on her shoulders, his grip warm.

"You there?" he said.

He had asked her that before, dozens of times. Their handler, Bert, had called her a lone wolf, and he rarely made her join the others in training or on missions. *Let her do her thing,* he had told Matt once it became clear that Matt was their leader. *You'll get better results that way.* And Matt had, checking in with her only when he had to.

You there? Over the phone, in a whisper, in the dead of night, or right to her face when she spaced out on something. Sloane had been annoyed by the question at first. *Of course I'm here, where the fuck else would I be?* But now it meant he understood something about her that they'd never acknowledged: she couldn't always say yes.

"Yeah," she said.

"Okay. Stay here, all right? I'll get your medicine."

Sloane braced herself on the marble counter. The knife lay at her feet, but she didn't dare touch it again. She just waited, and breathed, and stared at the swirl of gray that reminded her of an old man in profile.

Matt came back with a little yellow pill in one hand and the water glass from her bedside table in the other. She took them both with shaking hands and swallowed the pill eagerly. Bring on the coasting calm of the benzodiazepine. She and Ines had drunkenly composed an ode to the pills once, hailing them for their pretty colors and their quick effects and the way they did what nothing else could.

She set the water glass down and slid to the floor. She could feel the cold through her pajama pants—the ones that had cats with laser eyes all over them—but it was grounding this time. Matt sat down next to the refrigerator in his boxers.

"Listen," she started.

"You don't have to say it."

"Sure, I just almost stabbed you, but no apologies necessary."

His eyes were soft. Worried. "I just want you to be okay."

What had that awful article called him? "Quite possibly the kindest person alive"? She hadn't disagreed with Rick Lane, Creepmaster 2000, on that point at least. Matt had eyebrows that squeezed together in the middle in a look of perpetual sympathy and the heart to match.

He reached for the butcher knife that lay on the floor near her ankle. It was big, almost as long as his forearm.

Her eyes burned. She closed them. "I'm really sorry."

"I know you don't want to talk to me about it," Matt said. "But what about someone else?"

"Like who?"

"Dr. Novak, maybe? She works with the VA, remember? We did that talk together at the juvenile detention center."

"I'm not a soldier," Sloane said.

"Yeah, but she knows about PTSD."

She had never needed an official diagnosis — PTSD was definitely what she had. But it was strange to hear Matt say it so comfortably, like it was the flu.

"All right." She shrugged. "I'll call her in the morning."

"Anyone would need therapy, you know," he said. "After what we've all been through. I mean, Ines went."

"Ines went, and she's still booby-trapping her apartment like she's living out a *Home Alone* fantasy," Sloane said.

"Okay, so she's a bad example." The floodlight on the back stairs glowed through the windows, all orange-yellow against Matt's dark skin.

"You've never needed it," Sloane said.

He raised an eyebrow at her. "Where do you think I kept disappearing to the year after the Dark One died?"

"You told us you were going to doctor's appointments."

"What kind of doctor needs to see someone weekly for *months?*"

"I don't know! I figured something was wrong with . . ." Sloane gestured vaguely to her crotch. "You know. The boys or something."

"Let me get this straight." He was grinning. "You thought I had some kind of embarrassing medical condition that necessitated at least six months of regular doctor visits . . . and you *never* asked me about it?"

She suppressed a smile of her own. "You almost sound disappointed in me."

"No, no. I'm just impressed."

He had been thirteen and lanky when she met him, a body of sharp edges with no sense of where it began or ended, but he had always had that smile.

She had fallen in love with him half a dozen times before she knew she had—when he was screaming orders over the deafening wind of a Drain, keeping them all alive; when he stayed awake with her on long night drives through the country even after everyone else had fallen asleep; when he called his grandmother and his voice went soft. He never left anyone behind.

She curled her toes into the tile. "I've been before, you know. To therapy," she said. "I went for a few months when we were sixteen."

"You did?" He frowned a little. "You never told me that."

There were a lot of things she hadn't told him, hadn't told anyone. "I didn't want to worry anybody," she said. "And I still don't, so . . . just don't mention this to the others, okay? I don't want to see it in fucking *Esquire* with the headline 'Rick Lane Told You So.'"

"Of course." Matt took her hand and twisted their fingers together. "We should go to bed. We have to get up in four hours for the monument dedication."

Sloane nodded, but they still sat on the kitchen floor until the medicine kicked in and she stopped shaking. Then Matt put the knife away, helped her up, and they both went back to bed.

AGENCY FOR THE RESEARCH AND INVESTIGATION OF THE SUPRANORMAL

October 4, 2019

Ms. Sloane Andrews

██████

██████

Reference: H-20XX-74545

Dear Ms. Andrews:

On 13 September 2019, the office of the Information and Privacy Coordinator received your 12 September 2019 Freedom of Information Act (FOIA) request for information or records on Project Ringer.

Many of the requested records remain classified. However, due to your years of service to the United States government, we have granted you access to all but those requiring the highest level of security clearance. We searched our database of previously released records and located the enclosed documents, totaling 120 pages, which we believe to be responsive to your request. There is no charge for these documents.

Sincerely,

Mara Sanchez

Information and Privacy Coordinator

WHEN SLOANE'S ALARM went off the next morning, she took another benzo immediately. She would need it for the day ahead; that morning, she would attend the dedication of the Ten Years Monument, a memorial for the lives lost in the Dark One's attacks, and that night, the Ten Years Peace gala, to celebrate the years since his defeat.

The city of Chicago had commissioned an artist named Gerald Frye to construct the monument. Judging by his portfolio, he had taken a great deal of inspiration from the work of minimalist Donald Judd, because the monument was actually just a metal box surrounded by a swath of empty land where the unsightly tower in the middle of the Loop had been, next to the river. It looked small by comparison to the high-rises around it, glittering in the sun as Sloane's car pulled up on the day of the dedication.

Matt had hired them a driver so they wouldn't have to park, which turned out to be a good idea, because the entire city was swarming with people, the crowd so thick the driver had to blast the horn of their black Lincoln to get through it. Even then, most people just ignored the sound until they felt the heat of the engine behind their knees.

Once they got close, a police officer let the car through a barrier and they cruised down a clear stretch of road to get to the monument. Sloane felt her pulse behind her eyes, like a headache. The second Matt opened the car door and stepped out into the light, everyone would know who they were. People would hold up their phones to record video. They would thrust pictures and notebooks and arms past the barriers to have them signed. They would scream Matt's name and Sloane's name, and weep and struggle forward and tell stories of who and what they had lost.

Sloane wished she could go home. But instead, she wiped her palms on the front of her dress, took a slow breath, and put her hand on Matt's shoulder. The car eased to a stop. Matt opened the door.

Sloane stepped out behind him and into a wall of sound. Matt turned toward her, grinning, and said, right against her ear, "Don't forget to smile."

A lot of men had told Sloane to smile, but all they wanted was to exert some kind of power over her. Matt, though, was just trying to protect her. His own smile was a weapon against a gentler and more insidious form of racism, the kind that made people follow him through retail stores before realizing who he was or assume he had grown up in a rough neighborhood instead of on the Upper East Side or fixated on Sloane and Albie saving the world as if Matt, Esther, and Ines had nothing to do with it. It was in silence and hesitation, in careless jokes and fumbling.

There were harsher, more violent forms of it too, but smiles weren't weapons against them.

He walked over to the crowd pressed up against the barrier, many of the people there holding photos of him, magazine articles, books. He took a black marker from his pocket and signed each of them with his quick *MW,* one letter an inversion of the other. Sloane watched him from a distance, distracted from the chaos for a moment. He leaned in for a picture with a middle-aged redhead who didn't know how to work her phone; he took it from her to show her how to switch to the front camera. Everywhere he went, people gave him pieces of themselves, sometimes in the form of gratitude, sometimes in stories of people they had lost to the Dark One. He bore them all.

After a few minutes, Sloane walked over to him and put her hand on his shoulder. "I'm sorry, Matt, but we should go."

People were reaching for her, too, of course, waving copies of the *Trilby* article with her face plastered on one side of the magazine and Rick Lane's sexist assholery on the other. Some of them shouted her name, and she ignored them, like she always did. Matt's weapons were generosity, kindness, social grace. Sloane's were detachment, a tall stature, and a relentlessly flat affect.

Matt looked down the line at a group of black teenagers in school uniforms. One of the girls wore her hair in tiny braids with beads at the ends. They clattered together as she bounced on her toes, excited. She had a clipboard in her hand; it looked like another petition.

"One second," Matt said to Sloane, and he walked over to the group in the uniforms. She chafed a little at the brushoff, but the feeling disappeared when she saw the subtle shift in his posture, his shoulders relaxing.

"Hey," he said to the girl with the braids, grinning.

Sloane felt a small ache in her chest. There were parts of him she would just never access, a language she would never hear him speak, because when she was present, the words were gone.

She decided to go on without him. It didn't really matter if he got to the ceremony on time. Everyone would wait.

She walked down the narrow aisle the police had whittled into the crowd. She climbed the steps to the stage, which faced the metal box of the monument—about the size of an average bedroom, standing in the middle of nothing.

"Slo!" Esther stood on the stage in five-inch heels and black leather pants, waving. Her white blouse was just loose enough to be elegant, and from afar, her face looked almost the same as it had when they'd defeated the Dark One—but the closer Sloane got, the more she could see that the poreless glow was achieved by foundation and highlighter and bronzer and setting powder and God knew what else.

It was a relief to see her. Things hadn't been the same for the five of them since she'd moved back home to take care of her mom. Sloane walked up the steps to the stage, shaking her head at the security guard who offered her an arm to help her up, and pulled Esther into a hug.

"Nice dress!" Esther said to her once they separated. "Did Matt pick it out?"

"I am capable of choosing my own clothes," Sloane said. "How—"

She was about to ask how Esther's mother was, but Esther was already taking out her cell phone and holding it out for a selfie.

"No," Sloane said.

"*Slo* . . . come on, I want a picture of us!"

"No, you want to show a picture of us to a million other people on Insta!, and that's much different."

"I'm gonna get one whether you smile for it or not, so you might as well not fuel the rumors that you're a turbo-bitch," Esther pointed out.

Sloane rolled her eyes, bent a little at the knee, and leaned in for a picture. She even managed something like a smile. "That's the only one, though, okay?" she said. "I'm not on social media for a reason."

"I get it, you're so *alternative* and *authentic* and whatever." Esther flapped a hand at her, her head bent over her phone. "I'm going to draw a mustache on you."

"How appropriate for the ten-year anniversary of a horrible battle."

"Fine, I'll just post it as is. You're so boring."

It was a familiar argument. She and Esther turned toward Ines and Albie, who were seated beside the podium wearing almost identical black suits. Ines's lapels were a little wider, and Albie's tie was more blue, but that was the only difference as far as Sloane could tell.

"Where's Matt?" Ines asked.

"With his royal subjects," Esther replied.

Sloane looked back. Matt was still talking to the teenage girl, his brow furrowed, nodding along to something she was saying.

"He'll be a minute," she said when she turned back to the others.

Albie looked bleary-eyed, but that could be because it was eight in the morning, and Albie didn't usually get up until at least ten. When he looked at her, he seemed focused enough, just tired. He gave her a wave.

"Saved you a seat, Slo," he said, patting the chair next to him. She sat down beside him, legs crossed at the ankle and tucked back, the way her grandmother had taught her. *Do you really want to flash your underwear at strangers? Well, then, cross your goddamn legs, girl.*

"All right?" she said to him.

"Nah," he said with a half smile. "But what else is new?"

She gave a half smile back.

"Hey, kids." A man was crossing the stage. He wore charcoal slacks and a blazer paired with a powder-blue shirt, and his salt-and-pepper hair was combed back neatly. He wasn't just any man, but John Clayton, mayor of Chicago, elected on a campaign of "Not as corrupt as the other guy, probably," which had been the motto of Chicago politics for a few years running. He was also possibly the blandest man alive.

"Thank you for coming out," Mayor Clayton said, shaking Sloane's hand, then Albie's, Ines's, and Esther's. Matt climbed the steps to the stage just in time to take the mayor's hand too. "I'm just going to say a few words, then you can all walk through the monument. Kind of like blessing it, eh? Then we'll get you out of here. They're going to want a picture of us all. Now? Yes, now."

He was gesturing to the photographer, who positioned them so the monument was just visible behind them, and Matt was in the middle, his hand steady on Sloane's lower back. Sloane wasn't sure if she should smile for the ten-year anniversary of the Dark One's defeat. The entire world would be celebrating today. Even the city of Chicago, which had lost so much—they would dye the river blue, and Wrigleyville would teem with beer, and the el would turn into a cattle car. The merriment was good, Sloane knew that, had even participated in it for the first few years after the event, but it was harder to do that now. She had been told that things got easier with time, but so far it hadn't been true. The burst of joy and triumph that had come after the Dark One fell had faded, and what was left was this niggling sense of dissatisfaction and the awareness of everything lost on the way to victory.

She didn't smile in the picture. While Esther explained boomerang videos to the mayor, Sloane sat back down next to Albie. Meanwhile, Matt was talking to the mayor's wife, who wondered if he might come to the opening of a new library in Uptown, and Ines was jiggling her leg, frantic as ever. Albie put his hand on Sloane's and squeezed.

"Happy anniversary, I guess," she said.

"Yeah," he said. "Happy anniversary."

AGENCY FOR THE RESEARCH AND INVESTIGATION OF THE SUPRANORMAL

NATIONAL SECURITY ACTION MEMORANDUM NO. 70

TO: AGENCY FOR THE RESEARCH AND INVESTIGATION OF THE SUPRANORMAL (ARIS)

SUBJECT: UNEXPLAINED DISASTROUS EVENTS OF 2004

In approving the record of events of the February 2, 2005, meeting of the National Security Council, the president directed that the disastrous incidents of 2004 be studied in case a pattern exists among them. As the incidents are thus far unexplained by conventional means, this task falls under the purview of the Agency for the Research and Investigation of the Supranormal (ARIS).

Accordingly, it is requested that ARIS undertake this study as soon as possible, presenting their preliminary views at the next National Security Council meeting. Attached are the articles thus far amassed by the National Security Council regarding said events.

Shonda Jordan

Chillicothe Gazette

OFFICIAL REPORTS OF DISASTER IN TOPEKA REMAIN VAGUE

by Jay Kaufman

TOPEKA, MARCH 6: At last count, the death toll in Topeka, Kansas, for the disaster on March 5, 2004, is 19,327 —but officials don't seem to know what caused the significant loss of life. Or, if they do, they aren't telling.

Weather reports on the morning of March 5 predicted overcast skies and a high of 40 degrees, with a mere 10 percent chance of rain. Witnesses from nearby towns describe pockets of sunshine and low winds. At exactly 1:04 p.m., everything went haywire. An account from an employee of the National Weather Service described the environment in the office as "utter chaos," citing "screeching monitors and shouting.

"For a couple minutes, it was like there had been a tornado, an earthquake, and a hurricane all at once. The air pressure changes were insane, and tremors were felt as far as Kentucky. I've never experienced anything like it," the source reported. The employee requested to remain anonymous out of fear of losing their job. The National Weather Service has since released a statement that they can't provide any further details to the public, as there is an investigation ongoing.

The federal government has maintained a similar position. The Department of Homeland Security, including the Federal Emergency Management Agency, has been silent. The Federal Bureau of Investigation has said their investigation does not currently suggest either foreign or domestic terrorism behind the incident, but they aren't presently able to rule it out. Even at the local level, the mayor of Topeka, Hal Foster—who was vacationing in Orlando, Florida, at the time—has expressed condolences and sorrow but has not voiced so much as a theory about what occurred.

The most we can gather about the event so far comes from private citizens. Andy Ellis of Lawrence, Kansas, drove to the area surrounding Topeka with a drone he usually used to monitor the ongoing construction of his new house. His images of Topeka, which Ellis provided to every national news network simultaneously, are harrowing. They show the skeletons of buildings, bodies in the streets, and, most peculiar of all, not a shred of living plant matter. All the trees in Topeka, according to these images, are now just shriveled branches and dead leaves.

Left without any concrete explanations, the public has turned to conspiracy theories such as an alien invasion, a government experiment gone awry, a new weapon of mass destruction, and a new kind of weather event resulting from climate change. Hysteria has spread as well, moving some people to begin construction of bomb shelters in their homes or develop new evacuation plans that advocate for spreading out from a city's center instead of seeking shelter within it.

"We need answers," said Fran Halloway, a resident of Willard, one of the surviving towns just outside of Topeka. "We deserve to know why our loved ones are dead. And we're not gonna rest until we get them."

Portland Bugle

DISASTER STRIKES PORTLAND; DEATH TOLLS IN THE TENS OF THOUSANDS

by Arjun Patel

PORTLAND, AUGUST 20: A weather event tentatively classified as a hurricane struck Portland, Oregon, on August 19, causing widespread flooding and destruction of homes and buildings. If the classification stands, this would be the first tropical hurricane in recorded history to hit the West Coast.

With death tolls estimated to be as high as 50,000, this would be the deadliest natural disaster in the history of the United States, second to the Topeka Calamity earlier this year, which at final count claimed almost 20,000 lives. No definitive explanations for the Topeka Calamity have yet been offered.

The weather event has so far baffled scientists, who cite the low temperatures of the Pacific Ocean as the reason for the lack of hurricane activity on the West Coast. "Hurricanes feed on warm water temperatures," says Dr. Joan Gregory, a professor of atmospheric science at the University of Wisconsin–Madison. "One thing that *might* account for this is climate change, but we haven't heard of anyone recording significantly higher temperatures in the Pacific Ocean recently. This seems like a freak occurrence."

More information will likely become available as the recovery effort continues. A candlelight vigil for those lost will be held in Pioneer Courthouse Square at 8:00 p.m. on Thursday.

Rochester Observer

FIGURE SPOTTED IN THE MIDST OF DISASTER; CONSPIRACY THEORIES SPREAD LIKE WILDFIRE AS REPORTS OF DARK FIGURE EMERGE

by Carl Adams

ROCHESTER, DECEMBER 7: "Everything was bedlam," says Brendan Peterson of Sutton, Minnesota, one of the survivors of the attack on Minneapolis that claimed almost 85,000 lives earlier this year. He was right in the center of the destruction and describes a hellscape of wind and flying debris. "I saw a woman come apart right in front of me," he recounts, his hands trembling. "I've never seen anything like that before, never, not even in movies."

Brendan credits his survival to "sheer luck," and he is not alone. Several of the more outspoken survivors of the attack have offered similar tales of horrific death, each more gory than the last. But they all have one thing in common: each survivor saw the figure of a man moving confidently through the destruction.

"I guess it could have been a woman," says George Williams, another Sutton resident and neighbor of Brendan Peterson. "But anyway, it looked like a person. Eeriest thing I've ever seen."

The disasters are being classified as "attacks" by the U.S. government, but the perpetrators have not yet been identified. Theories have surfaced on the internet, ranging from the plausible (terrorists, agents of hostile foreign governments) to the downright absurd (aliens, a wrathful divine being).

"He was hard to see, though," Brendan clarifies later, referring to the figure he saw during the Minneapolis attack. "Dark from head to toe. I'm not crazy. I saw what I saw."

THE MAYOR'S SPEECH was a collection of trite phrases about moving on from grief and the triumph of good over evil and honoring the dead. Halfway through, Ines leaned over to whisper a quote from *Friday Night Lights*—"Clear eyes, full hearts, can't lose"—and Sloane had to cover her mouth so no one in the crowd could tell that she was laughing. Albie faked a coughing fit, and Esther elbowed Ines in the ribs. Matt schooled his face into a serious expression. For just a moment, Sloane felt like she had gotten something back.

Cameras flashed everywhere as the speech concluded, and the crowd applauded. Sloane joined them, clapping until her palms started to itch. Next came a series of firm handshakes, and finally, it was time for the Chosen Ones to bless the Ten Years Monument with their holy footsteps or whatever the hell Mayor Clayton had said about it. Sloane wondered if she could use that as an excuse to take off her shoes, because they were pinching her toes. Surely you couldn't bless something with uncomfortable high heels on.

The land around the metal box had been paved with concrete. Sloane walked down the steps of the stage and felt the warmth of it through the soles of her shoes. She felt like she was standing on the surface of a gray sea, the monument a bronze island one hundred yards ahead of her. It was the only spot of warm light in the midst of desolation—ethereal, mirage-like. Staring at it, she was surprised to find tears in her eyes. In time, the bronze would age, its luster giving way to flat green tarnish. Their memory of what happened would flatten, too, and become dull, and the monument would be forgotten, something for school field trips and bus tours for the history-minded.

And she would tarnish too. Always famous but always fading, the way old movie stars were, carrying ghosts of their younger selves in their faces.

It was a strange thing, to know with certainty that you had peaked.

She walked in Albie's wake to the box, the others at her back. She couldn't help but look across the river to where Matt had stood during their last stand, the Golden Bough held aloft, casting supernatural light on his face. One of a handful of moments in which she had fallen in love with him.

There was a narrow opening in the wall for people to step inside, and Albie went straight through it. Ines was about to follow him in, but Sloane stopped her with a hand. "Let's give him a second," she said.

They all fit together in different ways, knew different pieces of each other best. Esther knew how to make Albie laugh, Ines could almost read his mind, and Matt knew how to get him to talk. But Sloane was the Albie expert on his bad days, and there was no way today wasn't one of them.

"This thing is totally going to get peed on," Ines said.

"You don't need to fill *every* silence," Matt said.

"I'm gonna go in and see if he's okay," Sloane said. "Give me a minute or two."

Matt said, "Sure."

"Yeah, it'll give Esther time to figure out the right camera angle or whatever," Ines said.

Esther smacked her arm, then took out her phone. Sloane fled the scene before Esther could talk her into another selfie, finding the gap in the wall and slipping into the monument.

Tiny letters—the name of every person killed by the Dark One —were carved out of the metal walls. It had taken years to find and cut them all, according to the artist, and most names were so small you could barely read them. The artist had set up panels of light behind the metal sheets so each name glowed. It was like staring at a night sky somewhere deep in the wilderness, where pollution didn't interfere with the light of the stars.

Albie stood in the middle of the cube, staring at one of the wall panels.

"Hey," she said to him.

"Hey," he said. "Pretty in here, isn't it?"

"The bronze was a good choice. Almost cozy this way," she said. "Did you find your dad's name?"

"No," he said. "Needle. Haystack."

"Maybe we could ask the artist."

Albie shrugged. "I think the point is, you're not supposed to be able to see the individual names. You're just supposed to get an impression of how many there were."

So many it stopped mattering, Sloane thought. She already knew the number of people lost to the Dark One. Anything from one hundred to one million was just a number, her mind too limited to really comprehend it.

"I like it this way," Albie said. "It reminds me that we're just a handful of people who lost something among thousands of other people who lost something. Not hurting any more or less than any of the families of these people."

He gestured to the panel in front of him. Albie was only thirty, but his hair had gone feather-light and was receding at the temples. There were creases in his forehead, too, deep enough that she had noticed them. Time was wearing on him.

"I'm tired of being special," Albie said with a shaky laugh. "I'm tired of being celebrated for the worst thing that ever happened to me."

Sloane went to stand next to him, close enough that their arms touched. She thought of the stack of government documents in the bottom drawer of her desk, of Rick Lane discussing her like she was a slab of meat at a butcher, of the nightmares that chased her from sleeping to waking.

"Yeah," she said through a sigh. "I know what you mean."

Or at least, she thought she did. But when she watched Albie's hand tremble as he brought it up to scrub at his face, she wondered if she really did know.

"Knock-knock!" Esther said. She was holding up her phone—at a flattering angle, of course—as she walked into the monument, her hair arranged perfectly over her shoulders. She turned so the shot included Albie and Sloane. "Say hi to my Insta! followers, guys!"

"Is this live?" Sloane asked.

"No," Esther said.

Sloane glanced at Albie and then put up both her middle fingers while Albie put his palms up to his cheeks to make a loud farting noise. Ines walked in after Esther, looking nervous, to see Sloane waving her middle fingers around Albie's face. Esther put the phone down, scowling.

"That was supposed to be a live capture of my first time through the Ten Years Monument!" she said. "Now I'm gonna have to do it again and *act* like it's the first time."

She stormed out, passing Matt on her way.

"What'd I miss?" he said.

"Hold on," Albie said, touching a finger to his lips.

Esther came in again, the phone held up and away from her face, her eyes wide in faux-wonder as she looked at the glowing names. Albie darted forward and tipped his head so he was in the shot with Esther and said, "This is her second time doing this! Don't let her lie to you—"

Esther shoved Albie away and put her phone down. "What is *wrong* with you guys?"

"Us? You're the one who basically has a phone grafted to your hand!" said Sloane. "You're worse than Matt."

Matt put up his hands. "I am not involved in this."

"I'm not the first person to use social media!" Esther said. "It's my *job,* you don't have to be so freaking judge-y about it."

"This is supposed to be a somber occasion," Matt pointed out. "And it *could* have been a good bonding experience—"

"Recording it doesn't take away its somberness," Esther said.

"It does when you're recording from the ideal selfie angle," Ines said, miming holding up a phone. She posed with her hip thrust to the side. "'Here's the names of the dead and also my hot ass.'"

Sloane couldn't suppress a giggle. It came out so high-pitched, she clapped a hand over her mouth, embarrassed.

"Sloanie Sloanie Macaroni just made a girlie noise," Albie said, eyebrows raised.

"Don't you dare call me that," she said.

"Don't pretend we haven't all seen you in those home videos Cameron made," Esther said. "You may be into this tough-girl-don't-give-a-fuck thing now, but deep inside you will always be the kid who did a dance to 'Diamonds Are a Girl's Best Friend' in a tutu made of tinfoil."

Sloane cursed her late brother's video camera and was about to respond when Matt spoke up. "I found Bert."

Bert's real name wasn't Robert Robertson, of course. He had told them his real one in confidence a few months before his death so they could find him if they lost contact with him. But none of them thought of him as Evan Kowalczyk; to them, he would always be Bert.

They all moved to stand behind Matt and followed the line of his finger to a small name: EVAN KOWALCZYK, all in capital letters. She had no idea how Matt had found it among all the names, all the panels. It was like finding a particular tree in a forest of identical trees. Matt's hand fell away, and Robert's name disappeared into the wall again, blurring together with all the others.

All these losses—each one for nothing. A dark lord and his insatiable hunger.

"I wonder what he'd be doing now," Matt said.

"Probably refusing to enjoy his retirement," Ines replied.

Sloane turned toward the door before her expression gave her away. She didn't want to tell them what she had read in the files she had gotten from the FOIA request, hints of a Bert she had never known.

"Let's go," Sloane said. "They're going to start to wonder where we are."

4

THE INVITATION to the gala was taped to their refrigerator: CELEBRATE TEN YEARS OF PEACE. As if the defeat of the Dark One had brought harmony to the entire world. It hadn't, of course, but for the United States, at least, it had been a reason to withdraw from everything. A new era of isolationism, the headlines had called it. The reactions had been . . . mixed. One side had celebrated withdrawing troops from other countries but protested pulling out of international peacekeeping organizations. The other side had cheered the closing of borders but resisted the decreased military presence abroad. Regardless of where on the spectrum they fell, everyone had shared the same paranoia. No one knew where the Dark One had come from, which meant he could have come from anywhere. He could have been a friend or a neighbor, a refugee or an immigrant. Even Sloane's mother had gotten a licensed handgun and practiced at the shooting range once a month, as if that had ever helped anyone against the Dark One, who had made guns collapse from within, like imploding buildings, warping and twisting the metal without even touching it. Sloane couldn't help but wonder how long it would take ARIS to harness the same power for themselves. If they hadn't already.

Sloane took her dress out of the closet and hung it on the door. It was a gold-beaded gown that looked like something out of the twenties. It would be heavy on her shoulders, so she didn't intend to put it on until the last second. On a normal day, she wouldn't have bothered with anything so fancy, but Sloane loved formal occasions —not that she would have admitted that to anyone. Earlier, she had even hidden in the bathroom to watch one of Esther's Insta! beauty tutorials for winged eyeliner. If Esther ever found out, Sloane would never live it down.

The unfortunate formfitting nature of the beaded dress meant she had to find the item of clothing she most dreaded in the world: shapewear. The greatest wrangler of women's minorly imperfect torsos since the corset. The last thing she wanted was to wake up to gossip websites showing increasingly zoomed-in pictures of the bubble of fat around her middle, speculating about the state of her womb. Pregnancy rumors had haunted her as long as she and Matt had been together.

She couldn't find the shapewear in her underwear drawer or her sock drawer, so she turned to Matt's armoire. Sometimes it got lost amid the sea of black boxer briefs that he favored. She dug around in the spandex, and her fingers brushed something small and hard.

A box, small enough to fit in her palm. Black.

Shit.

Sloane glanced at the door—still closed, with no audible movement in the hallway beyond it. Good. She opened the box. Inside was a ring, of course, but not just any ring—it was old-fashioned, dotted with pyrite instead of diamonds. He had remembered what kind of jewelry she liked even though she never wore any.

She snapped the box closed and shoved it back in the drawer, her throat tight. She knew what it meant, of course: he was going to propose to her. Soon, probably, because he wouldn't trust the underwear drawer as a good hiding place for long. Given his fondness for dramatic gestures, he would likely do it at the gala that evening.

Sloane felt sick with dread. She opened the door and peered down the hallway. Matt was on the phone with his assistant, Eddie. His calendar was stuffed to bursting with causes. This week alone, he was moderating a panel discussion on mass incarceration, attending a fundraising event for a school on the west side, and meeting with a senator about state-funded counseling services for Dark One survivors with PTSD. He would likely be on the phone for a while.

She shut the door again and sat on the edge of the bed, staring out at the two-flat across the street, the one with the gaudy blue fairy lights hanging from the eaves all year round.

Sloane took out her phone and dialed a number she hadn't used in years. Her mother's number.

"Hello?" June Hopewell said, her voice sharp as ever.

"Mom?"

"Sloane?"

Sloane frowned. "Yeah, it's me, unless you've got some other kids running around I'm not aware of."

"Saw you on the TV this morning," June said. "You sure you don't want to rethink that whole 'no autographs' policy? Looked like you were being chased by wolves."

"Yeah, Mom. I'm sure." Sloane didn't think her mother actually cared whether she signed autographs or not, but ever since the defeat of the Dark One, she had weighed in on everything Sloane did, maybe in an attempt to make up for her nonexistent parental influence when Sloane was growing up. She had, after all, missed out on Sloane's entire adolescence due to not giving a single shit when the government came to take her away.

"Listen, there's something I want to talk to you about," Sloane said. "I just found a ring in Matt's underwear drawer. An engagement ring."

Her mom was quiet on the other end of the line. Then: "Okay. And?"

"And?" Sloane clapped a hand to her forehead. "And I'm freaking out!"

"Slo, you've been together for ten years."

Sloane's face got hot. "We've never even talked about it! Don't you think that if he wanted to marry me, he would, you know, bring up the subject of marriage casually at some point? For all he knows, I hate the entire institution on principle."

"While that would not be at all surprising, given the number of things you do hate," June said, a hint of amusement creeping into her voice, "maybe he wanted to keep it a surprise."

Sloane watched a cat prowl along the curb outside.

"Sloane." Her mother sighed. "He's the best you're gonna find. Trust me."

Sloane didn't respond.

"I gotta go," her mom said.

To do what? Sloane didn't say. She hung up without saying good-bye. That wouldn't surprise June. They usually spoke only once a year, on Christmas, for about five minutes. They hadn't exchanged "I love you"s since Sloane was a child. Since before her dad left, then turned up dead in a morgue in Arkansas — killed by a Drain — and June had to go identify the body.

He's the best you're gonna find. She was right, obviously, because Matt radiated goodness so hard, you wanted to punch him sometimes. Not loving him was like not loving freedom. Or puppies.

But there was something about the way June had said it that grated on Sloane. *He's the best* you're *gonna find.* And that, too, was true — what was she supposed to do, join a dating app? Pretend to have a regular job? At what point would she mention that she was one of the five saviors of humankind? Was that a third-date conversation or more of a fifth-date one?

But it would have been nice, she thought, for June to say something kind and reassuring for once.

Sloane sat with her phone in her hands. The sun was setting, and the eye-searingly blue fairy lights had turned on across the street. She felt uneven, like the room had shifted around her. But she also knew that whenever Matt proposed to her, she would say yes, because it was the only rational thing to do. They would get married and he would take care of her and she would try as hard as she could to be good enough for him.

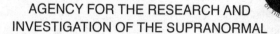

AGENCY FOR THE RESEARCH AND
INVESTIGATION OF THE SUPRANORMAL

SUBJECT: UNEXPLAINED DISASTROUS EVENTS OF 2005,
TRANSCRIPT OF DEBRIEFING SESSION WITH LEAD OFFICER
████████████, CODE NAME BERT

OFFICER S: Please state your name for the official record.

OFFICER K: My name is ████████, but for the purposes of this mission I have been assigned the code name Robert Robertson.

OFFICER S: Noted. We are here today to make an account of your collection of Project Ringer Subject 2, Sloane Andrews.

OFFICER K: Correct. I received notice on 17 October that Subject 2 had been identified and her retrieval was to occur immediately.

OFFICER S: The record shows that there was a twenty-four-hour delay on action, despite this order. Can you account for this?

OFFICER K: Yes. I requested a delay of one week to allow Subject 2 to attend her brother's funeral. My request was denied, but I was granted a delay of twenty-four hours. I deemed this to be insufficient but did as ordered and arrived at the Andrews residence on 18 October at 1500 hours.

OFFICER S: And how did you find the Andrews residence?

OFFICER K: As anticipated. Our intel indicated that the Andrews family was of relatively low socioeconomic status, so I was prepared for the dilapidated house as well as the worn quality of the rest of the neighborhood.

OFFICER S: And you made contact with Subject 2 directly upon arrival?

OFFICER K: She was sitting on the front steps. Her appearance was disheveled. I confirmed her name and introduced myself with my code name.

OFFICER S: And her reaction?

OFFICER K: She said, "That sounds like a fake name."

OFFICER S: Astute. Your reply?

OFFICER K: I confirmed that it was indeed a fake name. I thought I might begin to gain her trust if she felt that I was being honest with her.

OFFICER S: Noted. Go on.

OFFICER K: I asked if her mother was home and if I could speak with her. She looked uncomfortable. She asked me who I was and what I wanted, and I said I could only talk to her if her mother was present. Her reply was that if I was waiting for her mother to be "present," I would be waiting a long time.

OFFICER S: Ah.

OFFICER K: At that point I deemed it necessary to change my procedure. Typically with the subjects of Project Ringer, I speak with the parent and the subject at the same time, but this was a special situation. A dead father and brother and what appeared to be an incapacitated mother. The subject was essentially alone. So I decided to speak with her alone. I asked if we could go inside, and she refused. Said she wasn't about to let a strange man into her house. So I simply stood where I was.

OFFICER S: How did you begin?

OFFICER K: She asked who I was again. I replied that I was with a clandestine part of the government, the exact nature of which I was unable to disclose, and that I was there about a prophecy.

OFFICER S: Let the record reflect that the officer is referring to Precognitive Vision #545, regarding the Dark One and his equal, colloquially known as the Chosen One. How did the subject react to the notion of a prophecy?

OFFICER K: She said, "I don't believe in that stuff. I just stick to what I can see and touch." I asked her how she was able to account for what the Dark One had been capable of. It was perhaps a poorly timed remark, given that her brother had just been killed by the Dark One earlier that week —

OFFICER S: Did she become upset?

OFFICER K: The opposite, actually. She took on a flat affect. No expression. And she said, "I don't know." I decided that it might be best to appeal to her logical side and suggested it was the word *prophecy* she didn't like. I then cited Newton's third law.

OFFICER S: Let the record reflect that Newton's third law states that for every action, there is an equal and opposite reaction.

OFFICER K: . . .Thank you for that.

OFFICER S: Not everyone remembers physics, Officer.

OFFICER K: I explained that the prophecy simply predicted that for the Dark

One, there would come an equal and opposite individual. We had, in other words, received a list of criteria for who that person would be. We had acted in cooperation with Canada and Mexico to narrow down our options, since the attacks have thus far been exclusive to North America. When Sloane's brother died at the Dark One's hands, she became one of those options.

OFFICER S: You don't mince words.

OFFICER K: It was my theory that a young woman forced to be so independent due to parental negligence would interpret my bluntness as respect for her autonomy. It seemed I was right — she took in this information with no apparent reaction. I further added that my job was to prepare all five potentials for this eventuality so that humanity had our best chance of survival.

She asked me, "Are you saying I'm . . . 'the One'?" With finger quotes around the phrase "the One."

I answered, "Yes and no. I'm saying you *might* be the One." I cited some of the criteria she met — the death of her father and brother, her birth during a harvest moon, a mother who did not share her last name, the rare blood type AB negative —

OFFICER S: Also known as the preliminary identification criteria, or PIC.

OFFICER K: Correct. I would characterize her reaction to that as "incredulous." She asked who'd made the prophecy and why the government would pay attention to, I quote, "some crazy person spewing poetry."

I had been given clearance to disclose details about the clairvoyant. I said that her name was ██████, and this individual had repeatedly demonstrated a talent for knowledge beyond our ability to comprehend. That she had made 746 predictions that had come to pass in our observation.

OFFICER S: The subject's reaction to this?

OFFICER K: It's strange — the other subjects had demonstrated disbelief or fear or even, in the case of Subject 1, steely determination. But Subject 2 was the first one to ask what would happen if she said no.

OFFICER S: No?

OFFICER K: Yes — no. No to fighting the Dark One.

OFFICER S: [Laughing] Did you tell her she didn't have much of a choice?

OFFICER K: I believe that would have been unwise. She reminded me a little of a stray dog — if you try to grab it, it might bite you. But if you are careful, you might be able to persuade it to come to you.

OFFICER S: If you know what it eats.

OFFICER K: Correct. And I think in this case, respect was the right bait, so to speak. So I said, "I think that if you said no, you would dramatically increase the chances of the world ending." Citing repercussions rather than restrictions — a choice without an acceptable outcome.

OFFICER S: It did the trick?

OFFICER K: It did. She was very still for a while. I had rarely encountered a person of her age who could be that still. But she simply said, "This sucks," and started discussing the logistics with me.

OFFICER S: Profound.

OFFICER K: Contrary to what you may have seen in movies, our Chosen Ones rarely make poetic declarations. In this case, I believe she was the only subject who truly grasped what was ahead of her.

OFFICER S: What logistics did you go over?

OFFICER K: The training that awaited her at ███████ in ███████, the preparations she would need to make before she left, and when I would return to pick her up for the move. I asked her how long she would need to prepare, and she told me a day. When I asked if she would prefer to take more time to bid farewell to family and friends and explain the situation to her mother, she said it wouldn't take that much time. "In case you haven't noticed, I'm alone here," I believe she said.

OFFICER S: She didn't think her mother would object to her child being taken away by a government agency she'd never heard of to fight the Dark One?

OFFICER K: No, she didn't. And by all accounts, she was right. When I came back a day later, she was sitting in the same spot with a backpack and an old banker box.

OFFICER S: I gotta be honest with you, she's not the Chosen One I'm betting on. My money's on Subject 4.

OFFICER K: Let's just hope we got at least one of them right.

TOP SECRET

5

SLOANE STUFFED another bite of spanakopita in her mouth. She stood with Esther at one of the high tables near the buffet in the ballroom where the Ten Years Peace gala was taking place. They had their heads bent toward each other as if they were having a serious conversation. It was the only way anyone would leave them alone long enough for them to get some food in their mouths. Being one of the Chosen Ones at the Peace gala was like being the bride at a wedding.

They were in the grand ballroom at the Drake Hotel. The room was white and gold—a white marble floor lined with pillars decorated in gold filigree with chandeliers casting white-gold light over the space. Along one wall, floor-to-ceiling windows showed the bend of Lake Shore Drive and the lights of the buildings along it and the stretch of dark that was Lake Michigan at night.

All around them were men in tuxedos and women in gowns, forming little clusters, clutching glasses of champagne by their stems. Sloane made eye contact with one of the guests and immediately turned away, not wanting to provoke conversation.

"You keep wincing," Esther said to her.

"I gave myself armpit razor burn this morning, and sweating is like literally rubbing salt in a wound," Sloane replied. A bead of sweat had just rolled across the raw part of her armpit, and she did not appreciate it.

Esther grimaced. "The worst."

Esther was wearing something only she could have pulled off, a drapey, elaborately pleated gown in a muted mint color. Her hair was tied back in a simple knot. She wore a thick layer of makeup, as usual, but tonight it suited the occasion, her eyes framed in gray eye shadow, like a puff of smoke had settled on each lid.

"I miss it here," Esther said. She was poking olives from a pasta salad with her fork, trying to get them all on one tine. Her hyperfocus on her plate was part of what made their disguise complete; when you were looking down, people thought you might be crying, and they avoided you. That combined with Sloane's effortless death glare would keep them safe for at least a few minutes.

"How's your mom doing?" Sloane said.

"Not great." Esther shrugged. "Her oncologist says there's not much we can do at this point except . . . delay things."

"I'm so sorry, Essy," Sloane said. "I wish I had something more profound to say, but it just . . . sucks."

It didn't seem right, really, that they could save the world by taking down an entity of supreme evil *using magic,* but they still couldn't keep their families safe from mundane dangers. To humanity, they were Chosen Ones, saviors, heroes—but cancer made everyone equal.

"Better to be honest than profound," Esther said distantly.

Over Esther's shoulder, Sloane spotted a trim young man in a tuxedo with a blue bow tie who was watching Esther with interest. Sloane narrowed her eyes at him and shook her head when he glanced at her. He moved away.

"We miss you, though," Sloane said. "Grumpy as we might seem."

"Oh, do *we* seem grumpy?" Esther raised an eyebrow. "Slo, I can see all the way from California that you're losing your shit. What's going on with you lately?"

Sloane gave her a sideways look. She thought about calling the man with the blue bow tie back over so he could distract Esther from this conversation.

"Don't think you can glare me into submission," Esther said. "I asked you a question."

She and Esther always had conversations like this. They both communicated like battering rams, for better or worse, which meant they frequently collided with each other, to catastrophic effect. But they also didn't waste each other's time. If Esther was thinking something, she would say it, and there was no guesswork involved.

"I requested some documents from the government," Sloane said. "Reading them has been . . . eye-opening."

"You know," Esther said, "sometimes it's better to keep your eyes shut." She sipped her champagne. "Okay, get that chunk of spinach out of your teeth, because I'm pretty sure Matt's about to call attention to you."

Sure enough, the musicians in the corner had stopped playing their cellos and violins and . . . was that a standup bass? They were all looking across the room to where Matt stood in his immaculate tuxedo with the gold bow tie, his smile wide. He tapped a champagne flute with a butter knife, trying to get everyone to quiet down.

"May I have your attention, please!" His voice boomed through the space. Commander Matt, they had called him when he spoke like that during their fight against the Dark One. There was no way anyone else could have led them but him; none of the other four could have been heard over the din of the Drain.

Sloane hurriedly stuck her fingernail between her two front teeth to free the chunk of spinach.

The room finally quieted. Everyone turned to Matt, as obedient as students in a classroom.

"Thank you, and I'm sorry for the interruption," Matt said, softening from Commander Matt to Politician Matt. "I was hoping you would all indulge me for a moment. Where's Sloane?"

Sloane pulled her finger out of her mouth and straightened up. Matt beckoned to her, and she joined him in the middle of the ballroom under one of the chandeliers. Her chest was so tight, it hurt. He took her hand. She looked at him expectantly, noting that her hands had gone numb. She *knew* she should have had a third glass of champagne.

"I knew I was in love with Sloane about eleven years ago," Matt said. "There was this little kid near one of the Drain sites where we had gone to investigate the Dark One, and he had lost track of his parents. And Sloane was carrying him around to every person she could see."

Sloane remembered the kid. She had picked him up because he had refused to move, and she didn't feel like arguing with him. She had been surprised by how easily he fell against her hip, given that she had never held a child before.

"She was just interrupting conversations to ask if anyone knew him. In that way Sloane does—if you know her, you know." A low laugh spread through the crowd. Even the people who hadn't met her could likely imagine, if they had read the dozen profiles that had been written about her in the past ten years calling her unstable, taciturn, moody, grouchy, a bitch. An antiheroine. Her cheeks flushed hot. Why was he making a joke of that now?

Matt went on. "Sloane's like one of those Easter chocolates—she's got a hard shell, but once you crack it, you get to the marshmallow-y good stuff in the middle." He smiled, his eyes sparkling.

It was supposed to be sweet. Instead, Sloane felt like a child standing in a woman's dress.

He took the ring box from his pocket, opened it, and got down on one knee. A few people around them gasped.

"Sloane, I love you. I've loved you for a long time." His eyes were on hers, but all around them, people had taken out their phones and were aiming them in Sloane and Matt's direction. This footage, like most videos of Sloane taken by strangers, would likely appear on television shows and in newspapers and on gossip blogs and be analyzed half to death. Her expression, her posture, her outfit, her goddamn lipstick.

Matt continued. "And I want to spend the rest of my life cracking that hard candy shell. Will you marry me?"

The crowd was like a giant animal, sighing as one.

Don't let them see you, she told herself, the same thing she had told herself when the Dark One's minions—all dead now; they had died with him—crept close in the middle of the night. But in this case, it didn't mean that she should run away; it meant that she should hide in plain sight.

Sloane summoned everything she had ever learned about pretending from all the post-battle interviews she had done and smiled wide, hoping her eyes were sparkling. "Yes." The word came out almost as a gasp, making her sound choked up — which was perfect, because then Matt leaped to his feet, hugged her, and spun her around, and no one was analyzing her expression anymore.

Everyone cheered, and there was a chorus of digital clicking sounds from all the smartphones, and news cameras rotated around them, capturing them from every angle — Matt in his tuxedo, Sloane in her beaded dress. The Chosen One and his blushing bride.

Who was, apparently, a goddamn piece of Easter candy.

Sloane was there, wishing there were a socially acceptable way to sponge sweat off one's armpits so they would stop *stinging,* but she also *wasn't* there.

She was by the river, the cold air burning her lungs, as she stared across the bridge at the Dark One right before their last battle. Part of her always would be.

6

S LOANE HAD HARDLY gotten the ring on her finger when the crowd swallowed her in congratulations. Someone thrust a champagne flute into her hand, and she looked for Matt, hoping she could plead with her eyes for an escape. But he was talking to an older gentleman in a suit and sipping a similar flute of champagne. Sloane's face was hot. She smiled at a woman who told her—tears in her eyes—that they were a "perfect couple," thinking of one of the recent articles about Matt that had called their relationship "perplexing." It was affixed to their refrigerator because Matt had thought it was amusing.

Sweat rolled down her stomach to her bellybutton. She searched the crowd for Albie and found him near one of the large pillars, talking to a woman in a tight black dress with her hair pinned up on one side. Sloane excused herself from the teary-eyed woman—who was recounting the story of her own engagement, twenty years before—and set her champagne down on one of the empty tables on her way to Albie.

When she reached him, she drew him in close so she could speak right into his ear. "I have to get out of here," she said. "Want to come?"

"Uh," Albie said, looking over his shoulder at the gala. "Yeah. Sure. What about Matt?"

Sloane looked for Matt in the crowd. He wasn't hard to find. His smile alone was a beacon, and then there was the glittery gold of his bow tie. Fondness pierced the mire of anxiety within her. He was good at this. He had always been good at this. "He'll be fine," she said. "Coat check. You got a five?"

Albie was digging in his pocket for his billfold as they marched out of the ballroom together. The coat check was a gap in the wall manned by a postadolescent with gel in his hair playing a game on his phone. As he shuffled away to find their coats, Sloane hiked up her skirt to undo the delicate straps of her shoes. She would be faster on flat feet.

"Spotted," Albie said under his breath. Coming out of the ballroom was a couple in matching white tuxedos, their eyes fixed on Sloane. She grabbed her stomach impulsively and hunched, pretending to be sick. Albie grabbed the coats from the shuffling attendant, tipped him five dollars, and put a hand on Sloane's back reassuringly.

"Let's find you a bathroom," Albie said as they passed the two men near the ballroom doors. He glanced at them. "Avoid the spanakopita."

The men looked at each other, stricken. She and Albie limped along toward the hotel restaurant, bent and huddled into each other, and once they were out of sight of the ballroom doors, she laughed and dragged him toward the kitchens.

Both of them had had their strengths, and Sloane's had been getting out of bad situations. She was always looking for exits, even when there weren't any. On a few occasions when Matt had dug in and decided it was time for them to make their heroic last stand, she had helped them escape instead. It was the only time she had ever felt like she really was a Chosen One.

And now that skill was helping her escape conversations. Not exactly how she had imagined putting it to use.

"Hello, hi! Ignore us, official hotel business!" she chirped once they were in the kitchen. She slipped behind one of the line cooks, lurched away from the heat of a pan fire, and ducked under the arm of someone opening the deep freezer. Albie apologized in her wake. She pushed the door to the alley open and drank in the cold air, her shoes dangling from her fingertips by their straps.

"God, don't tell me you're going to walk barefoot in an alley," Albie said, offering her her coat.

"I mean, I'm going to try to avoid broken glass," she said, shrugging the coat on. Her smartphone was in the pocket. She took it out to use the flashlight on the ground and found a hopping path over garbage and puddle and early frost. They went past a line of dumpsters, and when they reached the corner where alley met street, Albie grabbed her elbow to stop her.

"Okay, there's a shitty dive bar around the corner," he said, pointing to a pin on his phone map. "But we'll probably have to take it at a run so nobody spots us."

Sloane grinned. "This feels like old times, doesn't it?"

"Yeah, except without the threat of imminent death," Albie said, snorting. "Let's go."

Together they ran down the sidewalk and around the corner toward the sign for Fred's that was rendered in green neon lights in a window. The place was empty and smelled like a gym. Peanut shells cracked under Sloane's bare feet as she and Albie walked to the bar. Her barstool was ripped down the middle, with duct tape stretched across it to contain the stuffing.

"Perfect," Sloane said.

"Whiskey," Albie said to the bartender, an older man whose expression communicated profound lack of interest. Albie glanced at Sloane. "Make that two doubles. Old Overholt, if you've got it."

The bartender raised his eyebrows but turned away to pour them their drinks. Sloane took the pins out of her hair, lined them up on the bar in a neat row.

"I take it that proposal didn't go the way you'd hoped," Albie said to her.

"If this night had gone the way I hoped, there wouldn't have been a proposal at all," Sloane said.

"Then why the hell did you say yes?"

"There were five hundred cameras documenting every second of it," Sloane said. "What did you want me to do, completely devastate and humiliate the goddamn Chosen One of Chosen Ones on national television?"

Albie considered this. "Fair enough."

"Anyway, it's not that I don't want to marry him." She paused and frowned. "Okay, I guess I don't, but I have no idea why." She groaned and put her head down on the bar.

"Ugh, okay, either the feet or the head have got to stop touching every surface in this place," Albie said. He grabbed some paper napkins from the end of the bar and thrust them at her. "I feel like I might know why you don't want to marry him."

"Oh?" Sloane unfolded one of the napkins and wrapped it around one foot before balancing it on the rail again. It stuck there without difficulty. "Enlighten me."

"Well," Albie said, scrunching up his nose, "it seems like he doesn't really know you, Slo. You aren't squishy in the middle—"

"Technically *everyone* is squishy in the middle—"

"—which is *okay*. Many fine generals and responsible, emotionally distant fathers have also been un-squishy. We even call some of them heroes."

"I've always wanted to be an emotionally distant father." Sloane slid a napkin over on the bar and hit her forehead against it. "Fuck, Albie, what am I gonna do?"

"I mean," Albie said, "you already know what to do, don't you?"

Sloane sighed and looked at the ring she wore on her left hand, sparkling in the yellowish lights of the bar.

The bartender set two whiskeys down in front of them. They picked them up at the same time, then tipped them back in unison, both swallowing most of the whiskey at once.

"He wants me to just get over it, I can tell," she said. "He feels like we all went through the same thing, so if he's okay, I should be okay."

Albie pressed his lips together and finished his whiskey. He signaled the bartender for another round.

"Do you think he's right, that I should just . . . get over it?" she said.

"Well, if you figure out how," Albie said, "let me know."

She sipped the last dregs of her whiskey and stared at the array of multicolored bottles behind the bar. "We never talked about it," she said hollowly. She meant the day she and Albie had spent as captives of the Dark One. The only day, of all the dark days they had endured, that neither of them ever mentioned.

"What's there to say?" Albie said.

"Yeah," Sloane replied. "He also told me to go to therapy."

Albie snorted. "Therapy. Is that all anyone can tell us to do?"

"Didn't help you?" she said.

"It did. And it didn't. I don't know. I just wish people would stop talking about it as if just going fixes everything," Albie said. When he picked up his fresh glass of whiskey, his hands were shaking. He looked at her. "Why did you request those documents, Sloane?" he said. "It seems like it's only made things harder."

Sloane was quiet for a moment. "I've always wondered something," she said. "I wondered if they found more potential Chosen Ones than just us. I know the criteria were specific, but there are like three hundred million people in this country alone, so—maybe there were a few others."

"And this bothers you."

She nodded. "What if," she said, tilting her glass with a fingertip, "what separated us from them—what made us Chosen—was just that our parents said yes, and theirs said no?"

She remembered the conversation with her mother. The dim bedroom, with the heavy curtains closed. The clothes she had stepped on as she crossed the room to the bed. And the shape of her mother's body under the blanket, curled in on itself like the dead bugs in the light fixture over the kitchen table. The way everything had smelled like unwashed body and liquor.

And the way she had told Sloane to do whatever she wanted.

Albie gave her a sad look. "It would mean we have shitty parents," he said, "which, to be honest, I pretty much already knew."

"No, that's not how it went." Sloane was laughing through each word. "Bert took me aside and he was like, 'You don't seem to work well with people watching you.'"

"And then he told you to be the rogue assassin!" Albie exclaimed. "I'm telling you, that's how it went."

"How could you tell me how it went—you weren't even there! Plus, I never assassinated anyone."

"I'm telling *you,* you were a much more badass Chosen One than I was," Albie said. "I was like . . . cannon fodder. Like what Bert said to me—'You're a good man in a storm, Albie. Matt's lucky to have you.' To die in his place so he can go on to save the world, you mean."

Sloane shook her head. "You know that's not what he meant."

Albie shrugged.

"You motherfuckers." Esther stalked over to them. Sloane hadn't seen her come in. She wore a faux-fur coat that puffed up around her face like an old-fashioned ruff. Behind her were Ines and, brushing snow off his shoulders by the door, Matt. "Next time you're going to bail, you better tell us first. I was talking to some woman about her trip to Florence for *twenty minutes.*"

She dropped her clutch on the bar, signaled the bartender, and ordered a small fleet of gin and tonics.

"Hey there," Matt said, putting his hand on Sloane's shoulder. His fingers were cold. "This is a weird way to celebrate our engagement."

"Oh, boy. Fun's over," Sloane said to Albie.

"Shh," Albie said. "He can *hear you.*"

"Geez. Tell me how you really feel, Sloane," Matt said stiffly.

"I feel like I wish I hadn't worn these spandex undergarments," Sloane said. "Sit down, have a drink."

"Why are your feet wrapped in napkins?" Esther asked her.

"If Albie had his way, my entire body would be wrapped in napkins," Sloane said. "Nap wraps. Wrapkins."

Matt was looking at her in a way she didn't like. Like she was a car that had broken down on the side of the road and he was looking under the hood to see what the problem was. Like there was something wrong inside her that he could make right. And maybe that was the entire problem with them—he didn't see her; he saw who she could be with a few adjustments, and all she wanted was to stay busted and be left alone.

"You know," she said, propping her cheek on her hand, "I like being this way, actually."

"What, drunk? Yeah, lots of people do, Slo," Matt replied. His hand was still on her shoulder, but it was warm now, from her skin.

"Not drunk," she said. "The way I am all the time. I am that way all the way through. No marshmallow center. Anybody else'll tell you."

Albie was nodding along. "Maybe like . . . a lemon-juice center. Or a licorice center."

"Maybe other people don't know you like I do," Matt said gently.

"Except this is me, telling you," Sloane said, her voice suddenly firmer. "The Dark One sucked out all my insides. I know it. Everyone knows it. Except you."

"Sloane . . ."

"I'm going home," she said. She peeled the napkins off her feet and put them on the bar. She stumbled outside, holding her shoes by the straps. Matt followed and hailed them a taxi. He didn't try to talk to her, and he didn't even object when Sloane cracked the window open and stuck her head out as they cruised down Lake Shore Drive. By the time they got home, her nose and cheeks were numb.

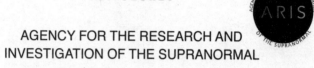

AGENCY FOR THE RESEARCH AND INVESTIGATION OF THE SUPRANORMAL

MEMORANDUM FOR: COMPTROLLER

ATTENTION: FINANCE DIVISION

SUBJECT: PROJECT RINGER, SUBPROJECT 5

Under the authority granted in the memorandum dated 4 March 2008 from the director of Central Intelligence to ARIS on the subject AR/CO-2 Project Ringer, subproject 5, code name Deep Dive has been approved, and $763,000.00 of the overall Project Ringer funds have been allocated to cover the subproject's expenses.

Charlotte Krauss

Director of Artifact Research

ARIS

7

THE FUMES FROM MATT's old diesel BMW combined with the hangover were making Sloane a little sick, so she leaned her temple against the cool window. Esther had left earlier that morning. They had dropped her off at the airport on the way, with a promise to fly out to California and visit her soon. Albie was in the front seat playing DJ and navigator at the same time, a phone in each hand. Ines was next to her in the back, tap-tap-tapping on her knee, which was also jiggling.

"My God, Ines," Matt said. "You're like one of those toys that buzzes when you wind it up."

"Well, if you didn't drive like you've got nothing to lose, I'd probably be calmer."

"Indoor voices, please," Sloane called out. "Slo's gonna vom."

"And what? If we're loud, we'll miss it?" Ines said, raising an eyebrow.

"Yes," Sloane said. "I require an audience."

Ines laughed and offered her an empty potato-chip bag. Sloane tried to catch Matt's eye in the rearview mirror, but his phone rang. "Eddie?" he said, answering it. Not that he would have met her eyes anyway—he hadn't so much as glanced at her since the night before.

Sloane glared at Ines, but she took the bag and angled even more toward the window so she couldn't see Ines's leg jiggle. She watched the trees smear past. They were an hour north of Chicago, where the city turned into peaceful suburbs with perfect lawns and mailboxes shaped like barns and dogs and boats. She wondered what it was like to carry lunch money to school instead of a faux-cheese sandwich wrapped in paper, to drive a car your parents bought for you to learn on, to go on school field trips to the city and stare up at the towering skyline. All these safe little lives going on uninterrupted.

"I gotta go, Ed, we're approaching a dead zone," Matt said. A second later, he hung up and put his phone back in the cupholder.

Bert had taught her how to drive when she was fourteen, out in the fields behind the house where she had learned about the Dark One. She had almost rolled the old Accord taking too sharp a turn in the mud. She hadn't needed to go to the DMV for the driving test like everyone else—Bert had snapped a picture of her against a blank wall and then one day just handed her a license out of the blue, along with a passport and a Smoothie Fiend BUY 10, GET ONE FREE! card with two stamps on it already.

Sloane smiled at the memory. She still had that card in her wallet.

"Better download that map, Albie," Ines said.

"Already done," Albie said. "All these years and you think I still don't know that GPS doesn't work around Drain sites?"

"You knew it at one time," Ines said. "But you had a couple hard years in there—"

"'Hard years' is a nice euphemism for 'so, *so* high'—"

"And as a result, I don't like to count on your memory."

"Fair enough."

A shiver crawled down Sloane's spine as Matt turned off the main road. She checked her phone—no bars, and they weren't even within a mile of the Drain site yet. They didn't even know why they'd been summoned, but when Agents Henderson and Cho summoned them, they went. It was easier to keep an eye on ARIS when they were invited.

It was quiet in the car as the first signs of the Drain appeared in the land around them. People had resettled in areas like this after the destruction, but the homes here weren't the kind with manicured lawns and novelty mailboxes. This was a sea of temporary dilapidated structures that had never been properly repaired after the Dark One destroyed the place. People were living without water or power and sometimes with massive holes in their floorboards. Matt had dragged Sloane to volunteer here once, and she'd had to pick her way across a collapsed porch just to get to the front door of a house.

Trees had grown wild and tangled, their roots crowded with weeds as tall as Sloane; long grass collapsing under its own weight hung over broken sidewalks. The road itself was full of potholes thanks to rough Midwestern winters, so Matt's driving became even more erratic, and Sloane started to contemplate the potato-chip bag again.

"Oh, boy," Albie said. "Fun times ahead."

Sloane craned her neck to see out the front windshield, almost knocking skulls with Ines as she leaned in too. Up ahead, the road appeared to come to an abrupt end, and there was just a sea of brightly colored tarps, like the bumps of moguls on a ski slope. And past them, on a small hill, stood the temporary government structure that surrounded the center of the Drain, a white geodesic dome roughly the size of a football stadium. Sloane's phone lit up as cell service came back.

There were always people camped around Drain sites, but Sloane never got used to them. They were all fanatics, but there were distinct groups among them—wannabe magic-users, usually, but also those who were desperate with grief and seeking spiritual healing and, the worst of the bunch, Dark One acolytes who wanted to bring him back.

Matt was on the phone, calling Agent Henderson for help, Sloane assumed, because there was no way they could drive through the wall of tents ahead of them. He stopped the car and waited at a safe distance from the crowd.

"Agent—yes, hello, it's Matt Weekes," he said. "Fine, thanks, and you? Great. We're here, but there's a bit of a problem—ah. Okay, thank you." He hung up. "They're sending a golf cart."

"I am not diving into that bowl of mixed nuts in a *golf cart*," Sloane said. "Can't they clear a path or something?"

"Apparently they've tried that and were unsuccessful," Matt said. Those were the first words he'd spoken to her since an "Excuse me" that morning in the kitchen. "So we either go on foot or in the golf cart."

"You forgot about secret option three," Sloane said, "which is to turn around and go home because HenderCho never wants anything we want to give them anyway."

"Slo, it's not gonna be that bad," Ines said. "Promise. We'll even let you sit up front."

"Oh, joy," she said.

"Bring your potato-chip bag," Ines suggested.

The golf cart arrived a few minutes later, one of the long ones with multiple rows of seats. The driver was in his early twenties, an eager man with sandy-blond hair and a firm handshake. He introduced himself as Scott, then directed Matt to a parking area and invited them all to climb into the cart. Sloane took the front seat she had been promised, sliding across the squeaky beige vinyl so Scott could get in beside her. The others piled in, and the cart lurched toward the tents.

"Sure is lively out here, huh?" Scott said, grinning. "Reminds me of a music festival, only—"

"Even worse outfits?" Sloane said, grabbing the handle on her right to steady herself as Scott whipped around a corner.

Up ahead was a circle of people in loose-fitting clothing sitting cross-legged. In the middle was a young woman lying with her hands over her heart. As Scott drove past, Sloane spotted a purple crystal in the woman's hands, held against her sternum. Sloane rolled her eyes. A séance, probably. A lot of people thought that the barrier between life and the afterlife was thinner at places like these, places where so many had died, so they came here to speak to their lost loved ones.

Just beyond the séance was a tent with an altar in front of it, a stick of incense dwindling in a dish atop it. At another tent, a besom—a kind of broom used in Wiccan rituals—was leaned up against a massive pentagram painted on the side of it. All around were different-colored stones wrapped in twine or laid on low tables. The smell of patchouli was thick.

"The air always feels weird here," Matt said. "Like a storm is coming, only it never does."

"Possibly you're just getting a contact high," Albie said. "Pretty sure that's not all just incense."

"No, that's not what I mean," Matt said.

"I feel it too," Ines said from the very back of the golf cart. "Makes me dizzy."

They drove past a shirtless old man playing a pan flute. He spotted them and, startled, dropped the instrument into his lap. Sloane saw Matt touch his finger to his lips to ask for silence. He always did that to stop people from going wild at the sight of them. It worked about half the time.

For all that Sloane was annoyed by people like this, people who thought being close to such horror and destruction would give them superpowers or make their wishes come true, she didn't have a real problem with them. And that was because the third set of people who gathered around Drain sites were so much worse by comparison: Dark One acolytes.

These were no well-meaning Wiccans, no modern druids in robes, no tarot-reading psychics or astrologists trying to figure out the position of Mercury (in retrograde at the moment). They were the kind of people you could walk past on the street and never look twice at, mostly men, almost all of them white, wearing blue jeans, and running secret websites about how the Dark One was misrepresented by the media, how all he had wanted to do was balance out the world's population so they wouldn't continue to devour Earth's resources or cleanse North America of its impurities, all racist vitriol disguised as reverence for a dead man. And worse than all that was that they wanted to bring him back, as if he wouldn't just murder every last one of them if he returned.

Sloane spotted a group of them roasting hot dogs over a portable grill and gritted her teeth. The tent behind them bore the motto that made Sloane choke on bile: MAKE THINGS RIGHT — BRING HIM BACK.

Make things right was the worst part of it. They thought Matt — the rest of them too, but mostly Matt — was the wrong that needed to be righted, the real evil that the Dark One would eradicate, ushering in some kind of white supremacist utopia.

Right before they passed out of sight, one of the Dark One wor-shippers recognized them, pointed his hot dog in their direction, and shouted, "Murderers!"

"Fantastic," Matt said over Sloane's left shoulder. "Scott, can this thing go any faster?"

"No, we're pretty much maxed out," Scott said. "But we're almost there, don't worry!"

Sloane felt her heartbeat behind her eyes. One of the men was coming toward them, hot dog in hand, ketchup smeared all over his fingers, and maybe he was shouting, she wasn't sure, because her ears were ringing.

Hello, Sloane. Did you get some sleep?

"What did you say to me?" she yelled at the guy with the hot dog.

"You heard me!" the man snarled. "Fucking bit—"

"Slo." Ines's hands were on her shoulders. "Don't jump out of the cart, please."

"Those—*fucking*—"

"Yeah, I know," Ines said. "But everyone and her mother has a smartphone and the ability to record video of you wasting some pasty idiot with an inferiority complex, so—"

"Here we are!" Scott chirped like nothing at all had just happened. "We'll just whisk you through security, and I'll get in touch with Agent Cho."

Sometimes Sloane wondered if the world had been worth saving.

8

S OMETHING WAS THERE.

Sloane felt it as soon as she passed through the doors.

Being inside the geodesic dome that housed ARIS's public-facing front corporation, Calamity Investigation and Restoration (CIR), felt like being inside a giant golf ball. The structure was massive and white, the roof made of small triangular panels that held together in a curve. Fluorescent lights shone between the panels, so the whole place glowed like a Halloween decoration, making everyone's skin appear green. The people who rushed back and forth inside it wore either the standard government garb — black or gray suits with boring ties and sleek hair — or white hazmat suits with the hoods down.

Agent Henderson waited for them by the entrance, checking his bulky watch. He held a leather file folder against his chest. When Sloane had first met him, right after Bert's death, he had been the definition of *strapping* — tall, muscular, and energetic — but he had gone soft around the middle since the Dark One fell. There was gray mixed with the red-brown of his beard now. He had a wife and two children, a mortgage, and a retirement plan.

"Hey, guys," he said with a grim smile. Sloane squinted at him a little. He looked . . . not right. Or maybe that was just the unsettled feeling inside her talking.

Something was there, in the Dome. She could still feel it.

"How was the golf cart?" Henderson asked.

"One hell of an engine in that thing," Albie said.

"Yeah, how much torque does it get, like three hundred and sixty-nine foot-pounds?" Ines said. "And the RPMs!"

"I forgot about this little comedy tag team," Henderson said, waggling his finger between Ines and Albie. "See anything weird out there?"

"We passed a séance in progress, but that seems fairly standard for that crowd," Matt said. "Has anyone managed to speak to the dead yet?"

"Allegedly," Henderson said, shrugging. "Pretty sure it was a hoax, but I won't rule anything out anymore. You okay, Sloane? You don't look so good."

Magic, that was what it was. It had to be. She felt that tingling in her chest, right behind her sternum. But she had never felt magic at a Drain site before. She was more likely to feel the opposite, a kind of limpness in the air, like something had wilted.

"Thanks," she managed to say to Henderson. "Just what everyone likes to hear."

They said goodbye to Scott, who gave a cheerful wave before returning to his golf cart, and Henderson led them across the springy temporary floor—gray—down an equally gray hallway with temporary walls hemming them in on either side. It had been ten years, but the structure still looked like it had been set up only to be taken down. There were no offices, just long tables packed with computer monitors and tangled cords.

If the Drain site was a bicycle wheel, they'd started off walking its circumference, then turned down one of the spokes and were walking toward the center.

As they neared it, Sloane saw that the middle of the site was surrounded by glass panels from floor to ceiling. Clusters of floodlights aimed white beams inward. Whatever was left of the Drain site, ARIS wanted to get a *very* close look at.

But it was not the source of the magic Sloane felt. The prickling spread from Sloane's chest to her abdomen. She tried to focus on the meeting room Henderson had taken them to, where his partner—

Eileen Cho—waited. She was spinning a closed laptop in circles on a table. The right wall was all windows, showing the Drain site, where dozens of workers in the typical white hazmat suits walked along the edge, gesturing at each other and taking samples with metal tools.

The Drain had driven a crater deep into the ground, so deep that some of the workers looked child-size from where she stood. When Sloane first saw a Drain site, she had expected it to be a uniform substance, like the surface of the moon. But there were still remnants of what had been there: broken planks, crumbling bricks, chunks of asphalt, bits of old fabric. They were reminders that this place had once been a suburban street. People had lived here. And they had died here.

"—Ten Years Peace celebrations," Cho was saying. "We wish Bert could be here to see it."

Ines and Matt were nodding, but all Sloane could think of was the stack of files in the bottom drawer of her desk, the ones she was reading early in the morning before Matt got up. The Bert that appeared in those files wasn't quite like the one she remembered. The Bert she remembered would never have called Sloane a "stray dog."

"All right there, Sloane?" Cho asked her. Her hair was in a loose knot at the base of her neck, and her buttons were askew. Cho always looked like she had gotten dressed in the dark. It was part of what made her good at her job—she was warm and clumsy, and you felt like she was someone you could trust. Bert had had the same quality when he turned up on Sloane's front lawn in his decrepit Honda.

Sloane was tapping each tingling fingertip against her thumb in turn, trying to press normal feeling back into them somehow. "What's going on here?" she said.

"I see your small-talk skills are ever improving," Henderson said. "Let's sit."

Once they had all settled in their chairs, Henderson pointed a remote at the wall of windows. They all lit up blue, showing a desktop with a white cursor. Cho had opened the laptop, and was clicking on a video file labeled *1IC145G*. They all stared at the pinwheel as the file loaded—as ever, Sloane was blown away by how finicky government tech was, and she might have commented on it if she hadn't been focused on how tingly her fingers felt—and then the footage played across all five windows at once.

"This is footage taken from a fishing boat west of Guam in the Pacific," Henderson said. "Five days ago."

The video wasn't crisp, played on such large screens, but it was clear enough for Sloane to get a sense of the waves that stretched in all directions, the swollen bellies of clouds about to unleash rain, the sway of the boat as it charged through the water. It almost looked like it had the last time she was on the ocean—but she wasn't going to think about that now.

Then the sea went flat as a pond, the boat stilling. She saw something dark moving just beneath the surface. It pierced the calm and shot up straight into the air. Another followed, and then another, too fast for Sloane to identify the objects, which were each as big as a man—no, bigger; the perspective was just flattened by the camera angle. Whatever the things were hovered in midair over the water, which began to move again, the boat bobbing along like a rubber duck in a bathtub.

The camera zoomed in on the objects, and Sloane realized they were *trees*. Not just trees, but pine trees, dark needles heavy with water. There were maybe thirty, all hanging at different heights, like wind chimes.

"What," Ines said, "the fuck."

"That's what I said," Henderson replied. "Would you open the second one, Cho?"

Cho closed the first and clicked on the second, labeled *2ICI45G*.

"Australia," Cho said to introduce this one. The footage opened on a rocky beach with the sun just beginning to set over the water. The land around it, even the dry grasses that grew on the slopes, glowed orange.

"Are you sure?" a male voice asked from behind the camera.

"Yeah!" came the chirped reply. The camera swung to the side, showing a massive boulder as tall as a house with others leaned up against it, as if part of the slope had crumbled off at some point in history and the rubble had been left there. There were silhouettes of lithe bodies on the boulders, beer bottles balanced next to them.

Sloane spotted the ties of bikinis, the frayed hems of jean shorts, the brim of a baseball cap.

The camera zoomed in on a girl no older than sixteen with a red-and-white-striped bikini top and a flat, tanned stomach. She wore her sun-streaked hair loose around her shoulders. She had turned toward the camera and was waving.

"If it doesn't work this time, I'll just fall in the water," she said with a shrug. "You recording?"

"Yep!" the man with the camera replied. "Go on!"

"Okay, watch!"

The sun burned orange behind the girl as she lifted one foot, skinny arms held out from her sides, and stepped into the air next to the boulder, over the water. She then lifted up her other foot so she stood on nothing at all. Sloane could see the light of the sky beneath her heel—there was only emptiness beneath her, yet she wasn't falling.

Half a dozen voices crowed with amazement, fists in the air, bottles clinking together, the camera shuddering as the one who held it gave a shout.

"I'm gonna take another step!" the girl called out, and before anyone could object, she did, leaning out, seemingly into the sky—

Her body tipped, not forward, but sideways, her feet ripped from beneath her. She screamed as her hair dropped toward the water in a sun-bleached curtain. She fell, but not toward the ocean—she fell *up,* toward the clouds, her arms flailing, her screeches echoing over the rocks. The camera followed her as she grew smaller and smaller, a tiny black shape against the clouds. And then she was gone, and the man with the camera was screaming. "Barbara! *Barbara!*"

The footage ended, leaving the screen blue again. They were all silent this time.

"The third, please, Cho," Henderson said.

The file was *3ICI45G.* And the footage had been filmed underwater; it was blue, cloudy, and dreamlike, the surface undulating with light. Sloane thought again about the Dive, her last trip to the ocean, the smell of salt and seaweed on the air—and she felt the tingling again, not just in her fingertips this time, but all the way up to her elbows, as if her arms were asleep. She shook them out, watching as a diver entered the camera's line of sight, eyes shielded by the reflective mask. The figure jabbed a finger down, and the camera swung in that direction.

Sloane saw what she thought was a bunch of seaweed growing along the ocean floor; the person holding the camera swam closer, the movements smooth. Shafts of light shone through the surface, refracted by the waves, onto neat rows of plants, their long, sharp leaves shifting as the water did. The diver swam closer, and Sloane saw a large metal structure on wheels with a bar arching gently away.

She recognized it. It was an irrigation pivot, like the kind used to water the fields around her hometown.

Sloane leaned closer to the windows as she realized the neat rows of plants along the ocean floor were not seaweed, but stalks of corn. The shadow of a tractor loomed in the distance. The diver swam over the corn, zooming in on the intact husks among the leaves, then under the metal arch of the irrigation system, where the tractor was in full view. As was the man still sitting atop it, trapped there with his knees under the steering wheel, his arms floating toward the surface.

Cho stopped the footage so that image stayed frozen on the screen for a few seconds before she closed it.

"That was in Hawaii, three weeks ago," she said. "We haven't been able to identify the man, but the girl from the second clip, Barbara Devore—she's been missing for a month now."

"It has to be magic," Matt said. "Right? There's nothing else it could be."

"It certainly falls under the category of the supranormal," Henderson said. "We have done extensive investigations on each of these incidents as well as hundreds of others that have occurred over the past decade. We've been able to confirm that these are not hoaxes."

"There are always supranormal occurrences here and there," Cho said. "But they seem to be happening closer and closer together, and they're becoming more numerous."

"Do you . . ." Albie swallowed so hard Sloane could see his Adam's apple forcing its way down. "Do you think the Dark One is back or something? Is that why you asked us to come here?"

Sloane felt a burning in her chest, and she wasn't sure if it was the same thing causing the tingling in her arms or if it was just run-of-the-mill terror. She couldn't sit still anymore—she got up, stepped around her chair.

"What is it?" Cho said.

"Can't a gal do a good, old-fashioned pace back and forth without getting questioned?" Sloane replied.

Henderson chuckled a little and said, "No, we don't think it's the Dark One. We haven't seen any evidence of his return—there are no actors present at any of these incidents, see? No one *wielding* magic—but magic is happening anyway. It seems to us . . . well, the prevailing theory in ARIS, anyway, is that it's like a malfunctioning radio. It's creepy when it starts playing music out of nowhere, but it doesn't mean anything sinister."

"You're saying that our planet is like a malfunctioning radio," Matt said, "and that doesn't alarm you?"

"Obviously it alarms us," Cho said. "But I'll take the source of Earth's magic being busted or . . . whatever this is . . . over the Dark One any day."

Sloane was moving, now without meaning to, toward the double doors across the room. Her body was burning, and as she drew closer, she smelled something sulfurous and chemical and familiar. Her hands had smelled that way after she did magic.

With the artifact.

The Needle of Koschei.

She hadn't known when she went with a crew of ARIS agents to the middle of the Pacific Ocean how much the Needle would cost her. In the end, she had been so desperate to get rid of it that she had chewed it out of her own hand.

The others had gone quiet. Or maybe she just couldn't hear them over the pulse in her ears. She didn't try the handles of the doors, just pressed both palms against them and drew a long, slow breath.

She felt Matt standing behind her. She didn't need to look to know it was him; she knew the shape of him, the heat of him. How close he dared to stand, so their arms were almost touching. And not because they were dating—no, *engaged,* she reminded herself—but because that's how Matt was: not afraid to get close to anyone.

"What is it?" he asked.

"You don't feel it?" she said.

"It feels weird in here, but no more than usual for a Drain site," Matt said. "Why? What do you feel?"

Sloane stared at the scar on the back of her right hand. A web of thick tissue, paler than the rest of her skin. "It's been bothering me since we got here. They made something new," she said. "And it's through these doors. Somewhere."

"Okay," Matt said, touching her shoulder. "Okay, let's go sit down and ask them about it."

Sloane nodded. On some level, she recognized that she would feel embarrassed later. But for now, she just let Matt take her hand and lead her back to the table. Henderson, Cho, Albie, and Ines were still sitting there, looking confused.

"Well, I guess that's as good a segue as any," Henderson said, scratching at his beard. "Uh—since these incidents have been increasing in frequency, we've stepped up certain programs we were already working on. It seems important to understand what exactly magic *is* and how to use it, so—we've developed a device that we believe channels magic. You reacting to it that way, Sloane, is actually really encouraging."

"You haven't tested it?" Ines said.

"Not yet," Cho said. "We were hoping you might agree to help us. You are, after all, the only people we are aware of who have successfully wielded magic before. You're less likely to cause a catastrophe."

Sloane tasted copper. She wished she had kept the empty potato-chip bag with her.

"Did you go for a wand?" Ines said. "Or, like, an orb? Or is it a giant hammer? Please say it's a giant hammer."

"No," Sloane said.

"Yeah, you're right, it's the government, so it's probably a boring box," Ines said.

"No," Sloane said. "No, we aren't going to help you test your fucking weapon."

"Slo," Matt said. "Just because it uses magic doesn't mean it's a weapon."

Cho sat down in the chair across from Sloane and folded her hands on the table. Her fingers were thick at the knuckle, and callused. Sloane had heard her say, once, that she liked rock climbing.

"In order to know how to fix whatever it is that's broken," Cho said, "we need to understand how magic works and how it's used. So we have made a tool—that's all."

"You expect me to believe you developed this thing so you could keep teenage girls from falling into the sky?" Sloane scowled. "You were already making it before you realized something was wrong— you *just* said that."

"We are a branch of the government concerned with scientific advancement—" Cho began.

"I studied history," Sloane interrupted, swallowing down the flavor of blood in her mouth. "And I know what motivates the government to invest in scientific advancement. We only have rockets that go into space because you guys were trying to blow up Soviets. This is just another Space Race."

"Even if it is a weapon," Henderson said, "would you rather Russia or China figure it out first, Sloane? And do you think they won't be racing to harness magic themselves?"

"I would *rather* governments stopped playing the who-can-destroy-each-other-faster game," Sloane snapped. She knew by the ringing in her ears that she was panicking.

"Yeah, well, I'd rather open up a goddamn ice cream shop," Henderson said. "But we all have to deal with reality."

"Countless people have died because of magic," Matt said. "Right here, in this spot, actually. It's happened right in front of us. And you want us to be complicit in something that might bring more of that?" He sounded choked. Sloane hadn't heard him sound that way in a long time. "After what we've seen—after what we've done?"

He didn't know the half of it, Sloane thought. He didn't know a damn thing about what she had done, and it would stay that way.

Beside her, Albie was staring at his hands, curled over the edge of the table. His fingers had once been nimble enough to fold the most intricate origami Sloane had ever seen. He had tried to teach her once how to make a crane, and the session had ended in a heap of crumpled paper. But the damage sustained from their time as captives of the Dark One had taken the feeling from his fingertips, so he had given up the hobby. Now those hands were trembling.

"Albie," she said.

He didn't look at her. "Isn't it . . ." He cleared his throat. Albie was shorter than average, with thinning blond hair that stuck up in all the wrong places and a hunched posture from the permanent damage done to his spine. He was nobody's Chosen One, not now and not ever. "Isn't it important to know how to use it, though?" he said. "So it can't be used against us again?"

"Albie," Matt said. "You can't mean that."

"Don't give me that Hero Voice," Albie said, his own voice shaking. "Nobody ever used magic against you — any of you! — the way the Dark One used it against me. Whether it's a tool or a weapon or a freaking plush toy, I'm not going to sit back and let the rest of the world figure out how to do it to us without us knowing how to do it back. Mutually assured destruction."

Sloane reached for words and came up empty. He had a point — she had been kidnapped by the Dark One, too, but he hadn't done to her what he had done to Albie, hadn't attacked her body and left her with no feeling in her hands and no way to rejoin the fight.

He had done something else. Damaged her without so much as touching her.

"If people die because of your help," she said finally, her throat aching, "you'll have to carry that around."

"And if people die because I don't help?" he said, meeting her eyes at last. "Either way, we'll carry it. We always do."

TOP SECRET

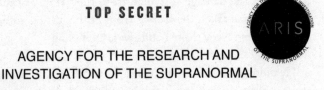

AGENCY FOR THE RESEARCH AND INVESTIGATION OF THE SUPRANORMAL

MEMORANDUM FOR: ROBERT ROBERTSON
OFFICER, AGENCY FOR THE RESEARCH AND INVESTIGATION OF
THE SUPRANORMAL (ARIS)

SUBJECT: PROJECT RINGER, SUBJECT 2, DEEP DIVE AFTERMATH

Dear Officer Robertson,

Attached is the document we discussed. Sloane and I developed this piece of writing in one of our sessions as part of her ongoing cognitive-behavioral therapy for PTSD. In our exposure-therapy practice, we need to reliably provoke Sloane's panic so that she can become habituated to the emotions it brings forth. As such, the following exposure is as detailed as Sloane could manage in order to most effectively simulate a re-experiencing of the event, which we refer to as "the Dive."

I must remind you to keep this confidential, as providing this to you is a violation of HIPAA. However, given how dire the situation is, I agree that an exception must be made.

Thank you, and have a pleasant week.

Sincerely,

Dr. Maurene Thomas

I'm on the ARIS ship. It's a cold morning. I see the glare of the sun on the water. As I pull the string attached to the zipper of my wetsuit, the fabric tugs in from both sides toward my spine. The mouthpiece tastes like chemicals. My nose feels blocked as I try to breathe only through my mouth.

All around me are ARIS officers, at first identical in their black scuba gear, but if I look closely I see the swell of Maggie's hips, or Marie's long, muscular legs, or the bristle of Dan's mustache. Their eyes are shielded by the goggles, which is a relief, since they've been looking at me skeptically since I met them.

And they have good reasons. I'm only fifteen. I got my dive certification in a hurry once Bert briefed me on the mission. I've only practiced a few times.

But I'm Chosen, and that means they have to follow my lead. So even though I'm shivering in the cold and squinting into the sun and so scared I want to throw up right into the ocean, I sit on the edge of the boat and slide into the water.

There's a rush of cold. I try to stay still. To breathe deep into the regulator. To exhale fully before inhaling, so I don't hyperventilate. All over me is something tingling and burning. It's not the sting of salt water on the skin around my eyes; it's more like feeling coming back to a limb that's gone to sleep. On the way here I asked the ARIS officers if they felt it too. They didn't. They don't. Just me. *Is she making it up?* I feel them wondering, and I'm wondering too.

The others are in the water now. Someone tosses me the line that will keep me attached to the boat, and I hook it to my belt, tug at it to make sure it's secure. All the ARIS officers wait for me to move. They look like aliens in their mirrored masks, polarized so they can see better underwater. The Dive is too deep for a beginner like me, but there's nothing anyone can do about it. I have to go.

I think of that Millay poem as I kick my flippers. *Down, down, down into the darkness of the grave.* I have a flashlight in one hand, held against my side. I swim away from the boat, checking over my shoulder now and then to make sure the others are following me.

What's ahead of me is just cloudy blue. Bubbles and particles of sand. The occasional piece of seaweed flopping past. A darker shape develops slowly in front of me, and I know what it is.

I wasn't expecting the boat to blend so well into the bottom of the ocean. It's coated in a fine layer of sand, the same muted blue as the ocean floor. It could have been a stretch of dead coral if not for the sharp bends of the radar aerials and the main mast, with its attached ladder, the rungs still white when I shine my flashlight on them.

I know this ship, the *Sakhalin*. I researched it right after the briefing, months ago. A Soviet spy ship, Primor'ye class, built sometime between 1969 and 1971. The Primor'ye-class ships had been converted from large fishing boats, outfitted to gather electronic intelligence and transmit it back to shore. They were not usually made for combat, but the *Sakhalin* was special. When I swim closer, I shift the beam of light back to the distinct bulges of weapons systems, one of them now wrapped in seaweed.

The tingling is in my chest now, right behind my sternum. Like heartburn. When I swim closer to the ship, it drops to my belly, right to the middle of me. I keep kicking, moving toward the energy. (I have no choice. I don't mean that ARIS is forcing me; I mean that whatever it is—the feeling, even though it's almost painful—won't let me turn back.)

Someone tugs on the line attached to me, a signal that I should stop. I don't. I swim over the deck gun and dodge the bulk of the aft superstructure. As I pass over the smoke funnel, I feel a stab of terror, like I'm going to be sucked into the blackness and disassembled. But I can't stop swimming.

I reach the aft mast, and I know I'm in the right place. The burning in my chest turns to a thump. Built in the base of the aft mast is a door fastened by a busted lock. Without thinking much about it, I slam the base of my flashlight into the lock, once, twice, three times. Already worn by time and exposure to water, the lock breaks.

The little door opens and I turn my beam of light toward it. Inside the mast there's a small trunk about the size of a toaster, elaborately decorated with gilt and enamel in a pattern of flowers and leaves that reminds me of babushkas and matryoshka dolls. I know I should swim with it to the surface, let the ARIS officers scan it with their equipment to make sure it's safe. But if I do that, they'll form a perimeter around it, and I have to be looking at it, holding it, feeling inside me the pounding of its heart.

So I open it.

Settled inside on a bed of black velvet is a silver needle about the length of my palm.

Koschei's Needle.

I read a lot of folktales to prepare for this mission. They say Koschei was a man who couldn't die. He hid his soul away from his body in a needle and put the needle in an egg, the egg in a duck, the duck in a hare, and the hare in a trunk. Only when a person broke the needle could they take his life.

I am trembling when I touch it. I think it trembles too.

And then—horrible pain, a flash of white. The tingling of returned feeling is gone, and in its place, I'm enveloped in flames. Scalding skin peeling away from muscle, muscle cooked away from bone, bone turning into ash, that's what it feels like. I scream into the regulator mask, and it pulls away from my face, letting in water. I choke and thrash, struggling to grab the line that attaches me to the boat, but my hands won't work.

And then it's like—a pang so deep I feel it in every part of my body, like the sounding of a clock tower at midnight. It feels like wanting something so much you would die to get it, more than craving or longing or desire—I am empty, and more than that, a black hole, so absolutely composed of nothingness that I attract all *somethingness* to me.

All around me the water swirls and churns, bubbles so thick they keep me from seeing anything. Pieces break off from the ship and enter the cyclone of water. Black shapes tumble past me—the ARIS officers in their scuba suits. I choke on water as I scream, and I feel like I'm pulling something in, like I'm drawing a breath.

The next time I open my eyes, I'm staring at the sky. All across it are clouds. I tip forward, water rushing down my back and into the wetsuit. The water that surrounds me isn't blue; it's red, dark red. My hand hurts so badly I can't stand it. I lift it up to look at it. Something hard and straight is buried under my skin like a splinter, right next to one of my tendons. I press against it. It's Koschei's Needle.

Something bobs to the surface next to me. It looks like a piece of plastic at first, but when I pick it up, it's soft and slippery. I scream, dropping it when I realize it's skin. All around me are pieces of skin and muscle and bone and viscera.

Everyone is dead. And I'm alone.

TOP SECRET

9

THEY LEFT ALBIE with Cho so he could try the device. She had promised to get him home when they were finished.

Sloane had no doubt that the device worked — she would not have felt its presence so strongly if it didn't. They all had their own way of relating to magic, and hers was with craving, and seeking, and understanding. She *knew* the device, and the device knew her.

Albie had been more straightforward in his use of magic. Albie with the Freikugeln — the bullets of German legend that struck their targets without fail — had just been a man with a tool, the same as a hammer or a saw. His artifact had not burrowed under his skin, becoming part of him, the way Koschei's Needle had done to her. He had simply held the bullets, and though they never did what the legend said they would — none of the artifacts they had collected had — they had allowed him to perform rudimentary magic, lighting fires, making objects float, things like that.

Ines, Matt, and Sloane walked back down the spoke of the bicycle wheel and around its circumference until they reached Scott in his golf cart. She didn't feel fear of the device anymore; instead, what she felt was numbness, a separation between body and mind. She knew that time would weld the two together again; she would just have to wait.

Scott took them out the same way they had come in, weaving a serpentine path through the tents. Hardly a minute into the drive, Sloane spotted the tent with MAKE THINGS RIGHT — BRING HIM BACK on it, and the ringing in her ears intensified. The distance between mind and body that she had maintained since sensing the magical device collapsed suddenly, like hands clapping together. She braced herself on the handrail that was keeping her in her seat and threw herself out of the golf cart to the tune of Ines and Matt crying "Sloane!" in unison.

She walked past a little altar made of a stump with what looked like a squirrel skeleton wrapped in beads and twine perched atop it, and a tent with a dream catcher hanging in the zipped-shut doorway, likely mass-produced in China and distributed in the Home section of a hipster clothing chain. These people wanted magic, but they had no idea what magic really was; they had never seen the great unraveling of the Drain, the way it had separated all living things into distinct pieces, bone, sinew, blood, and nerve flung apart so you could see the fine details that made up a body, all while said body was still conscious enough to comprehend it.

When she reached the little campfire of boys pretending to be men, they had finished cooking their hot dogs and were now listening to music, but Sloane could only hear the thump of the bass. The ringing in her ears was too strong at that point for her hear much of anything, including Ines calling out her name behind her.

She noted the hunting knife on top of a pallet of bottled water nearby and planted her feet in front of the portable grill, staring down at the man who had almost but not quite called her *bitch* earlier. It was not the first time she had been called that word, and it wouldn't be the last, but there was a certain violence in it — the way it made her anger small and petty, the way it reduced her entire self to some narrow, foolish thing.

"Hello there," she said, her voice sounding oddly unctuous all of a sudden. "Do you recognize me?"

She could tell by his wide eyes that he did. And just as they were narrowing, just as the word *bitch* was likely taking shape in his mouth again, she bent and picked up the hunting knife.

"What—" the man started, but she had already unsheathed the

hunting knife and plunged it into the side of the tent, right through the RIGHT in MAKE THINGS RIGHT.

"What the fuck?" the man shouted. They were all on their feet. Sloane only heard ringing.

"You idiot," she said. "You think he would welcome your loyalty if he came back, that he would reward you? If he comes back to life, he will rip your guts out just like everyone else's."

"He only targeted the weak," the man said. "Your boy over there got lucky the first time—"

His eyes shifted over Sloane's shoulder to the golf cart, to Ines and Matt. But she didn't hear what he said next. She just punched him in the face.

The ringing in her ears stopped. Pain crackled in every knuckle. She shook out her hand, gritting her teeth against the ache that spread all the way up her arm. The man's nose was bleeding, and his friends were on their feet around him, shouting obscenities at her but not quite ready to fight back. She was still a girl, after all.

She had thrown punches before, but she always forgot how badly it hurt. Ines grabbed her arm and dragged her away. She yelled "Eat shit!" over her shoulder before getting back in the golf cart.

Scott was staring at her when she sat down.

"What?" she said, and he just shook his head and drove on, going as fast as the little cart could carry them.

TOP SECRET

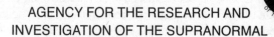

AGENCY FOR THE RESEARCH AND INVESTIGATION OF THE SUPRANORMAL

MEMORANDUM FOR THE RECORD

TO: DIRECTOR, AGENCY FOR THE RESEARCH AND INVESTIGATION OF THE SUPRANORMAL (ARIS)

FROM: OFFICER ████████████, CODE NAME BERT

SUBJECT: DEEP DIVE AFTERMATH

Dear Director,

I very much appreciated your letter regarding the Deep Dive incident. We are deeply saddened by the loss of some of our finest agents, and it has been difficult to carry on with Project Ringer without them. But as you noted in your message, we must soldier on for the sake of the cause. The Dark One is too potent a threat.

I understand your concern about Sloane Andrews's ability to move forward after such a trauma. I am writing only to give you my observations; the decision is, of course, up to you. I have thought it over carefully, and I must recommend against releasing Sloane Andrews from Project Ringer for the following reasons:

1. Despite costing the lives of multiple agents, whose value cannot be estimated, and upward of one million dollars (money we can't recoup, obviously), Project Deep Dive was technically a success. We were able to retrieve Koschei's Needle, which is currently buried in Sloane Andrews's hand. Which brings me to my next point.

2. Though we have discussed the possibility of removing the Needle surgically, everyone here at Project Ringer is reluctant to interfere with a force we don't fully understand. We don't know how the Needle will behave if it is disturbed. Therefore we can regard Sloane and the Needle as inextricably linked. To dismiss Sloane Andrews now would be a tremendous

waste of resources, as well as a waste of the lives lost retrieving the Needle.

3. Though Sloane herself has asked to be relieved of duty, I don't think it will be difficult to get her cooperation. I have been observing her for years now. She trusts me. She has come to regard me as something of a paternal figure. If I tell her to stay, she will stay.

4. The behavior of Koschei's Needle suggests that Sloane has a strong affinity for magic. Though the events of the Deep Dive were tragic, they were also indicative of tremendous power, which we may need to defeat the Dark One.

I suggest, therefore, that we encourage Sloane to employ the same techniques that soldiers (often unconsciously) use in active combat, compartmentalizing trauma so that they can continue in battle and suppressing those parts of their personalities that do not serve them in intense situations. Sloane Andrews functions well alone and with a high degree of personal responsibility and autonomy. I will foster her independent streak by assigning her solo missions while I form the others into a functioning team under the leadership of Matthew Weekes. We can instruct Sloane's psychotherapist, Dr. Maurene Thomas, to combine drug therapy with compartmentalization techniques so that Sloane is able to maintain a reasonable level of stability in the short term.

Let me know if you'd like to discuss this plan or offer any suggestions. Thank you again for your concern and for the flowers. We can but endeavor to move forward.

Sincerely,

███████

TOP SECRET

TOP SECRET

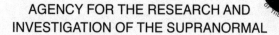

AGENCY FOR THE RESEARCH AND INVESTIGATION OF THE SUPRANORMAL

MEMORANDUM FOR THE RECORD

TO: DIRECTOR, AGENCY FOR THE RESEARCH AND INVESTIGATION OF THE SUPRANORMAL (ARIS)

FROM: OFFICER ███████, CODE NAME BERT

SUBJECT: RE: DEEP DIVE AFTERMATH

Dear Director,

In my previous letter, I offered my observations about Sloane Andrews in the aftermath of the Deep Dive incident and presented to you a plan of action. In response, you expressed frustration with my "psychobabble mumbo jumbo" and told me to "speak plain English." While I would appreciate a more amicable tone moving forward, I understand the necessity of simple language in matters such as these, so I will try to put this in terms you can understand:

I previously observed about Sloane Andrews that she was a bit like a stray dog. Feed a starved dog and you will have its loyalty, even if you don't treat it well. For Sloane, her need for approval will be the leash I keep her on even while she feels like she's roaming around free.

We can't lose our Project Ringer subjects. It's too late for that now. Either they defeat the Dark One for us or we all die.

I hope that this English is plain enough for you, sir.

Sincerely,

███████

TOP SECRET

10

SLOANE WAS AT THE ENTRANCE to the Modern Wing of the Art Institute of Chicago at 9:30 a.m.—time for her friend Rebecca to let her in, though the museum didn't open to the public for another hour.

She saw Rebecca through the glass doors, tying off the end of her braid. Rebecca yawned, unlocked the door, and waved Sloane in.

"You're too prompt," Rebecca said. "Why aren't you hung over like everyone else our age?"

"First of all," Sloane said, "'our age' is not a thing because you are twenty-two. And second of all, it's Tuesday."

"So?" Rebecca said. "Monday-night booze tastes just as good as Saturday-night booze."

Sloane's presence in the art museum at odd hours had become commonplace. The staff knew her, and no one had ever objected to someone letting her in early. It was, possibly, the only perk of being a Chosen One that she actually enjoyed.

This was part of her weekday rhythm. She didn't have a job. The government had paid them for their years of service, and Sloane had handed the money over to an investment bank. The interest would keep her going for a while, provided she spent carefully.

The others had found more financial stability, but at a cost. Matt had sold the rights to his autobiography and partnered with an experienced writer, and that money was plenty to coast on—not that he did. He was always traveling, speaking at conferences and universities, appearing at charity balls and philanthropic galas, meeting with politicians and community organizers. Esther, too, had turned her fame into money, cultivating her Insta! following as she would a garden. Ines had illustrated her own graphic novel about her story, rendering the Dark One's death in swirls of color. Albie, meanwhile, was in some commercials abroad, using his face to make back the money he had lost by going to rehab.

One day, Sloane would have to find a job for which her identity wouldn't be an issue—one that required no qualifications or experience—or she would have to sell off pieces of herself one by one, the way everyone else had. She didn't blame them for it—not much, anyway—but part of her felt like she would sooner live in her mother's garage than sacrifice what little privacy she had carved out of her own fame.

The Modern Wing was bright and open, a wide corridor of white with galleries on either side. She climbed the stairs to the third floor, which was where she always began the visitation, in the architecture and design gallery. The space was empty, of course—it usually was, regardless of how packed the rest of the museum was. She wandered past the chairs made of twisted wire and the vase that looked like spilled milk to the sketches of proposed Chicago buildings. Then she sat on a nearby bench and stared at the drawing from the Burnham Plan, the proposed city design for Chicago that had never come to fruition.

Her brother, Cameron, had been studying architecture when he answered the call to fight the Dark One. He had died in one of the Drains, in Minneapolis. They had fought over his decision to put school on hold, even though she had been young at the time, only twelve. *You're not a soldier,* she had told him. *You're a skinny nerd and you'll get yourself killed.* A rare moment of prescience, maybe.

She had taken all of Cameron's things from her mother's house and pored over the sketches in his journals so many times she had them all memorized. Everything from a child's drawing of a doghouse to a detailed, carefully measured floor plan of his dream home.

He had wanted to make places that felt interesting and warm. Places that didn't feel like home, she had joked with him once. At least, not like *their* home.

He had liked it here. So now Sloane came here, not to the Drain site where he had lost his life, not to their central Illinois haunts, but *here,* to visit him.

She rarely stayed long. A half hour, maybe, and then she would drift through the other exhibits. The new one downstairs was a series of photographs of big-rig trucks. After wandering through them for a few minutes, she said goodbye to Rebecca, who already looked bored out of her mind, and left. She turned right, walked to the lakefront path, and did a few stretches before jogging north, toward Ines and Albie's place.

The lake reflected steel blue back at her. It was a cloudy day, and there was mist over the water, blurring the horizon line. The run was about six and a half miles and would take her an hour if she kept up her usual pace. She passed a small fleet of spandexed people on bicycles and a woman in hot-pink leggings walking a spotted hound. A man in short shorts breezed past her.

She watched the crashing of the waves against the breakers, the dogs chasing tennis balls on the dog beach, the speed-walking women in visors with their fists pumping at their sides. No one paid any attention to her, not here, where she was just another jogger. She turned away from the lakefront path and toward Java Jam.

She ordered the coffees breathlessly, then carried them down the street to Ines and Albie's apartment, a second-floor corner unit in a grand two-flat. The stairwell carpeting was dark green and worn down the middle where too many shoes had trodden; the walls were covered with wallpaper that had tiny flowers on it in purple and red and blue.

Ines was already at the door when Sloane reached the landing, her glasses on and her hair piled on top of her head. "Little early, aren't you?" she said, grabbing her coffee from the tray and turning away from the door.

Sloane followed her in, sipping the coffee that was left. She got a mouthful of cinnamon. "Switch."

They traded cups. "Don't know how you drink that; it's pure milk."

Sloane's sneakers squeaked on the floor, which was the standard Chicago yellowish oak that creaked no matter where you stepped. Albie's door was closed, and so was Ines's, but in different ways. Albie's was closed like he just wanted to keep the noise of the hallway out. Ines's was locked and bolted from the outside, as secure as a bank vault. Up until a few years ago she had been booby-trapping it — even though it was illegal — and Sloane didn't have the heart to ask if she was still doing that. She pretended to be fine, but Sloane had seen the neat row of medications on her dresser, the twitch of her body at certain sounds and gestures.

The apartment was warm and comfortable, with a colossal bean-bag chair that was always leaking pellets; the curtains on the two windows facing the alley that were just a Canadian and a Mexican flag, respectively.

Ines went back to the stove, poking at her eggs with a wooden spoon. The whole room smelled like onions.

"You know, once you hit thirty, this whole living-like-a-college-junior thing is going to be less charming and more creepy," Sloane said.

"What do you mean, like a college junior? Are you referring to Frodo?"

"You mean the giant beanbag you decided to name Frodo Baggins? Yes, that's exactly what I'm referring to."

"Just because you refuse to enjoy your life doesn't mean the rest of us can't," Ines said. "You have white bathroom towels and you're invigorated by early-morning runs in the sleet. You're like the dad from *Calvin and Hobbes*."

"I always liked Calvin's dad."

"Of course you did." Ines snorted. "Have you talked to Matt yet?"

Sloane shook her head. "He had the mass-incarceration thing last night and a meeting this morning. Why?"

Ines sipped her coffee.

"I'm in trouble, aren't I," Sloane said.

Ines shrugged.

"If he thinks I'm going to apologize to him for punching that ass-hole . . ."

"I'm not here to have your fight with Matt before you have it," Ines said. "Just don't assume he's going to thank you for being his little white knight."

Sloane scowled at her.

"Yeah, I said it," Ines said. "Did you see the Essy Says update?"

"No. How bad is it?"

Ines took her phone out of the pocket of her sweatshirt and handed it to Sloane. Esther's Insta! account was already on the screen.

Sloane recognized the familiar setting of one of Esther's videos—her office, which was decorated like someone's Pinterest dream, draped in stylish fabrics with muted colors, a string of pale pink fairy lights, and an expensive camera that captured all the shine in her hair and every knickknack on her shelves. And in the middle of it all, Esther, dressed in a heather-gray sweater that bunched up at her wrists as she drank from a teacup with a little bird carved into the side. The video was titled "Essy Says Is Going Places!"

As Sloane watched, Esther introduced a clip from the day before, showing her skin care and makeup in fast-forward as she got ready. Sloane was always perversely fascinated by how many steps Esther's skin-care routine had. Sloane could never have remembered that many things in the morning. Not without coffee. And maybe amphetamines.

"I'm not watching her put on makeup; it'll give me hives," Sloane said, but Ines was already reaching over the island. She skipped forward on the video, past the impressive powdering and lining and staining, until there was Esther back in her gray sweater again, sipping from her teacup.

"I have some news to share," Esther said with a waggle of her eyebrows. She was talking in her video voice, chipper and unctuous—similar to her speaking voice, but *more*. "No, I'm not talking about the big punch from my girl Sloane—the link to that is in the caption."

Sloane sighed. "Fantastic."

"February thirteenth, I'll be launching Essy, my very own lifestyle brand!" Esther's perfectly lined eyes sparkled. "That's right, you'll now have a one-stop shop for all the product recommendations and reviews you could ever ask for! And you know you want to be an Essy girl."

"Well," Sloane said as Ines stopped the video. "That was inevitable, I guess."

Ines turned off the stove and tipped the eggs onto a plate that waited on the counter. "I invited her to come down with me in a couple weeks. You should come too. Get away from the cold."

"I love the cold," Sloane said. "It's my Nordic blood."

"No, it's your determination to love what everyone else hates and hate what everyone else loves," Ines said. She jabbed the rubbery eggs with the tines of her fork. "You should still come. I'm going to kidnap Albie."

Sloane winced at the word *kidnap*. "Have you seen him since . . ." Sloane said. "Did he tell you if the prototype worked or anything?"

Ines's brow furrowed. "No—he came home last night and disappeared into his room right away. But it worked. It must have."

Sloane felt the irrepressible need to sleep, suddenly.

"Maybe it's not so bad," Ines said, shrugging a little. "If the world is breaking—that girl floating toward the sky, my God—maybe we'll need magic to fix it."

"If anything, magic is what broke it," Sloane said darkly.

"You hate it so much," Ines said, nodding to the knot of scars on Sloane's hand. "But you've never explained why."

Sloane put her hand under the lip of the counter. "I don't hate it, exactly," she said. "I've just seen what it can do."

"So have all of us."

"Yeah." But Sloane didn't mean the Drains or the leveling of the tower or even the death of the Dark One. She meant the taste of copper and salt on her tongue as she had surfaced after the Dive.

Her coffee had run out, and only foam was left.

$$\boxed{\text{II}}$$

T HAT EVENING, Sloane got a text from Esther: *Nice jab. Bert would be proud.* She included a link to a blurry cell phone video of Sloane punching the Dark One acolyte. The still image in the article was of Sloane with teeth bared, her fist up by her face. Sloane looked herself over, the sheen of sweat on her pale face, the weird hollowness to her eyes. It was an expression she had seen in the mirror often since the Dark One's death.

"Shit," she said aloud. Matt had just gotten home from a coffee meeting with Eddie. He was hanging his coat up in the closet.

"There's a video of the punch online," she said.

"What a shock," Matt replied, closing the closet door. He had the sleeves of his powder-blue shirt rolled up to his elbows.

"I'm not sorry, you know," she said. "That guy was a piece of shit. He deserved it."

"That's not the issue."

"I was defending *you,*" Sloane said.

"Yeah, and that *is* the issue," Matt said. "I don't need you to defend me, Sloane. I can take care of myself."

"But you weren't going to," Sloane said. "You're so—*passive* about stuff like this—"

"Passive?" Matt laughed harshly. "*Passive?* What do you think I've been doing every day since the Dark One fell, exactly? Twiddling my thumbs?"

"No, of course not." Sloane scowled. "But guys like that—"

"Are not my problem," Matt said. "They're easy to spot and easy to avoid. My real problem is contented people who smile while refusing to lift a finger for anyone who isn't them. That's who I spend every day fighting, trying to get them to fucking *do* something. And it would be really nice if my fiancée could understand that instead of making things harder for me."

"How the hell did I do that?" Sloane snapped. "It's *my* picture that's in the news, not yours."

"Yeah, it's your picture, but now those assholes and their 'message' are in the news again, and they get to be victims this time! You came at them out of nowhere, threatened them with a knife—"

"I didn't threaten anyone with a knife!"

"That's not what the picture of you *holding a knife* looks like. Do you think that shit doesn't come back on the rest of us? That if you're violent to protect me and Ines, that doesn't make *us* look violent too? And we don't get to bounce back the way you do! We get to sit here worrying if a bunch of extremists are going to burn our houses down."

"That's not going to happen."

"Well, it must be nice to feel that confident," Matt said. "But I don't. I don't get to lose my shit and punch a guy, I don't get to mess up. I am always failing someone, all the time."

All the anger seemed to go out of him at once. He sat down on the couch and slumped over his knees. The ice pack Sloane had been using for her swollen knuckles was wedged between the cushions, no longer frozen.

She wanted to comfort him, but she didn't know how. She had never seen him so tired, so . . . *disappointed*. In the world, in himself, even in her. She sat next to him on the couch, her hands clasped over her knees. The television was off, so she saw them reflected in the black screen, Matt's head hanging low, Sloane stiff and upright.

"He called you 'boy,'" she said quietly.

"Yeah," Matt said, turning his head so their eyes met. "What else is new?"

"What was I supposed to do, just let him talk down to you?" she said.

"I mean, for one thing, you were supposed to stay in the golf cart." He raised an eyebrow. "What's going on with you lately? You charged at him like a bull even before he said anything. It's like you want to set the world on fire."

Esther had asked her that too. *What's going on with you?* The answer, of course, was waiting in the bottom drawer of her desk, the stack of FOIA documents she had stashed there.

Like he had read her mind, Matt said, "Esther told me about your FOIA request."

"God, Esther." Sloane pressed her hands to her face briefly. "I'm never telling her anything ever again."

Matt waited. There was something about his posture that irritated her. The defeated sag to his shoulders. It would have been better if he had yelled at her.

"I requested the Project Ringer documents," she said. "I wanted to know everything I could. It's my life, and they have all these . . . *records* of it."

"I understand wanting to know," he said. "I just think it's weird you didn't tell me. And that you mentioned it to Esther before me."

"I was going to tell you right away," she said. "But then I read more and — it was upsetting."

"And what? You didn't want to upset me?"

She shook her head. "That's not it."

"Tell me about it, then." He sounded earnest, but Sloane knew him too well to be fooled. He had used this tone when they fought the Dark One. She remembered one particular evening — they had been trying to track the Dark One when he was just a man, not a shadow in the middle of a Drain. Ines had been following a promising lead that had yielded nothing. *Tell me what happened,* Matt had said. But it had just been a moment of quiet before he erupted. The struggle had drawn them all as taut as an overstrung harp. She had not realized that the strain of living with her lately, or maybe of the Ten Years Peace celebrations, had affected him so much.

"Sometimes," she said, taking her time, "when I'm upset about something, all you want to do is tell me why I shouldn't be."

"And that's bad?"

"It makes me feel crazy! Like I can't trust my own reactions to things."

"We all need people to help us see things from different perspectives."

She rolled her eyes. "You think I don't make myself consider things from other angles?" She had spent a lifetime reacting and then questioning the reactions—a lifetime of second-guessing, self-interrogation, badgering her brain into thinking about things the *right* way. "You think I *can't?*" Her volume was rising. "Did you ever consider that when I'm upset about something, it might be because it's worth getting upset about?"

"This explains why you haven't been yourself lately," Matt said. "I wish I'd known, I—"

"Your problem is you think this isn't myself," she said. "Just like you think a day imprisoned by the Dark One was a pleasure cruise and I should be over it by now and . . . getting giddy about wedding dresses or something!"

"Yeah, you know what? I think you should have spent the last ten years doing the *work* to move past everything instead of wallowing nonstop and holing up like a hermit." Matt had snapped, the harp string broken. "I have never once suggested that it should be easy. I have only ever asked you to try, and to stop acting like you're the only person in the world who has pain."

They both went silent. Sloane's cheeks burned. She warred with the impulse to storm out, knowing it would only make her seem even more like the child he had accused her of being but also desperate to hide from his chastisement. Every time she thought she understood what she didn't know about him, could never know, she remembered that was impossible.

Matt's phone buzzed, glowing through the pocket of his jeans. He turned off the ringer. She breathed deep, remembering the photo still of the punch, the emptiness of her eyes, her gritted teeth. The stray dog in her.

"Man, the way you see me." She huffed a laugh. "How can you want to marry someone you see as such a selfish child?"

"Sloane—"

Sloane's phone, face-down on the coffee table, sounded out the first few bars of "Good Times, Bad Times" by Led Zeppelin—her ringtone for Ines. She reached down and turned off the ringer.

A second later, Matt's phone started buzzing again. This time he answered it. "*What,* Ines?" Matt said.

He listened for a moment and then wilted, his body folding into his desk chair.

"Oh God," he said. He covered the mouthpiece of the phone. "Albie's in the hospital," he said to Sloane, then returned to the call. "No, I'm sorry, we'll be right there."

12

HAVE YOU SEEN him since the Drain site?" Matt asked.

They were in Matt's BMW on their way to the hospital, stuck at the world's longest red light. Or that's how it felt to Sloane.

She looked out the window. "No, I haven't."

It had rained, so the multicolored neon from the credit union on the corner glimmered on the road. The shush of car tires on wet pavement and the roar of the car's diesel engine started up again when the light turned green. Neither of them had put on the radio to fill the silence.

"I'm sorry if I—" Matt began.

"Please, don't," Sloane said, covering her face with a hand. "I'm just . . . let's just focus on Albie."

She had discovered an origami penguin in a bag of flour the week before. All the creases had been sharp, which meant it was one of his old ones. But still, he had thought to put it there, knowing it would make her smile. Sometimes she felt like Albie was the only person in the world who knew her. And it was because he wanted nothing from her, not sex, not love, not secrets. There was no currency between them.

Ines had not said why Albie was in the hospital, but Sloane had a few guesses. An accident, maybe; it was always possible. It could also have been unknown repercussions from the magical device he had experimented with at the Drain site; they understood so little about magic, it would not have shocked Sloane to know that it was actually harmful, like radiation, and only got worse with prolonged exposure. But the best guess was predictable and painfully human: Albie had relapsed and overdosed.

Matt pulled into the parking deck at the hospital, and he and Sloane fell into old patterns. She was better at navigating new places —spotting and interpreting signs—and had better instincts about the layouts of buildings and public spaces. Matt followed along, chasing her heels to the walkway that led to the emergency room, then the waiting room, where Ines was sitting, her eyes red.

"I found him an hour ago," she said, checking her phone to verify the time. "I guess he kept an old stash. Or went out for a new one when I wasn't paying attention, I don't know. The doctor said it's probably not more than he used to take, but he's been clean so long he can't handle that much anymore."

"So it was an accident? He wasn't—trying anything?"

"Can't say for sure. He's not an idiot; he probably knew it would be too much."

Sloane was listening, but she was also watching the other people in the waiting room. They were glancing over at them. Whispering. Shifting in their seats to take out cell phones.

"What was he like when he came back from the Drain site?" Matt said.

"Not good," Ines said. "But making a good show of it. He said he was just worn out, and it was late at night—I didn't think to check up on him—"

"It's not on you," Matt said. "You're not a mind reader. No one expects you to be."

"Hey," Sloane said, jerking her chin at a twenty-something man with gel in his hair and his phone held out like he was recording video. "What the fuck do you think you're doing?"

"Slo . . ." Matt said.

She crossed the waiting room and plucked the phone out of the guy's hand as he was fumbling to put it away, his eyes wide. She swiped to find the video, deleted it, then tossed the phone back into his lap. It hit him in the stomach, hard enough to make a slapping sound.

"Mind your own business," she said, voice low.

Matt went to ask the receptionist if there were any spare rooms where they could wait, and Sloane sat next to Ines in silence.

They spent the next few hours in an empty hospital room, Ines sitting on the bedside table, Matt and Sloane in the chairs. Everything was taupe and muted sea-foam green, the same colors as Sloane's kitchen growing up. Ines turned on the TV as soon as they walked in and changed the channel to late-night reruns of a sitcom she had liked as a child. Sloane's body still remembered how to sleep through anxiety, so she slumped in the chair, leaned her head back against the wall, and dropped into a doze within minutes, the sound of a laugh track in her ears.

It was around midnight when the door finally opened, admitting a middle-aged woman wearing a lab coat over slacks and a blouse, her hair pulled back and her expression grave.

"Hello," she said. "I'm Dr. Hart. You must be Albert's friends."

Ines was sitting up, pushing her hands through her hair. Matt was already on his feet—he had been changing the channel on the television. Sloane was just staring at the doctor because she knew what was coming by the tone of the woman's voice, by the hesitant curve of her shoulders.

"I have bad news," Dr. Hart said.

Everything after that was just static on a television screen, the hum of a busy signal. Sloane picked up the highlights: organ failure, Albie, who should contact his family. Dead. The doctor would give them some time, come back later to answer any questions. She was sorry for their loss.

Sloane was just blinking at the two trashcans in front of her, one red, for biohazards, and the other white, for other refuse. On the wall was a drawing of the circulatory system, a man made out of veins and arteries.

There was nothing quite like the Drain for reminding you what people were made of. Sloane had had that thought the first time she saw one happening. The way people peeled apart right in front of you, displaying bone and muscle and internal organs all pressed together in the moments before they came apart. Sloane had an affinity for the mechanical; she liked to see the way things worked. She had always gaped at the complexity of the human body, displayed in such gruesome fashion, in the moments before the reality of death dawned on her.

But the Drain also revealed fragility. How soft people were, how easily destroyed. She had no trouble believing that Albie was gone, factually. His body was like any other, yielding, breaking.

But understanding it, the space he would leave behind—she couldn't do it.

Dr. Hart had left them in silence. None of them cried. None of them moved. The clock ticked, and the TV droned the late-night news.

Finally, Sloane had to move, had to do *something* or she thought she might scream. She took her phone out of her pocket and opened her contacts list.

"I'll call Esther," she said to the phone screen rather than to Ines or Matt directly. "Can one of you get in touch with Albie's mother? She's never liked me."

Matt was staring at her like he had no idea what she was saying.

"I'll do it," Ines said weakly.

"Thanks," Sloane said. "I'll go in the hallway; you stay here."

She stood, her back aching from spending so long in the hospital chair. She thought about the ache, and the squeak of the floor under her sneakers, and the chemical-solvent smell of the air. A nurse gave her a pressed-lipped smile, and she returned it, a reflex.

At least there was protocol here. Call the family, the friends. Ask the questions they might find themselves wondering about in the coming weeks and months, even if they didn't care about the particulars now. Then go home, sleep.

Sloane didn't need to wonder about burial arrangements. They all knew what one another's preferences were—that was the sort of thing they had talked about in the days of the Dark One, the "In case

I don't make it" contingency. Albie's was cremation. Ashes scattered at a Drain site, didn't matter which one. No big funeral; he didn't like crowds.

Esther was at a club when Sloane called; it was hard to hear her over the thrum of the bass. Sloane had to shout at her to get her to step outside. She gave the news like the doctor had: straightforward, clear, concise.

After hanging up, she sank into a crouch, her back against the wall of painted cinder block behind her. She watched the nurses shuffle back and forth in their Crocs and scrubs. She thought of Albie's trembling hands and how he had shoved napkins at her that day in the bar so she could wrap them around her feet.

She stayed there until her legs went numb.

Chicago Tribune

CHOSEN ONE ALBERT SUMMERS DIES AT 30

by Lindsay Reynolds

CHICAGO, MARCH 18: Albert Tyler Summers, known to his loved ones as "Albie," died yesterday at Northwestern Memorial Hospital of a drug overdose. He was thirty years old.

Albert is survived by his mother, Kathy, and his sister, Kaitlin. His father and brother were killed by the Dark One in the attack on Edmonton, Alberta, in 2005.

Albert was one of the five Chosen Ones who famously defeated the Dark One on March 15, 2010. He was recruited by the Central Intelligence Agency, in a cooperative effort with the Canadian Security Intelligence Agency, at the age of sixteen, when the elements of a classified prophecy singled him out as a candidate for the Dark One's defeat. He was educated and trained in a secure facility with the other four Chosen Ones: Matthew Weekes, Sloane Andrews, Ines Mejia, and Esther Park.

He spent the next several years engaged in the struggle against the Dark One and his army, emerging unscathed from dozens of altercations, including, most notably, the Battle of Boise and the Springfield Stronghold. He suffered permanent spinal injuries as a captive of the Dark One in 2010 but still fought with the others in the final conflict.

Following the Dark One's defeat, Albert struggled with substance abuse for years before entering the Assurances Treatment Facility just outside San Diego, California. In an interview in 2013, he said of his addiction: "I didn't know what to do with myself after the fight was over, you know? It was like my brain was used to the adrenaline and kept looking for it afterward. It's hard to learn a different way of being, but I think I have now. One day at a time. Now I try to only look at what's in front of me."

His friends and family say that Albert was a kind, generous individual with unwavering loyalty to the ones he loved. He will be remembered for his sacrifices of inestimable worth.

Services will be private. Donations can be made in Albert's memory to the One Day Foundation, which funds drug-rehabilitation programs for low-income individuals.

13

SLOANE WASHED HER HANDS in the crematory sink. The soap smelled like Band-Aids.

Logistics had consumed the past day, with Ines dealing with Albie's family and Esther making arrangements for the funeral reception from afar. Matt helped where he could, but the grief had hit him harder than the rest of them, and he spent a lot of time blank, awake but empty-eyed. Eddie had canceled his events and meetings. Sloane thought she understood; Albie wasn't just one of Matt's friends, he was someone Matt had led, and, for better or worse, Matt always took responsibility for his soldiers.

Sloane's job was Albie's body. They didn't have to talk about who would do that part. She was the only one with the stomach for it.

She had signed all the forms and made all the arrangements. The hospital had given her a bag of the clothes Albie had been wearing when he came into the hospital, and inside it was his late brother's class ring, a paper clip, and a tiny, roughly folded paper airplane.

The airplane had confounded her at first. Albie had given up paper-folding of all kinds after his injury, frustrated by the inefficiency of his hands. Her instinct was to preserve the plane, just as she would keep his clothes unwashed and never use that paper clip. But something about it wasn't sitting right with her.

Sloane dried her hands with a paper towel, then looked at herself in the mirror. She didn't look well. Pale and exhausted, her hair greasy, her clothes rumpled. She tied her hair back, hoping it made her look halfway presentable, and went out to meet the crematory operator, who had agreed to give her a few minutes for a bathroom break before they started.

No one had to witness the cremation, but Sloane wanted to. She had identified the body beforehand, forcing herself to stare down at the face that was Albie but not quite Albie. The tuft of dark blond hair that stood out at an angle from his head was undeniably his, but without the life in his face, in his eyes, the body could have been a wax figure. Still, she had agreed it was him, and now the casket was sealed, ready on its cart next to the tray that would roll into the cremation chamber.

The crematory operator was named Walter, and he was about her age, soft around the middle with a pale, drawn look to his face.

"Ready?" he said.

She nodded. Walter showed her the button she would press to start the process.

"Don't be alarmed if the bottom of the casket catches on fire really quickly," he said. "It's really hot in there so the finish might light up too."

"Don't worry," she said. "I've seen worse."

Walter nodded, and looked away as Sloane approached the button. But she wasn't as ready as she'd thought. She reached over and rested her hand on the casket. The paper plane was in her back pocket.

"Actually, Walter," she said, "would you mind giving me a second alone?"

She could tell he was trying not to look annoyed. She had found that people fit into one of two categories when interacting with her post–Dark One: some went out of their way to be accommodating, and others assumed the worst of her. Walter had been sighing at her since she walked in, so she guessed he was in the latter category. But he nodded and slipped out of the room. Sloane waited until the door closed behind him, then took the plane out of her back pocket.

She unfolded it, and smoothed it out on the casket. Written right in the middle of the paper was *I'm sorry. I couldn't carry it anymore.*

Sloane's vision went blurry, and she crumpled the paper in her fist, squeezing it so tightly her knuckles ached. In the time that had passed since Dr. Hart had delivered the news, she hadn't cried, hadn't even come close. Not even when she was listening to Esther sob on the phone. Not even when she held Albie's shirt up to her nose to see if it still smelled like him.

Either way, we'll carry it. We always do.

Sloane slumped over the casket and sobbed, hugging the wood tight. She felt like she was losing her brother all over again, but it was worse this time, because she would remember more than the itchy wool dress she wore when they lowered the casket into the ground and the way Cameron used to wake her up for the first frost and drag her outside to make footprints in the grass.

With Albie, she would remember the Survival Beer they got after every altercation with the Dark One, the looks they exchanged whenever Matt went into hero mode, and the way they had held each other upright when they escaped captivity together. She had half a lifetime of memories of Albie. They had understood each other's pain in a way no one else had.

Now there was no one left who did.

The sobs subsided in a minute or two. They always did. Like something inside her didn't have the patience for such reckless emotion. But she rested her cheek on the casket for a while longer, the wood warm now from contact with her skin. Then she straightened and flattened the crumpled paper against the wood as best she could, folded it, returned it to her pocket. She wiped her eyes and called Walter back in from the hallway.

He took his place again, and she took hers.

Bye, buddy, she thought as she pushed the button, a metal disk the size of her fist. The door to the cremation chamber opened, sending a wave of heat over Sloane's body. The casket slid into it, and just as Walter had warned, there was a flash of light as it caught on fire. Then the door to the cremation chamber closed, and it was done.

Sloane took the train back from the crematory in her usual disguise: baseball cap pulled down low over her eyes, glasses, a scarf wound around her neck up to her ears. When she had first visited Chicago as a child, the trains had been a marvel, coasting high above the street and glinting in the sun. She still rode them when she could, preferring their potential anonymity to the certainty of being recognized by a ride-share or taxi driver. Today she chose a seat by a window and watched the sun go down behind the towering glass and metal of the Loop.

It was a short walk back to the apartment, but she took the long way around the block. There had been a crowd of reporters and photographers outside their building that morning, and Sloane had elbowed her way through them on her way to the car Matt had called for her, but she didn't feel like doing that again now. Instead, she walked down the alley, past overstuffed dumpsters, discarded furniture, and narrow garages to their building.

But before she unlocked the gate, she spotted movement in the courtyard beyond the fence, followed by a camera flash. Cursing, Sloane shoved her keys back into her pocket and went to the building next door. It was easy enough to climb on top of the dumpster and hop over the wooden fence into their patch of unmowed grass. She climbed three flights of stairs to the top of the three-flat, then used a nearby broom to nudge open the trapdoor to the roof.

There wasn't a ladder nearby, but Sloane could do a pull-up in a pinch. She had to stand on a chair — borrowed from someone's back patio — to reach it, but she managed to climb onto the roof. It was level with her building's, the gap separating them only three feet wide. Sloane had made the jump before when reporters had gotten a little too gutsy. She ran, leaped, and landed with a stumble on her own roof.

It was all second nature now, finding new exits and new ways to approach a problem. Sloane was a picker of locks and a solver of puzzles. She had defaulted to practical means to get things done even after they could use magic; it just seemed safer, given what had happened the first time she wielded it.

Sloane heard a voice when she opened the back door, a sharp soprano that didn't sound like Ines or even Esther, who wouldn't be landing at O'Hare until that evening anyway.

Agent Cho was sitting on the sofa, a cup of tea in her hands. She looked different outside of the geodesic dome, wearing jeans and a black turtleneck sweater, her hair loose around her shoulders. After what had happened, it probably shouldn't have surprised Sloane that she had turned up, but it did. Neither Henderson nor Cho had ever come to their apartment before.

But then, none of them had died before.

"Hello, Sloane," Cho said, looking grave.

Matt, sitting across from Cho on the old rocking chair that had belonged to his grandmother, looked up at her like he had only just realized she was there.

"How'd it go?" Matt said. He got up and pressed a kiss to her cheek. The familiar smell of cedar and aftershave washed over her, and she wanted, suddenly, to curl up with him on their bed, to find comfort in the rustling of their clothes coming off — to feel anything except this yawning hole inside her where Albie used to be. But the strict metal of the ring around her finger reminded her that when this funeral was over, she needed to end their engagement. It wouldn't be fair to Matt to let herself find comfort in him now only to break his heart later.

"It went," Sloane said. "What's going on?"

"Eileen came to . . . offer her condolences," Matt said, settling back into the rocking chair.

"Oh." Sloane looked at her. Cho's mouth twitched into a frown that looked less like grief and more like . . . guilt. "Really," Sloane said.

Cho played with the string of her tea bag, wrapped around the handle of her mug. It was the one Matt had gotten from NASA as a child, decorated with stars and rocket ships, the name MATTHEW around the rim like a banner.

"There's something else," Cho admitted. "Although it's classified, and I . . ." She looked out the window. The neighbor's painful blue fairy lights were blinking rapidly enough to give someone a seizure, and Sloane could see the family of four in the apartment across from theirs sitting down to dinner.

"I'm not supposed to say anything, but I think there's a code of honor that needs to be upheld here," she finished. "So."

"This is about the device, isn't it?" Sloane said.

Cho nodded. "Something went wrong. Well—technically the device worked, so ARIS considered it a success, but—"

Sloane noticed the rapid rise and fall of Cho's chest, the tendons standing out from her neck.

"Albie was always good with fire," Cho said. "So we agreed that he would try to use the device to light up a ball of paper in a controlled environment. We had technicians standing by with fire extinguishers, and Albie was in a flame-retardant suit—all the precautions we thought were necessary. So he pointed the device at the ball of paper and . . ." Cho shook her head. "The fire was out of control," Cho said. "It enveloped three of our technicians. Two of them got out with minor burns, but Darrick, the one who was directly in the path of the flames . . ."

"Dead," Sloane supplied.

"Yes," Cho said.

Sloane had seen Albie manipulate fire before. He put the Freikugeln in his left hand, squeezed in his fist, raised the right . . . and light and heat, tongues of flames, danced around his fingers. None of them had really figured out how to control their artifacts, so sometimes tiny flickers were all he could muster, and other times he could level an entire building. Their use of magic had always been unpredictable, which was why it had been good for all five of them to be present at any given time, to maximize their odds of success.

If people die because of your help, she had said to him, *you'll have to carry that around.*

Like a prophet.

Sloane let out a laugh.

"Slo," Matt said, eyes wide.

"Well, thanks for that little revelation, Cho," Sloane said. "You can go now."

"Sorry, Eileen," Matt said. "She doesn't . . ." He lost the sentence right in the middle and fell silent.

"I understand," Cho said, getting to her feet. "Let me know if you have any questions. I can't answer them on the phone, obviously, but you can just ask me about tea, and I'll know what you mean."

She handed her half-empty mug to Matt, avoiding Sloane's eyes, and picked up her coat and purse, which sat on the low table next to the front door. Matt went to walk her out, but before exiting the apartment, he shook his head at Sloane.

When the door closed, she grabbed her keys, hat, and sweatshirt and ran to the back door.

Avoiding the reporters had seemed important ten minutes ago, but she didn't care anymore. She ignored the flashing and clicking of cameras as she ran down three flights of stairs and then around the corner to the basement steps. Each unit had a small storage space there. Matt and Sloane's held mostly decorations for each major holiday, even Valentine's Day. Sloane generally made it her business to hate things like that, but she had a soft spot for cheesy decorations.

As she approached the door to their storage space, her body began to tingle and burn. She unlocked it and pulled the chain for the light. A stack of identical plastic crates, labeled with a label maker, greeted her. She shoved them aside and knelt in the corner where there was a loose chunk of concrete. A second heart beat in her chest, its rhythm counter to her own.

Under the concrete was a sewing kit small enough to fit in Sloane's palm, and in it, a box of sewing-machine needles of various sizes and thicknesses. A few were broken in half, jagged at the break. She plucked two medium-size pieces from the box and held them up to the light, her hands trembling.

Koschei's Needle.

TRANSCRIPT OF THE U.S. SENATE SELECT COMMITTEE ON INTELLIGENCE AND SUBCOMMITTEE ON DARK ONE ATROCITIES

MEETING REGARDING PROJECT RINGER, THE ARIS (AGENCY FOR THE RESEARCH AND INVESTIGATION OF THE SUPRANORMAL) PROGRAM OF TARGETED ACTION AGAINST THE DOMESTIC TERRORIST KNOWN AS "THE DARK ONE"

Washington, DC
Thursday, October 28, 2010

Testimony of Matthew Weekes, Subject 4 of Project Ringer; Sloane Andrews, Subject 2 of Project Ringer; Esther Park, Subject 1 of Project Ringer; and Ines Mejia, Subject 3 of Project Ringer.

MATTHEW WEEKES: Thank you, Mr. Chairman. I'd like to thank you and the committees here for inviting us today to speak on our own behalf, which has happened somewhat rarely since the beginning of all this. And I'd like to thank you for your commitment to keeping an accurate public record of what happened so it's not easily forgotten. That's something that's really important to all of us.

The four of us came here today to give an account of the events of March 15, 2010, the day of the Dark One's defeat. We consulted with each other on this prepared statement, and when I finish, we will be available for questions.

So . . . I'll just get started, then.

In the weeks leading up to March 15, the Dark One and his followers were quiet. The Dark One had kidnapped two of our number for a period of twenty-four hours, during which Albie — I mean Albert Summers — sustained serious injuries. Albie was still in the hospital, and since we weren't sure the extent to which he would recover mobility, we had to change our plan of attack significantly.

We had done a year of reconnaissance work, with the help of ARIS, trying to discover the Dark One's origins. But we found no record of him whatsoever. It was as if he had just . . . appeared. But one of us —

ESTHER PARK: Me. I did.

MATTHEW WEEKES: Okay, *Esther* pointed out that that in itself told us something —

ESTHER PARK: It told us that at the very least, he didn't want to be traced. Which meant he had likely gotten one of his followers to do everything for him. After all, he needed food and lodging just like anyone else. So we gave up on learning anything about his origins, and instead we focused on investigating his most loyal followers. It was slow going. They covered their tracks really well.

MATTHEW WEEKES: But about two weeks after Sloane and Albie got back —

SLOANE ANDREWS: [inaudible]

MATTHEW WEEKES: We finally got a break. Esther successfully identified one of the Dark One's followers as Charles Wright, who worked as a ▮▮▮▮▮▮ at ▮▮▮▮▮▮ and lived in one of the condos at what was then Chicago's Trump Tower.

INES MEJIA: So I went to have a look, posing as one of the janitors. A couple people went in and out of the apartment while I was cleaning the windows, didn't give me a second glance. One time, when the apartment door opened, I spotted him in a crowd of them — the Dark One himself was *there*. Which was huge — before this we hadn't known where the Dark One was between attacks.

ESTHER PARK: The rest of us were visiting Albie at the hospital. And it was lucky that we were, because otherwise we might not have gotten Sloane's idea . . . Sloane?

SLOANE ANDREWS: Yeah?

ESTHER PARK: You want to tell this part?

SLOANE ANDREWS: Okay. Um — I suggested we set a trap. I would do a work of significant magic at the base of Trump Tower on the Wabash Avenue Bridge — the Irv Kupcinet Bridge is technically its name. I figured if I made it visible enough, the Dark One or his followers would be able to see me from the condo.

SENATOR GOO: Pardon me for interrupting. We very much appreciate your testimony on this matter. But before you proceed, I'd like to ask Ms. Andrews a question.

MATTHEW WEEKES: Um. I don't think —

SLOANE ANDREWS: Go for it, Senator.

SENATOR GOO: Thank you, Ms. Andrews. I was wondering — I've always wondered — how did you know that the Dark One would fall for such a trap?

SLOANE ANDREWS: Well, for one thing, I figured if he saw one of the people fated to destroy him — or whatever the prophecy says — making an open challenge, he wouldn't be able to resist going out to kill them.

SENATOR GOO: Yes, I've heard you give that reasoning in several interviews since the Dark One's defeat. But I can't help but think that it was just as likely he would know you were setting a trap.

[silence]

SENATOR GOO: Ms. Andrews?

SLOANE ANDREWS: Sorry, I — it's hard to explain. I had had — I guess I'd had a very specific experience of the Dark One, a unique experience, when I was in captivity. It was only twenty-four hours, but . . . it was the closest anyone had ever been to him without dying or being in his thrall. Even his followers, the ones we'd gotten to question, didn't seem to know much about him.

SENATOR GOO: I understand this is hard for you to talk about, Ms. Andrews. I was hoping that you might try so that the official record can reflect reality as accurately as possible.

SLOANE ANDREWS: Yeah. Well — the real explanation is a little more complicated than the one I've given before.

SENATOR GOO: I think everyone here understands that you have shared what you were able to thus far, Ms. Andrews.

SLOANE ANDREWS: I guess so. Well — it wasn't so much that I thought just *any* of us down on that bridge would be able to lure him there. And that's what it was — luring. Figuring out what bait he wouldn't be able to resist. Which, uh . . . was me. I was the bait.

SENATOR GOO: Because . . .

ESTHER PARK: Because he was kind of obsessed with her, okay?

SLOANE ANDREWS: I think he — he said we were similar. Can we move on? I don't get it either, I promise. The guy was —

ESTHER PARK: A couple bananas short of a bunch.

INES MEJIA: Or a couple bananas in excess of a bunch.

SLOANE ANDREWS: It doesn't really matter why it worked, anyway; we just knew it would. So we all suited up —

MATTHEW WEEKES: Which is to say, we got our artifacts, which we had all acquired as part of our previous work with ARIS —

SENATOR GOO: And these artifacts were intended for what purpose?

MATTHEW WEEKES: Weapons. Magical weapons, to be exact. ARIS had outfitted us with objects of legend, most of which had been generously provided by other governments around the world. The Golden Bough and the Ring of Gyges were on loan from Greece; the Gjallarhorn came in from Sweden; the Freikugeln — magic bullets — had been taken from Germany during World War II by ████████, so they were easy enough —

ESTHER PARK: ████████ prefers if you say "allegedly."

MATTHEW WEEKES: Allegedly taken, sure. And Sloane had Koschei's Needle. It turned out that the Ring of Gyges was useless to us, but the other items channeled magic somewhat reliably, so we figured if we used them all at once, we'd have a higher likelihood of actually doing something. We'd gotten better at consistency, but it doesn't hurt to have a contingency plan —

INES MEJIA: I stayed where I was, to make sure nobody left the condo. I must have cleaned that window twenty times, almost ran out of Windex —

ESTHER PARK: Matt and I took hiding spots at either end of the bridge. I was in the tower north of the river, and Matt was south of it, on the river walk. Albie wanted to come, but since he was still pretty beat up, we left him behind. Tried to, anyway.

SENATOR GOO: And where is Mr. Summers today?

MATTHEW WEEKES: He's — he wasn't feeling well. He was really sorry to miss this, but he cleared me to tell his part of things. Anyway, Esther and I had taken up our positions, and Sloane —

SLOANE ANDREWS: I set out alone, on foot. I stopped in the middle of the bridge. With the Needle. I wanted — my intention was to do something that was hard to ignore in order to lure him out. I wasn't sure what it would be, but magic sometimes takes a shape of its own, as if it doesn't matter what we want from it. A bright light came out of the Needle, kind of like — a thread, I guess. Golden. Up to the sky. There's footage of it in the official record —

SENATOR GOO: Several bystanders submitted footage of this incident in advance of this hearing, and they are labeled Exhibit 23, A through E.

SLOANE ANDREWS: Anyway, it worked. He came down. He wasn't subtle about it either. Blew open the side of Trump Tower and floated down like he was wire-flying in a stage play or whatever. Landed right in front of me. He spoke to me. I don't — I'm not sure what he said. Something about me summoning him, about how he knew it was a trap but he needed something from me. But I never found out what that was because —

ESTHER PARK: We weren't going to give him time to do anything to her; we acted right away. I had the Horn, and Matt had the Bough, and Ines was —

INES MEJIA: Running as fast as fucking possible down five million flights of stairs, because the goddamn elevator stopped working the second he blew out the windows —

MATTHEW WEEKES: The Horn was letting out this frequency, too low for us to hear but vibrating in the street — it drove a massive crack through the pavement right under Sloane and the Dark One, and I was adding to it with the Bough, but we could both tell it wasn't going to be enough. The Dark One had set up some kind of protective barrier around him and Sloane, and she was screaming —

SLOANE ANDREWS: I'm not sure what he was doing to me. It felt like he was trying to rip me apart. It was all I could do just to hold on to the Needle. No chance of me actually thinking straight long enough to use it.

MATTHEW WEEKES: But then — from the bridge just west of the one we were on, the one that State Street runs across —

SLOANE ANDREWS: The Bataan-Corregidor Memorial Bridge.

MATTHEW WEEKES: Yeah, that one. Anyway, it was Albie. He had the Freikugeln in his fist and he was aiming them out the open window of a taxi. I think you guys gave the taxi driver the Medal of Honor. One of a handful of private citizens to get it. Anyway, then everything just . . . broke.

SENATOR GOO: I will refer everyone to Exhibit 24, A through R, for footage of this event from a . . . wide variety of angles, submitted by civilian bystanders in advance of this hearing. Essentially, the entirety of Trump Tower pulled free of its moorings, taking along with it the Wabash Avenue Bridge with the Dark One and Miss Andrews on top of it. For approximately 1.23 seconds, everything remained suspended in midair and then radiated outward from a central point inside the . . . floating building. The steel and glass projectiles caused forty-five casualties and upward of two hundred injuries as well as a significant amount of property damage.

ESTHER PARK: We're . . . sorry?

SENATOR GOO: We'll be expecting your reparation money any day now, Ms. Park.

[silence]

SENATOR GOO: That was a joke.

MATTHEW WEEKES: We all got knocked out at that point, so none of us remember —

SLOANE ANDREWS: I remember something. I remember — falling. Into water. The river. I sank all the way to the bottom with the concrete from the bridge. That was when I blacked out. I woke up on the lake shore. Still not sure how I got there, why I didn't just drown. And the Dark One, he was . . . gone.

14

SLOANE WALKED a winding path through the tents that surrounded the Drain site. It had rained earlier, so the ground was soft beneath her boots. There were fewer people milling around than when she had come during the day, and those who were still out were gathered around portable grills and small fires with lanterns hanging above their heads or floodlights attached to the front of their tents. She heard a few bars of "The Times They Are A-Changin'" coming from one of the sites, and the words chased her, as if carried on the cold wind, all the way to the Dome.

Sloane stopped at the security barrier that separated the crowd of seekers — no matter what they were here for, they were all looking for *something* — from the Drain site. She was not far now from the cluster of tents she had stomped over to a few days ago to punch that guy in the face.

But it felt like a dream to her now. Albie was gone, which meant it didn't matter what some Dark One acolyte called her or what he wanted. Albie was *gone,* and now there was only what needed to be done and the one willing to do it.

No one had recognized her, nor would anyone. She had changed into new clothes in the car. They were shapeless and black, disguising anything feminine about her figure. She was tall enough to be mistaken for a man. A hood was secured over her hair, and over her nose and mouth, she had on a neoprene mask she wore when running in the dead of winter. She was glad she hadn't put on makeup that day —nothing to wipe off. ARIS would suspect her, she was sure, as soon as they realized what she had done. But the disguise would buy her some time.

Sloane took the broken pieces of Koschei's Needle from the container in her back pocket. She had broken it herself. After Bert came after her and Albie, unnecessarily, and died because of it, and after being a captive of the Dark One, she was repulsed by the Needle in her flesh. She had argued with the people at ARIS when they refused to remove it; they'd said there was no way to know how it would behave if they disturbed it. So one night, with one foot in a nightmare and one foot in reality, Sloane had gnawed the Needle out of her own hand and ripped it loose with her teeth. Then, with the taste of coppery blood in her mouth, she had snapped the artifact in half—but it hadn't been as easy as a needle snapping in a sewing machine because you hadn't threaded it properly. It had taken every ounce of her strength, every ounce of the Needle's own *magic*. She had collapsed afterward, all her energy exhausted, and woken up in a hospital, her hand bandaged, a week later.

She hadn't touched the Needle bare-handed since then, afraid it would somehow leap back under her skin. But it seemed that, broken, it didn't have the same power it had possessed when she had found it at the bottom of the ocean. She felt its magic like the simmer of water about to boil. It tingled and burned inside her, but the pull of it wasn't irresistible.

Magic was not a weapon or even an amoral source of energy—it was an infection. Wherever it was, people died, places turned rotten, and the order of things was disrupted, sometimes irreparably. But there was no other weapon against the magic ARIS had developed than magic itself.

Sloane held the two pieces of the Needle up to the light from the security station. Two pinpricks of white glinted on its surface. It was like two magnets with opposite polarity—she could feel the bond that formed between the two ends and the irrepressible need to join. But she wouldn't let them. Then what felt like fire raced down her fingers and the back of her right hand, her arm, her shoulder; it boiled in her blood and singed her spine, and she felt the tug of the Needle, knew it wanted to join with her, too, just as it wanted to mend itself.

She gritted her teeth and pushed back. The pieces of the Needle resisted, struggling toward her, and she turned them, held them like knives in the center of her fist.

Her palm felt like she had poured acid over it, but she held tight to the Needle fragments and walked toward the security station. The guard—not the same one who had been there the last time she visited but wearing the same bland uniform—called out for her to stop. She walked straight toward the gate.

What came next felt like a reflex, the same achy tickling that followed a doctor's mallet striking the knee. She jerked the two halves of the Needle up, and the gate lifted—frame and all—high above her head. It stayed there, unwavering, as she and the guard both looked up at it. The wind shivered through the chain links, but otherwise everything was silent.

Sloane raised an eyebrow at the guard. He didn't tell her to stop again.

The gate remained suspended even after she passed under it. When she looked over her shoulder, it was still there, hanging fifty feet above her head as if strung from the clouds.

The front entrance of the Dome met the same fate. The doors pulled effortlessly from their hinges and burst through the roof. The hole they left behind was slim and rectangular, like the cut of a knife.

The Dome ceiling was dark now, but emergency lights glowed here and there, showing the spokes of the Dome's bicycle-wheel interior, paths to the emergency exits. A guard with a Taser stood in Sloane's path.

"Sir, put your . . . weapon . . . down," he said.

The Needle seemed to know that he was talking about it—Sloane winced as the burning in her palm intensified. Her voice would give her away, so she didn't speak, just shook her head.

He held out the Taser.

She held out the broken Needle.

The Taser exploded into fine particles of black dust. A thread of light wrapped around the security guard's hand, making him scream.

Sloane gave him a wide berth. There was no time for sympathy or wonder. She ran toward the room where she had felt the prototype. She felt it again now, pulsing, like the heart beneath the floorboards in that Edgar Allan Poe story. It called to something inside her and something inside the Needle. Magic beckoned to magic, as it always did.

As the Dark One had once beckoned to her.

Hello, Sloane. Did you get some sleep?

I hope so, because you have a big decision to make today.

She pushed the Dark One's words out of her mind and chased the feeling down, only then allowing herself to articulate what she had always known: That the feeling of magic speaking to her was the feeling of something coming back to life. A new pulse, new circulation in an unused limb.

It made her into something new.

The doors to the laboratory where the prototype was held shot up and stayed, stable, just beneath the curve of the Dome. Sloane walked through the door frame, more cautious now than she had been before. The laboratory was white: white walls, white floors, white tables. There was a row of microscopes on one table, slim computer monitors on another. An eyewash station, an emergency shower. Sturdy ducts twisted together in the ceiling — which was also painted white — terminating in massive vents.

Sloane took all this in, but her focus went right to the prototype, which sat on its own lab table on a metal platform. Someone had put red tape around it. It was, as Ines had predicted, a box. Narrow enough to fit in a palm, but about a foot long, made of matte metal. Her body trembled as she approached it, the broken Needle held out.

And then: A feeling as familiar to her as air in her lungs. She had felt it only once before, that hunger, that emptiness that demanded filling — just before the Needle killed everyone on the Dive with her. Then, it had been shapeless, just a *want* so potent she'd been forced to give in to it.

And now she wanted only one thing: to destroy this piece of shit before it could hurt anything—or anyone—else.

Her want caught on the Needle like thread going through the eye of it, and then—

Light—

She smelled like dust and smoke.

When she came to, after, it was still dark. In a perfect circle around her body, the laboratory floor was intact and just as clean as when she had first walked in. But beyond that was rubble. The Dome was still mostly whole, but there was a huge dent in the side, like a bite taken out of an apple. The laboratory—and the prototype with it—was now just gravel and metal fragments that were too small to piece back together.

For a long time, she sat on the circle of clean floor and shook. But the sun was rising. So she forced herself to stand up, then stumbled out of the wreckage. On her way out, she saw a security guard lying on the ground near an exterior door. She was lucky she had woken up first.

Assuming he was unconscious, not dead.

She didn't see any others. Maybe they had fled at the first sight of magic. She didn't blame them—after all, the Dark One was the only magic-user most people had ever heard of, so the Drains had taught people that if they saw any evidence of magic, it was best to run.

The light and the sound had woken the seekers in their tents, and now they were standing as close to the security barrier as they could get. Sloane walked past a séance and a group of men talking excitedly about "his return." No one paid any attention to her.

She got into her car and drove to a nearby forest preserve. It was still hours until the funeral. She walked deep into the woods to set a fire, gathering kindling as she went. She stacked it in one of the metal trashcans that were staggered along the paths, lit it with a match, waited for the flames to build and catch the thicker logs she added, and then stripped to her underwear.

She burned the clothes she had worn to the Drain site and changed into yesterday's outfit. As the fabric burned down to cinders, she walked out of the woods, branches scratching her neck and ears and shoulders, underbrush grazing her ankles. She shook the dust from her hair, then braided it tightly. When she looked at her reflection in the dark screen of her phone — turned off since the night before — she couldn't help but feel like all her efforts to look normal had been wasted. She looked crazed, her eyes too wide, her jaw bulging with tension. Matt would know something had happened. It didn't matter.

Sloane set her GPS to take her to the monument site in the Loop and drove in silence.

TOP SECRET

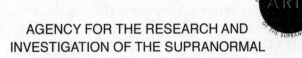

AGENCY FOR THE RESEARCH AND INVESTIGATION OF THE SUPRANORMAL

MEMORANDUM FOR THE RECORD

TO: DIRECTOR, AGENCY FOR THE RESEARCH AND INVESTIGATION OF THE SUPRANORMAL (ARIS)

FROM: OFFICER ███████████, CODE NAME EDWINA

SUBJECT: REPORT ON PROJECT RINGER ARTIFACT 200

1. For the purposes of this report, I will be referring to Project Ringer Artifact 200 by its common name, Koschei's Needle.

2. The Needle is an object of significance in Slavic folklore, with Koschei (also known as "Koschei the Immortal" and "Koschei the Deathless") typically taking the form of an antagonist who has a fear of death. He therefore places his soul inside an object that is nested in other objects: for example, he places it in a needle, then buries the needle in an egg, then hides the egg inside various creatures or, in some stories, a trunk. He is unable to die if the needle that contains his soul is intact.

3. ARIS has been paying attention to so-called mythical objects since the agency's inception, particularly to those objects to which other governments ascribe value. There has been chatter on and off about the Needle for a few decades, but the Cold War brought it to the fore, according to our field officers in Russia. We managed to trace the Needle to a Soviet spy ship, the *Sakhalin*, that sank somewhere in the Pacific Ocean in 1972. Surveillance technology revealed the ship's exact location in 2007, and we deployed a Project Ringer task force, including Subject 2, Sloane Andrews, to retrieve the Needle in 2008. The events of that mission are detailed in the enclosed documents following this report.

4. ARIS certainly does not subscribe to the belief that the Needle truly contains a person's soul, that there has ever been an immortal person, or that a man named Koschei ever existed; how-

ever, we do not at this time have an explanation for the Needle's origin. The Needle is not, in fact, made of any metal that we can identify, though it appears metallic. It is only about two inches long, and its somewhat jagged edges suggest it is a fragment of something larger, but we have not located anything else that resembles it. We have been able to match certain microscopic particles to deep ocean material, especially the pelagic sediment particular to the Mariana Trench. More information about pelagic sediment as it relates to analysis of the Needle is attached. Further investigation into the trench will be necessary if we are to understand the Needle's origins.

5. Additional examination of the Needle's properties is ongoing, though it is clear that we can categorize this object as an active channel of supranormal energy. We hope that in the future, we will be able to devote more time to this task; as it stands, the Needle is one of our most powerful weapons in the fight against the Dark One.

TOP SECRET

15

SLOANE WORE SUNGLASSES, though the sky was dark with clouds, and made her way through the crowd.

Lake Shore Drive had been a parking lot. She had given up near the Michigan Avenue exit, pulling her car over to the shoulder and leaving it there. Sweat dotted her hairline, and she was breathless from half walking, half jogging all the way downtown.

But she had made it to the monument site — or at least to the security barrier that the police had set up there.

She walked up to the nearest police officer and took off her sunglasses. The woman gave her an odd look, but nodded and gestured for her to go through.

"Thanks," Sloane mumbled, and she put her sunglasses back on, stepped around the barrier, and speed-walked away before anyone in the crowd behind her figured out why she had been let through. She spotted Esther ahead, dressed in a long black coat that just brushed the pointed toes of her patent-leather boots. Esther raised a perfectly penciled eyebrow at her.

"Where the hell have you been?" Esther demanded, then she wrapped Sloane in a hug. "Matt said you freaked out."

"I guess that's one way of describing it," Sloane said. "How did word get out?"

"Don't give me that look," Esther said. "I haven't been on social media since yesterday."

Sloane snorted.

"It was Matt," Esther said. "He contacted the police to let them know we'd be doing this today, just in case anything weird happened. One of them probably has a big mouth."

She should have known it was Matt's fault. He had never understood why she wanted to stay so private. He didn't mind sliding his name into dinner reservations to get a better table or winking at people who gave him a second look on the sidewalk. *We have to pay the price of this life all the time,* he had said to her once. *Might as well get something good out of it when we can.*

She spotted him standing next to the monument. When he saw her, it was like a big knot unraveling. He grabbed at her, as if testing to see that she was real, and then held her for a few seconds, his breath shaking in her ear. He had thought she was dead, Sloane realized, her sunglasses crushed against his shoulder. Somehow, it hadn't occurred to her to reassure him.

"I'm sorry," she said, but she wasn't sure what for — for leaving, for the fight they'd had before Albie died, for destroying the Dome, or for what she would have to do next, fleeing ARIS, maybe leaving the country . . .

"Yeah," he replied, avoiding her eyes. It meant he didn't forgive her, and that was what she had expected. Even Matt had limits to his mercy. His eyes were red. He had been crying. Maybe awake all night.

Ines stalked over to them and punched Sloane in the arm, hard enough to make her wince.

"God, Sloane!" Ines snapped. "You're such an asshole."

"Yeah," Sloane said, breathless. "Can you — give me just a second? You can yell at me when I get back."

She slipped past Ines and walked toward the edge of the monument site, where the concrete dropped off to the river. She pressed her stomach into the railing. The mildew-and-mud smell of the river overpowered the smoky scent that clung to her hair.

She put her hand in her pocket and felt for the pieces of the Needle. They numbed her fingertips on contact. She put her elbows on the railing, leaning out as if to get a better look at the bridge where she had lured the Dark One to his death. She tipped her hand, and the Needle pieces fell into the water.

She looked down just in time to see the metal glinting as the pieces fell to the river bottom. She didn't need to see their resting place to know where they were. Even broken, the Needle hummed at the same frequency as she did. She would always be able to find it again.

Sloane returned to the others and found Ines scowling at her.

"Just needed to look again," she said.

They hadn't found the Dark One's body. Ten years later, they had all accepted that it lay buried under the concrete, steel, and glass from the old tower, packed into the river bottom too densely for anything to be retrieved. But initially they had all been afraid that he wasn't really gone. Sloane had even joined the divers who searched the debris for any trace of him, not satisfied until she found a few things: a gold button that looked like it came from his coat, a rotten shred of fabric that resembled his shirt cuff.

Even after that, she had come back every few weeks to remind herself that the river was his grave, that he was really dead. Ines had gone with her.

Sloane spotted a familiar figure in the doorway of the monument, a girl with crooked features and light brown hair so fine and frizzy, it hovered around her face like spun sugar. Albie's little sister, Kaitlin. It hurt to look at her.

Sloane took off her sunglasses. Kaitlin gave her a little smile. Albie's mom—Mrs. Summers was the only name Sloane knew her by —appeared behind her, clutching a floral handkerchief against her chest. She nodded to Sloane and stepped past her daughter, out of the monument.

Mrs. Summers had never liked Sloane, probably for the same reasons that other people didn't. She was the kind of person who followed celebrity gossip religiously and believed what she read in chain e-mails that warned of new viruses and internet curses. Every time the Sloane of gossip rags cheated on Matt, Mrs. Summers was on the phone with Albie, asking if it was true.

Today, though, all she said was "Thank you. For taking care of the . . ." Mrs. Summers's eyes filled with tears. Thinking of the cremation, no doubt.

"Uh . . . sure. I mean, of course. I—" Sloane shook her head. She didn't know what to say.

Luckily, Esther was there to help. "Hey, Mrs. Summers," she said. "My mom sent this with me."

She offered Mrs. Summers an envelope with elegant cursive writing on it. Mrs. Summers turned away from Sloane, looking relieved.

Next to Sloane, Matt was frowning at his phone. "I just got a news alert," he said. "Something happened at the Dome." He looked up at Sloane.

She stared back steadily. If he asked her, she decided, she wouldn't lie. She was done with that. Maybe it was her fault that Matt thought she was better than she was; she had spent so much time pretending, for his sake. Maybe it was time he knew what he was really dealing with. Heat rushed into her face, and she was ready, ready for him to ask, ready to tell him—

"Well," Ines said. "Shall we?"

She was holding the little can the crematory had given Sloane. A heavy silence fell.

"Um—before the last stand, as it were, we all talked about what we wanted if we died," Ines said. She sniffed. "Albie said he didn't want a big thing, just for his ashes to be scattered somewhere the Dark One had hit with the Drain. He felt like—I don't know, he felt connected to the people who died in the same fight. It was a comfort for him, in a way, knowing that if he died, he wouldn't be alone."

Sloane stepped to the side so they were all in a circle: Kaitlin and Mrs. Summers, Matt and Esther, Ines and her. Ines opened the lid of the canister. Inside it were the gray ashes, and on top of them, something yellow and bright. A paper crane.

Mrs. Summers spotted it first. And started to laugh.

They all laughed, then, not because it was funny but because it wasn't, because laughter was a full-body hiccup, wild and strange, and death was wild and strange, too.

"I can't believe he's gone," Sloane said when silence fell again.

Kaitlin took the canister from Ines and turned west, away from Lake Michigan. She tossed the ashes in a wide arc, toward the monument. The yellow crane tumbled to the ground.

A hand in a houndstooth-patterned mitten wrapped around Sloane's. Esther. And on her other side, a sturdy leather glove. Matt. All four of them were clasped together, with a few of the ashes dancing around their feet. Sloane's vision went blurry with tears.

And then she heard a gentle voice. It seemed to speak right into her ear, too quiet at first for the words to be intelligible. She felt the tingle and burn that she associated with the Needle and with magic and looked around her. The others had their heads bowed, and they weren't moving. Esther's and Matt's hands still held hers, the pressure steady.

"Sloane," the voice said, and it was Albie's. She searched for him, scanning the monument, the river, the crowd beyond the barrier, but she couldn't see him. She felt something tugging at the back of her hand, where the scar from the Needle was.

"Let's go," Albie's voice said, from in front of her now, a whisper against her cheek.

It was stupid to think he might be there, even in some small way, just because his ashes were here, just because this was a place where they had done powerful magic. But she had seen and felt and done impossible things, ripped doors free of their hinges and sent them sailing toward the clouds, watched trees hover over the ocean, burst a skyscraper like a grape. She had opened herself to wanting things that could never be hers, and she had gotten them. What was so different about this?

The Dark One had died here. Maybe Albie could be alive some-where else.

She took one step toward the voice —

—and then regretted it, tried to step back, to *go back,* but it was too late. Everything had gone dark.

PART
TWO

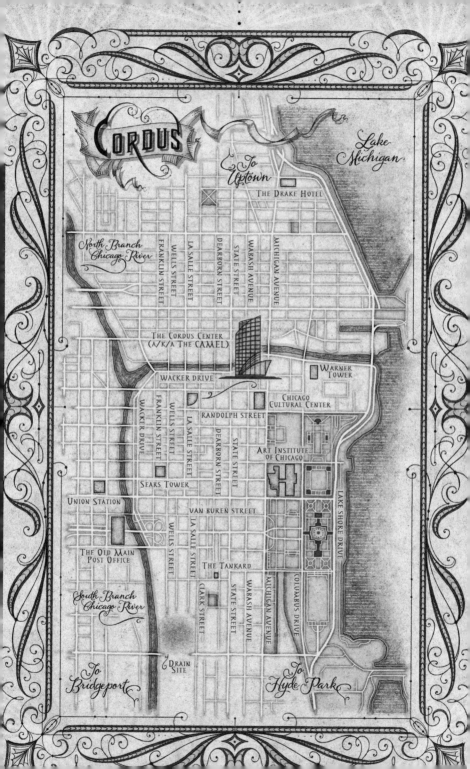

It's a Magical World Out There! An Elementary-Schooler's Guide to Magic, 7th Edition

by Agnes Dewey and Sebastian Bartlett

Did you know that the world used to be a whole lot less magical? Well, it's true! Up until 1969, most people didn't think magic really existed. It was just fairy-tale stuff. But in 1969, something called **the *Tenebris* Incident** (more on that in chapter 3!) happened, and magic spread all over Genetrix. People all across our planet saw some amazing — but scary! — things, like certain parts of the ocean boiling for no reason [fig. 2], glowing balls of light floating around neighborhoods [fig. 3], and whole buildings turning upside down [fig. 4]. One person even took a picture of a whale floating in the clouds [fig. 5]!

After magic spread, a lot of people also got really sick. Their bodies weren't used to the magical energy in the air! And since there was no cure for the magical plague, those people all died, which was really sad. But if you're here, that means that you're immune to the magical plague! So you don't need to worry about it. All you need to know is that magic is part of our world now, and it's time for you to learn how to use it! You won't be able to do very much until you're older, but even what you can do now is pretty cool. First, though, you have to learn how magic works.

The truth is, we don't even really know how magic works! We're only just starting to understand it. Isn't that exciting? Maybe one day, you'll be the person who discovers all of magic's secrets!

The Manifestation of Impossible Wants: A New Theory of Magic
by Arthur Solowell

In the burgeoning field of magical theory, we often speak of *intent* being a central component of the magical arts. A siphon, for example, cannot function without a person to wield it and direct its power; it is fundamentally inert, no more than a blunt instrument without the living form to fill it. And certainly intent is important—how else would a person be able to control the results of a siphon's work? How else would someone be able to, say, reliably freeze an object rather than set it on fire? Certain types of siphons are indeed attuned to particular tasks—an eye siphon is most often used for visual workings, an ear siphon for auditory ones, etcetera—but each offers a great deal of flexibility even within those categories. Intent then ensures that flexibility does not mean unreliability.

However, I would argue that while intent is a *component* of a magical act, and certainly a significant one, it is not the *essence* of what distinguishes a magical act from a mundane one. Any man with a hammer can intend to hit a nail—that itself is not magic, and a siphon is no hammer. Instead, it is the argument of this text that the essence of a magical act is *what a person wants*. Or, to be more specific, what a person wants that is not easily achieved within the realm of the mundane. Desiring that a nail sink into a board is a want, but it is not magic. Wanting the boards to hold together with no nail at all—*that* is magic.

In other words, for something to be magic, it must be an *impossible want*.

Senator Amos Redding's speech
in support of the Haven Act
September 17, 1985

I take the Senate floor today to share my thoughts on a most contentious issue, that of the proposed Haven Act, which, if passed, would enable the citizens of a city to vote to prohibit the use of magic as well as the establishment of businesses that sell devices that make use of magic or otherwise facilitate its use. I intend today to vote yes on the Haven Act, and I will tell you why.

Ladies and gentlemen, magic is a shortcut. It is the easy path. And we do not know where it leads or what may come of it. It is one thing to be excited by its possibilities, but it is another to allow it to spread uncontrollably through our nation, rendering our young people unable to perform the slightest practical task, leaving no space clear of its influence. We must maintain the skills we have fought so hard—over so many years of human history—to learn. We must honor the past as we look toward the future.

I ask you, colleagues and friends, to consider the future you would like to have and the future you would like this country to have. Magic has long been regarded with suspicion, going all the way back to our earliest myths and legends. This distrust and even loathing for the practice of magic is not merely due to ignorance; it speaks to something at the very core of us, something that says we should be working the land we live in, that great accomplishments should be hard won by the labor of our hands . . .

16

SHE REMEMBERED, right after the building blew apart, right after the Needle had sent light into the sky, right before the Dark One disappeared, the taste of river water and the pale glint of his cheek in the moonlight.

Sloane tried to scream and choked on water instead. Esther's hand slackened in hers, then slipped free; Matt's soon followed. Sloane waved her arms wildly, trying to find either of them again, but her movements were slow, and the darkness around her was absolute.

She coughed silent bubbles. Water — she was surrounded by water. Her lungs burned. She kicked. She was moving, but she didn't know where she was going; for all she knew, she was swimming deeper.

She put a finger up to her lips and blew a bubble. It tickled the underside of her fingertip, which meant she was upright — bubbles always moved *up,* toward the surface. She kicked harder. Her coat, soaked through, dragged behind her, and she wriggled free of it, then pulled the strap of her bag over her head, so it crossed her chest.

She opened her eyes, ignoring the sting of the water in search of light.

Nothing; there was nothing.

With both hands empty, it was easier to swim. Cameron had taught her to swim when they were children, at the park district pool. One summer, they had gone there every day. They had competed against each other for the biggest splash, cannonballing into the deep end.

She pulled herself up, and up, and up.

Ahead of her was a glimmer of light. Just a hint, at first, and then a circle of bright teal, blurry. She swam toward it. One of her shoes fell off. She kicked harder, legs, arms, and chest burning.

She broke through the surface with a gasp. She tilted back to float, her heartbeat sounding in her ears.

Above her was a waning crescent moon, thin as a toenail clipping, surrounded by a sky purple with light pollution. She could have sworn the moon had been waxing when she was walking toward the Dome with Needle in hand. It was as if almost a month had passed in a single breath. She slapped a hand over her eyes and rubbed them to clear them.

Not to mention the fact that Albie's funeral had been in the morning.

She knew where she was. The smell of river water rotten in her nostrils was familiar, as was the irregular outline of the corncob building in the distance, partly obscured by the strict lines of 330 North Wabash. But in place of the monument to the Dark One's defeat was a tower. Not Trump Tower, gleaming blue and scratching the sky with its needle, but a building unlike any she'd seen before — half straightforward glass cylinder, half undulating steel panels, like a breath of smoke spilling down the western side.

No longer desperate for air, Sloane straightened up and noticed, for the first time, a line of people standing on the shore. In the light cast by the old-fashioned globular fixtures along the river walk, she saw clothes in dark, rich colors and heavy fabrics, artfully draped. Sloane kicked to keep herself afloat as she pushed her hair away from her face. Every muscle in her body ached, but she wasn't sure she wanted to move closer to the edge, closer to *them*.

"Who . . ." She spat, her voice coming out rough and guttural. It carried across the water and echoed off the concrete walls on either side of the river that held the streets back from the water. "Who are you?"

A woman — dark, thick hair, light brown skin, dressed in green —

stepped forward and seemed to be about to speak when Esther burst through the surface of the water, mascara streaking down her face. Matt followed, his head emerging right at the edge of the river. He grabbed the barrier to steady himself as he vomited water at the woman's feet. She hopped back. Her shoes were shiny and came to a point.

"What—" The woman turned to someone else, a blond man standing away from the river's edge cradling a thick book against his chest. "Why are there more than one?"

"I don't . . ." The man was gaping at Sloane, Esther, and Matt in turn. "I don't know."

"Where's Ines?" Sloane asked Esther and Matt.

Esther shook her head. "I didn't see her."

Sloane gave up on treading water, swam to the edge, and hoisted herself up, her arms trembling under her weight. She fell, almost cracking her head on the sidewalk, but got her knees under her and stood. She was taller than the woman, but not by much.

The woman stepped back.

"I asked you a question," Sloane said. Unfortunately, some of the menacing effect was lost because she had to bend over to cough up more water. It tasted like moldy peach.

"Calm down, please," the woman said. "We—"

"The fuck she will!" Esther said from the water. She was fighting to free herself of her coat. Sloane saw the white trails of her breath in the moonlight.

Matt had managed to haul himself over the side and sat with water leaking from his pants legs. Esther made it to the edge and pushed her hair away from her face.

Sloane scanned the line of people now just a few feet away from her. Their styles of dress were varied, but they had one thing in common: a gold pin about the size of a mandarin orange fastened to their chests. Several of them also wore elaborate jewelry, somewhat mechanical in style, around their throats or on their hands. One woman had a piece covering her left ear, red-plated, like it was made of rubies.

"Where are we?" Matt asked them in the low voice he used when he meant business. He thought it was intimidating, but to the rest of them, it just sounded like a Batman impression. They had all agreed not to tease him about it, since he seemed to enjoy it.

"Which of you is the Chosen One?" the woman said, scanning each of them in turn.

They made a dignified bunch, Sloane thought. Esther was on the edge of the river now, rubbing her hands over her face to get rid of the mascara streaks. Matt was yanking off one of his soaked leather gloves with his teeth. And Sloane's pants were so heavy with water, she was sure her ass was showing.

"You don't get to ask questions until you answer some," Sloane said, pulling her pants up by the belt loops.

Matt raised his hand. "Me. I'm the Chosen One."

Esther snorted.

"What?" Matt shrugged. "She asked a simple question."

"I mean, we were sort of *all* the Chosen One," Esther clarified. She had managed to smear the mascara tracks sideways, toward her ears. Sloane realized that she hadn't seen Esther without a thick layer of makeup on since the last battle. She looked . . . tired. As tired as Sloane felt.

"One of us is missing," Sloane said. "Where's Ines?"

The woman frowned at her. "We were expecting *one* of you, not three. And certainly not four. And to answer your previous question, you are in the exact same place you were a moment ago, with the notable difference that you are now . . . one dimension to the left. So to speak."

"Like an alternate universe?" Esther said. "Are you high?"

A long time ago, Sloane had learned about parallel dimensions, about string theory and infinite possibilities branching off from one another into an eternity no human being could comprehend. Ever since, she had avoided thinking about it, not wanting to consider that for every decision she made, there was an identical Sloane on another Earth making the other decision, the universes branching off forever. Who was she, really, if there was no stability in her identity, if there were that many Sloanes walking that many paths, nudged this way and that by minor alterations in circumstance?

"Who are you?" Sloane said again.

In any universe, in any dimension, her first concern was always people.

"My name is Aelia," the woman said. "I am praetor of Cordus and tribune of the Army of Flickering."

"Did she just say words?" Esther asked Sloane. "Did you just say words, lady?"

They were old words, and strange ones, with the lights of a modern city glittering behind the woman's head. But Sloane caught the meaning of them. "She's Aelia, and she's in charge," she translated.

"Another dimension," Matt said. "How is that possible?"

"Your people are not aware of other dimensions?" Aelia said, frowning. She wore stiff fabric draped around her shoulders, narrow trousers tapered at the ankle, and a shirt with a short, upright collar. Styles Sloane recognized, but also didn't. The gold pin on her chest stood out against the gray and green of her clothes, and she wore an apparatus on her hand that looked like a mechanical, bejeweled glove.

"In the abstract only," Matt replied.

Aelia looked again at the blond man, scorn in the scrunch of her nose. "Then this must be quite a shock," Aelia said.

Sloane snorted.

"I know you have questions, and I promise to answer them," Aelia said, narrowing her eyes at Sloane. "But in order for me to do that, you will have to trust us enough to come with us somewhere."

Matt twisted the hem of his coat in both hands to squeeze out some of the water. He had the casual air of someone shaking out an umbrella after coming in from the rain. "Okay," he said.

"No!" Sloane glared at him. Her pants were slipping down her hips again. "We're not about to just . . . go somewhere else. Not until we know what the hell is going on."

Matt's lips quirked at the corner. For a few years, while they hunted the Dark One, that was the only smile he had ever worn. But after the Dark One fell, she had seen it less and less often as he softened and relaxed, no longer responsible for any life but his own.

The return of that smile meant he was working Aelia, and Sloane was getting in the way.

You must let them play to their strengths as they let you play to yours, Bert's voice told her from her memories. They each had a place in their small platoon, and though it grated on her now that she and Matt were engaged, Matt was the leader. He made the calls. They had to trust him or the system would break.

"I intend to tell you," Aelia said, "but some things are better explained by seeing them for yourself."

Esther, coming to stand beside Sloane, looked just as wary as Sloane felt. But she caught Sloane's eye and nodded, lips pursed.

"Fine. Show us," Sloane said.

Sloane stayed in Aelia's shadow as they climbed the wide steps of what was, on Sloane's Earth, the River Theater, a wide, minimalist staircase made of polished stone. Here, however, the space was arranged into terraces, like steps, but with trees growing from each flat area, giving the impression of a forest right in the middle of the city. Aelia wove around the trees, and Sloane, Matt, and Esther followed her up to street level.

The other observers fell into step behind them. Their silence unsettled Sloane, their presence behind her pricking at the back of her neck. She felt like she was being herded.

She was almost afraid to lift her head, to be confronted with the *wrongness* of the place. But Wacker Drive, at least, was the same street she remembered, with cars careening around the bend ahead of them, and there was the Seventeenth Church of Christ, Scientist, which looked like a grounded spaceship, standing where the two branches of Wacker separated. There were no pedestrians on the sidewalks, and it wasn't until the group of people behind her fanned out that she realized why. One of them lifted his hand and let out an inhuman trill. A wall of iridescence appeared in front of him, forming a barrier across the walkway one hundred yards from where Sloane stood.

Aelia cleared her throat. She stood beside a boxy, wine-colored limousine with chrome wheels. Aelia opened the wide back door, then pulled the center panel open from the left so she could slide inside. The blond man waited beside the car. He raised a hand, and with the sleeve falling away from his wrist, Sloane got a closer look at the apparatus he wore. It was simpler than the one Aelia had, but no less beautiful; it looked like a glove, but it was made of copper, with articulated joints. Dense organic patterns—vines of tiny leaves—were carved into each plate, and unlike a bulky gauntlet from an old set of armor, it was streamlined, clearly made to fit him and him alone.

"I can dry you off, if you like," he said.

Sloane glanced at Esther.

"We would not have brought you here simply to harm you a moment later," he said. "My name is Nero. Who wants to go first?"

It took a few seconds for Matt to volunteer, though he had been the one insisting that they go along with this. He stood in front of Nero, fidgeting a little. "What do I do?" he said.

"Stay still, please," Nero replied. He held his hand up, fingers spread, palm facing Matt. He hummed a low note, and Matt's shirt shifted, almost imperceptibly, as if hit by a breeze.

Nero hummed again, and droplets of water pulled away from Matt's head and dangled in the air. He stared at them, dazed. Sloane looked around, just to make sure time hadn't frozen and kept the water from falling. It would not have been the strangest thing to happen that day.

Nero hummed the same steady note as he moved his hand down to hover over Matt's shoulders, abdomen, and then pelvis. Water tugged free from the fabric of his coat and shirt and hung suspended in the air.

When Nero finished, he hummed a different note, moving his hand in a circle. All the droplets that had been hanging in midair around Matt's body flew toward him and coalesced into a sphere of water. He ushered the ball of water forward so it hovered over the street, then dropped it into the gutter with a gesture. Once it hit the ground, it collapsed, becoming shapeless liquid again.

Sloane had seen magic before: a force like a hurricane that tore people apart from every direction; an unstable leap of flames in Albie's hands; even the strange light that had emanated from Matt's Golden Bough. But she had never seen it manipulated with such delicacy, such magnificent precision.

Matt was dry now, his shirt crisp. Nero turned to Esther and Sloane.

"Who's next?"

Matt, Esther, and Sloane crammed into the back seat of the limousine. Sloane pinched the burgundy velour between her thumb and index finger and looked out the window. They were driving around the bend of Upper Wacker toward Lake Shore Drive. Moonlight rippled on the lake. The jagged skyline was mostly unfamiliar but with some touchstones Sloane recognized: the vertical white lines of the Aon Center; the glass slant of the Crain Communications building, like a carrot cut on the bias; the Ionic columns of the Field Museum.

"What are those things?" Matt said, pointing at the apparatus on Nero's hand and then Aelia's. Aelia's hand rested on her kneecap, so Sloane could see in better detail the thick cuff wrapped around her wrist, with delicate chains attached to it that followed the lines of her fingers, finishing in a thimble-like cap at the end of each fingertip. Red beads were scattered along each chain, and a red jewel was set into the middle of the cuff.

Aelia held up her hand. "These are called siphons," Aelia replied. "They channel magical energy."

"Magic," Matt repeated. "But they look like tech."

"Actually," Esther pointed out, "they kind of look like jewelry."

"They are all three," Aelia said, looking puzzled. "Magic, technology, and adornment. Are these things at odds where you are from?"

"Our technology doesn't use magic," Matt said. "We're some of the only people who have ever wielded it, and even we were only just beginning to understand how to manipulate it."

And it had killed Albie, Sloane thought bitterly.

Aelia turned to Nero and arched an eyebrow at him. Nero ducked his head.

"Fascinating," Aelia said. "Our integration of both elements is not seamless. There are some who insist that technology should advance without magic in case magic proves to be a finite resource. And there are even some who view the use of magic as the work of the

devil. But this is a siphon, a triumph of technology and magic both."
She turned her hand over, made a fist, then unfurled her fingers. She
whistled, and sparks danced in her palm.

"Originally invented by Liu Huiyin in Xiamen, China, in 1980,"
Nero chimed in. "Magic was not widespread on Genetrix until 1969."

Sloane stared at Aelia's hand. The sparks were already gone, but
they had left her with a crooked afterimage.

"What happened in 1969?" Matt asked.

"The *Tenebris* Incident," Nero replied.

"We'll have time for history lessons later, I'm sure," Aelia said.

"You call your planet Genetrix?" Esther asked. Her hands were in
fists on her knees, her knuckles white.

Sloane looked out the window again. She knew enough about architecture to understand that some of these buildings didn't fit the
usual categories. The modernist structures that had become so ubiq-
uitous as to be unremarkable to her were gone. In their place were
strange shapes lit in an array of colors. Before she could comprehend
any of them, the limo had already driven past. They exited Lake
Shore Drive and plunged into the South Loop.

"When magic became common, we began using two names for
places, one for the mundane and another to refer to the magical aspects of those locations," Aelia said. "We use the names Earth and
Genetrix both, just as we refer to this city as both Chicago and Cordus, which means 'second.'"

"Right — the Second City," Matt said. "Rebuilt after the fire."

"I feel like I'm dreaming," Esther said in a low voice to Sloane.
"Like the first time I saw footage of the Drain."

Sloane nodded. They drove past the yellow arches of a McDonald's, unchanged from the ones Sloane knew.

"You weren't holding hands with Ines when we . . . came here?"
Sloane said.

Esther shook her head. "I had just let go. I don't remember her being in the water with us."

"She's probably back on Earth, then," Sloane said. "Maybe there's
a way to contact her."

They stopped at a traffic light, and Sloane peered into the car next to theirs. There was a woman behind the wheel, a siphon on her left hand, her right hand twisting the radio knob. The glow from the dashboard was orange, analog instead of digital. There was a clock between the air vents, with hands pointing at 10 and 12. It was 10:00 p.m.

"What can you do with that thing?" Esther asked Nero. There was still a smear of mascara on her temple.

"Siphons can be attached to most parts of the body, and their placement affects what they do," Nero said. "Wrist siphons, like this one, tend to be used for the practical—electrical manipulation, as well as water, air—"

"Fire?" Sloane asked.

Nero nodded.

"So it's a weapon, then," she said.

"Anything can be a weapon," Nero replied. "If you're trying hard enough."

"I'm just trying to figure out to what extent we're being held hostage," Sloane said. She was surprised that Matt didn't jump in to chastise her for sounding so harsh, but he kept quiet. Maybe he wanted to know the same thing.

Nero's mouth twitched into a mild smile. *Mild* was a good word for him overall, Sloane thought. His voice had a silky quality, not persuasive, but delicate. His movements, from his footsteps to his smallest gestures, were careful, as though he were consciously selecting each one. He turned his hand over and unfastened a clasp on the underside of the siphon glove. A light flickered between the metal plates as he undid it. He slid it off his hand, set it on the floor of the limousine between them, and showed her his palms.

"We do not intend to threaten you," Nero said.

"And who is *we*?" Matt said. "You and her?"

"The group that summoned you is the special council of Cordus," Aelia said. "We were assembled to address . . . a particular problem that I will describe to you in full. I am the leader of that council as well as an elected official in city government. Praetor, as I said."

Sloane frowned at the device on the floor. She didn't feel the burning, tingling *pull* of magic here the way she did at home. She stretched out a hand toward the siphon, waiting for something, anything, but she felt nothing. Maybe here, magic suffused the world so completely that she couldn't feel it, the way a person stops hearing white noise after a few minutes. She brushed her fingers over the siphon, and it felt warm from skin contact but otherwise inert.

"It requires intent," Nero said to her.

That was what she was afraid of.

The car stopped. Aelia opened the door and gestured for them to follow her.

On their side of the street were old-fashioned gas lamps with elegant black bases and glass spotted brown from the flames. On the other side of the street was rubble. Broken chunks of concrete piled up against cracked wood beams, which were fraying where they had split right down the middle. Twisted girders reached upward. Broken glass shone in the moonlight.

Sloane heard Esther's footsteps behind her, then felt her cool, dry hand. Sloane grabbed it, held it tight, and both women stood shoulder to shoulder, staring. One building's remains tumbled into another's, and on and on, as far as Sloane could discern in moonlight alone. Where a street had been was carnage and destruction—a curl of yellow-white, the spine of a squirrel; a woman's blouse, patterned with flowers, trapped under a rock; a bit of stuffing from a plush toy in the mouth of a scurrying rat.

"The Drain," Esther said.

Sloane felt like time had run backward, and she was at the edge of the site where the Dome would later stand, surrounded on all sides by worshippers of the Dark One and seekers of magic. The Drain was like a fingerprint, distinct from all other forms of magic she had witnessed. And only one person could leave that particular mark.

If this was a Drain site, then the Dark One had been here.

Nero moved away from them to set up the same barriers Sloane had seen on Wacker Drive, intended to keep pedestrians away. But Aelia stayed beside them. "In your world," Aelia said, spreading the fingers encased in her siphon wide so her hand looked like a metal claw, "there was a force of evil at work—one that you defeated?"

"The Dark One," Matt replied quietly. "Yes. I—we, actually; all of us—killed him."

"Wonderful." Aelia smiled, and it looked almost sinister in the dim light of the gas lamps; shadows pooled beneath her prominent cheekbones. "We too have a kind of Dark One. Our name for him is the Resurrectionist."

"*Is,*" Esther said. "Present tense."

"Yes," Aelia said. "Our Resurrectionist is still alive. Still terrorizing us. Still doing *this*."

She gestured to the dark expanse before them. Sloane saw dark shapes moving ahead, darting in and out of the broken buildings. The area had the trademark pattern of a Drain site, the bits of concrete and wood and steel growing smaller the farther in you looked. At the center, everything would be fine as sand.

"This happened last year," Aelia said. "The closest the Resurrectionist has ever gotten to our city center. They grow more powerful by the year, and they inch closer."

"Is that *they* singular or plural?" Esther asked.

"Did your Dark One work alone?" Aelia's mouth twisted into a wry grin. "There are followers; there are always followers. But the Resurrectionist's followers are where the nickname comes from. They are the walking dead."

Across from them was the skeleton of a house, stripped of siding and drywall. Insulation tumbled in the wind, pink and puffy as cotton candy.

"Like you, we had a Chosen One," Aelia said. "He was valiant and a talented worker of magic. Young too. Too young, perhaps."

"He *was?*" Esther asked.

"He is dead." Aelia's voice cracked. "He was defeated."

It should have been obvious, Sloane thought. Even expected. If there was a universe in which she and her friends had won, of course there were universes where they had lost. Where they had died. Where they had never even existed.

"But he's *the Chosen One*," Esther said. "He can't be *dead*. Are you sure you got the right one?"

"We are certain," Aelia said curtly. "We had a prophecy. It was quite specific. And we used its magical signature to summon you here."

"Magical signature?" Matt said at the same time Esther said, "Why did you summon *us?*"

Matt stepped back. Hers was the question he really wanted answered, Sloane assumed.

"Isn't it obvious?" Sloane said bitterly, her voice trembling. "She wants us to take on her Dark One for her."

"He isn't *my* Dark One," Aelia snapped. "And I assure you, I would not have resorted to such measures unless the situation was truly dire. I can't allow more people to die. I can't allow more of our world to fall into ruin."

"Oh, well, if the situation is *dire,* then it's okay to kidnap people from other dimensions," Sloane said. Her throat felt tight with rising hysteria.

"Yeah, here I was thinking the direness quotient wasn't high enough," Esther added sourly.

"I assure you, it is!" Aelia said, her voice becoming almost shrill.

"I don't think she's very good at sarcasm," Esther said to Sloane.

"She's going to love us, then," Sloane replied.

"You have to understand," Matt said, raising his voice a little to talk over them. "We've already been through this, and we're not eager to go through it again, especially for a place that doesn't even belong to us."

"I'm afraid it's not that simple." Nero spoke from a few yards away, in the middle of the street. His fingers twisted together in front of him, metal siphon glove wrapped around flesh. "The fates of our worlds are no longer as distinct as one might hope."

"Uh," Matt said, "what?"

"Our worlds are connected," Nero said. "We can see it, the connection. The use of magic has made both of our worlds unstable. The Resurrectionist preys on this instability to accomplish his destruction."

Sloane narrowed her eyes. "How?"

"We don't know. We don't know anything for certain. All we

know is that *this*"—Aelia gestured to the rubble that confronted them—"is not something he should be able to do. It's not something anyone was able to do until he came along."

Sloane thought about touching the Needle for the first time, how it had turned her into an empty stomach, a black hole of wanting. How she had taken everything—*everything*—into herself, indiscriminate and frantic, churning water into froth and bones into particles of sand. How she had burst through the surface of the ocean, soaked with blood and roaring with power.

"No," she said. The word came out broken. "No, it can't be. This can't be happening."

"Sloane," Matt said softly.

"We *killed* him," Sloane said. "I saw him, under the water; I saw him die."

"In one world," Matt said. "Apparently not in every world."

"Well, that was *my* world! I did my part, I fought my Dark One. I did my job!" She was crying. She *hated* crying. "You can stay and help if you want. But I'm not going to do it again. It was hard enough the first time."

Matt's hand fell on Sloane's left shoulder, then her right, so she was looking at him. She needed a benzo. She needed a mother who didn't suck. She needed to be *home*.

"I can't," she said again, this time only to Matt.

"I know," Matt said, nodding. "Me either, Sloane. Except I think we might have to."

Sloane looked over Matt's shoulder at Aelia. Asking her a question without asking.

"It is a huge feat, to send or summon between universes," Aelia said. "We will only be able to accomplish it once more, to send you home. Which our urgent need compels us to do only after we have received your help."

"So you kidnapped us," Esther said, "and now you're holding us prisoner until we help you."

Aelia looked down, didn't answer.

"Just wanted to be sure I was clear on the situation." Esther sounded bitter but tremulous.

Sloane looked over Matt's shoulder at the stripe of darkness in front of her flanked by intact buildings, cheerfully lit. An entire city block, obliterated. Aelia had brought them here to gain their sympathy, Sloane was certain. Show them a tangible sign of the destruction they were dealing with. *This is just the beginning,* this place said, *of the horrors I will show you.*

It's a simple choice, my dear, the Dark One had whispered.

Sloane tasted bile.

"I am sure you need time to process all of this," Aelia said. "We have prepared rooms for you to stay in while you're here. We can speak again tomorrow, after you've rested."

Esther reached for Sloane's hand and squeezed it gently. She felt warm and steady and familiar. They had fought side by side before, in situations they thought they would never escape. Sloane remembered the two of them staying up to keep watch, their spines pressed together as they each watched a different horizon.

Sloane let the heat of her friend draw her back to herself. She knew how to do this. Knew how to search dark landscapes for enemies, how to fall only half asleep, how to booby-trap a house with a jar of marbles, how to march inexorably toward a single end and a near-certain doom.

It was like a dance, and she would never forget the steps.

Life and Death: Scholars on the Resurrectionist and His Army

by Garret Rogers

From "The Possibility of the Impossible: An Interview with Marwa Daud, Professor of Magical Theory (University of Chicago)"

DAUD: Magic has confronted us all with many utter impossibilities made possible. But thus far it obeys certain rules. A person cannot, for example, make herself fly through the air like a bird or conjure food out of nowhere. Up until the emergence of the Resurrectionist, we believed that bringing the dead to life was another one of those limits. But the Resurrectionist's army is, as I'm sure you know, composed of individuals that appear to be corpses. Yet they walk, talk, and even produce magic themselves on occasion. How can this be? How can this terrorist raise an entire army when the world's most talented magic-users cannot reanimate anything larger than a housecat? Is he—assuming the Resurrectionist *is* a he—that much more powerful than the rest of us?

ROGERS: A housecat—you're referring to the experiment by the German Franz Becker about five years ago?

DAUD: Yes, Becker. He was a brilliant scientist. So tragic that he was able to bring his recently deceased pet cat back to life only for the act to kill him shortly thereafter. He is a fine example of what I am saying, which is that other people have indeed tried to raise the dead. Magic is still relatively new, so I am not positing that no one else ever *will* walk in the Resurrectionist's footsteps, but it seems to be a long way off. That doesn't mean that we can't learn something from his army in the meantime. Quite the contrary—on a theoretical level, his army is significant. Outliers and anomalies are always central to my thinking, because they expand our understanding of theory—the practical informing the possible. That giving some form of life to the dead is even possible tells us something important about the nature of magic itself. About its origin or perhaps about the way we use it. The Resurrectionist is alone in his ability, for now, but why? Does he have access to a particular magic source or channel? Is his enhanced ability innate, instinctual, or is it learned? All of these answers, when found, will tell us something profound about magic.

ROGERS: Such as?

DAUD: Well, if magical skill is innate, then we exist in a world where power truly is inherited. We can therefore begin to ask if the use of this power is genetic, and if so, does it follow certain bloodlines more closely than others? This kind of thinking—that there are certain superior bloodlines—has led humanity down dark paths more than once. But if the Resurrectionist *learned* his ability, then we can assume that magic is a resource from which any person may draw, in which case we must know if it is a limited resource or if it renews itself. If it is finite, we might begin to allocate magical use to particular people in positions of prominence or influence. This would reinforce existing structures of power in our society. The wealthy and famous become the most magical, which brings further wealth and fame.

If magic is an endless resource, however, there will be no inherent limit to its use. The human race will change on a fundamental level as we stop performing everyday tasks "the old-fashioned way," so to speak—

ROGERS: So you don't see a positive outcome no matter what the answers are, do you?

DAUD: I guess I hadn't really thought about it that way. But no, regardless of what power humankind has access to, I suppose I never see it as having a good outcome. We are animals, after all. And don't let your housecat fool you into thinking that animals are nothing more than fuzzy, whiskered creatures who wish us no ill. Nature is bloody, and as a whole, it favors strength over compassion.

17

WE JUST PASSED CITY HALL," Sloane said to Esther, as the car pulled up to a curb again. "This must be the Thompson Center."

"That big curved glass building?" Esther gestured to the stone façade that confronted them. "Doesn't look like it."

"I mean, I think the architecture is different, but we're in that location." Sloane frowned. "So to speak."

They passed through a dark, spacious lobby to an elevator bank. It was too dark for Sloane to see how high the ceiling was. Nero pulled a grate of tarnished bronze across the elevator doors before pressing the button.

"This building is in the Bygoneist school," he said as the elevator rose. "Which means it's made primarily without magical intervention but represents styles of many periods combined without concern for accuracy."

"Without magical intervention," Matt repeated. "Is that . . . rare? To build something without magic?"

Nero shrugged. "In Chicago, yes. Architecture is an industry heavily influenced by magic, and people here love their architecture."

Cameron would have loved it, Sloane thought.

The elevator came to a stop on the seventh floor. Nero led them to a balcony that overlooked a dome made of stone—the Hall of

Summons, he explained, as if it were obvious what that meant. They walked to the back of the building and climbed a winding staircase made of wrought iron up another two flights to what appeared to be a wall of solid wood.

Nero pressed his siphon-covered hand to the wood, then took it away, leaving a bright white handprint behind. It faded into the wall within seconds, and then the polished wood parted down the middle and opened to a long hallway with doors on either side.

"These rooms are occasionally used as apartments for important guests of the Cordus Center," Aelia said, gesturing toward one of the doors. She whistled. The door opened and slammed against the wall behind it with a shudder. "They're intended to showcase the work of up-and-coming designers, so they are a bit . . . odd."

Nero set about opening the other doors with a gentler effort from his siphon.

"The Cordus Center," Matt repeated. "Is that where we are now?"

Sloane walked the perimeter of the hallway, passing rooms in different styles. She took in only quick impressions of each: one done in spartan simplicity, another a Gothic cathedral in miniature with windows of stained glass, and the last full of delicately carved wood furniture.

"Yes," Aelia said. "This building is primarily an academic institution, the Cordus Center for Advanced Magical Innovation and Learning."

"Camel," Nero said.

"Camel?" Sloane frowned.

"C-A-M-I-L," Nero said, "or, as the students fondly call it, the Camel."

Aelia gave him a look, and Nero shrank back. "We will meet again tomorrow to further discuss things," she said. "Please, try to rest. Nero." She jerked her head to the side. "A word?"

Nero gave them all a nod and followed Aelia back down the hallway to the elevator. Sloane's instinct was to go after them and find a way to listen to their conversation, but the hallway went straight to the elevator with no bends or curves or alcoves to hide an eavesdropper, so she stayed where she was.

"I call the church room," Esther said at once.

"Go for it," Matt said, glancing at Sloane.

Surely he wouldn't want to share one.

He turned and walked into the room filled with carved wood.

Sloane's room, her only option, was white: white walls, white sheets, a wood floor painted white. But when she slid her fingers into the wide seams between wall panels, she discovered drawers, a small closet, and a hidden bookshelf. The last occupant had left a few books there: *The Manifestation of Impossible Wants: A New Theory of Magic; A Society Divided: The Cold War Between Magic and Science;* and *The Mysterious Magical History of the Throat Siphon.* Sloane was just weighing the last one in her palm when someone knocked.

"Team meeting," Esther said. "My room."

Sloane set the book down, leaving the white wall panel open. When she went next door, Esther was already sitting on the bed, her back against its elaborately carved headboard. Matt was tapping on one of the stained-glass windows as if testing its stability. His face was dotted with multicolored lights in the shape of the Virgin Mary.

Sloane leaned against the base of one of the flying buttresses.

"So," Matt said. He looked weary. "Thoughts, anyone?"

The request was a cue for her to tumble right back into the person she had been when they first fought the Dark One. She found herself speaking.

"The overlap between our universe and this one seems to be substantial," she said. "I saw a lot of familiar buildings on the drive to the Drain site. My guess is there's a relatively recent point of departure between this world and ours."

Esther looked lost, so Matt explained. "There's a theory in quantum physics that there is an infinite number of possibilities for how any event might turn out, and each of those possibilities creates a different universe. Think of it like . . . a fork in the road. You could go down either path, so there's a universe where you choose left, and another universe where you choose right. Slo's saying that the fork in the road for Genetrix and Earth happened pretty recently."

"Is that good?" Esther asked.

"I think so," Sloane said. "It means a lot of things will be familiar."

"Except—and I feel like this is a pretty crucial point that you're downplaying right now—we don't know how to get home," Esther said. "And they do. So we're trapped."

"I'm not downplaying it," Sloane said. "I'm saying it's good that if we had to end up in a parallel universe, it's one where people speak English and aren't, like, growing a third nostril or sleeping in vats of goo or something."

Esther snorted, and they all fell silent for a moment.

"They were surprised by how many of us came out of that river," Sloane said. "They expected only one. A parallel Chosen One."

"Yeah, could you have claimed that title any faster, Matt, by the way?" Esther said.

Sloane crossed the room and opened one of the windows. A gust of cool air hit her face, making her shiver. Across the street was a building made of brown stone with a row of columns set into it. City Hall. She heard the rush of cars across pavement and the roar of a distant train in motion. It sounded like the Chicago Sloane knew.

When she turned back, Matt was shrugging. "Sloane getting pissed didn't seem to be helping, so I decided to be cooperative instead."

"Sorry for being a little startled that we got *sucked into another dimension,*" Sloane snapped.

"Startled." Matt raised his eyebrows. "That's one word for it. *Hostile* is another."

"Hey," Esther said, sounding tired. "We need a united front if we're going to get through this." She bit her lip. "Are we really gonna do this?" Her stare was blank, fixed on the opposite wall—or something beyond it. "Fight the Dark One again?"

"We did it before." Matt's head was framed by the stained-glass window, so it looked as if the Virgin Mary were gazing down at him, her eyes half closed, the very picture of serenity. "And we learned a lot from it. We can do it again—better this time, maybe."

"No," Sloane said. "No, we won't be fucking better at it."

Matt was ready with an objection. "Slo—"

"No! I'm not going to stand here and let you give us a pep talk

when we're in a goddamn living nightmare," she said. "Albie is dead,
Ines is a universe away, the Dark One is still alive, and this world is
stuffed with magic we don't know how to wield!"

"I'd say *you* know something about how to wield it," Matt said
coolly. "How else could you have blown up the Dome last night?
Pipe bomb?"

Sloane didn't answer. She didn't know how.

"You think *Slo* is the one who attacked the Dome?" Esther said.
"Matt—"

"He's right." Sloane kept her eyes steady on Matt's as she spoke.
"I did it. I dug up Koschei's Needle and destroyed the magic prototype."

"Fuck, Slo," Esther said. "I thought the Needle was destroyed
years ago."

"It wasn't," Sloane said. "I just didn't want ARIS to have it."

"But you thought it was fine if you had it?" Matt said. "Because
you're more trustworthy than ARIS?"

"Yeah," she replied. "I am."

"You probably killed people, you know that?" Matt said. "Janitors, security staff."

Sloane looked down at the raised scar tissue on the back of her
hand, the jagged lines caused by her crooked teeth. "Wouldn't be the
first time." She lifted her head.

"What?" Matt said.

"Why do you think I gnawed the Needle out of my own hand?"
Sloane brandished the back of her hand at Matt like it was a weapon.
"Because all the other people who were with me on the Deep Dive
mission to get it are dead. I killed every last one of them." She was
tense, her shoulders up by her ears. Bracing herself for impact, she
thought. "ARIS wouldn't remove the Needle even when I begged
them to," she said. "So I did it myself."

She remembered the x-ray of her hand taken after the Deep Dive
incident. The bones, stark white against the black background, grayish in places where they weren't as dense. And then right in the middle, the thick Needle, tapering to a sharp point.

It's really stuck in there, the doctor had said. *Like it thinks it belongs or something.*

Sloane had gone her entire life never getting what she wanted. No one had ever even asked her what she wanted. She didn't make any Christmas lists or birthday requests, that was a given — but there were also no signed field-trip forms, no clubs or sports or musical instruments, no lunch money — hell, no *food* in the kitchen half the time, especially after Cameron joined the fight against the Dark One. As far as her mom knew, Sloane had no desires beyond physical necessities. And sometimes she wasn't even allowed to want those.

So when it came to getting the Needle out, she had decided that this one time, she would get what she wanted for herself, even if she had to do it with her teeth.

"That was for your own safety," Matt said. "ARIS didn't know how the Needle would react—"

Sloane laughed. "ARIS never gave a shit about our safety as long as at least one of us survived to fulfill the fucking prophecy. They made me keep the Needle because it served their purposes. That's all."

Matt's eyebrows knit together like they always did when he pitied someone. She hated it.

"And now here we are again," she said, "another wall of flesh between the people in charge and the Dark One. So how are we going to survive this time?"

Neither of the others answered. Esther seemed unwilling to even look at her. Sloane thought of the bloodstained waves crashing around the ARIS boat, now empty. Thought of how she had hauled herself back onto the deck and padded on flippered feet to the controls to activate the distress signal, tasting copper on her tongue.

She thought of the sting of water hitting her shins as she did a cannonball off the diving board. Cameron waiting for her at the edge of the pool.

And the taste of river water, the pale glint of the Dark One's cheek in the moonlight, before he disappeared.

Sloane opened the door and was about to leave when Matt spoke again.

"We'll find a way," he said.

"Yeah," she replied, and she walked out.

Sloane wasn't surprised when Matt followed her into the hallway.

Their first kiss had happened something like this. After the fall of the Dark One, he had asked her out a few times. Each time, she had refused. They were friends, she said. She didn't think of him that way.

But it had just been an excuse, because she had no longer known how she thought of him. The image of him when she first met him —all elbows and knees—had vanished, and the one of him conquering the Dark One had replaced it, the light from the Golden Bough warm on his face, his arm taut and muscular as he held it out to cast the killing blow, his chest heaving, his jaw clenched—

Her hero. Everyone's, really, but hers most of all.

He hadn't accepted her refusals, which had bothered her. His persistence was just insulting, she insisted. As if he believed she didn't know her own mind. But in this particular case, he had been right. Because at one of Ines and Albie's parties, she and Matt had talked until three in the morning, arms draped over the back of the sagging couch, beer bottles dangling in their fingers long after the beer was gone. Matt had asked her again, and she had avoided the question and gotten up to use the bathroom. And he had followed her into the hallway and kissed her.

"Think of me another way," he had said as he pulled away.

She couldn't remember that feeling of fire in her belly that had driven her to press him up against the wall next to the bathroom and push her tongue into his mouth. She didn't feel it anymore.

"I know it's not a good time," Matt said. "But we have to—"

"Talk. I know."

He was dressed in preppy funeral clothes: a white collared shirt, a tie, a black sweater. Wool slacks, pressed so they'd had a sharp crease earlier that day. Now he looked rumpled and exhausted, like this conversation was just another task at the end of a long list.

He said, "I'm not even sure where to start, honestly."

Sloane laughed. It felt more like a cough. She didn't need him to start. As if drunkenly mocking Matt's proposal with Albie hadn't been enough, there was blowing up the Dome, lying about the Dive, hiding the FOIA request, burying the Needle in their storage unit . . . and the line of little deceptions that made up their days, every time she felt one thing but said another or indulged him in some fantasy of her that bore no resemblance to reality. There was almost nothing about them that was real anymore, and it was her fault.

But her throat was tight at the thought of what was coming, because he would be another person who didn't want her. As if her parents and Bert and every journalist and Chosen One fangirl in existence weren't enough. "You and I are all wrong," she said. "You don't need to convince me of that."

"You're not even going to argue with me?"

"There's no point."

"So you have no desire to fight for us at all," he said, volume rising. "You've just—what, been waiting around for me to break up with you because you didn't have the guts to do it yourself?"

She shook her head. "That's not it. I—I know that when you find something good, you should hang on to it. That's all."

"That's so . . ." He blinked rapidly. "That's so fucking selfish, Sloane."

"What?"

"Ten years," he said. "Ten years I could have spent with someone who actually gave a shit about me instead of someone who lies to me and can't even *pretend* to care when we break up."

"I *care*," she said. "Just because I'm not the sobbing type doesn't mean I don't care!"

"If you cared, you wouldn't have bolted right after I proposed to you and made fun of me to Albie," he said. "If you cared, you would have called a goddamn therapist after you almost sleep-murdered me in the middle of the night."

"I wasn't making fun of you to Albie," she said. "He said it sounded like you didn't know me, and I agreed. That's all."

"Like I didn't *know* you?"

"Yeah!" Sloane threw up her hands. "You're acting like all this shit comes as a surprise! Well, I am exactly who I've always claimed to be. And you've just been walking around with your fingers in your ears for ten years."

"So in other words, it's my fault because I believed in you."

"No, it's your fault for acting like you know me better than I know myself!"

She realized, belatedly, that he had said *believed*. Past tense. She hadn't understood how much his belief in her—foolish as it had been—had permeated her until it was gone. She felt like a cored apple, gutted of all the things that could bring life or a future. All shiny skin and juicy flesh and nothing else.

She slipped the ring from her finger and held it out to him. Her hands were steady, but she couldn't meet his eyes. If she did, she would remember how warm they had been whenever they looked at her. How they sparkled a little when he smiled at one of her jokes. How fierce they could be when something threatened the ones he loved. She would be very little to him now. An old friend, an ex-girlfriend. She would fade into his memory. That was how it always was—she faded away for people once she had served her purpose. "I really am sorry," she said quietly. "For not being more."

"Yeah." Matt put the ring in his pocket. "So am I."

He closed the door behind him. Sloane sat at the end of the bed, listening to Esther thumping around in the room next door and the cars rumbling past on the street below, a *shush* sound audible even from this high up. When she could move again, she crawled toward the headboard, her shoes still on, and curled up on her side. She could feel them coming, the wild, fierce sobs that took her over when the hollow feeling inside her was too much to bear. She grabbed the pillow and buried her face in it, falling asleep when she was too tired to feel anymore.

MEMORANDUM FOR THE RECORD

SUBJECT: Project Delphi, Subproject 3

1. Subproject 3 is being set up as a means to
   continue the present work in the field of
   Divination Verification and Validation at
   ███████████ until 4 April 1999.

2. This project will include a continuation of the
   study of the predictions of ██████████, code
   name Sibyl, with an aim to verify the accuracy
   the End of the World Prophecy made on 16
   February 1999 as well as associated predictions
   from alternate "sensitives" (defined as those
   with an innate perception of times other than
   the present). A detailed proposal is attached.
   The principal investigators will continue to be
   ██████████, ██████████, and ██████████.

3. The estimated budget of the project is
   $156,200.00. ██████████ will serve as a cover
   for this project and will furnish the above
   funds to ██████████ as a philanthropic grant.

4. ██████████ are cleared through TOP SECRET and
   are aware of the true purpose of the project.

APPROVED:

██████████

MEMORANDUM FOR THE RECORD

TO: Director, Central Intelligence Agency

FROM: James Wong, Praetor of the Council of Cordus

SUBJECT: Project Delphi, Subproject 3

Dear Director,

It is with a heavy heart that I write this report, knowing the implications of our findings. Let me get on with it.

1. Per your instructions, we investigated all eighty-seven prophecies that had allegedly been made by ████████, code name Sibyl, prior to the End of the World Prophecy made on 16 February 1999.

2. We were able to verify that eighty of the eighty-seven prophecies had indeed been made prior to 16 February 1999, according to witness testimonies, phone records, journal entries, and various other forms of physical evidence. We then pursued the results of said prophecies and were able to confirm that all eighty of said prophecies had indeed come to pass, within a time frame ranging from seven days to thirteen years.

3. It is the opinion of the Council of Cordus that the fulfillment of fifty of these prophecies was both unambiguous and specific; i.e., that they are not predictions of the fortuneteller variety

(which are so vague as to be widely applicable).
We defined *specificity* as details that apply to no
more than 30 percent of the population. At least
five of these specific details needed to be stated
in the initial prophecy and met.

4. Therefore we are forced to conclude that the End
   of the World Prophecy, being the most specific
   of Sibyl's prophecies, is overwhelmingly likely
   to be valid and imminent. The Council of Cordus
   therefore recommends that the search for the
   prophecy's Chosen One must be undertaken with
   the greatest haste.

I am sorry to be the bearer of bad news. I am
available for further discussion or inquiry should
you require it.

Sincerely,

James Wong
Praetor, Council of Cordus

TOP SECRET

18

Sloane dreamed that the Dark One was standing at her bedside, dragging a cool finger along her cheek. She woke with a start, grabbed the glass of water on her bedside table, and gulped it down.

Few people had seen the Dark One's face without dying immediately afterward. Even his followers only saw something out of fantasy novels and space epics: a man of cloak and shroud, mask and mystery. So the startling thing about him, in Sloane's memories, was always his face: young and pale, a swoop of mousy-brown hair over his forehead, watery eyes. He looked like the preserved corpse of a handsome man, his eyes empty, his skin waxy smooth.

Sloane had seen his face and lived.

She dove for the bag she had brought with her from Earth and turned it upside down on the white floor. It was morning, but only just, so the light coming through the frosted windows was blue. She squinted at the pile she had created. There were soggy receipts and gum wrappers, wet matches, a pocketknife, her wallet. She poked her fingers into the corners of the billfold. There, wedged between a dollar bill and the leather, was one last benzo.

She held it up so she could stare at it. Just one left. She could take it now, trusting that this—the morning after finding out she was trapped in an alternate universe—was the worst it would get. Or she could save it for when she was insensible with terror. There were surely harder times ahead.

Sighing, Sloane put the pill on the bedside table and stuck her head between her knees to breathe.

It was a little brighter in the room when Sloane had collected herself enough to stand up. She left the wet matchbook and other scraps on the floor, shoved her feet into her boots, and walked down the hall. The others were still asleep. She went to the bathroom to force her tangled hair into a braid and rinse the sleep from her eyes. They hadn't given her a toothbrush, so either they didn't use toothbrushes anymore because they cleaned their teeth with siphons or they had simply forgotten to leave her one. In any case, her teeth felt fuzzy.

After making herself somewhat presentable, she walked to the elevator, but she didn't know how to summon it. The night before, Nero had done it with his siphon. But even magical elevators had to break down sometimes, she thought, so she went in search of stairs.

She found them around the corner, through a door with a sign saying EMERGENCY USE ONLY, which seemed more an idle threat than something to be concerned about. And sure enough, when she turned the handle, no alarm sounded, no lights flashed to warn of security guards coming.

The stairwell didn't appear to get much use. The steps were decorated with black and white tiles in wedges and triangles, and the railings were wrought iron shaped into tight curlicues. She descended to the lobby, skimming the iron with her fingertips all the way down. She thought of her morning runs along the lake back in her Chicago, the cold air and the foam that gathered on the beach sand from the crashing of the waves. That, at least, would be the same on Genetrix.

But when she reached the lobby, which was all marble, gold trim, and art deco diamonds combined with Frank Lloyd Wright lines, she saw a sign pointing toward the library. The thought of an endless supply of information was irresistible, so she followed the arrow down a hallway of stained glass. The multicolored panes were arranged in a pattern of fanned half-circles layered over each other, each segment a different shade of green. The rising sun cast green spots on her shoes.

The hallway opened into a massive space that smelled like old paper. Sloane stopped and closed her eyes just for a moment, pretending she was home, in the library down the street from her apartment.

Books smelled the same no matter what dimension you were in.

The library was C-shaped, as if the room were curled around something to stay warm. Two stories of bookshelves towered over her head on either side of the somewhat narrow space, with walkways on the second level. In the center of the room were tables and desks, and the place was lit from above by skylights and by old-fashioned lamps with multicolored glass shades glowing in the center of each table. It didn't much resemble her library back home. For one thing, there were no computer banks crowding out the bookshelves.

She frowned. She hadn't actually seen a computer in Genetrix yet, and the people she had seen in the passing cars the night before hadn't been staring at smartphones either.

Did Genetrix even have the internet?

Sloane walked along the inner curve of the library looking for a computer. The place was empty and silent; there was nothing keeping Sloane from running off with a stack of books. Nothing she could see, anyway. But then, she didn't know what Genetrix magic was capable of.

"Can I help you find something?"

She recognized the voice as Nero's but jumped at the sound anyway. He emerged from the stacks on her left, his hands held up in a placating gesture.

"I'm sorry," he said with a smile. He wore a pair of round glasses, and the cloak that had been fastened at his shoulder the night before was now loose, like a cape. "I didn't know how to avoid startling you."

She was glad she hadn't taken off her bra the night before. "Did you follow me here?" she asked.

Nero raised an eyebrow. "Not exactly," he said. "You know, there are some dangerous places you could stumble across in this building if you wander unaccompanied. I myself am working on half a dozen volatile experiments at any given time in my workshop. But more frightening still for you would be coming across Aelia before she's had her third cup of coffee in the morning."

"Well, thank goodness you just happened to come across me, then," Sloane said flatly.

"It's no coincidence," Nero said. "I made sure that I would be alerted if any of you began wandering."

"If your intention was to make us feel like we *hadn't* been kidnapped," Sloane replied, "that wasn't a great thing to share with me."

"I thought you might be more suspicious if I pretended to have simply happened upon you."

"I would have been." Sloane smirked a little. "What tipped you off? The door to the stairwell?"

"Not telling," Nero replied.

The sun was climbing higher now, piercing right through the skylights above them. If she listened carefully, she could hear horns honking outside. Morning traffic beginning.

"Were you looking for something in particular?" Nero said. "When I was a student, I worked here, so I know my way around."

"Maybe." Sloane sighed. "Do you guys have . . . computers?"

"Computers," Nero repeated. "Yes, we have them. But I'm not sure what good they would do you."

"Oh, I don't know. The accessibility of information?" Sloane said. "I'd like to know at what point our universes diverged. It'll be easier for us to acclimate if we know."

"This is a *library,*" Nero said. "Computers are for engineers and scientists; if history is what you want, this is where you'll find it."

"So does the internet exist?" Esther was going to be so upset if it didn't.

"It exists, but I don't know anyone who uses it," Nero said. "Why do you ask?"

"At home, people carry the internet around in their pockets," Sloane said. "Everything you could ever want to know, in any language, is right there. That's how I'm used to getting information."

"And you say you don't have magic."

"It's not *magic,*" Sloane said.

"I know." Nero smiled a little. "It wouldn't do us much good, I suppose. It's difficult enough to communicate about magical theory in written form; I can't fathom trying to share techniques your way. It's much simpler to gather in person."

Sloane couldn't imagine something that couldn't be taught over the internet. The year before she had learned how to replace a sink drain from a YouTube video. She had survived shopping for groceries in Germany by using an online translator. Even now, with her waterlogged phone back in the bedroom, she felt its phantom buzz in her back pocket, alerting her to an e-mail or reminding her about a doctor's appointment. She had never had to explain to anyone why it might be useful. It was like having to explain why it was useful to drink water.

"Everything here seems backward to us," she said. "Like traveling back in time."

"You seem somewhat backward to us as well," Nero said. "Let me show you. Tell me something you want to search for. Anything."

"Okay." She didn't know what to say at first. There were so many things they needed to know about Genetrix in order to find a way home—even if they did it by defeating their Resurrectionist, which Sloane still wasn't sure about. But she didn't want to ask Nero to look up something about magic. She didn't want Nero to be responsible for the information at all when she wasn't sure that she could trust him. So maybe she could look up something he had said. Just to make sure he had been honest with them. "You said there's a connection between this universe and ours," she said. "I'd like to find some proof."

"I'm not sure you'll be able to do that here," Nero said. "Our knowledge of the connection is rooted in analyses of magical energy fields and—"

Sloane wasn't paying attention. She was thinking of the footage ARIS had showed them in the Dome, the footage that was supposed to prove that the world was breaking. The trees hovering over the water, their origin unknown; the cornfield that had appeared on the ocean floor and no missing-persons report to match the farmer trapped in his tractor. If she assumed that Nero was correct about the connection between universes, maybe that farmer hadn't been from Earth but from Genetrix.

"What's the date? Day and year?" she said.

"April twenty-ninth, 2020," he replied.

"Shit," Sloane said. "It's only March back home."

"Time discrepancies seem to be common when traveling between universes," Nero said. "We've found some ways to stabilize it, but we can only approximate."

Sloane indulged in a moment of terror when she realized that even if they managed to get Nero and Aelia to send them back home, they might be thrust millennia into the future or, worse, into the past. Then she pushed the thought aside. She couldn't worry about that now. "I'm looking for a missing-persons report from about . . . a few months ago, I guess, our time," she said. "An odd case—a farmer from somewhere in the Midwest. A corn farmer. Just . . . disappeared while on his tractor. A John Deere, so probably American."

Nero raised his eyebrows but didn't ask her anything. Instead, he put his whistle between his lips and turned toward the stacks. He raised a hand, then waved it carelessly as he let out a high, sweet note like the trill of a bird. "Certain frequencies are like pathways for particular workings," he said, taking the whistle out of his mouth to speak. "And there are a lot of categories for workings. But once you find the right pathway, intent is what guides the magic, not striking the right note. So I must know my heart's intent and be able to shape it. I want to find this for you. But I need a more specific intent. The missing tractor, I think, is more specific than your date range."

He tucked the whistle between his lips and blew it again, a long, slow note. His eyes closed, and Sloane waited for something to happen. But when Nero opened his eyes and spat out the whistle, nothing in the library seemed to have changed. He smirked and gestured for her to follow him.

He led her away from the towers of books and into a back room, where newspapers were stacked in neat piles on every surface. Most bore the name *Chicago Post,* which wasn't a newspaper Sloane was familiar with, although the *New York Times* made an appearance too. But what Sloane had first dismissed as reflected daylight was a glow coming from a few of the piles as particular newspapers lit up within them. She moved toward one of them, eyes wide and hands outstretched, and searched out the right issue from the layers that had dulled its brightness. She read headlines as she flipped through the papers: "Resurrectionist Sighted Near South Side Grocery Store"; "New Siphon Regulations Issued by European Union Might Cause Problems for Refugees"; "Birmingham: The Next Haven City?"; "Airborne Killer Whale Spotted Near Alaskan Coast."

The glowing newspaper was the *Peoria Chronicle,* and on the front page was the headline "Farmer in Iowa Goes Missing — Along with Half His Crops." The text beneath it read:

Trevor Sherman, who owns a corn farm in central Iowa, disappeared while driving home in his tractor one week ago, as did an irrigation system and a square quarter-mile of corn. The *Chronicle*'s Midwest correspondent was able to verify this in person.

Beneath the article was a half-page photo of a circle of bare dirt and half an irrigation pivot in the middle of a cornfield. Something had sliced cleanly through some of the remaining corn stalks, cutting them at a neat diagonal. The same was true of the metal irrigation pivot.

Sloane said, "Before we came to Genetrix, we saw a report of a man and his tractor appearing on the ocean floor out of nowhere. I wondered if that man was from Genetrix. Looks like the answer is yes."

"Not our first disappearance," Nero said. He tapped the newspaper she held. "Keep reading."

Sloane skimmed past descriptions of the man's children (three of them, all teenagers) and the quotes from his wife to one of the later paragraphs:

Disappearances and reappearances of this nature have been occurring across the globe in recent months, including the incident on the Sunshine Coast in Australia just last year in which a large iceberg appeared on the beach. Some magical theorists have proposed the multiverse theory as an explanation, but scientists reject this, as there has not been any concrete proof that any contact between multiverses is possible at this juncture, much less evidence that matter can be removed from one universe and inserted into another.

Sloane looked up at Nero, who had been reading over her shoulder. "People here don't know that you've figured out how to access another universe," she said.

"It seemed prudent to be discreet until we understand the repercussions," Nero said. "We can't have just anyone trying to poke their way into another universe, after all."

There was a section in the *Peoria Chronicle* called "Magical Oddities." Most of the content sounded like something from the *National Enquirer*: people growing wings and tails, alien-abduction stories, disappearing vehicles (that later turned out to have been towed or stolen). But some of it seemed more believable: a mailbox launching into the sky like a rocket, a cat clawing its way out of a grave, another sighting of the Resurrectionist—this time in Iowa.

"So you're an 'I'll tell you only what you need to know' kind of guy, then." Sloane set the newspaper down. Her fingers were gritty with ink. The light was beginning to fade from behind the headline letters, leaving her vision spotted. "How do I know you're telling me enough?"

Nero sighed. "I know I owe you—all of you—an apology," he said. "It's inadequate, of course, but—I can't emphasize enough how desperate we were after the Chosen One's defeat. It was like . . . the world was ending."

Sloane remembered the nights the five of them had thought the world was ending. There had been a few. The one after she and Albie returned from captivity was the worst of them, with Albie and Sloane in the hospital and Matt pacing the hall between their rooms, unable to sleep. Esther's mother had been diagnosed with cancer just two days before. So they had wheeled Sloane into Albie's room, and everyone had gotten drunk.

The feeling was what she remembered best. The exhaustion, but also the frantic need to escape, like she was fighting her way out of a straitjacket. There had to be a way out, a weakness they hadn't discovered, an avenue they hadn't explored —

They had never considered a parallel dimension. But if they had, she was sure that in her fevered state, she would have kidnapped someone to save the world.

"This Resurrectionist," she said. "He's powerful?"

Nero nodded. "Anyone can use a siphon and do *something,* but there's plenty of variation in skill levels. I say *skill,* but skill really has little to do with it. *Talent* is perhaps more accurate," he said. "Wrist siphons are the simplest. Throat siphons are expensive and require a natural affinity. The others suggest a high level of innate magical ability. Ear, eye, mouth. Chest." He shrugged. "You can put one almost anywhere, though some are illegal because of the type of magic they produce."

"Such as?"

"Ah, well. Placing one on the spine is said to render the wearer subject to another person's control," he said. "And placing one on the crotch causes horrific disfigurement."

Sloane cringed. "People really will put anything down there, won't they?"

Nero nodded sagely, but he was smiling. "In any case, siphons are difficult to master, and most people can't wear more than two at once or they will fall into a coma," he said. "The Resurrectionist wears five."

Sloane let out a low whistle.

"His innate ability combined with his nature is . . . catastrophic," Nero said darkly.

"What do you know about his nature?" She spoke with care, sensing a shift in Nero's mood.

Nero was quiet. The sun was high above the edge of the skylights now, spilling into the stacks and shining between the books. It reached them even in the back room where they stood among the newspapers.

"My sister assisted the Chosen One," Nero said. "One night, she was . . . taken. Tortured. And her body was left hovering over this building. It took days to figure out how to get her down so I could bury her."

Sloane remembered the day they brought her brother's body back from the Drain site. In a government-issued casket. It hadn't fit in any room in the house, so they'd had put it in the garage for the night before the funeral. She had gone there after her mother was asleep, just to sit with him. She hadn't wanted him to be alone, as foolish as that was. She knew he wasn't there anymore, that whatever was inside that casket was just rotten flesh and bones, but she had stayed there all the same. No one ought to be alone in death. "I'm sorry," she said.

"Her name was Claudia," Nero said. "As you have likely noticed, names from ancient Rome experienced a swell of popularity here about forty years ago."

"I wondered about that," she said. "Most people don't have positive associations with the name Nero."

"My mother just liked the sound of it." His smile was small and forced a sharp crease into his cheek. "I don't like to discuss my sister, but I thought you should know why you were taken from your home. Or, specifically, why *I* assisted in taking you from your home."

"Well," Sloane said. "Thank you."

"I think I should take you back to your room, don't you?" he said. "Or Aelia will have my head."

"She seems a bit grumpy with you."

"She blames me for having summoned three of you instead of just one," Nero said. "Though I wasn't the only one doing the working."

"What kind of siphon opens up another dimension?" Sloane said.

"Guess," Nero said.

"Butt siphon," Sloane said immediately.

Nero snorted. "No," he said. "It's actually not a body part at all. It requires multiple people standing around a massive siphon built into the floor, called a siphon fortis. There are some moderately large ones in haven cities, but the only ones that boast this particular size are here, in the Hall of Summons, one in Los Angeles, and one in Maine."

"*Maine?*"

Nero smiled. "Our most prestigious magical university is in Maine, right on the coast. It's very nice there. Expensive, though." He checked his wrist — the one not covered by a siphon — to see the time. "Let's go. I'm sure you'd like a shower and a change of clothes. And maybe breakfast."

Together they walked to the elevator. They got back to the Chosen Ones' hallway just as Matt and Esther were waking up.

Chicago Post

NATIONWIDE SEARCH FOR "CHOSEN ONE" BEGINS

by Lucia Arras

(from the archive, August 11, 2009)

CHICAGO, AUGUST 11: When word of a verified apocalyptic prophecy leaked to the press last month, fear and chaos ran rampant. But there was one ray of hope: rumor of a "Chosen One" who might be able to stop the prophecy's foretold doom in its tracks. Now an anonymous source inside the Council of Cordus, the government's "magic" branch, has revealed that the council will be aggressively searching for this individual in the days to come.

"The criteria listed in the prophecy is quite specific," the source said. "We'll be looking at a selection of children, mostly ones who have already displayed an advanced magical ability."

Religious groups across the nation are divided regarding the doomsday prophecy, with some denouncing it as a false teaching or a heresy, and others declaring it to be a message from the divine. People dwelling in haven cities, which prohibit the practice of magic, have begun protesting the government's perusal of their children's records for the purposes of finding and honing magical talent, citing privacy laws and the separation of church and state.

The Council of Cordus declined to comment on this story and has not released an official statement on the matter of the Chosen One or the prophecy. In the past, however, the council has acknowledged some unique expressions of magical ability in the population, including "demonstrations of raw power (i.e., without a siphon), such as telekinesis, the creation of short-distance portals, mind-reading, and divinatory gifts."

PROJECT DELPHI, SUBPROJECT 17

EXCERPT from the official log of ▇▇▇▇▇▇▇▇, code
name Merlin:

I will begin by stating that I am composing this
report a week after the fact, upon verifying that
subject ▇▇▇▇▇▇▇▇, code name Mage, is, indeed, the
most likely subject of the Sibyl Doomsday Prophecy
who is "the last hope of Genetrix," commonly referred
to as "the Chosen One." This will inevitably account
for some bias in the retelling, as I am unable to
separate myself from my current knowledge. However, I
shall endeavor to be as objective as possible.

My first impression of Mage came from his file, which I
scanned prior to entering the examination room. There
was a list of the usual facts: his name, ▇▇▇▇▇▇▇▇;
age, ten; hair color, ▇▇▇▇▇▇▇; eye color,
▇▇▇▇▇▇▇; birthplace, ▇▇▇▇▇▇▇. When I opened the
door, he was sitting with his hands in his lap and
his legs swinging. Average height for a ten-year-
old but somewhat scrawny, as if he had been mildly
food-deprived, though it could have simply been his
natural build.

I experienced none of the signs that others have
reported upon seeing our Chosen One for the first
time—no tingling, no existential satisfaction, no
blinding lights, choirs of angels, or impulses to
prostrate myself before him. I find those reports
to be ridiculous, as they elevate meeting Mage to

a religious experience when it is in fact just
encountering a child who has raw magical ability.

"Hello," I said to the boy, and I sat across the
table from him. Someone had brought him the magic-
development game Perception Interception. It can
be programmed for a single player and had been for
Mage. As far as I could tell, he hadn't used it or
even touched it. He had instead been sitting in the
examination room unoccupied for the better part of an
hour.

"You didn't want to play?" I said.

Mage shook his head.

"All right," I said. "What have you been doing in
here?"

"Watching," he replied.

"Watching?"

"Yeah, the—strings." He wiggled his fingers. "If I
concentrate, I can see them."

"Strings," I repeated. "What do they look like?"

"They're like when you see the sun through fog," he
said. "In rays. Bright, a little hazy."

"And you've always been able to see them?"

Mage's eyes narrowed. "You think I'm crazy, don't
you?"

"I don't," I replied. "I think maybe you are
describing an experience with magic that we simply
haven't documented yet. Magic is new to us, and we
are only just beginning to understand it. So I am
inclined to believe you."

"Oh." Mage brightened at that, but then, almost in the same moment, he deflated. "My mom and dad told me not to talk about it."

"I think your mom and dad were just trying to keep you safe," I said. "Because there are some people who get mad when they hear things they don't understand."

It was a shame, really, to see how readily he accepted that, to know how young we learn these lessons.

"Can you tell me more about what you see? How long have you been able to see them?"

He shifted in his seat.

"A long time?"

"Since I can remember," he said. "Not always, though, just when I try really hard."

"Well, that makes sense," I said. "When we talk about a work of magic, we often use the word *intent*, which is like having a goal or a purpose. Magic doesn't work without intent. So when you concentrate on the strings, as you call them, your intention is to see them. Understand?"

"Yeah."

"Have you ever tried to touch one?"

He shrugged, but even crafty children are not skilled at keeping secrets. It was clear to me that he had, in fact, experimented with his unique ability. And since one of the major criteria of Sibyl's prophecy was that the Chosen One would have a magical ability heretofore unseen on Genetrix, I needed to pursue it further. "Will you show me?" I said.

Mage nodded. He lowered his eyes, so he was no longer staring at me but instead at the table. He drew a slow breath, in and out through his nose. It was clear to me that he had spent a great deal of his idle time doing this trick, because there was a process to it already, even though he was a mere ten years old. In and out he breathed, steadily, until a kind of energy came into his eyes, like the answer to a tricky problem had just come to him.

He reached out with his left hand . . . and *pinched*.

As to what happened after that, please refer to the video footage for a more complete understanding. Gravity failed, and everything in the room—myself included—began to float. The chair I had been sitting in bounced off the ceiling. I specifically remember one of the game pieces from Perception Interception, a glass eyeball, drifting past my face.

But sitting in his chair below, as if nothing had changed, was the young man we came to know as the Chosen One.

TOP SECRET

19

Shortly after Sloane returned from the library, a young woman named Cyrielle knocked on her door and introduced herself as Aelia's assistant. She was dressed head to toe in purple, the only exception the silver glint of her throat siphon, which Sloane now recognized as a status symbol. It was a simple cuff around the woman's neck with a string of purple beads at the back.

Sloane spent the rest of the morning receiving deliveries from Cyrielle: food, shampoo, soap, an old-fashioned straight razor, a pile of clothes, an assortment of shoes. By the time Sloane was dressed—in a high-necked black sweater with sleeves that stopped just above her wrist and a pair of loose pants, also black—and fed, it was almost noon, and Cyrielle had gathered them all and was taking them to the Hall of Summons for what she called their "orientation."

Sloane took one look at Esther and groaned. As Sloane should have anticipated, Esther had taken to Genetrix's extravagant fashion immediately. She was swathed in layers of muted pink, cream, and beige. Her shoes—also beige—came to a sharp point. Her face had been restored to its former made-up glory, her skin dusted with powder, lips stained the color of wine, eyeliner winged to her temples.

"All dressed up and no one to see it," Esther said with a sigh.

"We see it," Sloane pointed out.

"I meant Insta!" Esther said. "You guys don't count."

Matt walked beside Cyrielle, smiling and asking questions. He had not opted for the dramatic cape or voluminous cowl of the Genetrixae men they had seen the night before, but the jacket he wore was snug around his broad shoulders, and Cyrielle obviously approved, judging by the way her eyes lingered on him.

He hadn't so much as looked in Sloane's direction that morning. Sloane felt like something in the center of her had hardened into a tight knot of muscle. Esther hadn't given her much acknowledgment either. It was as if Sloane were someone Esther recognized but she couldn't remember from where.

But dealing with situations like these, Sloane knew, was just a matter of knowing the right procedures. She had learned how to disappear after Cameron died and her mother burrowed into her bed and never came out again. You dealt with it the same way you dealt with the cold when you didn't have the right jacket: you let the chill pass through you, digging deep into your bones, until you could no longer feel it.

The Hall of Summons was huge and empty. The walls, concentric circles of stone, curved up to a covered oculus at the highest point of its domed ceiling. Sunlight streamed through the stained glass, casting bright spots of blue and green on a far wall, where there was a rusted door.

Directly beneath the oculus, set into the floor, there was a metal plate, a little like a drain cover but larger, maybe six feet in diameter. There were decorative flourishes in the plate, curlicues twisting together like vines. Sloane thought back to what Nero had said about there being a powerful siphon fortis in Chicago. This had to be it. The room felt strange, like the air was too close.

When they walked in, Aelia was using her siphon and a whistle to guide a large stone table to the center of the room. Nero was at her shoulder, showing her a page from a book that barely fit in the cradle of his arm, it was so large.

"Ah," Aelia said when she had set the table down. "Thank you,

Cyrielle. Good morning to the rest of you. I can't stay long, but I stopped by to make sure that your accommodations were satisfactory."

"Well," Sloane said, "it's hard to be satisfied with what is essentially a prison cell, but sure. Great pillows."

Esther gave her a sideways look, familiar. Then she seemed to realize she wasn't supposed to do that and angled her body away so Sloane couldn't see her face.

Sloane let that pass through her. Soon she wouldn't even feel it.

Aelia pursed her lips. "Well. As you may have observed, it is essential that you be able to do small workings with a siphon in order to get by in this building, let alone to pursue your mission. Therefore Nero will be teaching you how to do some things with the siphons before we move forward with your mission. Nero will be—"

"Actually," Matt said, "before we start, I have a request."

Aelia's mouth puckered like she had just tasted something sour. "Yes?"

"I want to know more about this connection between our universes," Matt said. Sloane had told Esther and Matt about the article she found in the library, and they agreed that it was enough to tentatively trust what Nero and Aelia had claimed but not enough for them to risk their lives. "Everything you know, basically."

"Also," Esther added, "no offense, but if there *isn't* a connection, then it'll feel like you're lying to us to get us to risk our asses for people and a place we don't even know. And I, personally, have done enough risking of my ass for one lifetime."

"I am not sure how to demonstrate what we know about the connection," Aelia said. "At least, not without all of you attaining a somewhat advanced understanding of magic."

"Well," Matt said with a smile, "I suggest you figure something out."

Aelia shot a look at Nero. He cleared his throat.

"I will commit myself to it," Nero said. "In the meantime, perhaps you would still be amenable to learning a few siphon skills so that you can move more freely through the building?"

"How about outside this building?" Sloane said. "Or does our leash not extend that far?"

Aelia was not provoked. "At this time, we don't think it would be safe for you to leave the building," she said. "You don't know anything about our world, and you don't know how to use siphons—"

"But after we learn more," Matt said, "surely your policy will change."

Sloane covered her mouth to hide a grin. Aelia reminded her of a wind-up toy; each demand they made twisted her up a little more.

"We will evaluate it as the situation develops," Aelia replied. "I will leave you in Nero's and Cyrielle's capable hands."

Aelia rearranged the fabric of her stiff cowl, smiled with pursed lips, and walked out of the Hall of Summons, her shoes snapping all the way down the hall. As the sound faded away, Cyrielle approached the box that was on the stone table and started laying out its contents: a line of handheld devices that resembled recorders, the kind that Sloane had seen reporters use during interviews. Cyrielle placed one next to each siphon and switched each one on. A small screen lit up green at the top of the device, right below what appeared to be a microphone.

"Well, shall we begin?" Nero said, bringing his hands together in front of him. "The purpose of today's lesson will be to master something very simple, something we teach children on Genetrix—we call it a magical breath. But in order to do that, you need to know the basics of what makes a working, which is what we call any act of magic, no matter how small."

"Like . . . a spell?" Esther said.

"No incantations are involved, so I think that was deemed inaccurate," Nero said. "What is involved is *sound*. If magical energy is like water, then certain frequencies are like channels in stone that provide pathways for particular workings. And we help you to find the right frequencies with one of these." He picked up one of the devices from the table. "It's formally known in the magical community as a praecontograph, but it's just a modified oscilloscope—it measures frequencies with the attached microphone. A sophisticated praecontograph can be set to tell you what category of working your frequency falls in."

"Does that mean . . . men and women do different kinds of work-ings, usually?" Matt said. "Because men's voices are usually lower?"

"Yes—when the sound comes from the voice," Nero said, smil-ing. "There are an array of small instruments that can be used to pro-duce a wide range of frequencies. And though some people do make their workings quite musical, even someone with a horrible ear for music—or someone who can't hear at all—can still make sound at the correct frequency."

"That's a relief," Esther said, "because I've been told that when I sing, I sound like a drowning cat."

"The range of workings possible with the human voice are quite limited anyway," Nero said. "But the magical breath is one of them, which makes it ideal for children. Unfortunately for male adults"—here he looked at Matt—"the frequency is somewhat high. One hundred seventy megahertz. I have a whistle if you can't quite man-age it."

"My falsetto isn't bad," Matt said.

"Excellent. Well, first, everyone take an oscilloscope, and we'll all try to find the right frequency."

Sloane went up to the table with the others to pick up one of the devices. While she was there, she looked over the siphons. They were simple, made of a black, grainy metal, with a plate for the back of the hand and one for the palm, like a glove without fingertips. A standard-issue siphon, Sloane guessed, whereas Nero's and Cyrielle's were for the wealthy. A logo was stamped on the back: a beast with a bird's head, a man's torso, and a serpent's tail instead of legs. The tail was curled around a large *A*.

"Abraxas," Nero said when he saw her staring at it. "They make the highest quality siphons."

Sloane stepped back, an oscilloscope in hand, into the line with the others. Cyrielle then sang a note. Her voice was unwavering—not especially beautiful, but the sound was consistent, easy to mimic. Nero gestured for them to repeat the noise.

Sloane's cheeks heated up. She had never sung in front of people. She didn't even sing in the shower. She wasn't tone-deaf—she just . . . didn't do it.

She held the oscilloscope's microphone up close to her mouth and hummed. A wavy line appeared on the device's screen, as well as the number 165. It took a few tries to hit 170 MHz on the nose, but once she found the pitch, she was able to do it again without too much difficulty. Next to her, Esther was rolling her eyes at the oscilloscope, her lips pursed as she whistled. Matt, however, was singing "Ah" like he was doing a vocal warm-up. Sloane wondered if he would have been in choir if he had been allowed to live a normal life.

Her chest felt tight at the thought.

"Good!" Nero said. "Now—siphons. Put them on your dominant hands, but don't make any noise just yet."

The siphon was cold against her skin, and loose. Cyrielle saw her fussing with it and stepped over to tease a small wire from the space between the plates. When she pulled it tight, the plates drew together around Sloane's hand, and she wrapped it around a small hook to keep it secure. Sloane flexed her fingers. The siphon was clunkier than the one Nero wore, but it wasn't uncomfortable, and the metal warmed the longer she wore it, like a wristwatch.

"You may have noticed Aelia or me making a small gesture when we do a working," Nero said. "That doesn't actually have an impact on the working itself—it's more of a way of getting your mind to realize that you are trying to *do* something. So gesture or don't, it doesn't matter, whatever helps you to focus your intentions. What we call a magical breath is just a small puff of air emitted magically by the user. When I tell you to, you will make your sound at the correct frequency, and you will try to have that tricky, nebulous thing we refer to in magical study as 'intent.'"

He glanced at Sloane. That was the word he had used the day before to explain why the siphon on its own wasn't dangerous.

"Nailing down exactly what constitutes intent is the subject of the majority of magical theory," Nero said. "But there is a reason it's easier to teach someone magic if they've been learning since they were a child. Children don't need explanations or details in the way that adults do — they can just *want* something . . . and *do* it. So I can't tell you exactly how to have the right intent — you just have to figure it out. The less thinking involved, the better, at this stage."

"This should be easy for Esther, then," Matt said.

"Kindly shut the hell up," Esther replied. She held up her hand in the siphon and whistled while flicking her hand in a dismissive gesture. Esther's hair fluttered and she stepped back, eyes wide. A moment later, a grin crept over her face, revealing a small splotch of lipstick on her teeth.

"I did it!" she said in something like a shriek. The grin took years away from her face, so Sloane felt like she was looking at the Esther who had not been through the war, who had not fought the Dark One, who had not been caring for her sick mother.

Matt gave Esther a high five, and Sloane, not sure her congratulations would be welcome, opted for a smile.

"Yes, well done," Nero said. "Now the rest of you."

Sloane stared at her hand, sheathed in its siphon. *Don't think,* she thought. She hummed and the oscilloscope read 175 MHz. Another hum got her closer to her target. *Don't think. Do a gesture that feels natural.* She wasn't sure that any gesture could feel natural with a metal glove on her hand. She tried flicking her first two fingers. That seemed simple enough.

Nothing happened.

Across the room, Matt was singing his "Ah" and waving his hand through the air like he was conducting an orchestra. She would have laughed if things weren't so bad between them. Esther's whistling was accompanied by a finger waggle, and she was holding the oscilloscope up to her face to read her pitch.

Don't think, she scolded herself, and she hummed again. *Intent,* she reminded herself. Well, maybe that was the problem. She didn't *intend* anything at all. She had no idea why a person would want to magically conjure a puff of air when you could just as easily make one with your mouth.

She closed her eyes and instead tried to think of how it had felt when she had faced the ARIS prototype in the Dome with the Needle halves in hand. The great yawn inside her, and then the gnaw of hunger, as essential to her body as the need for air or the lure of sleep. Sloane focused on that gnawing, not even knowing what she hungered for, with breakfast still sitting in her belly. The desire was shapeless still, but she felt it.

She *always* felt it.

She held up her hand and hummed. And then she felt it, at last, the first tingle of magic she had detected on Genetrix. A moment later, it was more than a tingle; it was as if she had opened a door a crack to see who was knocking and found an inferno waiting at her doorstep. Burning consumed her body, stinging her eyes, scorching her throat. She screamed and thrashed against it, but the burning kept coming.

She couldn't see—her hair had blown across her eyes, and her clothes had pulled away from her; air swirled around her like a skein of silk at first and then like tight threads, binding her, lifting her—

A sharp *crack* sounded. The window that covered the oculus had broken, and glass was spilling down like a waterfall in the center of the room. Someone shouted, "Slo!"

Something hit her in the head, and the fire went out. Sloane fell back and landed hard on the tile; her head slammed into the ground, making her wince. Esther, who was also on the floor, crawled over to her, her hair clinging to her painted lips. Light was streaming into the room from above.

"You all right?" Esther said, pushing her hand under Sloane's head to feel her scalp. "Shit, Sloane, you don't do anything halfway, do you?"

"Essy," she said, "Slo's gonna vom."

At least she had enough presence of mind to turn her head away from Esther before she did.

THROAT SIPHONS ARE HERE — BUT AT A COST

by Corey Jones

MagiTech Mag, no. 240

Ever since Abraxas (then operating under the name of its former parent company, IBM) first dipped a toe into siphon manufacture in the United States in the 1970s, it has dominated the tech sphere in North America. This latest release, the first consumer-focused throat siphon, is no exception—yet its prohibitive cost of more than $5,000 per unit has many complaining about the company's priorities. They have left cost-cutting efforts to smaller, inferior manufacturers and instead focused solely on innovation. The narrowness of vision seems to have paid off. Abraxas's presence in the market has never been greater.

Researchers at the Cordus Center have estimated that only 20 percent of the population possess the magical faculties necessary to make use of a throat siphon, so the development of the device has been controversial since its inception—it seemed unlikely that manufacturing them would be profitable for any company, large or small. But Abraxas's current CEO and founder, Valens Walker, insisted. "We don't need to sell every siphon we produce to every consumer," he said in an interview with the *New York Times* last winter. "We just need to sell the best ones available." So far, they do. *MagiTech Mag*'s reviews of Abraxas products have yielded As across the board, whereas the closest Abraxas competitor, Trench, averages a B-, with its startlingly cheap wrist siphon as its standout product.

So what about Abraxas's throat siphon? Well, it came to me in a sleek gold box, so clearly Abraxas is playing up the exclusivity angle. The object itself is far from inconspicuous—it's a seamless metal plate, copper in color, that's engraved across the front with one of three patterns, floral brocade, herringbone, or damask. It's two inches high, so there's no way to hide it behind a collar; this thing is meant to be displayed, and I'm sure fashion designers will accommodate with neck-revealing clothing, as they did with shortened sleeves when wrist siphons were first released.

The look is a little bit much for me, to be honest, but it's lightweight and adjustable, so I hardly noticed it while I was wearing it. As to its performance, though—well. If you've ever attempted a throat working before, you know why those who can, will, almost exclusively, use this type of magic. A throat siphon is particularly attuned to those who hum or sing their workings, being so close to the vocal cords; it picks up the vibrations from the skin, which means workings can be done quietly and discreetly; it doesn't broadcast one's intent with an ostentatious whistle, as other siphons do. And the range of what is possible with a throat siphon is, obviously, expanded. All the basic workings are effortless—opening doors, lighting candles, moving objects—and I finally performed some complex ones without being in a classroom. I set a timer on a working that kept my pencil spinning, with the help of an oscilloscope, in the privacy of my apartment.

That's one of the downsides: the necessity of the oscilloscope. Throat siphons are more sensitive to minor deviations in pitch, so you have to be *precise,* and unless you have perfect pitch, you're going to need extra equipment. If you want to set an indefinite clock, you'll still need to find an assembly to support your efforts, but the force of your workings should mean the assemblies can be smaller and take less energy. If you're doing a sequential working, you don't have to break between pitch changes, as you would with a wrist siphon, but you have to be decisive about your shifts or you'll end up with unexpected outcomes. As with any new siphon, the government's going to be keeping a close eye on new users, so don't try to raise your own undead army just yet. (That's a joke, guys. One Resurrectionist is plenty, don't you think?) But this tech could very well change magic forever.

Abraxas's throat siphon 1.0 will be available on Friday, February 3.

20

SLOANE FELL ASLEEP almost immediately after the incident in the Hall of Summons, and when she woke up, it was the following morning.

Matt and Cyrielle had helped her back to her room. She had counted their footsteps and tried not to think of the destruction she had left behind. All the siphons and oscilloscopes, scattered wide. Cold air rushing into the bared oculus. Glass strewn across the floor in blue, green, and red. Nero's cape, blown free of its clasps, flapping on the floor. Cyrielle's braided updo ripped from its pins.

They had sat her down on the mattress, and when Matt left to get her a glass of water, she looked up at Cyrielle and said, "What does it mean, that I did that?"

"I don't know," Cyrielle replied. "But no one was hurt. You'll try again another time, and we'll take . . . precautions."

"There won't be another time," Sloane said, and she fell asleep without taking her feet off the floor.

She didn't know what time it was now. She woke like someone who had been blackout drunk the night before, putting herself together in pieces. She sat up. Swiped her fingers under her eyes. Combed them through her hair. Straightened her clothes. Matt had set a glass of water on her low white bedside table and she drank it in a single gulp, searching the room for her shoes. Someone had taken them off for her and put them next to the door.

Sloane put them on, pulled the laces tight, and checked the hallway for any sign of the others. Their doors were closed, their lights off. They were still asleep. No one would notice if she stepped out for a while.

Aelia didn't want them to leave the building, so naturally, that was exactly what Sloane had decided to do.

Sloane knew Nero had some way of checking up on them, but she didn't know what it was. She couldn't summon the elevator regardless, so she decided to take her chances again with the stairwell. If stealth couldn't be her ally, then she would have to opt for speed. Sloane reached the end of the hallway, where she could see the stairwell door, and *ran*. She pushed through the door and took the stairs three at a time, then four, as she got her bearings.

She hadn't gone for a run in a while, so the pounding of her heart and the ache of her limbs were a welcome distraction from everything that had happened. She was eager for cold, fresh air and the feeling of pavement under her boot soles. When she reached the ground floor, she noted the emergency exit, but the ALARM WILL SOUND sign put her off trying it. She went through another door to the lobby instead.

She had passed through it a few times with the others. It was a wide-open space that felt, with all its ornate decoration (Baroque, Sloane thought) and its flying buttresses (Gothic) and its hints of gilded geometry (art deco), like the sanctuary of a church. The heavy wooden doors leading outside only enhanced that feeling. Cameron would have approved, she thought. She walked straight toward the doors, her path, for the moment, clear of obstacles—

"Sloane."

A man she didn't recognize stepped in front of her. Military, she decided, judging by his impeccable posture, ample musculature, and —right, the uniform. Navy-blue pants, casual, tucked into his boots. Long-sleeved gray shirt, sleeves pushed up to his elbows. The same symbol that the others by the river walk had pinned to their chests was stitched on the right side of his chest.

She considered sprinting for the doors, but she decided the time wasn't right for such an act of desperation—not yet, anyway. So she just made a show of not being intimidated.

"Listen," she said, "the more determined you are to keep me here, the more determined I'm going to be to leave. So why don't we skip the whole ramp up in tensions?"

"Okay," the man said. "What if I told you that my job is not to stop you from leaving but to accompany you to ensure that you don't get into any trouble?"

Sloane looked out the windows to the street beyond them, the view obscured by the thick ripple in each pane of glass. She could almost taste the air coming off the water of Lake Michigan.

"I should add," the man said, "that if you don't agree to let me do my job, there will be a lot of fuss and tedious arguing."

"All right," she said. "Fine."

"My name is Kyros," he said, offering his hand for her to shake. *Firm grip,* she thought. Not surprising. "I'm a captain in the new Army of Flickering. Not that that will mean much to you."

He wore a siphon on his wrist, simpler than the ones she had observed thus far, just polished metal plates covering the back of his hand and palm but leaving his fingers free. The logo she had seen on the siphon she had used the day before—the creature with the head of a bird, torso of a man, and tail of a snake—was etched into one of the plates.

"Magic army," she said. "Right. What makes it new?"

"The previous army was massacred by the Resurrectionist," he replied. "Where would you like to go?"

Guess we're just going to breeze past the massacre, then? she thought. "To the lake," she said.

The lakefront had always been a kind of anchor for her; if she ever lost her way, all she had to do was find it, and she would know which way was east. She could name the streets that ran parallel to it: Lake Shore, Columbus, Michigan, Wabash, State, Dearborn, Clark, LaSalle, all the way to the river. Going there, to the water, might help her find something steady inside her, even in Genetrix.

Kyros flicked his index finger at the double doors, and they opened.

His control, she noted, was impressive; the doors opened just enough for both of them rather than flying apart as they had done for Aelia. But regardless, it seemed like a frivolous use of magic.

"For future reference," she said as she passed through them, "I can open my own doors."

"My apologies," Kyros said. "It's just a reflex."

A world of magic at your fingertips, she thought, *and you're using it to open a door.*

Outside, they fell into step right away with the rest of the population on the sidewalk. Sloane noted their shoes—they favored pointed toes with hard bottoms that made sharp sounds, almost like tap shoes—and the heavy drape of fabric around their necks and shoulders, which left their throats bare to display throat siphons; the wide sleeves that stopped in the middle of their forearms to show off wrist siphons; the intricately braided hair that revealed bejeweled ear siphons, the most ornate kind, by Sloane's observation. Across the street was the comforting sight of the Daley Center, a dark brown block of a building that had, evidently, made it through the splitting of their two universes. But across the street, where at home there had been a tall, modern structure with pale blue windows, there was a cluster of spires that reminded her of the church in Barcelona, La Sagrada Família, made of dense and ornate stone.

The thought brought a familiar pang. Cameron had once brought home a book on architecture from the library and he must have forgotten to return it, because Sloane had found it in his bedroom after he died, the pages with his favorite buildings dog-eared. La Sagrada Família had been one of them.

"So this Resurrectionist," she said. "If I see him—and I assume I'll know him when I see him—what should I do?"

"What you *should* do is learn basic defensive maneuvers with your siphon," Kyros said. "There is a shield that is simple to learn that seems to buy people time when they face him. It keeps him from performing his favorite working."

"And what's that?"

"He collapses lungs," Kyros said, in the same frank way he had told her about the army massacre. "It is difficult to get them to reinflate before a person suffocates, and they are unable to do it themselves since they can't make noise."

Sloane suppressed a shudder. "Okay," she said. "So—shield."

"Here," he said. "I'll show you."

He put a hand on her elbow and steered her into an alley clogged with cardboard boxes and sacks of trash. She would have protested if she hadn't been so eager to see the shield. Kyros held his hand out from his shoulder, palm facing Sloane, and whistled between his teeth at a pitch so high she clapped her hands over her ears. Sloane wondered how such a sound was possible until she saw something glint in Kyros's mouth. A false tooth? A piercing? She couldn't tell.

Whatever it was, at its whistle, the air appeared *thicker,* the way it did when gas leaked from a stove. Sloane watched it ripple in front of Kyros with each exhale.

She reached for it, almost unconsciously, the child in her always eager to discover by touch. It felt viscous, silky, like still water.

"It won't stop him," Kyros said, his voice muffled by the barrier between them. "But it will delay him."

"Too bad I'm such shit with siphons," she said.

"You should endeavor not to be 'such shit'," Kyros said, a determined set to his jaw. "Or you put yourself and everyone around you in danger, particularly if you insist on leaving the safety of the Cordus Center unaccompanied."

"Point taken." She got the feeling Kyros didn't like her very much.

Kyros dismissed the shield with a grave look, and they kept walking.

They passed some businesses that looked familiar: bakeries, sandwich shops, pizza places. It wasn't until she walked past a coffee shop with a blue awning that she realized she was looking for a Starbucks . . . and wasn't finding one. This place was called Jack's Magic Beans, and the logo was, of course, the white outline of a beanstalk disappearing into a cloud.

At the intersection of Randolph and State, she realized the Walk signal was not the glowing white man she was used to but rather a piece of metal that flipped over every time the signals changed, displaying a series of layered circles. The Stop image was a solitary circle. She wondered how they were visible at night.

As they approached Michigan Avenue, Sloane tilted her head back and looked for the black building that stood at the bend in Lake Shore Drive, but she couldn't find it. In its place was a wide glass tower with a hole in the middle — and hovering in the center of the hole, with space on all sides, was a sphere made of the same glass and metal as the rest of the building.

"How . . ." She felt strange, like she wasn't standing in her own body anymore. "*How* —"

"Oh, that. I'm not sure how it works," Kyros said, sounding amused. "Magic, obviously, but I'm unclear on the specifics."

"It's not an illusion?"

"No. Would you like to go in?"

Sloane shook her head. No, she did not want to stand in a giant floating glass sphere. She put a hand to her aching temple. Across the street, she spotted something familiar — the Chicago Cultural Center — and walked straight toward it, not even glancing at the Walk signal to make sure her path was clear. It was too much, too fast. She needed to sit, needed to breathe.

Kyros chased her across the street and up the stone steps. The cultural center was old — which, she was realizing, meant that both universes would likely have it in common — a neoclassical building with a row of arches topped by a row of columns, like layers in a cake. But it was the inside that made it one of her favorite places, the domes of Tiffany glass that glowed colorful and beautiful in the morning sun. That and the space's persistent quiet.

Just inside, she found a bench made of cool marble and sat, putting her head in her hands. Kyros sat beside her — not too close, thankfully, or she might have punched him — and stayed quiet as she took deep breaths through her nose.

"It's a lot," she said once she felt calmer.

Kyros nodded. "I'm sure it is."

"Would you mind if I went up there —" She pointed up the stairs toward the Tiffany dome. She could see only a sliver of it from where she sat, glinting green, but it promised familiarity and—if Kyros would allow it—solitude. "By myself? I just need a few minutes."

Kyros narrowed an eye at her.

"I promise I won't go anywhere else," she said.

"All right," he said. "But in a few minutes, I'll come up to check on you."

Sloane stood, feeling steadier now. She climbed the steps, then paused on one of the landings to look up at the Bacon quote— *The real use of all knowledge is this: that we should dedicate that reason which was given us by God for the use and advantage of man*—set in tiny tiles into the mosaic that covered each wall, framed on every side by green and yellow and blue patterns, spirals and diamonds and draped ribbons.

When she turned the corner, she saw the Tiffany dome aglow in the sunlight. The walls arching up to meet it were covered in small tiles formed into organic shapes, vines twisting and coiling together, bright green. The dome itself was simpler, divided into rectangular sections that shrank as they drew closer to the middle. Within each rectangle, the glass was arranged in small blue-and-green semicircles, like the scales of a fish, and in the center, the symbols of each astrological sign. A chandelier hung over the space, mirroring the shape and pattern of the dome itself.

Across from her, three canvases were set up in front of the back wall. The two on either side were featureless from a distance, like Rothkos, massive and empty. The one in the center showed hints of light, like something cracking open to reveal something luminous inside it. She drew closer to see the label fixed to the wall near the paintings and found herself standing directly beneath the chandelier.

And then—something caught her by the ankle, its fingers cold and strict, and jerked her foot up toward the ceiling. Sloane gasped as her body flipped upside down, thinking of the teenager who had floated into the clouds in the video HenderCho had showed them, and the walls began to turn around her—or *she* was turning, guided by the hand around her ankle, the hand that didn't seem to be there at all. Her clothes floated away from her body but didn't fall down all the way. Her hair, too, was adrift around her, like she was in a pool of water instead of dangling in midair, staring at the floor as if it were a ceiling.

Quiet, she found herself thinking, her default thought when panic set in. Because quiet had helped her to escape the Dark One with Albie; quiet had helped her escape death dozens of times. She clenched her jaw and went still, letting herself turn, dangling, like a Christmas ornament just placed on a branch. She thought if she could just jerk her leg free . . . but then she might fall headfirst onto a hard floor that had to be more than six feet below. She stared at her captive ankle as if the invisible force holding her might speak up and tell her what to do.

"Hello," a voice beneath her said.

She flinched and looked up. Or rather down.

She was still turning, but the man's face was right beneath hers, separated by a few feet—she was higher than six feet above the ground, then, because he appeared to be tall—so he was like the center of a pinwheel.

"Do you need help?" he said. His voice was low but oddly musical for such a serious face. He was pale, with a nose that could politely be described as "pronounced" and dark eyes that had not shifted from hers from the moment she first looked at him. The focus was unnerving.

"What," she said, "the fuck. Is this."

He smiled a little. "An Unrealist prank, I think," he said. "Here, take my hand, and I'll get you out of the trap."

The last thing Sloane wanted to do was hold hands with a strange man in a parallel dimension, but she didn't see that she had any other choice. She reached up—down—and they clasped hands firmly. He raised his other hand, which was encased in a black siphon that looked like a glove with no fingertips. It, like all of the siphons she had seen, was made of metal, but it had once been painted green. The paint was peeling at the edges, and there were large scuff marks and scratches across each plate. There were noticeable screws around its edges and visible hinges made of different colors of metal, suggesting that it had been repaired more than once.

He hummed, a low rumble that she thought she might feel buzzing in her fingers. She felt the tension around her ankle break, like a cord snapping. He kept his hand outstretched and continued to hum, though he changed the pitch somewhat. Her leg slowly lowered, her body righting itself by degrees. Soon she stood in front of him, her hand still held in his for a moment before they both realized it was no longer necessary.

Now that she was on the ground, she could see that he was a head taller than her, which was no small thing, given that she was tall herself. And he wore dark, muted colors, gray and navy and black, with that odd swath of fabric around his shoulders like a hood. It was pinned at his shoulder, not by the gold finery of Aelia and her peers but by what looked like a large bolt. She smiled faintly at it. It almost seemed like a joke, to mock the same people who had summoned her to Genetrix.

"Thanks," she said. "You said that was a . . . prank?"

"Yeah, the Unrealist artists' collective have been setting up traps all over the city for a couple months now. Snares, they call them. I read their manifesto the other day—someone wallpapered a train with them."

She was about to ask what Unrealists were but then she remembered she was supposed to be blending in as much as possible and swallowed the question. "What did it say?" she said instead. It seemed like a safe thing to ask.

"They contend that the introduction of magic unmoored us from the practical and therefore from reality itself," he said. "And question whether there's such a thing as a fact when half the things we used to regard as facts are being upended. Hence the reversal of gravity that you just experienced."

They had a point, she thought. Gravity was a law, and magic upended it. Unraveled it. What else did magic unravel?

Time. Space. Whole dimensions, maybe.

"Well," she said. "Interesting or not, I hate them."

He laughed. His entire face crumpled when he laughed, and his mouth opened to reveal a row of slightly crooked teeth. "They're a nuisance," he said, "but a harmless one most of the time." His eyes shifted down to her hands. "No siphon of your own? A bold choice."

"It's being repaired," she lied as smoothly as possible. She was the worst of all of the Chosen at lying—even Albie had been more convincing than she was—but she had practiced enough now that she wasn't completely hopeless. "It's a piece of shit," she added for authenticity.

"Sounds like mine," he said, wiggling his fingers. "I know someone who does cheap repairs, though."

A silence fell between them. Sloane knew she should stop the conversation there, thank him again, and go back downstairs to meet Kyros. But it had been a long time since she had spoken to someone who didn't know who she was or *what* she was. A lifetime, in fact. She wasn't so eager to give it up.

"So—you like the paintings?" he said, gesturing to the three canvases.

She stepped closer to read the placard on the wall: *"Tenebris,"* *Charlotte Lake, 2001.*

"I heard the artist speak last night," he said. "She said people assume they're a view from the USS *Tenebris* before the incident, but they're actually from the perspective of magic, looking through the veil at the lights of the *Tenebris*."

Sloane didn't know what to say. She didn't know what the USS *Tenebris* was—aside from a naval ship, obviously—or what the incident was, though it sounded familiar.

"I don't know how to look at art," she said. "There hasn't been much room in my life for it."

"What's been taking up all the room?"

She considered that for a moment, then replied, with a hint of a smile, "Mayhem."

He laughed a little, but his eyes lingered on hers, like he knew she wasn't quite kidding. "I'm Mox," he said, holding out his siphon hand for her to shake.

"Sloane," she replied, wrapping her fingers around the metal. It was cool to the touch. "So . . . you're into art, then."

"Not particularly," he said. "I repair and customize non-Abraxas siphons, so I'm just here to deliver a finished product to a friend."

"Ah," she said. "So the cheap repair guy you know is . . . you."

"Lucky me," he said.

"Well, maybe I'll look you up if my repair guy does a shit job," she said.

For the first time in a long time, Sloane was standing in her own skin. She was not a Chosen One or Bert's stray dog or Sloane Andrews the turbo-bitch who some *Trilby* reporter wanted to hate-fuck. And the second she had a little bit of herself back, she was desperate to get the rest.

"I better go," she said. She didn't want Kyros to come upstairs and spoil the moment.

"Well, if you want something to do later," he said, "I sometimes pick up shifts at a bar in Printer's Row. The Tankard."

"The Tankard, huh?" she said. "I'll see if I can escape."

She smiled. He smiled. And she started toward the staircase.

But on the first landing, she couldn't help but look back. He was standing right where she had left him, staring intently up at the Tiffany dome, his face rendered even paler by its light.

MEMORANDUM FOR: COMPTROLLER

ATTENTION: FINANCE DIVISION

SUBJECT: Project Delphi, Subproject 17

Under the authority granted in the memorandum dated 9
March 2004 from the director of Central Intelligence
to the Department of Magical Oversight on the
subject of Project Delphi, Subproject 17, code name
Flickering, has been approved, and $1,000,000.00 of
the overall Project Delphi funds have been allocated
to cover the subproject's expenses. Flickering is
here defined as a small military force intended to
serve and protect the valuable entity known as
Mage until such a time as his purpose, dictated by
the predictions of ▉▉▉▉▉▉▉, code name Sibyl, is
fulfilled.

Fatima Harrak
Director of Security
Department of Magical Oversight

21

T HE *TENEBRIS* INCIDENT?" Kyros frowned and held the door for her as they exited the cultural center. "No one's told you about the *Tenebris* Incident yet?"

"Should they have?"

"Well, it's the foundational event of the modern world," Kyros said. "So . . . let's see. It happened in 1969. The USS *Tenebris* was a naval ship that set out to test the response of a ballistic missile to the intense pressures of Challenger Deep."

Sloane waited for the walk signal to flip. "Um—the deepest part of the ocean, right?"

"The deepest part of the Mariana Trench, which is itself the deepest part of the ocean," Kyros said. "They wanted to demonstrate naval strength after World War Two. Due to a minor equipment malfunction, the *Tenebris*'s deep-water submersible had to touch down on a particularly precarious spot in Challenger Deep. The rocky expanse it settled on collapsed, revealing an even deeper part of the deep later known as the Tenebris Gorge. No one is certain of what happened next, but the ballistic missile they had set out to test fired into the gorge, and the men in the *Tenebris*'s submersible were buried alive in rubble. After that, magic spread throughout the world, sometimes with . . . catastrophic results."

The sidewalks were busier now, and *louder*. Whistles, hums, and sung vowels came from all directions in an array of pitches. Most of the workings, from what Sloane could see, were small and practical: a flash of light to hail a cab, a tiny flame to light a cigarette, a bubble of a shield to keep coffee from spilling. A group of teenagers sitting outside Jack's Magic Beans linked pinkie fingers and hummed in unison, like they were performing a séance. Judging by the way they shed outerwear afterward, though, the working had been for warmth.

"What kind of catastrophic results?" Sloane said, still craning her neck to look at the teenagers. One of the girls was using her siphon to shoot bubbles out of her fingertip at one of the boys. He whistled and poked one of the bubbles as if to pop it. Instead, it turned solid and gleamed like glass.

But Kyros was talking again. "The earliest recorded incident was a sighting of the leviathan, but it could have been a false report. Everyone is always spotting monsters. But then there was the Graves Disturbance—gravity failed over the gorge, and a massive fishing boat just floated away along with a lot of water and, by some accounts, a baleen whale."

"A *whale?*"

"Evidently. Electrical storms caused power outages across large regions—all of England, actually, and one left the entire state of Florida without electricity for two weeks. Parts of the ocean boiled all the sea life alive—that was quite unpleasant to clean up after, though I'm told we discovered some interesting delicacies in that time too. And then there was the plague that killed one-eighth of the world's population."

The Camel was across the street, and from this angle, she could see the inner building, with its Hall of Summons, poking out where the outer walls dipped low enough to reveal it. There was nothing cohesive in the design of it; it looked like dozens of ideas had been thrown in a blender and poured out while they were still chunky.

"Kyros," Sloane said, "has anyone ever commented on the way you talk about catastrophe?"

"No. Why?"

"No reason."

Cyrielle was standing right in the middle of the lobby. Today she wore only blue: blue lipstick, a blue feather stuck in her hair, tight blue trousers, and a billowing blue blouse with a high neck. She wore a hand siphon made of delicate gold chains that crisscrossed over her knuckles and wrapped in a dense cuff around her wrist. She didn't look pleased. "We've been looking for you," she said tersely.

"I went for a walk," Sloane replied. "Kyros was kind enough to join me."

"Nevertheless, you should clear it with someone before you—"

"I wasn't aware I needed permission to leave this building."

"The issue is not *permission,*" Cyrielle said. "If you don't care about my reaction or Nero's and Aelia's, then you might spare a thought for your friends, who had no idea what happened to you."

Sloane couldn't think of anything to say to that.

"You're missing another training session," Cyrielle said. "Come."

Kyros nodded at Sloane, who reluctantly followed. Apparently she needed to learn a shield, at least.

"A very hearty what-the-fuck to you," Esther said when Sloane walked into the room where they were training.

The Hall of Summons, Cyrielle had explained to Sloane as they walked, was closed for repairs after Sloane's "stunt"—Cyrielle's word for what had happened the day before. Instead, they were in a bare room on the fourth floor of the Camel that was typically used as a meeting space for students. There were no windows, and the furniture—a few beat-up couches—was pushed against the walls, leaving a clear stretch of beat-up wood floors for their practice.

Matt didn't even look in her direction when she walked in, just continued to hum into his oscilloscope.

"Sorry," Sloane said, feeling somewhat helpless. "I just—"

"Whatever," Esther said, raising her siphon hand. "Just get to work."

Sloane took the siphon Cyrielle offered her, determined to do something useful with this session. She pulled the cord tight with her teeth and flexed her fingers.

Unfortunately, *determination* and *intent* didn't seem to be the same thing, because the only thing she accomplished in the next two hours was reliably humming at 170 MHz. Meanwhile, Esther had figured out how to modulate the strength of her magical breath, Matt had enough precision to fill a balloon with a succession of magical breaths, and Nero had cleared them both to move on to something else. Cyrielle, who had been working one on one with Sloane, seemed ready to hurl the siphon—or Sloane herself—at a wall by the time she called the session to a close.

After, Sloane went back to her room and flopped on her bed, her head throbbing. It was impossible to "stop thinking so much," as Cyrielle had instructed her to do, when you were thinking about not ripping your friends to shreds with magic while simultaneously worrying that the Resurrectionist would suffocate you if you didn't learn faster.

There was a knock on her door, and then Esther was leaning on the door frame, her arms crossed. She had adopted the thick eyeliner that people on Genetrix seemed to favor. Esther was nothing if not adaptable.

"All right, so," Esther said. "You're a selfish dick, and apparently you've killed people."

Sloane stared. She wasn't sure what to say to that.

"I just figured it would be better to get it all out in the open," Esther went on. "While you were on your little stroll this morning and everyone else was fretting about where you were, I accepted your certain demise and went down to the library and looked up some names."

"You accepted my demise pretty quickly."

"I was pissed at you," Esther said, picking at a cuticle. "Anyway, first I got the librarian to search for *our* names, just to make sure there weren't parallel versions of us running around out there—thank God she didn't find anything or I'd probably lose every last marble I had left."

Sloane had been so busy processing the other aspects of occupying a parallel universe that she hadn't spared a thought for AlternaSloane. Or her parallel parents. *Paralleloparents,* she thought, and it was a joke she might have made to Albie, who was remarkably patient with wordplay.

But Albie was dead.

Sloane sat up and pushed the thought firmly aside. "I think the universes may have diverged in 1969. Which means our parents would be alive here."

"I tried that next, obviously," Esther said. "Did you know the internet here is basically a glorified card catalog? Susan—the librarian—described it to me. Anyway, it would take a huge effort to figure out if my or Matt's parents are alive and well, since they're in different states."

"What about my mom?"

Esther shrugged. "I kinda figured that was your business, whether you wanted to know about her or not. But I looked up Bert."

Sloane hesitated between hope and scorn. Reading the letters Bert had sent to his superior about her had curdled her fondness for him like sour milk. But he had been a better parent to her than the ones she was born with, and his death, just a few months shy of the Dark One's defeat, had been devastating.

"Parallel Bert lives in Chicago. Hyde Park. I remember our Bert saying he had an aunt there. Seems like he lives in her old house, if the public records are accurate."

Sloane got to her feet. She hadn't bothered to take her boots off before falling into bed. "So are we going to see him or what?"

Esther walked over to Sloane's bedside table and picked up the book she had started reading, *The Manifestation of Impossible Wants*. The cover was plain white with a sketch of a wrist siphon on it in black. She flipped through it, too quickly to see any of the pages. "Matt thinks that's a dumb idea."

"Matt doesn't have to come," Sloane said, shrugging. "Don't you want to know what he's like?"

"Yeah, but . . ." Esther bit her lip. "I don't know. He's got nothing to do with our Bert except that he has the same combination of genes."

"That's not nothing."

Esther put the book down. "We would have to be really clear on the fact that he's a different person from the one we knew. No expectations. Do you think that's even possible?"

"Sure it is," Sloane said, even though she wasn't sure at all. "Essy, if parallel selves are similar, that means the Resurrectionist could very well be a parallel version of the Dark One. Which means we already know more about him than anyone else does. So this is an important test case. More information is always better."

"The older I get, the less I believe that."

"But we're going, right?"

Esther sighed. "Yeah, we're going."

PROJECT DELPHI, SUBPROJECT 17

SUBJECT: Transcript of Debriefing Session with Cordus Council Member ███████████, Code Name Merlin, Witness to Destructive Incident

OFFICER L: Can I get anything for you, sir? More water?

MERLIN: No . . . no, thank you, this is plenty.

OFFICER L: Can you state your name for the record? [Silence.]

OFFICER L: Sir? Your name?

MERLIN: Oh, yes. My name is ███████████, but for our purposes I am known as Merlin.

OFFICER L: Thank you. We are here today for an official account of what you saw on the night of July 2, 2006. Today is July 3, 2006, so let the record show that these recollections are recent and thus less likely to be subject to manipulation. We will be using a memory-sharing working, a technique with which Merlin is particularly adept. Sir, what frequency do you need from me?

MERLIN: 65.4 MHz.

OFFICER L: Before we begin, can you describe the technique you'll be using?

MERLIN: Yes. This working is mental magic, involving a minor alteration of consciousness in which we temporarily share a so-called mind's eye. I will supply our shared mind's eye with the memory of the . . . incident. And you will describe, for the record, an account of what you see. You will form the connection at 65.4 MHz with your handheld

whistle, and I will maintain it at 63.2 MHz as you
describe the images, using a dental implant.

OFFICER L: Thank you. Shall I begin?

[Low tone.]

[Second low tone joins in.]

OFFICER L: I am in an office, looking out a window.
It's dark outside, but I recognize a couple of
the buildings from their lights. City Hall—I
know it from the pillars. If I had to guess, I'd
say I'm in the Camel—er, in the Cordus Center
for Advanced Magical Innovation and Learning—
facing south. There's a glass of whiskey on the
table in front of me on top of a stack of old
books. There's a lot of books stacked everywhere,
actually.

Somebody's knocking. I turn around and whistle,
flicking my fingers. The doors open, and the man
runs in. He's dressed in military sweats, the kind
we sleep in. He's out of breath, too out of breath
to talk. He gestures for Merlin to follow him, and
Merlin does. They go to the elevator and down to
the fifth floor. Everybody at the Camel calls it the
Chosen Floor, because that's where the Chosen One
lives and where his army trains. Almost nobody's
allowed on that floor, so I've never seen it before
myself—this fellow has to scan his badge before
the elevator will move.

[Low tone continues.]

Elevator opens to an empty hallway. Only it
feels off, somehow. Sort of—stuffy, like the way
the air feels when there's way too many people
in one place, except here there's not a soul in
sight.

"I'm on night patrols. I went up—heard
something—" The soldier's recovered enough of his
breath to explain the situation. "Saw—didn't know
who else to call—"

"You did the right thing," I say. Merlin says,
I mean. "What's happened?"

"The army's gone," he says. They reach the
end of the hallway, where there's two doors with
crash bars on them. Above them is a sign that says
training area. He lets Merlin open them. The floor
is squishy, like a gymnasium. Rubbery, too, so it
squeaks under his shoes. But it's dark in there,
only the emergency lights are on, so all I can see
is dark shapes here and there, little bumps on
the floor. It maybe looks like—looks like someone
left a bunch of mats out, forgot to put them away.
Merlin whistles, waves his siphon hand. All the
lights go on at once. They're so bright he shields
his eyes for a second, and I . . .

[Low tone continues.]

    . . . I wish he'd kept shielding them.

[Low tone continues.]

They're all lying there in their training
clothes. White shirts and gray pants. They all
fell in different positions, some flat on their
backs, some flat on their faces, some on their
sides, their arms under them, their legs twisted,
like they were running and tripped before dying.
Their eyes are open—nobody tells you that
sometimes, people die with their eyes open.
Somebody has to shut them, only no one has, here.
So there are just these stares coming at me from
all sides, empty stares. Slack mouths too, open,
drooling. God. It's—

There's one alive. Coming to his feet right
in the middle of the room. Not a military man
—dressed in civvie clothes. Tall. *Really* tall.
The kind of guy you wouldn't start a fight with.
He sees us, and I can't get a good look at his
face because his hair's falling in front of it,
and then he lifts his hand and there's sound and

light—it *hurts*, God, so loud I can't help but
stagger back and shield my head. It's over in a
second, though, and I blink hard to get my vision
back, but it takes a minute for the splotches to
disappear.

The soldier who brought me here is lying on
the ground now, and I reach for him, shake his
shoulder. He doesn't move. He doesn't move—he's
dead, and the tall man is gone, and I'm alone with
the dead.

[Low tone ceases.]

OFFICER L: Who was he? Do you know?

MERLIN: Sibyl said there would be another. A Dark One
who could end the world, just as the Chosen One
could save it. I think we have finally met him.

TOP SECRET

22

AN HOUR LATER, Esther and Sloane stuffed themselves into a taxi with Kyros and a fellow soldier, a buxom woman named Edda. Sloane looked through the raindrops at the Merchandise Mart, wide and squat, lit from beneath. She almost, in the moments before she remembered where she was, felt like she was at home—in the car with Matt, on their way to a restaurant where they would sit in the back, in a booth, so no one could see their faces. They would have a steak, a glass of wine. Tell each other stories they had both lived through already. That time they went to an old farmhouse where they thought the Dark One was staying and found only an old lady with rollers in her hair and a shotgun on her hip. That time they pranked Bert with sugar in the saltshaker, and he pretended he liked the taste so he wouldn't give them the satisfaction. That time—

"Matt's gonna be pissed," Esther said.

"We left a note," Sloane replied.

"Yeah, I'm sure that will make it all better."

"Just blame it on me. He already hates me."

"Yeah." Esther sighed and leaned back. "You made sure of that, didn't you?"

The cab was the size of a small boat, boxy, with a hood ornament in the shape of a discus. It looked like a flying saucer to Sloane, but

Kyros had struck up a conversation about college shot-put front-runners with the driver as soon as he sat down. Genetrix had, apparently, experienced a resurgence of interest in track and field in the last ten years. It had eclipsed baseball.

"So there's only one baseball team here?" Sloane couldn't get over it. "What do they call them, the Cubsox?"

"Chicago Cornhuskers," Edda said.

"*Cornhuskers?*" Sloane couldn't imagine the city without a cross-town rivalry, let alone the city rallying behind the cornhusker as a mascot.

"Sloane, you don't even like baseball," Esther said.

"Living in Chicago means liking baseball by proxy," Sloane said.

"We need to come up with a plan." Esther sounded impatient. "We can't just show up on the guy's doorstep and tell him we're from . . ." She lowered her voice, checking the rearview mirror to make sure the driver was still talking discus with Kyros. "A parallel dimension."

They coasted down Lake Shore Drive. Lake Michigan was the color of steel, and restless, crashing hard against the wall that held it back from the road. Esther drummed her fingers on her knee. Her fingernails had been manicured at Albie's funeral, but the paint was flaking off now.

"We could call it a military thing," Sloane said, glancing at the badge of the Army of Flickering on Edda's jacket. "Say it's top secret or something?"

Esther rolled her eyes. "Sure, that doesn't sound at all absurd."

"Don't you know this man?" Edda chimed in. "Make your reason personal rather than official."

"We know him, and we don't," Sloane said. "But I guess we could try to use information we have about him from before the likely point of divergence between universes. So—before 1969."

"He got married when he was eighteen," Esther said. "Had an older brother who drowned when he was sixteen. Born in Idaho . . ."

They went over everything they could remember from Bert's early life as the taxi passed the Museum of Science and Industry, green dome and stately columns standing on pristine grounds, the same as it was on Earth. Beyond it were sprawling red-brick buildings with cracked sidewalks in front of them; long, low municipal buildings with glass-block windows; trees with bare branches that twisted among the power lines, all familiar sights. But every so often they passed something she would never have seen at home: a picket line outside a siphon retailer with people carrying signs that said MAGIC FOR ALL and ABRAXAS: ENEMY OF THE POOR and even MY MOM SOLD A KIDNEY TO GET AN ABRAXAS SIPHON; a fast-food restaurant with a drive-through that appeared to be a Howard Johnson's, long defunct in her world; a high school called the Timuel Black School for Magic Theory and Practice.

They turned off 57th Street onto a side street packed with houses, and the taxi pulled up next to an old Craftsman home with the numbers 5730 painted above the front door. Esther and Sloane both stared at it while Kyros paid the driver with what appeared to be two twenty-dollar coins. Sloane had noticed people jingling as they walked or wearing little pouches hanging from their belts, but she hadn't connected them to currency before.

They got out of the car, and the taxi pulled away from the curb. Sloane stared up at the old house, which was gray with white trim, the paint peeling, the lawn dull green and dusted with frost.

"You guys had better stay out here," Esther said to Kyros and Edda. Kyros looked dubious.

"If something bad happens, I'll let out a bloodcurdling scream and you can come running. How's that?" Sloane said.

"He's just an old guy," Esther said, more reassuringly.

"Fine," Kyros said.

A shiver coursed through Sloane, and she forced herself to follow Esther down the front walk. A small collection of lawn gnomes stood around one of the stone planters, each of them wearing a red hat.

"So you're his niece through his wife's sister," Esther said. "I'm ninety percent sure her name was Shauna."

"That or something Polish neither of us can pronounce," Sloane replied, and they were at the door.

I have a niece your age, Bert had said to her once. *Haven't seen her in years.*

She had a clear memory of Bert getting out of his Honda Accord outside her house wearing an ill-fitting suit. Gray slacks, black shoes, a blue tie. His hair short but not too short, neither blond nor brown exactly, his eyes some middling shade of hazel. He had been so regular-looking that she could barely describe him after he left. The only thing that had been distinct about him was that one of his eyes watered, and he had dabbed at it with a folded handkerchief every few minutes.

Evan Kowalczyk of Genetrix had a handkerchief pressed to his eye when he opened his door.

"Can I help you?" he said, and Sloane's throat tightened. She couldn't speak. His voice was the same, just a little monotone.

"Sorry to bother you," Esther said, jabbing Sloane hard in the side with her elbow.

"Oh! Yeah." Sloane cleared her throat. "I'm . . . your wife's sister's daughter. Uh—your niece. Shauna."

"Shauna." He scratched behind one ear with one hand while stuffing his handkerchief in his pocket with the other. "It's been a while, hasn't it? Since you were maybe eleven."

"Twelve, I think," Sloane said, because it felt natural. "I was just visiting the city. Looking at schools. Grad schools. Esther is helping me decide. And I remembered that you lived here. So—"

"So we're just stopping by for a visit," Esther said. "If you're not busy."

Evan was quiet for a moment, then said, "I have time for a cup of coffee, if you'd like."

"Perfect!" Esther smiled.

"Yes," Sloane said. "Coffee. Sounds good."

Esther gave her a look that said, as clearly as if she'd spoken the words out loud, *Why are you acting like a robot?*

He stepped away from the door, letting them inside. The foyer was cramped, only large enough to accommodate all three of them if they huddled together. They followed the creak of Bert's—no, Evan's—footsteps across the dark wood floor and into the living room. A fire crackled in the fireplace, and a record spun on a nearby turntable: the strumming guitar and the high, tight voice of Neil Young's "Harvest Moon."

Sloane remembered getting into Bert's beige Honda Accord, the kind with the headlights that popped up out of the hood of the car when you turned them on, so he could drive her to the training facility to meet the other Chosen Ones. She had asked about music, and he had directed her to the glove compartment, where three Neil Young CDs, two Neil Diamonds, and a Phil Collins awaited her. *Could you be a more boring white dude?* she had asked him.

She looked at Esther, whose face had gone slack, staring at the turning record.

"Not sure where you got your height," Evan said to her, frowning.

"Neither are we," Sloane said. She was straining to remember something, *anything,* about Bert's sister-in-law, her supposed mother. "Some have suggested a milkman's-baby situation, but . . ."

"But you've got your dad's eyes," Evan supplied. "I'll get the coffee."

Sloane had never been more grateful for having blue eyes in her entire life. She suppressed a hysterical giggle and turned toward the bookcase that stood next to the fireplace. The top shelf was packed with old novels: *Moby Dick, White Fang, The Sound and the Fury, Catcher in the Rye.* Like the entire syllabus for an Intro to American Literature class. Next to them was *For the Living to the Dead* with *Lee* on the spine. When she slipped it out to see the cover, she read the name Harper Lee.

The next shelf down was even more interesting. *Monsters and Madness in Russian Folklore. Mythical Objects of Ancient Greece and Rome. The Ark of the Covenant: Fact or Fiction?*

"Were you studying to be an archaeologist?" Sloane called out to the kitchen, where the coffee machine was groaning.

"No," Evan called back. "Just a hobby. Lost its charm when magic became a reality."

"Why?" Sloane turned to face him as he came back into the living room, her hand still hovering over the Russian folklore text.

"No mystery left in anything, I suppose," Evan said. He was carrying the coffeepot in one hand and three mugs, his fingers through the handles, with the other. He set all of them down on the coffee table on top of a book about castles, its dust jacket marked with rings from old cups.

"What do you do, Mr. Kowalczyk?" Esther asked.

"I work for the post office," he said, sitting down. "Don't you remember, Shauna? You sent me letters for Santa Claus when you were a child."

Sloane smiled. "That's right. I thought you knew his address."

Evan smiled back. "It's strange for a child to understand that it's helpful to be well connected."

Sloane moved to the pictures arranged on the mantel. Their Bert had lost his wife in a mysterious incident—he had never been specific—that had later motivated him to join ARIS, in search of explanations.

"I've never seen this picture of Anna," she said, picking up one of the frames. In the photograph, a young Evan Kowalczyk sat beside a plump woman—Anna Kowalczyk—her hair tied up in a scarf and a pile of knitting on her lap. The picture of domesticity.

"Ah, you wouldn't have. I was never very good at sending your mother copies." Evan's mouth pressed into a line. "Or staying in touch."

"It's a two-way street," Sloane said, hoping it was true.

"How did she die?" Esther said.

"You don't know?" Evan raised an eyebrow. "She was killed by the Resurrectionist."

Esther's and Sloane's eyes met. Sloane thought of the rubble of the Drain site, a tomb of bodies and memories that would never be recovered.

"How is your mother doing?" Evan asked her. "I know the anniversary was always hard for her."

"Oh, she's all right." Sloane shrugged. "Dad's driving her crazy, as usual."

It had seemed like a safe comment in her head, but it came out sounding wrong, like a dissonant chord. Evan froze with his cup of coffee on his lap, his eyes on her. Sloane didn't dare to look away.

"I mean—" Sloane began.

"Pete's been dead for ten years." Evan set the coffee down on the table, his hand trembling. "You're not Shauna, are you?"

He had gone rigid. Sloane felt her heartbeat all through her body —chest, fingers, throat, cheeks.

"Shit," Esther said.

"No," Sloane said. "I'm not."

"Who are you?" Evan stood and stepped toward her. She stumbled back toward the front door. Esther was on her feet, too, inching out of the living room.

"Someone who knows what you could have been," Sloane said coldly. "There are plenty of mysteries left in the world, Evan."

"Who are you?" Evan demanded again. "How do you know me?"

Her eyes burned suddenly, like she might cry. Violence flared inside her, so similar to the burn of magic in her chest that she worried she would cause another gale like the one in the Hall of Summons that had shattered the oculus window.

She raised her voice: "The Resurrectionist killed your wife, and here you are delivering mail, living in your dead aunt's house, like there's nothing to avenge!"

"How do you know whose house this is?" Evan's face had gone white. He blinked a stray tear down his cheek, forgetting to dab it away with his handkerchief. "How do you know anything about me?"

"She has some latent . . . clairvoyant . . . abilities," Esther said, grabbing Sloane's arm. "She's also kind of an asshole, so sorry—"

"Get out," Evan said.

"How can you be so—" Sloane started, but Esther was dragging her toward the front door.

Sloane gave in to Esther's grip, letting herself be wrestled outside and down the steps to the sidewalk. She heard the door slamming, the lock sliding into place. Esther said something to Kyros and Edda, who were still waiting for them by the curb, but Sloane couldn't make out the words.

She sat on the concrete and tried to breathe. Esther's hand was on her back, steady and warm. The sun was setting, and with it came the brutal wind coming off the lake, like daggers on her skin.

They all stayed still for a long time, until Sloane's ears burned from the cold and Esther was shivering.

After a while, Sloane said to Esther, "I wouldn't read those FOIA documents if I were you. It's not a Bert you'd want to know."

"So why did you read them?"

Sloane shrugged and tilted her head back to look at the sky. The moon was rising behind the clouds. "More information is better, right?" She laughed. "Fuck."

"Fuck," Esther agreed. "Want to get a drink somewhere?"

"Yeah," Sloane said, and she let Esther help her to her feet and hook her elbow around Sloane's. "I know a place."

Esther laughed, her crisp voice echoing down the empty street. Edda was standing on the corner of the street, her siphon hand raised and shining with ethereal light. Hailing a taxi.

"We're in an alternate universe!" Esther said. "How do you know a place?"

Sloane managed a smile.

23

THEY PULLED UP to the Tankard, which didn't have a real sign, just an old beer mug rendered in pink neon shining through the front window. Inside, it looked like a pub, wood paneling everywhere, sticky but warm. Sloane raised an eyebrow at Esther as they walked in; the man sitting on a stool by the door was uninterested in their IDs. Sloane ran both hands through her hair to push it away from her face as she scanned the place for Mox.

"Looks like a movie set," Esther said with a snort. She was right. The dark alcoves, the stone walls, the tables with candles burning on top of them—it was a scene from a fantasy movie or a place in a theme park. Except here, the magical effects were real: a lemon wedge floating over a gin and tonic, squeezing every time a woman took a sip; a martini with a bouncing, glowing olive; a glass of flaming whiskey whose fire didn't burn out when a man drank from it.

Esther found a table in the back where they could all huddle together on low wooden benches, and Sloane went to the bar. The bartender wasn't dressed like the people in the Camel, that much was certain. Her clothes were tight, for one thing, and ripped every which way, artful tatters. Her nose was pierced horizontally with a metal rod that expanded when her nostrils flared.

"Hi," Sloane said when the bartender came closer. "I'm looking for Mox."

"Mox, huh?" the woman said. "Who're you?"

"Sloane," she said. "He told me I might find him here."

"I'll see if he's around."

"Can I also—" But the woman was already gone. "Order a drink? No? Okay." Sloane walked back to the table, where Esther and Kyros were talking.

"So they follow me, which means every time I put up a video or a picture, it shows up in their feed—"

"Feed?"

"Yeah, like a big list of all the people they follow mashed together."

"And following someone just means you want to see videos of them talking."

"Yes."

"Why not just talk to the people around you?"

"An excellent question," Sloane said, sliding into a chair.

"Because that's harder," Esther said, laughing. "You have to do the whole social rigmarole. But on social media, you can be at home in your underwear and still feel like you have a social life." Esther was wearing Barbie pink lipstick and the standard siphon that Sloane had struggled with earlier that afternoon. It wasn't decorative enough for Esther; it was at odds with the pale yellow swirl of fabric around her face, which dissolved into a diamond-patterned dress that tapered to her ankles.

"I'm not sure I'd *want* antisocial, naked people to watch videos of me," Kyros said.

Sloane glanced at Edda. She was scanning the bar. Her siphon was rudimentary, like the one Esther wore on her hand, but hers was on her ear, giving her a lopsided appearance. She saw Sloane looking at it and arched an eyebrow.

"What? Do I have something on my face?"

"No," Sloane said. "Just not sure what the ear ones do."

"Enhanced hearing," Edda said. "Distant sounds, sounds too quiet for the human ear. Some people use them to interpret a person's tone better, but I'm no good at that."

Sloane saw him then, ducking under the low door frame behind the bar, his dark, wavy hair pulled back into a low knot, his eyes finding hers right away, as if drawn by magnetism.

"Hey," she said when he was close enough to hear her. "Told you I'd escape."

Mox was so tall that when he sank into a crouch beside her stool, he was almost at eye level. "Welcome."

"I'm Esther. This is Kyros and Edda," Esther said, sticking out her hand for Mox to shake. "Heard you helped my girl out of a jam."

"Unrealist snare," Mox said.

"Unrealists." Edda snorted. "Bunch of pretentious art students."

"They can be brilliant, though," Mox said. "Even the snare is an advanced working, likely requires an assembly of at least five people with a high level of dissonance. Hard to maintain."

"Just because something is difficult," Edda said, "doesn't mean it's worth doing."

"If we're going to talk about this, I'll need a drink," Kyros said. "Or seven."

"Right." Mox stood. "What does everybody want?"

"I want that thing with the glowing olive," Esther said.

"The genie martini," Mox said. "A fine choice."

Kyros and Edda both ordered beers that were obviously familiar to them. Mox looked at Sloane.

"I . . . will go up there," she said. "I want to look at what you've got."

"Sure you do," Esther said, and Sloane glared at her. She was glad to step away from the table and away from Esther's assessing stare. Mox slipped behind the bar, and Sloane leaned against it from the other side, making a show of squinting at the bottles lined up behind him.

She raised an eyebrow when Mox grabbed a sheet of paper and dragged it over. On it were written the ingredients for the genie martini.

"Bad memory," he said. "Forgot how to work the olive."

"That sounds like a euphemism," she said.

He laughed and grabbed the jar of olives. Sloane watched with interest as he scooped one out with a spoon and put it in the bottom of the shaker. He covered it with his siphon hand, and she heard his low hum, much deeper than she was expecting. A wet bounce came from the shaker, and it shivered, with just his siphon hand keeping it still. He hummed again, this time higher, and when he pulled his fingers away from the shaker top, just a little, the olive was glowing blue. It bounced up, almost escaping, so he covered the top again.

"I bet a lot of things get smashed when you guys figure out new recipes," she said. "Do you serve anything that doesn't bounce, float, or continuously burn?"

"I could make you an OF OF—old-fashioned old-fashioned," Mox said.

"Sounds good," she said.

"Still no siphon for you?" he said, nodding at her bare hands. He scooped some ice into the shaker, careful to cover it until the last second so the ice could pin the olive to the bottom. He poured some gin and vermouth on top of it, at which point the olive had wriggled free of its icy prison. He covered the top and let the olive do the shaking.

"For all you know, I could have one on my right breast right now," she said. "How do you get that thing to settle down enough for someone to drink it?"

"If you were rich enough and powerful to have a chest siphon, you would be cutting holes in your clothing to show it off," he said with a laugh. "And it's a dwindler, this working. All it needs is time."

She tried not to give him a blank look, but she wasn't entirely sure she managed it. "Maybe I'm not showy about my siphons," she said.

"It's not a character assessment, it's a survival instinct," he said. "We display our best assets to attract mates or to warn off predators. Like the peacock. Are you claiming to be better than millions of years of evolution?"

"I'm the pinnacle," Sloane said, solemn. "Congratulations on meeting me."

"I feel so honored." He picked up a strainer and poured the drink into a martini glass, then added the olive. It danced at the bottom of the glass, no longer threatening to become a dangerous projectile.

"My siphon's still getting repaired," she said. "It's only been a day."

"Which would drive most people insane," he said. He tossed the ice and rinsed out the shaker, then started on the old-fashioned old-fashioned with a muddler and a sugar cube in a fresh tumbler.

"I think it's nice not to rely on magic for everything," she said.

"You're in the wrong place, then," he said. "Might want to go to a haven city instead."

Sloane didn't know what that meant. "You ever been to one?"

"I was born in one. Arlington, Texas," he said.

"No accent, though?" she said.

"I had some trouble with magic pretty early in life," he said. "Moved here as a child to learn how not to destroy things with it."

He paused with the tumbler in one hand and the jigger of whiskey in the other, his dark eyes fixed on her. She felt like he was waiting for something, and the longer she went without giving it to him, the more of a misstep she was making. But she was missing all the vocabulary for this place—the unspoken words for what a haven city was and what it meant that he had destroyed things with magic as a child and even what it suggested, that she could go a day without a siphon. "Did your parents stay here?" she said, knowing it was the wrong thing to ask but not coming up with anything else.

"Nancy and Phil, live in a magic hub? Perish the thought!" He spooned a cherry into the tumbler on top of the whiskey, ice, and sugar. "No, they never came to begin with."

"Ah." She searched, desperately, for a new subject. "Well, I'm from the middle of nowhere. High-school graduating class of twenty-three students."

It had been a middle-school class in another dimension, but he didn't need to know that.

"And now you're here in the big city," he said. He still had that look in his eyes like he was waiting. She knew the smart thing would be to end the conversation, go back to her table, and never see him again. But she stayed sitting on the barstool. "Doing what, exactly?"

"I already told you," she said. "Mayhem."

He didn't laugh. The blue glow of the olive reflected in his eyes, which in the dim bar looked almost black. She watched the blue ricochet in his irises as the olive moved in the glass. Finally, he smirked.

"I guess you did," he said. "Here's your drink."

She took the old-fashioned old-fashioned off the bar and sipped it, then followed him back to the table, where he handed out Esther's drink and the two beers like nothing had happened. But something had—Sloane just didn't know quite what it was.

Edda and Kyros were singing. The four of them were walking from the bar to the nearest hotel, where it was easier to hail a taxi. It was dark, and Esther had noted that at least half of the streetlights they passed were the old gas-burning kind. It seemed to Sloane that with the spread of magic had come a deep affinity for the past, but she wasn't sure what one had to do with the other. Maybe it was like the movie-set feel of the Tankard—all their magic stories were set in old-timey fantasy worlds or eras so ancient the magical acts were associated with old gods and angels and demons, so they reached backward to figure out how to be magical instead of forward.

Esther hooked her arm around Sloane's elbow. "So that Mox," she said.

"I know what you're thinking," Sloane said. "And you're off base."

"All I was going to say is, if you want to have a rebound fling with that hot praying mantis, you don't have to hide it from me," she said. "That's all."

"Good to know," Sloane said.

"I'd hide it from Matt, though."

"Obviously."

Esther cocked her head to the side and looked up at Sloane like she was trying to remember the title of a song. "You seem better here," she said.

"Better?" Sloane laughed. "Tell that to Evan Kowalczyk."

"I didn't say you were *normal,* just . . . better. Steadier."

"Well," Sloane replied, "I know how to do this. Fight the big bad, dodge the government goons. Same script, different movie."

Esther nodded. She choked a little when she responded: "I don't *want* to do this again."

Edda and Kyros had finished their song, one they had both learned in army training, apparently. They stood under the bright overhang outside the hotel, talking to a man in uniform with a whistle in his mouth.

"What if I die here?" Esther's voice was throaty. "What if my mom dies at home without ever knowing—"

Sloane couldn't bear to hear the rest. She had met Esther's mother when they were both teenagers, and Esther's face had still been round as a dinner plate. Her mother had been warm but somehow aloof, like she was living in two worlds at the same time, and each took her attention away from the other. And then, years later, after her diagnosis, she had been half the size, her head wrapped in a scarf, and still always smiling.

None of their parents were the dream of what parents should be. Every one of them had given their child away. But of all of them, Esther's mother was maybe the closest, fussing over Esther's diminishing waist, always foisting cookies and tea on them even if she was in someone else's house.

Sloane squeezed Esther's hand hard and hoped the pressure would steady her. She wasn't good at consoling people; that had been Albie's job. "Your mom knows everything she needs to know," she said. "That her daughter saved the world. And loves her."

Esther's head bobbed. "Okay." She swallowed. "Yeah."

A taxi pulled up to the curb. They all piled in, quieting down on the drive back to the Camel. Sloane looked out the window, but she didn't see anything they passed. All she could think about was how everything that happened now—including getting pulled into a parallel dimension—would be After Albie. Like a new era. Sloane AA.

Some things split your life in half.

MEMORANDUM FOR THE RECORD

TO: Director, Project Delphi

FROM: Captain Kyros Stasiak, Cordus Protective Forces

SUBJECT: Elsberry, MO

Dear Director,

I understand your point of view regarding the destructive incident in Elsberry, MO—I initially shared it myself. However, after interviewing dozens of people and observing the aftermath myself, I want to assure you that the reports were neither imagined nor exaggerated. Witnesses did indeed observe a figure fitting the description of the man Merlin saw at the site of the massacre of the first Army of Flickering; he was followed by a troop of what appeared to be reanimated corpses. Whether there was actually anything supernatural about the supposed corpses remains to be seen, but the descriptions are consistent, specific, and reliable.

We are working to repair the town hall, which was obliterated, and we have offered modest reparations to the families of the dead to cover funeral costs. But what we would rather give them is an explanation of how their loved ones died and who killed them. They have begun calling him "the Resurrectionist." Let us hope he can be apprehended before the nickname catches on.

Sincerely,

Captain Kyros Stasiak
Cordus Protective Forces

MEMORANDUM FOR THE RECORD

TO: Director, Project Delphi

FROM: Captain Kyros Stasiak, Cordus Protective Forces

SUBJECT: RE: Elsberry, MO

Dear Director,

Two days ago, we received a report that there had
been a disturbance at Roe's Hill Cemetery on the
North Side of Chicago. The reports said that huge
amounts of earth had been displaced in an apparently
magical fashion, exposing countless graves to
the elements. The case had been tied up in local
(nonmagical) law enforcement for a few months before
they realized magic had been involved and referred it
to us. We sent an officer to investigate the incident.
What we discovered is that dozens of graves had been
dug up, their coffins opened, and the bodies therein
stolen. Upon further investigation, it seems that all
of the aforementioned bodies belonged to soldiers of
the first Army of Flickering.

I cannot help but make a connection between the
Resurrectionist's last attack in Peoria, Illinois
—where he was again seen with a small army of what
was described as reanimated corpses (to be specific:
skin rotted, bones exposed, fingernails clawlike, some
holding their own severed limbs)—and this incident.
The coffins were unearthed at approximately the
same time as the Resurrectionist's first attack. I
submit that perhaps the Resurrectionist has enacted
some sick magical working that we do not presently

comprehend—he has successfully raised an army from
the dead.

I trust you will find this as disturbing as I do.
Pardon my language, but what kind of twisted son of a
bitch massacres an army and then raises them from the
dead to take down their former leader?

I wish I had better news.

Sincerely,

Captain Kyros Stasiak
Cordus Protective Forces

TOP SECRET

24

THE FIRST TIME she had ever seen Matt was at the Farmhouse, which is what they called the building where they had trained to defeat the Dark One. He had been holding on to the chain of the porch swing, gangly, his hair in short dreadlocks. He had told her she had a weird name and asked her how she got it. When she told him she and her brother were named after characters in the movie *Ferris Bueller's Day Off,* he had laughed, and his smile had been so wide that she liked him right away.

There was something about Matt standing in the hallway holding the door frame that reminded her of the teenager she had known. But he had stopped smiling that way a long time ago. Long before they started dating.

He certainly wasn't smiling now.

"Nice note," he said, holding up the piece of paper Sloane had slipped under his door before they left.

> *Matt —*
> *We're going to meet Alternate Bert. Just have to know. Taking chaperones, so don't worry.*
> *— Slo and Essy*

He crumpled it up and threw it at her feet. It bounced up against her shins and settled near the wall.

"Well, I actually told you where I was going this time," Sloane said coolly.

"That isn't the issue," Matt said. "We're supposed to be a team, Sloane."

"You don't want a *team*," Sloane said. "You want obedience."

Matt flinched like she had hit him and stepped back. She felt a twinge of regret. But she was tired of bracing herself every time she wanted to do something, say something, go somewhere. And not just here in Genetrix, but anywhere. He was a kind man, but his disapproval was paternalistic, at best, and, at worst, oppressive.

"Wow, hey, none of this," Esther said before Matt could respond. She put herself between them, holding one hand out to Sloane and the other out to Matt. "It's not like Sloane dragged me along, Matt. I agreed with her that it would be helpful, and I knew you wouldn't want to come, so—"

"No, you knew that if you told me about it before you left, I would argue with you," Matt said, scowling. "You don't just get to go behind my back because you know I disagree with you! Have I ever done that to either of you?"

"Well, maybe if you ever wanted to *do* anything—"

"Sloane, shut *up!*" Esther snapped. "Stop being such a fucking child."

Heat rushed into Sloane's face. Esther pinched her nose as if forcing tension away. Sloane kept forgetting how tired Esther had looked when she dragged herself out of the river. Nothing was waiting for Sloane back on Earth except familiarity and an apartment she needed to move out of. But waiting for Esther was a dying parent. Every moment they spent here was, for her, a moment too long.

"You make a fair point," Esther said to Matt. "Right, Sloane?"

"You don't have to pressure her into agreeing with you," Matt said.

"She's not," Sloane forced herself to say. "It is a fair point. Sorry."

Esther sighed with obvious relief and kicked off one of her shoes so it landed somewhere in the bedroom she had claimed. The other one soon joined it, and she stood in flat feet, her pink lipstick faded everywhere but the outline of her mouth, her eye makeup smeared under her lower lashes. The Essy of Insta! fame was gone.

"Okay," Matt said. "Well, how was he?"

"A dick," Sloane said.

"He was not a dick," Esther said. "He was a mailman with a dead wife. No interest in government work or magic."

"So he *wasn't* like Bert." Matt looked triumphant. "I told Esther earlier, just because someone's got the same genes as their parallel counterpart—"

"He was a lot like Bert, actually." Sloane crossed her arms and leaned against the wall. "He was listening to Neil Young. He had all these books on magical objects of legend. He talked like Bert, teared up like Bert; he had fucking gnomes in his front yard. He *was* Bert, but the spread of magic derailed him."

"How could the spread of magic derail him? Bert was fascinated by magic," Matt said. "He would have loved for it to become widespread."

"No, Bert was fascinated by *mystery*," Sloane said. "He liked knowing things that no one else knew and finding out that myths were real, so once magic became this known quantity that you could control with tech and frequencies, he lost interest." She stared at her shoes, covered in dust and dirt and puddle water. "He was similar enough that I lost it a little," she said. "He was similar enough that I think it's possible—maybe even likely—that the Resurrectionist could be the alternate version of the Dark One."

"Our Dark One was just making use of magic that most of Earth didn't believe existed," Matt said. "I guess it makes sense that in a world where magic is widely known to exist, he would delve deeper into what was possible—like bring an army back from the dead."

Sloane nodded.

"I mean, if a normal person knew how to bring someone back from death, they wouldn't build a freaking army. They would bring back loved ones, family, friends," Esther said.

Sloane thought of Cameron at the community swimming pool, teaching her how to backflip into the water. There were so many things she hadn't said to him. Things she could say if she figured out how to raise the dead.

Esther's voice sounded strained as she continued, as if she was thinking of her own father, lost to the Dark One, and her mother, who wouldn't be around much longer: "But the Dark One wasn't — isn't normal."

"The good news — well, the slightly better than horrible news," Sloane said, "is that we *do* know the Dark One a little. So we're not facing a completely unknown enemy here. Like you said the other day, Matt — we've done this before."

It was a better apology than the earlier one, in a way; it acknowledged that he had been right to find hope in the idea that they had experienced this already. She was remembering, only it didn't feel like memory, not really. It felt like becoming something she had already been. A pared-down Sloane, whittled to her essential elements. A clenched jaw and a clear head and a single purpose: the end of the Dark One.

"I know you hate the siphons, Slo, but you have to keep working on it," Matt said. "We all do. That's the next step for us here — learn how to use magic, because it's the best weapon we have."

"Never thought I'd wish I still had the Needle stuck in my hand," Sloane said. "But I'm starting to."

Over the next week, Sloane grew to despise the siphon. She hated its weight, its coldness, the feeling of the strings that pulled it tight to her knuckles. It was useless and inert on her hand no matter which working she tried. Cyrielle had given up on the magical breath and had attempted to teach her half a dozen small workings, each of which had the same result: nothing. The Resurrectionist was just a specter, a legend, but the siphon was an enemy she could see and touch.

The others were mastering theirs without much difficulty. Matt had a knack for moving objects without touching them. Esther had been clumsy with all wrist-siphon workings, but Cyrielle, in a stroke of genius, had gotten a throat siphon for her, and now Esther could mimic anyone's voice at will.

Every morning, Sloane considered smashing the siphon with one of the books at her bedside. The only thing that stopped her was fear of the Resurrectionist and the thought of the Drain.

Sloane considered going back to the Tankard to see Mox again but decided against it. Instead she found other ways to occupy herself. She took Kyros running along the lakefront despite the frosty air. She read the stack of books she had found in her room. She even managed to drag Esther to the Art Institute, where there was now an entire wing dedicated to Art Workings. She had wandered for hours through an exhibit of photographs that turned into three-dimensional scenes when you drew close, to make you feel like you were walking around inside them. She was beginning to understand the Unrealists—how could you trust reality when reality was so easily manipulated?

The only upside to the constant siphon frustration was how tiring it was. The heavy sleep kept her clear of the worst of her nightmares, though nothing could entirely protect her from them. More often than not, she dreamed about Albie, about chasing him through empty streets or up and down staircases. In one vivid dream, he ran out into traffic on the interstate and got crushed between two semis heading straight toward each other. The whole scene had erupted into flames.

When Sloane woke up from those dreams, she gave up on going back to sleep and tried to soothe herself by reading. The three of them had gathered all the books left in their rooms and piled them in the hallway, making a little library. Sloane kept *The Manifestation of Impossible Wants: A New Theory of Magic* for herself, but she also picked up a collection of poetry from Matt's room and a history text from Esther's.

The history book covered the period after the end of World War II, the establishment of the Iron Curtain and a Cold War Sloane both did and didn't recognize. She waited for the development of satellite technology, the Space Race, but it didn't come; in its place, there was technology to plunge deeper underwater, to hear farther across the SOFAR channel—the level of the ocean at which sound traveled fastest—to place hydrophones deeper in the ocean without losing their efficacy. And all this resulted, of course, in the *Tenebris* Incident, an accident of underwater-missile testing that had spread magic throughout the world.

Sloane was sitting in the hallway one morning, the book in her lap and a half-empty cup of coffee next to her, when she heard a soft *ding* —the sound of the elevator arriving. Nero exited, his hands in his pocket, one thumb covered in the chrome of his siphon. His hair was combed back from his forehead, revealing lines she hadn't noticed before. She wondered, for the first time, how old he was.

"Yes?" she said to him as he came closer.

"I have been alerted of your wandering the halls every single night this week," Nero said to her. "I finally came to find out if you were sleepwalking."

"So whatever magical alarm you've rigged, it's on my room," Sloane said. "Are you watching me sleep, Creepmaster 2000?"

"Creep—what?" Nero crouched next to her, his elbows on his knees. "No, I am not watching you sleep. I am simply made aware that someone has exited their living space."

"I have insomnia," Sloane said.

"Always?"

"Since my brother was murdered by a world-destroying lord of evil," Sloane said. "I usually take medication for it, but I left it at home."

Nero tilted his head as he looked at her. "Did it not occur to you that we also make medicine on Genetrix?"

Sloane laughed a little. "I guess it hadn't. Do you guys have benzodiazepines?"

"Like Valium?" Nero said.

"I guess that would work," she said.

"I will request some for you," Nero said. "I know how frustrating it is to not get enough sleep on a regular basis."

Sloane hadn't realized it would be that simple. "Well . . . thanks."

"Of course." Nero nudged her book so he could see what was on the cover. It was a sketch of the baleen whale Kyros had mentioned, adrift in the clouds above Challenger Deep.

"History," Nero said. "I suppose that makes it easier to sleep."

"You don't like history?"

"Not particularly, no." Nero shrugged. "On a grand scale, per-haps—the birth of the world, the first living organisms, the begin-ning of humanity. But the details of squabbling between nations—*That's my land; No, it's mine; Let's kill each other over it*—no. That does not interest me."

"Without those little squabbles, you wouldn't have magic," Sloane said. "There wouldn't have been a ballistic missile to accidentally fire into the Mariana Trench."

"And magic for magic's sake, that's such a good thing?"

"No," Sloane said. "But—don't you like magic? You work here, after all."

"Sometimes I like it," he said. "It's given me knowledge of the universe beyond anything my ancestors would have dreamed. But that knowledge is never enough to prevent catastrophe, it seems."

"It's not your responsibility to stop all bad things from happen-ing."

"Only some things. I know." He smiled a little. "But I bear the weight of them."

She wondered if he was thinking of his sister, lured into the Res-urrectionist's clutches. The horror of her death, her body suspended above the Camel, stiff and cold. Sometimes Sloane thought of Cam-eron that way too, lying dead in his casket, dusted with powder from the mortician that made him look plastic, like a doll. She had been young when he joined the fight against the Dark One. Too young to stop him, probably, but she hadn't even tried.

"I understand that, I think," she said.

"I didn't mean to interrupt your reading with my moroseness," Nero said. "I hear that your siphon efforts have been considerable."

"But fruitless."

Nero acknowledged that with a nod. "There's a book that may help you to understand more about magical theory. It's called *The Manifestation of Impossible*—"

"—*Wants*. Yeah, I read that one," she said. Maybe she was flattering herself, but she thought he looked a little impressed. "Magic is all about desire, not just intent, blah-blah. Didn't do me much good — you can't make yourself *want* something."

Nero cocked his head to the side again. "Can't you?"

She had never considered that before. She had lived half her life wanting only one thing — to save the world — and the other half wanting to be left alone, which was almost the same thing as wanting nothing at all. She didn't know what it was like to desire something between those two extremes. She wasn't sure she was even capable of it.

"I don't know," she said.

"Well, then, that's the central question," Nero said. "You will never be able to do magic unless you find a way to want to." He got to his feet with a groan, his knees creaking. "I'm a little too old to sit on the floor, I'm afraid. I'll talk to a doctor about your medicine once the world is awake."

"Thanks again," she said.

Nero walked down the hallway, humming.

25

Sloane stopped on the corner and looked up, trying to see the corkscrew spire on top of the tallest building in Genetrix's Chicago, Warner Tower. It was the one with two faces, one flat, the other undulating. It had been made, according to Cyrielle, "without magic, but influenced by the Unrealist school nonetheless."

If Sloane had believed in souls, she would have hoped that Cameron's existed in Genetrix, that he was an architect building houses that defied logic and sense. But she didn't.

Sometimes she still hoped anyway.

Cyrielle was walking with Matt at the front of the group. Esther was teaching Edda and their third chaperone, Perun, how to say something in Korean. Kyros saw Sloane lingering by Warner Tower and stayed behind to wait for her, his hands in his coat pockets.

"Did you have any luck today?" he asked.

"As far as I'm concerned, my siphon is just a really expensive paperweight," Sloane said. She glanced over her shoulder, sure she had just heard something buzzing. But the street behind her was empty.

Kyros smiled grimly. "Well, at least you know you *can* do something. Some people don't have the ability at all."

"What do they do?" She jogged a little to catch up to him. The streets were packed with cars, some as old-fashioned as the taxi she had taken with Esther and some that looked like little bubbles with wheels. "Move to haven cities?"

"Oh, so you know about those?"

"Mox—you know, that bartender friend I made?—said he was from one." She had stayed away from Mox since that conversation, sensing that she had made a critical misstep but not understanding what. It hadn't occurred to her that she could just ask Kyros what she had done wrong. "He said he had to learn not to destroy things with magic as a kid, so he moved up here."

Kyros raised his eyebrows. "Oh."

"I don't understand," Sloane said. "He seemed to be expecting me to react in a particular way, and I . . . didn't. That's why I haven't been back."

"That's probably a wise decision," he said. "Children having un-controllable magic is quite rare. If it were more common, we might not need siphons to channel magic at all. So those few talented children were the ones they summoned when they were looking for the Chosen One of Genetrix. If you didn't react to that information, it's an indicator that you aren't from around here."

"He wouldn't suspect the truth, though, right?" she said. She felt an odd pressure against the sides of her head, like she had just dived to the bottom of a swimming pool.

"Unlikely," Kyros said. "People here know there are other dimensions, but they don't know that they are accessible."

Sloane pressed her fingers to her temples. The pressure still hadn't gone away.

"What is it?" Kyros said, setting a gentle hand on her shoulder.

"I don't know. I just feel like something is *wrong*," Sloane said.

And that was when something behind them exploded.

The onset of the Drain was sudden. A change in pressure, and then, in the space of a blink: the tornado. A wall of opaque debris from street to sky. Only it wasn't wind, it was something else, whipcords of energy that dragged everything in their path into the center of the funnel. And while people were moving toward that point—the core of the destructive force—they came apart, piece by piece, vivisected by magic. Sometimes too quickly for the body to catch up and die, so a person's last moments were spent in segments.

The first time Sloane had gotten close to a Drain, she had turned and run away. All of them had. There were no thoughts of bravery when the Drain was coming. There were no thoughts at all; there was only survival. She had considered running away from ARIS, fleeing the country and the Dark One. But the prophecy had tied her to him, and when her own honor failed her, that fact kept her in ARIS's employ. If she fled the Dark One, he would find her, because she was Chosen.

So, because escape was not possible, Sloane learned not to turn and run.

She ducked under Kyros's outstretched hand and grabbed Esther's arm right below the elbow. Esther's arm twisted as she grasped Sloane in the same place, locking them together. Cyrielle was screaming, her hair askew and her cape blown back, the mandarin-size gold pin now up against her throat.

"Retreat! Three groups!" Matt shouted. "Perun and Cyrielle! Sloane, Esther, and Kyros! Me and Edda! Sloane, you there?"

The question made her chest ache. Sloane nodded. It was a familiar procedure: Never go near a Drain with more people than you had weapons. Don't rush into a fight—live to fight again. They were tenets she had worked into her muscles, mapped into her brain.

"Eyes open. Meet back at the Camel."

Matt cast a wild look over his shoulder as the group split into thirds. Sloane couldn't think of him—couldn't think of anything except the rush of concrete and steel and flesh and earth ahead of them.

Sloane's grip on Esther shifted as she took the lead. She bent low, pressing against the power that tried to throw her back. She had learned the way the Drain felt, how it pushed you until it pulled you, how the pressure in her head would release when she had gotten too close, how it smelled like ozone and dust at first, then wet earth and blood. She checked behind her for Kyros, who had his siphon outstretched, fingers spread wide.

Eyes open. The only real thing they had known about the Drains before they encountered one was that the Dark One had been spotted at each one—meaning he likely had to be present to control them. And though he was a being of great magical power, he was also still a man. Where their own magic failed, they had reasoned, knives and bullets would do the job just as well. If they looked for him, maybe they could find him. Maybe they could kill him.

Sloane rounded a corner and ran down an alley toward the funnel. As she watched, the Drain inhaled a huge wave of water from Lake Michigan and sent it scattering. Some of it escaped the thrust of the Drain's power and splattered *out,* wetting the street, the brick walls of buildings that hadn't yet crumbled, and Sloane's cheeks. She took one step too far, and the Drain's magnetism tugged at her legs and arms; she lurched away, knocking Esther back.

"Left!" she shouted. She could hardly hear herself over the roar of magic and power, the screams of those caught in the Drain's grasp, the hooting of car alarms and the wail of sirens. She jerked Esther to the side, back to the street, and Kyros tumbled after them both. She still couldn't see the Drain's center, where the Resurrectionist likely was, grounded by his own magic. He would be the eye of the storm, and to find him, to kill him, she would need to go somewhere open. One of the wider roads, where she could see farther, unobstructed.

Clark, Wells, Franklin, Wacker, she thought. The last street sign she had seen had been ripped from its moorings, but Warner Tower had been on Franklin, so it was only one block north to Wacker Drive. It was the smarter path to take whether she saw the Resurrectionist or not—small streets were crowded, hard to navigate.

She bent low and ran, pulling Esther behind her. The air was thick with dust; Sloane pulled the collar of her shirt up over her mouth and nose to keep from breathing it in. The sidewalks were now full of people running away from the Drain, their faces in grimaces of horror, soot-stained and tear-streaked. The crowd was too dense to penetrate; Sloane led them to the middle of the street instead, where cars stood abandoned. She climbed over two taxis crushed nose to nose and sidestepped the back of a bus, the front of which had collided with a brick building. The seats inside were all empty, purses and briefcases abandoned on the floor.

"Slo!" Esther said between coughs.

"Wacker!" Sloane answered, and she almost laughed at the word despite herself.

Her shirt clung to her back, soaked with sweat, and her legs burned as she climbed over another car. As she stepped on the hood, she saw that the driver was still behind the wheel, blood bubbling from his mouth. She stood for a moment, watching him. His chest was still.

Move on. She jumped down and found herself at the junction of Monroe and Wacker. Wacker Drive, the great double-decker confusion of Chicago, with its upper layer and its lower. Here it was wide with a landscaped, raised median, and tall buildings, titans of glass and steel, bracketed the road. Behind her was the spiral horn of Warner Tower and the twin prongs of the Sears Tower, and in front of her the Drain. As she watched, a woman in one shoe, hobbling away from a building entrance, stepped too close to the inexorable pull of the Drain's power. A whipcord of energy upended her and dragged her, screaming, into the gray wall of destruction.

But moving away from all the people and cars and uprooted trees and massive bricks of concrete was a solitary figure.

The weight of inevitability settled on Sloane's shoulders. Cold crept up her spine. Through the cloud of dust and dirt, she saw a face plated with metal siphons with only thin strips of pale skin visible at their seams. The hands that hung heavy at his sides were also metal-plated, as well as what she could see of his throat above the high collar of his robes. A hood covered his hair, and the rest of him was shrouded in the bulk of fabric.

The Resurrectionist.

"Retreat!" Esther screamed, her voice hoarse.

But Sloane couldn't move. If the theory she had proposed to Esther and Matt after visiting Evan Kowalczyk—that the Resurrectionist was the parallel version of the Dark One—was correct, this was the man she had lived her entire life to kill. This was the man who had painstakingly broken Albie's body. This was the man who had tested Sloane's heart.

It's a simple choice, my dear.

"Sloane!"

She was barefoot, in the Dark One's house. He had taken her boots.

She had to find something heavy or something sharp. She saw a rock the size of her fist, a crumpled soda can. And in the planter, in the median, an old metal rod, the kind used for street signs. She picked it up. It was flaky, rusty in her palm. Two feet long. She would need to be closer. She would need to swing hard, at his head—just to stun him, so she could escape—

She couldn't breathe. He was coming toward her, his steps confident. Hand raised, as if in greeting. Head cocked like a bird's.

She was barefoot, in the Dark One's house, and Albie was screaming.

"Sloane!"

Sloane screamed and charged, drawing the metal rod back like a baseball player with a bat. She swung, putting the full weight of her body behind it, and waited for the crack, the feeling of metal connecting with metal—

But all she heard was a low, tinny note coming from the Resurrectionist's facemask. He flicked his fingers as if dismissing her, and the rod burst into a cloud that covered her palms with silver dust. Then his hand was lifting, closing into a fist—she remembered Kyros telling her the Resurrectionist's favored method of execution, collapsed lungs that wouldn't reinflate—

Something heavy hit her from the side, sending her headfirst into the median. She saw dirt between her palms and used the momentum to propel herself over the planter and into the street on the other side of the barrier. Before diving into an alley, she looked over her shoulder. Kyros had taken her place in the street, his siphon hand held out and the air rippling in front of him as he let out a sharp, high whistle. But the Resurrectionist hissed through his mask, batted the barrier aside, and clenched a hand into a fist.

Kyros choked. And fell.

"Es—es!" Sloane tried to scream, but her throat felt like it was coated with sand. Esther was in the street, bent over Kyros's body.

Sloane turned back with a strangled scream, but the Resurrectionist was already walking away from Kyros and Esther and toward *her*.

If there was one thing she had learned from her day of captivity, it was that when it came to the Dark One, she was the only bait he wouldn't fail to take. And it seemed to be the same with the Resurrectionist.

She forced one foot back, then the other. Stepping backward over abandoned high heels. A briefcase that had fallen open, its papers spilling all over the street. A half-eaten hot dog covered in relish, still in its wrapper. She stepped back faster, making sure the Resurrectionist was still moving toward her and away from Esther and Kyros—

Kyros, who was probably dead—

She took another step back and ran into something solid. Sloane turned and saw—a person. But the greenish skin had peeled away from its jaw, revealing a white streak of bone and the clench of teeth. Sloane watched a tongue work between them as the thing licked its pale, purplish lips.

Not a person.

"Is this the one?" A raspy, metallic voice.

"Yes." The answer came from a distance with the same tinny sound as the note the Resurrectionist had emitted to turn steel into dust.

The dead thing moved fast, forcing a white cloth against Sloane's nose and mouth. She struggled against the inhumanly strong grip, but only for a moment. Then she passed out.

Chicago Post

CHOSEN ONE: STILL ALIVE?

by Alexander Marshall

CHICAGO, MARCH 3: are we doomed? reads a sign propped against the City Hall building. A "Chosen Truther"—a member of a movement demanding transparency from the Department of Magical Oversight in Chicago regarding the Chosen One—has stopped for a cigarette. Chosen Truthers have been protesting outside Cordus Center since Tuesday. Why? Because they think the Chosen One is dead.

The nation celebrated the day Cordus announced it had found the Chosen One, destined to save humankind. But ever since the massacre of the Army of Flickering three years ago, the Chosen One has remained under lock and key. Perhaps it's not surprising that people are starting to speculate.

"What if he's dead?" asks Eleanor Green, mother of two from the Chicago suburb of Deer Grove. She's the founder of the Chosen Truth movement, though she reminds me several times that she's not the first one to want proof of the Chosen One's life. "What if he died in the massacre and they just don't want to tell us? Has anyone seen him since then?"

Most of the Chosen Truthers hold signs that bear the illustration of the Chosen One that was released after he was discovered. Or "allegedly discovered," as the Chosen Truthers would say.

"They told us they found him," says Althea Grange, a self-described "neighborhood grandma" from Rockford. "And then they told us he was too young to have his picture in the paper, and we should just trust them? I don't think they ever found him. They're just trying to avoid a mass panic."

The Chosen Truthers have just begun to chant. "Chosen One, Hidden One!" is the refrain of the hour. Two hours ago, they were singing a parody of the R.E.M. song "It's the End of the World" with the lyrics "If it's the end of the world, we should know it! We know you're lying." Last night, they even brought in a minister to lead a prayer begging God to spare Genetrix.

After days of protests in front of her office, DOMO deputy director Aelia Haddox finally issued a response to the Chosen Truthers' concerns: "This isn't some kind of conspiracy. After the massacre we increased security around the Chosen One for his safety. He is still only eighteen years old, and he deserves a little privacy until he's ready to come forward. They need to go home and find something else to worry about."

26

S LOANE WAS SWAYING her hips to the music. Her hands were caked with flour. Albie popped the top of the jar of sprinkles and tipped his head back to pour them in his mouth.

"Gross!" Sloane said, still swaying. But she was laughing. In front of her was a line of cookies shaped like Christmas trees. She had dusted them with green sugar. "Decorate your damn cookies," Sloane said. "We're making a new tradition here."

Albie's cheek bulged with sprinkles. His lips were blue from the food coloring. Then the color drained from his face, leaving him ashen and pale. A blue-lipped corpse.

She woke up in waves. In the first, she noticed all the blood had rushed to her hands; her fingertips were pulsing. And in the second, she realized her stomach was pressed into something hard and faintly curved: a shoulder. In the third, she remembered the cloth against her face. And in the fourth, she opened her eyes.

There was fabric right in front of her. The hem of a shirt. She tipped her head up just a little to see the floor passing beneath her. It was checkerboard marble in taupe and white. Whoever—whatever —was carrying her wore brown work boots with untied purple laces.

With her ear against his back, she could hear his breaths rattling in and out. The hand clasping her leg felt unyielding as a vise. She thought of the rotten cheek, the gritted molars with the tongue undulating behind them that she had seen before she passed out. Aelia had told them how the Resurrectionist came by his name on Genetrix. His army was composed of the living dead.

Her instinct was to thrash and kick. Catch her captor by surprise, get away, and run as far as she could. But she didn't move. She didn't know enough about the one who was carrying her—did he feel pain? How strong was he?—and she didn't know where she was. Escape would have to wait.

Instead of running, she took note of the direction of the light (coming from windows on her right) and its slant (they were facing east, and it was morning, just after sunrise). A sharp pain in her chest told her she was panicking. She had woken up a captive once before. It had gone badly.

She listened to the murmur of voices around her, each one airy and dry, like a gasp. The Resurrectionist's army, surrounding her. The echoes and the reflection of high windows in the gleaming floor told her the space was large. The scent on the air was mildew and dust with a hint of the ozone the Drain carried in on her clothes, hair, and skin. She knew from experience that it would take days to fade, no matter how hard she scrubbed.

If she survived that long.

She was still wearing her boots. That was something, an anchor to keep her here instead of in her memories. She had worn flippers in the Dive. The Dark One had taken her shoes. But here, she had her boots.

"She's awake," someone—or something—said. The voice came from her right.

"Good," her captor grunted. "I'm tired."

He released her legs, and she crashed to the floor, her body battered by the tiles. She was in a long hall flanked by wide pillars and tiled with white marble. Geometric fixtures of blue glass hung in a line down the center of the hall. The tall windows on one side of the room were boarded up with plywood except for the top row of glass. Across from them, on the other wall, a line of morning sunlight glinted on tiny golden tiles.

Her elbows ached from hitting the ground so hard. She rolled over so she was on hands and knees and breathed through her nose as the pain subsided. She had been right about the Resurrectionist's army surrounding her. They were in every direction, standing in clusters or sitting with their backs against the wall, talking. They were dressed in uniforms, rich navy slacks and shirts with high collars, capes pinned at the shoulder by gilded buttons. If not for the unnatural greenish tint of their skin and the patches of rot on their faces and hands and throats, she might have thought they were just soldiers.

Sloane stood. The man—if he could be called that—who had been carrying her was tall and broad with milky blue eyes and only one ear. The woman with the bone-bare jaw who had knocked her unconscious was standing behind him, her dark, fraying hair worn in a braid over one shoulder. Sloane tasted bile.

"Move," the man said.

She wanted to do as she was told. She really did. But her legs were shaking, so she just stood there staring at them both.

The woman rolled her eyes, grabbed Sloane's elbow, and dragged her forward. Sloane's shoes squeaked as she walked down a hallway of broken tiles and peeling paint and up a metal staircase. The higher and deeper she went into the building, the less likely it was that she could escape. She tried to make a map in her mind—*West, you're walking west*—but it was all she could do to focus on her boots.

Boots meant now. Bare feet meant the past.

The woman stopped in front of a door and unlocked it with a key from the ring on her belt. Inside was a disintegrating laboratory. All the walls were painted azure, as was the front of each drawer and cabinet door, all of them dangling precariously from the lab table in the center of the room. The floor—wood under linoleum—was buckling in places and covered with bits of plaster and flakes of blue paint.

It wasn't a cell, not really. That was good. That meant it wasn't supposed to keep her in. That meant there was a way out.

The woman shoved her into the laboratory and shut the door behind her. Sloane listened as she turned the lock, then walked the perimeter of the room, getting a sense of its size. It was empty except for the lab table in the middle and a faucet on the back wall. She went to it. There was a pipe beneath it that must have gone to some kind of sink drain, but the sink was gone.

She turned on the water. It hissed for a moment before spraying a few orange drops in every direction, then spewing yellowish water that likely wasn't safe to drink. But she was covered in dirt and dust from the Drain and desperate to smell less like death. She stripped off her coat and turned it inside out so she could tear off one of the pockets with her teeth. It would make a good washcloth.

She scrubbed at the backs of her hands with the balled-up cloth until they were almost the right color, then rinsed out the pocket and used it on her face. She scrubbed until her cheeks tingled, then moved on to her throat and neck. Last was her hair, which made the water run black.

She turned off the faucet and wrung out her hair, then tied it in a knot at the back of her head so it wouldn't get in her way. She wrapped herself in the coat, rubbing her arms to generate some warmth. The water had chilled her, or maybe she was just afraid.

She crouched with her back against the lab table, facing the door, and took the deepest breaths she could manage.

It had gone this way before. Waking in a strange place and having to wait there until her captor, the Dark One, decided to do something. Falling asleep out of sheer exhaustion. She didn't know what had happened to her before she was taken to the room, while she was unconscious, and she wasn't sure how long he had stood at her bedside watching her before touching her face to wake her. The lost time had plagued her more than she would have expected it to — the idea that her body had no memory of its own, that she could not interrogate it for the answer.

She stayed crouched there, counting each breath so she could be sure that time was passing, until her feet went numb. She was just standing up to get her blood moving again when a key turned in the lock. Sloane backed up fast, moving until she hit the boards that covered the window frame. Her chest ached. She couldn't hear anything but the whisper of the Dark One saying her name.

The Resurrectionist stood in the doorway, the living dead woman visible just past his bulky shoulder. Nero had said that the Resurrectionist wore five siphons. He had miscounted. There was one over each of the man's eyes, one over his nose and mouth, one on his throat; a siphon for each hand; one over an ear. Each one was plain, made of dark metal that looked like pewter.

He had a loping gait, not quite a limp, unstable and predatory. He made a flicking gesture paired with a sharp whistle, and the door slammed behind him.

They were alone.

Her vision was going dark at the edges. She felt a tingling in her chest, in her hands, the same sensation she'd had when she encountered the Needle in the sunken *Sakhalin* and the magical weapon in the Dome. Whoever and whatever the Resurrectionist was, he was suffused with magic.

"Ziva was the one who noticed." His voice was distorted by the siphon and had that tinny quality she had noticed on the street when he'd whistled. He spoke as if they had been in the middle of a conversation. "All those sorcerers in their fine clothing scurrying about like rats. Something going on, clearly." He cocked his head. "I have eyes wherever I need them. And the things the eyes said about you. No siphon. Always in the company of that hulking soldier—"

"The one you *killed,* you mean?" The question came out hot and fierce. She drew a harsh breath.

"No apparent knowledge of our world." He continued as if he hadn't been interrupted. "Are you hyperventilating?"

"Fuck you," Sloane said, her fingers curling into the paint and plaster.

"No magic, not even when you had no other choice," he said. "Does that mean you can't use it? I wonder." He tilted his head to the other side. "But why would they summon a soldier from another dimension to kill me if she couldn't use magic?"

The plaster bit into the skin under her fingernails. He knew. He knew where she was from, what she was meant to do—

But how?

She remembered the look in Mox's eyes at the bar, how he had been waiting for something she hadn't given him. *I have eyes wherever I need them.* Mox had been the Resurrectionist's eyes, rescuing her from the snare, luring her to the Tankard, then asking enough questions to figure out she was in the wrong world.

Sloane cursed herself. She had been so stupid. Aelia and Nero wanted her to stay inside, stay safe, but she had been confident, cocky, a child playing at heroics. And now she would die for it.

"It would have been simple to end it, but then—*the others,*" the Resurrectionist said. "How many are there?"

"If you touch them," Sloane said, launching herself off the wall, "I'll—"

"Hit me with a pipe that turns to dust?" he said, voice turning unctuous. "You aren't being fair. You and your friends come to kill me and I'm not allowed to fight back?"

"You're destroying this world," she said. "And my world. What's fair about that?"

"Destroying the world? *Me?*" He laughed darkly. "I should be flattered, I suppose, that you think I can control that level of destruction while having a street fight."

Sloane thought of his dark silhouette against the turbulent blur of the Drain. It had not ceased even for a moment as he took Kyros down and chased her.

"This world, your world, they destroy themselves. All worlds do." He was shifty, restless, even, with the weight of siphons anchoring him. "They don't need me."

"Is that how you justify it?"

"How are you being compensated?" he said. "Pennies, nickels, and dimes? Power to take back with you? What?"

"*Compensated?*"

"Ah, you're a true hero, then." He sounded almost amused. "Scandalized by the mere mention of an exchange—"

"I didn't choose to come here!" she said. "And if I could get myself home, I would be gone already."

But it didn't seem like he heard her. He jerked his head to the side, like he was listening to something in the distance. Then he wheeled around and stormed out of the room. The door slammed shut behind him.

Sloane was still for a while after he left. Her fear had settled to a low flame. She knew the Dark One. She knew the gritty feeling of being near him, the twist of her gut when his focus found her. Didn't she?

Enough, she thought, and she turned to the boarded window behind her. It was her best chance at escape. Wood broke. Boards burned. Windows opened up to ledges and streets and the cold night air.

She started pulling out drawers and opening cabinets. They were made of flimsy plywood, and time had made them brittle. Good kindling, maybe, but that didn't help her unless she wanted to burn the room down around her. Still, she pulled the drawers free of their tracks and stacked them on top of the table. They were assets.

Blunt force was the first thing to try. She picked up one of the larger drawers and swung it hard at the window boards.

The drawer shattered, leaving Sloane holding only the drawer pull and half the front panel. She tossed it aside.

There were gaps between the boards in the window that were wide enough for her fingers. She grabbed one of the boards and put her feet up on the wall to give herself leverage. Sloane pushed with her feet as she pulled with both hands at the wood, straining with all her strength to break it, or even loosen it. But . . . nothing. Her hands ached, and she swallowed a frustrated scream.

She was not going to die here. Not in a rotten room in a parallel dimension.

What she needed, she thought, was more pressure than her body could apply. Which she could accomplish with either more force—something she couldn't get her hands on right now—or a smaller surface area.

Sloane stared at the boards for a few seconds, praising whatever had set the laws of the universe and also empowered her to remember them. Then she stood next to the drainpipe sticking out of the wall. The slip nut that held the drain extension to the U-shaped trap was old, simple to loosen with her hand. She held on to the drain flange and pulled hard. The piece—inlet, flange, and trap—separated from the extension and the escutcheon plate against the wall. The pipe was solid, heavy. She put it on the table.

She wriggled out of her coat and unbuttoned her shirt, ignoring the sudden chill. Once the shirt was off, she put the coat back on and buttoned it up to her throat. She twisted the shirt into a rope and shoved the tail of it through the gap between the boards.

It was annoying work, like threading a needle when you couldn't keep your hands steady. Even with her fingers stuck through the gap on either side of the board, she couldn't maneuver the makeshift rope to pull it through the other gap. She tried again and again, missing the fabric each time. Sweat was starting to bead on the back of her neck. The longer she spent doing this, she thought, the more likely it was that someone was going to interrupt her.

Finally she caught the rope on the other side of the board. Then she had to do it again. She needed to use two boards against each other, like the bars of an old-fashioned prison cell. It was easier the second time to maneuver the rope; she brought the end out on the other side of the second board and tied the two shirt ends together in a tight knot. She then grabbed the pipe, worked it through the center of the knot, and started turning it.

At first, she didn't notice a change. But the more she turned the pipe, the tighter the shirt fabric became around the boards, and soon it was difficult to turn the pipe at all. Sloane had to climb up, bracing herself on the window ledge, and force the pipe down as hard as she could. Her hand throbbed. But the boards were starting to creak.

Another turn, and the skin of her palms was starting to peel. The boards groaned.

Another turn, and they cracked.

Laughing, Sloane worked at the shirt knot to free the pipe, then used it to press into the weak spot in the boards, which were easier to bend now that she had made them give. Soon she had made a gap in the boards big enough for her body to fit through—but only just. She would have to crawl out.

Getting her head through was simple enough, though the broken wood scraped her scalp. It was still day, but the sun was getting low. The building had tiers, like a wedding cake, so she was above a lower level, the top covered in gravel. She wasn't sure how she would get down from *that* roof, but at least she could drop to the gravel without cracking her skull.

She forced her way through the boards, biting her lip to keep from screaming when the wood dug into her shoulders on either side. She sucked in her stomach hard, wriggled the rest of the way through, then toppled to the gravel roof, aching.

She knew better than to celebrate. She stood, brushed gravel off her clothes, and limped along the edge of the roof as she looked for a fire escape. Freedom was so close—just seven stories down—but out of reach unless she wanted to break her back. The Sears Tower was in full view, a dark giant against the clouds, and the Warner Tower wasn't far from it, the ripples of its western side reflecting gray back at her. She was facing the lake, and the building she was in sat on top of what would be Congress Parkway back home. She had driven beneath this building but didn't know what it was called.

Sloane walked the perimeter of the lower roof, but there was no ladder to be found. If she was going to escape, she would need to go back through the building.

At the other end of the roof was what she assumed was a stairway bulkhead with a door. It would likely lead to a stairwell not dissimilar from the one she had discovered in the Camel. If she was lucky, she would be able to get all the way to the first floor of this building, and then she could make a desperate run for it.

Sloane forced the door open—either it had been left unlocked or the lock had broken—and stepped into a dark stairwell that smelled like rot. She felt her way to a railing and held it tightly as she descended. It had been a long time since she'd had food or water. Her mouth was so dry it was starting to feel fuzzy. But she kept going, holding the thought of a glass of water in front of her like a carrot on a string.

She had made it past five landings when a light came on. Sloane jumped back against the wall, letting her eyes adjust. She heard footsteps. People talking. Close, and getting closer, as whoever they were climbed up the stairs. She went carefully down the last few steps to the door and tried to tug it open without making too much noise, but it was too heavy for that; she would need to pull harder.

Sloane counted down in her head, then yanked the door open. The hinges screeched, and she sprinted into the hallway beyond, where the linoleum was buckling just as it had been in the laboratory that had served as her cell.

Huge chunks of plaster were pulling away from the walls and in broken bits on the floor, and half the ceiling tiles were missing or dangling precariously overhead. She passed doors that opened to old offices with maroon carpeting and fluorescent lights. Charts still hung on one office's wall, tracking sick-leave trends in blue marker.

She looked out one of the few remaining windows to figure out which direction she was going. She spotted the Sears Tower, nearer now than it had been when she was on the roof, which meant she was moving north—closer to where she had first come in. Closer to the Resurrectionist's army.

She heard something behind her and ducked into one of the offices to hide. Except it wasn't quite an office—not anymore, at least. The walls that outlined cubicles and nooks were still there, but the debris had been cleared from the floor. In one corner was a mattress with a sheet patterned with faded flowers and a matching pillowcase. Stacked next to the pillow were a few books, only one of which she recognized: *The Manifestation of Impossible Wants*.

On one of the built-in desks near the front were neat piles of screws, wires, metal plates. In a box under the desk were old siphons in various stages of disrepair—one missing all the plates that would cover the palm, another missing all the fingers. A variety of screwdrivers were in a jar nearby, handles up, waiting to be used.

This was where someone lived.

She didn't know much about zombies—or whatever the proper term for the Resurrectionist's soldiers was, since they seemed too intelligent to be actual zombies—but she doubted they needed to sleep. So if this was anyone's bedroom, it was the Resurrectionist's. Which meant she couldn't have chosen a worse hiding place.

She heard voices again. Sloane slipped into another room that had clearly been a meeting space, judging by the long rickety table and the abundance of windows. These weren't boarded completely, giving her light to see by. In fact—

She was fairly sure she could open one.

Sloane wiggled the window by its handle, testing how loose it was in its frame. It shifted back and forth. She looked over her shoulder and paused to listen to the voices. They had gotten louder. She made out a few words:

"Stitch it back on, but—"

"Fuck," she whispered, and she shoved the window up as hard as she could. It slammed up in its frame, and she stuck her head out. She was two stories up. High enough that she would break a leg if she jumped.

She looked over her shoulder again. She couldn't see anything, but the voices had stopped. Sloane held her breath as she waited. There was a whine, the pressure of a foot against an old floor. The squeak of linoleum.

"Okay," she whispered to herself. "Okay, okay, okay."

She put her legs through the window and positioned herself on the windowsill.

Then, bracing herself for pain, Sloane jumped.

Sloane didn't look down at her right ankle. She didn't want to know.

Her eyes swam with tears. She bit down on her fist and limped as fast as she could, leaning against the alley wall for support. In a few yards, she would run out of wall, and she would have to put all her weight on her right foot.

Sloane stopped to wipe her eyes. She felt like someone was stabbing a knife repeatedly into her right leg. All her thoughts pulsed in time with the aching. She stepped away from the corner and screamed.

One more step, she told herself, gasping, even though she was at least one hundred paces from the river, where there was a railing she could put a hand on. She looked behind her, through a haze of tears, to see if any cars were coming. She saw nothing. Sloane stepped again. And again.

She walked all the way to the river, where she finally saw headlights.

At Long Last:
A Collection of Essays About the Chosen One

From the essay "Like a Dream"
by Laura Bryant

And it was there, watching my groceries spill across the street—
the onion rolling into the gutter
a bottle of milk broken and spilling into the cracks in the sidewalk
—that I first saw him.
The Resurrectionist's destructive gale had begun, the pull, the shredding,
    chewing of matter. And all around it, people screaming, screaming,
running.
Running for their lives.
I had toppled, twisting my ankle. One of the weaker ones of the herd, now
    vulnerable to attack by our world's most horrific predator, our would-be
    destroyer, our devil-made-flesh. My death was certain—
And yet.
Like a dream—
The Chosen One came forth. Golden hair glinting in the sun. The seal of the
    Army of Flickering beneath his shoulder, a tribute to his fallen comrades,
    his massacred men. A simple metal cuff around his throat, his siphon,
    his sword. A whistle clamped between his teeth, his shield. A new army,
    rebuilt on the ashes of the dead, at his back.
Our defender.
The Chosen One of Genetrix.

From the essay "My First Thought"
by Xevera Ibáñez

I saw a picture of him in the newspaper the day after the attack on Cordus. He
had fought, sung powerful workings into being, shaken windows, rattled doors in
their frames, but he hadn't won, and he hadn't lost. He was still among us, so we

were glad, but we were disappointed too. That he had not saved the world with one whistle.

It meant that more anguish awaited us. More streets split down the middle, more stonefaced mothers, children walking alone, men sitting on curbs and staring at nothing. More buildings torn apart by supernatural wind, more picking through rubble, torn curtains, shattered windows. More of all of this; more losing, more of having less.

I saw a picture of him standing next to a stop sign, golden hair, golden chain around his neck, golden band across his throat, lips pressed together, cheek dimpling, hand clasped in the mayor's hand in greeting.

My first thought was *I thought he would be taller.*

27

SLOANE LIMPED INTO THE STREET, waving her arms. The taxi screeched to a stop and she opened the door before the driver could decide she wasn't worth the trouble.

The driver, a clean-shaven, pale man in his early twenties, twisted in his seat to look at her. She propped her leg up next to her.

"Ma'am," he said, eyes wide, "are you—"

"I need to go to the Cordus Center," she said.

"I've gotta take you to the hospital, ma'am—"

"No," Sloane said, teeth gritted. She didn't want to navigate a Genetrix hospital by herself. "And if you call me ma'am again, I'm going to tuck and roll out of this car."

Sloane stared at the charms dangling from the rearview mirror for most of the drive back—a saint medal, half of a heart, a tiny plastic whistle. The radio was set to a Christian station, and one song's chorus—"Jesus, You did a working on my heart"—made her feel very far from home.

It was only when the car pulled up to the curb in front of the building that she remembered she didn't have any money. She was bickering with the driver at greater and greater volume when Cyrielle ran outside. Sloane had never been more relieved to see bright orange lipstick.

"Oh my God," Cyrielle said as Sloane stuck her swollen—*very* swollen—ankle out of the car. Cyrielle took a coin from the sack at her waist and thrust it at the taxi driver, then put an arm around Sloane to help her out of the car.

Sloane realized only then that she had done it. She had escaped.

She let herself relax once they were inside the Camel. Cyrielle sat her down on a bench near the main entrance, and Sloane watched orange diamonds scattered across the floor as the sun burned through the tiny panes of glass above her. The air was warm, and people rushed back and forth in front of her, stomping in heavy boots or snapping in fine, pointed shoes or squeaking in sneakers with marshmallow-white soles. Her right foot was bare—she had taken off the boot in the taxi upon realizing that the leather was pinching at her massive ankle—and turning purple. She hardly felt the pain anymore.

Something pricked at her attention. She lifted her head to see Matt half walking, half running across the lobby. His eyes were red—he had been crying. When their eyes met, he burst into a run, almost bowling over an old lady with tight gray curls. Sloane used the wall to push herself to her feet just in time for him to collide with her.

His arms wrapped around her middle, and he lifted her to her toes. It felt good to have his solid body against hers. The last time they had slept together, she hadn't appreciated it enough. Not just because Matt was all lean, finely tuned muscle, but because he was warm, and familiar, and kind. For the past few years, he hadn't exactly set her alight, but she had burned for him low and steady. She missed it, that fire, a pilot light that never went out.

Her hands had come up automatically to the middle of his back, which was damp with sweat. He set her down gently but didn't let her go. It struck her, suddenly, that he was trembling.

"Hey," she whispered into his ear. "It's okay. I'm okay."

"It was—all I could think was—" His voice was muffled by her shirt. He had buried his face in her shoulder. "All I could think was *Not again.*"

Not again. She had been thinking the same thing since they'd gotten to Genetrix: *Not again, not another Dark One, not another kidnapping, not another escape.* But she hadn't thought about what it might be like for Matt to watch her taken away a second time, not knowing if he would ever see her alive again, not knowing what she was enduring.

She hadn't actually thought about what he went through the first time either. Matt had been the leader of their group, unquestionably, and two of the people he led had been taken and tortured by their enemy. There was no way he hadn't blamed himself for it. He probably blamed himself now.

Sloane turned her face toward Matt's and spoke into the small space that separated them. "It wasn't the same," she said. She ran her hand over his short hair. "No one hurt me. Okay? I'm fine. Just . . . really smelly, probably."

A gurgle of a laugh—somewhat hysterical—was Matt's response. He relaxed his grip on her, and she offered him a small smile. She felt the first flicker of hope since she had returned the ring to him—hope that one day, when the pain dulled, they might be friends again.

Esther was waiting a few feet away. She had discovered Genetrix textiles, and she was wearing them all at once, a paisley scarf around her shoulders draped low enough to reveal her throat siphon; a checkerboard blouse; pinstriped pants; orange herringbone socks. When Matt and Sloane separated, she came forward and hugged Sloane a little more delicately than Matt had.

"Kyros?" Sloane said as Esther pulled away. The name came out soft. She could hardly stand to say it.

"Alive, but not conscious. They're not sure he'll ever wake up. I did a working. The breath. Got his lungs going again," Esther said, a sharp glint in her eyes that looked like pride.

An ache in Sloane's chest eased a little. She hadn't been able to think of Kyros since she was taken, but the sight of him falling at the Resurrectionist's hand hadn't left her.

"You're hurt?" Matt said, pointing to her bulbous ankle.

"Jumped out a window to escape," Sloane said. "Pretty sure I need a doctor. Or maybe a new leg."

"Cyrielle went to get one. A doctor, not a leg," Matt said. Sloane hadn't even noticed that Cyrielle was gone, but there was no orange haunting the edges of her vision. "She said someone could come to you."

"Good."

Esther stood on Sloane's left, Matt on her right. Both wrapped their arms around her waist to support her as she hobbled toward the elevator bank; she hardly even needed to put her feet on the ground. Esther sang the right note to summon the elevator.

There was relief in this too — that despite what she had kept from them and despite what they had all been through, they were still with her.

Not all was lost.

That night, she dreamed about stumbling barefoot across a field, her arm wrapped around Albie's waist as he wheezed in her ear. Her arm was slippery with his blood. She stopped, adjusting her grip on his body. Albie screamed into his teeth.

It was dark, but she knew it was morning by the dew on the grass. It wet her ankles.

She woke with a throbbing jaw, from gritting her teeth, and swallowed her last benzo.

Two days later, Sloane found herself in Aelia's office with crutches tucked under her arms.

The doctor had set up his equipment in Sloane's sparse room the night before and crouched at the foot of the bed with her foot in his lap. He had an elaborate whistle between his teeth, a modified oscilloscope that told him the frequency of the sound he made to the third decimal place, and a siphon over his eye that looked like half a visor. He'd used all three in concert, puffing the whistle to find the pitch on the oscilloscope and then gesturing to begin the working that let him see the break in her bone. In the haze of her sleep deprivation it had felt like a holy ritual.

He had set the bone with strong, cold hands and little apology and promised a cast the following day—and a siphon that would speed the healing of her bones.

Now both siphon and cast were wrapped around her leg, and she'd been told to use crutches for two weeks.

She was scrubbed clean of the soot and dirt of the Drain, but the feeling clung to her still, like a lucid dream.

Aelia's office was, in a word, clean. Wood floors, white walls, a single shelf with color-coded books. There were white orchids in large white planters by the window. The door closed behind Sloane with a heavy thump.

She had passed by Nero's workshop on the way to Aelia's office, and his doors were the same: thick and wooden, with heavy metal hinges and knobs, locked by magic. Their intimidating appearance made her wonder what was kept in the two spaces that required such tight security.

Sloane still caught phantom whiffs of sulfur every few minutes, even though her hair now smelled like the rosemary shampoo Cyrielle had brought them. She detected it now as Nero came forward to take her crutches and lean them against the wall so she could sit down. He settled in the chair beside her.

Aelia folded her hands on top of her clean white desk, the delicate metal plates of her wrist siphon tinkling as they touched each other. Her fingernails were painted a matte rose and filed into perfect half-ovals.

Sloane had written her statement the day before and passed it along to Aelia and Nero through Cyrielle. But they had summoned her here this morning anyway, citing the need to ask her a few follow-up questions. She couldn't imagine what more she could say about what had happened. She had already ripped herself apart for them.

"So," Sloane said, because no one had spoken for a few seconds. "You had some questions for me?"

"How are you feeling, Sloane?" Aelia's smile had to be forced. Sloane wasn't someone people smiled at, and Aelia wasn't someone who smiled.

"Peachy," Sloane said. "Your questions?"

Aelia glanced at Nero, who cleared his throat. He leaned toward Sloane, his legs crossed at the ankle. His socks had small magic wands on them. Sloane suppressed a smile.

"We were concerned for you because we detected a certain . . . sympathy in the tone of your statement," Nero said.

"Sympathy for the Resurrectionist, that is," Aelia clarified.

"What?" Sloane scowled. "He had me kidnapped; of course I don't have sympathy for him."

"But in your statement, you said something about him seeming . . . troubled."

"He's just different than I expected, that's all."

"Different how, exactly?" Nero cocked his head, reminding Sloane of the therapist she had seen after the Dive, all furrowed brow and tilted head.

"He's not the Dark One," Sloane said. "I thought maybe he was the parallel version of the Dark One from our universe. I see now that's not the case. That's all."

"Our concern is not without foundation," Aelia said. "The Resurrectionist has swayed people to his cause before. He has — a particular charm."

"Charm?" Sloane raised her eyebrows. "Where in my statement did you see a goddamn thing about him being charming?"

"Well, it doesn't begin that way," Nero said. "We suspect he may use some kind of persuasive working —"

"Who did he do this to before?" Sloane interrupted.

Nero and Aelia exchanged a look.

"Who she was is of no import," Aelia said.

"She was obviously of *import* or you wouldn't be warning me about it," Sloane replied.

Nero glanced at Aelia again. "As I said, we just wanted to check in with you to ensure that —"

"Well, I wanted to talk to you, actually," Sloane said. "Because it sounded like the Resurrectionist had dealt with someone in my position before. Another Chosen One, I mean. Did Genetrix's Chosen One ever meet him? You know — before dying?"

"We did not oversee our Chosen One's activities as much as we should have, perhaps because we believed everything would go according to plan, as the prophecy indicated," Aelia said. "As you can plainly tell, we won't be making that mistake again."

"But I notice you're still not volunteering to fight him yourself," Sloane said.

"It's not wrong to know your own limits," Aelia retorted, her cheeks going pink.

"Isn't it?" Sloane shrugged. "I've never had the luxury of knowing mine."

"Then you are as unwise as your predecessor," Aelia snapped. "She, too, believed the Resurrectionist was merely wounded, that an accord or some kind of reconciliation was possible. She was incorrect, and she paid the ultimate penalty for it. Is that what you wanted to hear?"

The words crashed into Sloane, one at a time. *She was incorrect.*

But when Aelia, standing in the rubble of the old Drain site, had told them that Genetrix's Chosen One was dead, she had called him "he." He *was valiant and a talented worker of magic.* He *is dead.* He *was defeated.*

"So the person the Resurrectionist manipulated before . . . it was your Chosen One," Sloane said, trying to sound casual. "You could have just said."

"Well, I didn't want to alarm you unnecessarily, particularly so soon after a traumatic event." Aelia straightened her crisp shirt.

Sloane leaned back in her chair. She had just caught Aelia using two different pronouns for the same person. But she didn't want to call attention to it—not yet.

"Do I seem alarmed?" Sloane said. "Or do I seem pissed that you're trying my patience when all I want to do is kill this asshole and go home?"

Aelia pursed her lips.

"Cool," Sloane said. "Now, if you'll hand over my crutches, I'll be limping back to my room."

"That's . . ." Esther furrowed her brow. "Odd."

Sloane sat in the doorway facing the elevator so she would see if anyone was coming toward them. Her right leg was stretched out on the broad boards of the floor of Esther's room; her crutches leaned against the inexplicable holy water stoup fixed to the wall that Esther was using to hold her jewelry.

"*Odd* is not the word I would have chosen," Sloane said. "*Alarming* or *suspicious*, maybe."

"I don't think I understand what's so alarming," Matt said. He had unbuttoned his shirt cuffs and was rolling up the sleeves. He wore his siphon all the time now—he and Esther both did. That morning Sloane had caught them turning their breakfast coffees into ice. "People misspeak all the time. It probably doesn't mean anything."

"Have you ever randomly started referring to me as 'he'?" Sloane said.

"Well, no," Matt said. "But maybe they were trans and Aelia just slipped up with the pronouns, or maybe she didn't really know them at the time, or—"

Esther interrupted him. "Why didn't you just ask her about it when it happened?"

"I figured if she told one lie, she might tell another," Sloane said. "Seemed safer to hold it in for the time being."

"I still think—" Matt began.

Esther cut him off again. "Don't be dumb," she said. "Aelia was obviously talking about two different people. Nero and Aelia have been lying to us. But we don't know why. It's just as likely it's for a good reason as a bad one."

"I can't believe you guys." Sloane slapped the floor with her palm. "These people kidnapped us from another dimension. They're holding us hostage until we fight their bad guy. And you're having trouble believing they would lie to us? Why—because they said please and thank you?"

"Always with the drama." Esther rolled her eyes. "All I'm doing is trying not to freak out; I'm not campaigning for them to get the Nobel Prize."

Matt was toying with the string that kept his siphon tight to his hand, turning it around and around his fingertip. "Even if Aelia did lie and it was for some insidious reason," he said, "what are we sup-posed to do about it? Our only path home is still through her."

He wasn't wrong, Sloane thought. No matter what Aelia was hid-ing, no matter what was really going on with Genetrix and Earth, wouldn't they still do whatever they had to to get home? The thought of spending the rest of her life here, surrounded by taffeta and the *clink* of siphon plates, made her feel suffocated. This was not her planet. Not her life.

Even if she had nothing but heartache waiting for her back on Earth—moving out of the apartment she shared with Matt, griev-ing over Albie, navigating the scrutiny of the media—at least that life belonged to her. But she couldn't forget the strange relief of hear-ing Aelia make her misstep, of finally having a name for what she had been feeling since she pulled herself out of the Chicago River: She was being lied to. And Sloane hated lies unless she was the one telling them. "I'll get proof," Sloane said. "And I'll confront her with it. She won't be able to lie to me then."

"I can talk to Cyrielle," Matt offered. "Just casually, not an inter-rogation."

Sloane recognized that as the peace offering it was and gave him a small smile.

"Nothing like a casual conversation about dead Chosen Ones over dinner," Esther said.

"Cyrielle, huh?" Sloane said. She meant to tease him, but it came out sounding flat, almost accusatory.

"Something else you'd like to ask?" he said quietly.

Sloane felt that awful swelling inside her—in her throat, in her chest, in her stomach—that meant she might burst into tears. She put her hands on the door frame behind her and pushed herself to her feet. "No," she said once she was steadier. "I'm gonna go. Tired."

It was obviously a lie. But Matt, in his infinite courtesy, let her tell it.

Le Quoi

by Artificielle

What is it?

Is it

IS it?

What is

is

Is itwhatit is

I

S

I

S

IT!

what

28

THE WEEKS THAT FOLLOWED brought Sloane boredom and frustration. The doctor had told her not to train with siphons for two weeks at least, so no one bothered her about practicing. She wasn't supposed to walk without crutches, and the crutches hurt her armpits, so she spent most of her time in one place, reading *The Manifestation of Impossible Wants*. That place was a small bench down the hall from Nero's workshop.

Few people approached the doors. Even fewer made it through them, and those who did were always escorted by Nero himself. It was as if the magic keeping the door secure responded only to him.

That was why she had chosen his office as her target instead of Aelia's. The praetor had at least granted Nero and Cyrielle access to her space. Nero had granted access to no one, which meant he was protecting something important.

At first, Sloane tried to think of an excuse for Nero to let her in. But Nero himself had become more elusive in the days since their conversation in Aelia's office. He had asked her why she liked to read on that bench the first day he saw her there, and she had gestured to the window across from it, which had a view of the Sears Tower. After that, he took another route to his workshop so he didn't have to walk past her.

It took two weeks for Sloane to hear it. She had gotten up when

she saw Nero approaching the workshop doors and rushed forward
—as much as she could, anyway—to engage him in conversation.
But he'd pretended not to see her and slipped into the workshop just
as she was close enough to speak to him. She watched as the heavy
double doors closed and then—the shift of a deadbolt.

She had been assuming that Nero secured his office through some
kind of working on the threshold. But what if his magic was applied
only to the lock?

After that, Sloane begged some money from Cyrielle and went to a
nearby hardware store—wearing a new brace that she didn't need to
use her crutches with—to buy a hammer and a screwdriver.

"I can't believe I agreed to this," Esther said.

"Don't act like I dragged you here," Sloane said, pointing at her
with the screwdriver. It had a royal-blue handle and the brand name
SIPHONA TECHNICA stamped in gold along the side. Sloane hooked a
finger around Esther's watchband and brought the watch face closer
so she could see the time. "All right, let's go. But remember our story
if Nero's there?"

"Your leg siphon thing is emitting a high-pitched noise and we
need him to have a look at it," Esther said. "You know he's not going to buy that, though, right? We could have just gone to Cyrielle."

"He's not going to be there anyway. I've been watching his ins and
outs for two weeks, and he never stays past five."

"You're such a creep."

Sloane smiled with all teeth and shoved the stairwell door open
with her shoulder.

Together she and Esther walked down the wide, windowed hallway that led to Nero's workshop. They passed the bench where
Sloane had spent so much time reading and a monochromatic pink
sculpture that reminded her of a kidney. The double doors of Nero's office looked like they belonged in a castle rather than in the
Camel, with huge pins in the old, rusty hinges. Lucky for her and
Esther.

"Just tell me if anyone's coming," she said to Esther, crouching awkwardly in front of the lowest of the three hinges. She stuck the end of the screwdriver up against the bottom of the hinge pin and hit it with the hammer, forcing the pin up. Once it stuck out above the hinge, she wiggled it free. One down, two to go.

"So the magic on the door doesn't prevent this?" Esther said. "That seems like a major oversight."

"You'd think so, wouldn't you?" Sloane moved on to the second hinge. "But all he does with magic is secure the lock—the working slides the deadbolt in place and holds it there. The magic isn't acting on the door itself, because if it were, why would Nero bother with a mechanical lock at all? It would be unnecessary. They rely on magic for everything here."

"And you thought of this . . . how?"

"I read the newspaper. You wouldn't *believe* how many robberies happen in this city just because people rely on magic security and forget that practical measures sometimes undo it—they've totally lost touch with how simple things work." Sloane finished the third hinge and stuck the flat head of the screwdriver between hinge and wall to wiggle the door out of place.

The magical deadbolt held, so the door dangled oddly from that one point like a loose tooth clinging to its last tender ligament.

"Success," she said. She turned sideways and slipped into the office.

"If we get stuck on Genetrix for some reason," Esther said, "you should consider a career as a criminal."

"I'll take it under advisement. Hurry, somebody's gonna notice this door pretty quickly." She turned to look at Nero's workshop for the first time. It was a large space with pale, moody light coming in from a ceiling that was structured like a greenhouse, a geometry of translucent white panels letting in daylight. The walls were covered in decorative stone friezes, making the room look like an ancient temple with holy symbols all around it. But the place itself was cluttered with books and equipment, bits of old siphons and the tools to fix them, texts in multiple languages lying open or stacked on top of each other.

Esther took something out of her pocket. It was a whistle, about the length of one of her fingers. Sloane had seen people on the street and in the lobby of the Camel with them between their teeth, puffing away as they did more complex workings.

Esther stuck the whistle between her lips and blew a long, low note. Nothing happened, so she tried again, her eyes closing and her brow furrowing as she focused her intent. Faint light pricked at the corner of Sloane's eyes, and Esther lunged at a nearby stack of books for a slim black journal hidden in the pile. She flipped to the glowing page and read aloud:

The Chosen One describes his unique perception of magic as fine strings of light, like threads in a loom, connecting people to each other, to objects, and to the ground. It is that last piece that most interests me — the magic that penetrates the earth must delve deeper than dirt; it must be connected to something in the heart of our planet, something we cannot yet comprehend . . . perhaps something broken apart by the missile fired into Tenebris Gorge, which would account for the promulgation of what we call magic throughout Genetrix.

"Nero's journal?" Esther stopped reading and asked.

"Looks like he's got a few," Sloane said, gesturing to a thin whisper of light in a stack near Esther. She wandered through the workshop looking at the books Nero had left open for any other glimmers she could find. *Advanced Siphon Repair*, volume 3. *Spine, Chest, Gut: A Study of the Lesser Used Siphons. String Theory for the Magical Mind.* She ran her fingers over the pages as she hobbled to the edge of the room. There she found a small alcove almost like a window seat, but instead of a cushion, as she'd expected, there was a table.

Esther started reading again.

Thus far I have been able to view other universes, but I have not attempted to act upon them. It is more important at this stage to find a viable universe within which to work. There are a few parameters: the presence of at least some magic, for one thing; no language barrier, for another; a point of departure within the last fifty or so years, to improve the subject's ability to adapt to Genetrix; and a champion or so-called Chosen One that is capable of completing the task at hand. It is incomprehensibly difficult to find a world that will suit . . .

She trailed off.

The table stood before a window with small, diamond-shaped panes. Through them, Sloane could see only the blurred shapes of the city turning black and blue as the sun set. There were a few small objects on the windowsill: a pocket watch with a broken chain, a small pair of pink spectacles, a ring with a purple stone. Beneath the spectacles—which were cat-eye-shaped—was a paper crane. Sloane pinched the beak between her thumb and forefinger and held it up to the light. It was as precisely folded as one of Albie's.

"Wait, I've got something else," Esther said.

I have spent days sorting through coalescing clouds of matter that have not yet formed Earth; molten worlds too toxic to sustain life; gaseous worlds embroiled in constant storms. I have seen Earths riven in two by massive asteroids, Earths overrun with feathered dinosaurs, Earths saturated with oceans. And I have even seen Earths that are barren from onslaughts of atomic bombs, Earths emptied of human life by some sort of plague — the houses still intact, the morning's breakfast rotten on the table.

Esther moved to another journal, this one red, the size of her palm.

My champion is dead. He was killed by the Resurrectionist last night, at a quarter past midnight, on the beach along the lakefront path. The victim of the Resurrectionist's favorite method of killing, the antithesis of the magical breath, a kind of magical collapsing . . .

The paper crane Sloane held was made out of notebook paper, wide-ruled. In the ridge of the crane's back, she saw a scribble of pink, like someone had tested a pen. After glancing over at Esther—now flipping through the red journal frantically in search of another glowing page—Sloane tugged the ends of the crane to unmake the origami.

The paper had been used to test all sorts of pens, she discovered.

But they were in bright colors, shimmering, neon, milky. The kind Albie had used, even after the rest of them teased him for it. But Sloane hadn't seen anything like them on Genetrix. People here used elaborate, old-fashioned instruments—feather quills, fountain pens, metal styluses retrofitted with ballpoints.

"Essy," Sloane said.

Esther's voice rang out: "'The second of my champions is dead.' Oh my God, Sloane."

Sloane and Esther locked eyes across the room.

"The *second*," Esther said.

"Isn't that supposed to be us?" Sloane said, forgetting the note-book paper in her hand for a moment. "Genetrix's Chosen One was first, and then they brought us here . . . right?"

"So the story goes," Esther replied, a distant look in her eyes.

"Keep going," Sloane said.

My search will continue — must continue — until a suitable candidate presents itself. I will scour the endless worlds for a lifetime if I need to . . .

"That lying sack of shit," Sloane said.

"How many were there?" Esther stared at Sloane. "Dozens? Hundreds? If they didn't survive, how the hell are *we* supposed to? We barely beat *our* Dark One, and that was on a world that didn't know magic—" She choked and fell silent.

"If he's lying about this, he could be lying about a lot of other things," Sloane said. "How hard it is to send us home, for one thing." She crossed the room and put her hands on Esther's shoulders. "Don't freak out. Not yet, anyway."

"What's that?" Esther was looking at the paper crumpled between Sloane's hand and her shoulder.

"It was a paper crane," Sloane said. "It reminded me of—"

"Oh." Something like pity softened Esther's eyes, and Sloane pulled away.

"We got what we came for," Sloane said, "now let's go, before Nero—"

"I'm afraid it's a bit too late for that," Nero said. He tapped the lock that held the door in place with a finger, and the door fell to the ground with a loud bang.

Sloane, acting on instinct, brandished the sheet of notebook paper in Nero's general direction. All three of them—Nero, Esther, and Sloane—just stared at the page she was holding like a sword until she put it down.

For just a moment, as Nero stomped on the fallen door, his teeth gritted, his blond hair spilling into his eyes, Sloane saw someone to be afraid of. But then he brushed off his gray sweater with both hands, flicked his hair out of his face, and again become mildness personified.

"I am not sure what I did to provoke suspicion profound enough for you to break into my workshop," Nero said evenly.

Sloane had a sudden, desperate desire to find whatever sensitive place she had just discovered in him and dig in as hard as she could.

"Well, there was the whole 'kidnapping-three-people-from-a-parallel-dimension' thing," Sloane said. "But most recently, it was Aelia referring to the Chosen One as alternately 'she' and 'he' in the span of one conversation."

"Ah." Nero ran his fingers over the door handle. "I told her you noticed that. She didn't listen."

"We came here for proof," Sloane said. "So unless your diaries are your first attempt at novel-writing—not great, by the way—"

"How many were there?" The question was sudden, and shrill. Esther lurched toward him, looking like she might strangle him. "How many Chosen Ones did you rip from their dimensions to fight your goddamned Dark One?"

"The only reason you weren't told is I didn't want to alarm you," Nero said. "Any of you. Not when you didn't know magic, not—"

"I take it these are really valuable books," Sloane said, picking up one of the journals and holding it open by the spine as if preparing to rip it in half.

"In fact—"

Sloane jerked the two halves of the journal apart, tearing it down the binding.

"There's no need to be—"

"I don't know, I kind of feel the need," Sloane said. "Considering you didn't mention that we're, what, tenth in line to fight your little death match for you?"

"You," Nero said, suddenly quiet, "are fifth."

"*Fifth?*" Esther shrieked.

"We summoned others because we did not *want* to summon inexperienced, barely competent magic-users to fight the Resurrectionist," Nero said, raising his voice. He clenched his siphon hand into a fist and sparks danced over the metal plates. "We mined universes with successful Chosen Ones who were also capable magic-users. All of them fell to the Resurrectionist. All for the sake of Earth and Genetrix. Finally we couldn't stand the losses anymore. We decided that a personal stake in the fight might compensate for a lack of magic experience. So we took you. Yes. Ten years of battles, and finally we took you."

He scowled down at his hand as if it were disobeying him. The sparks faded.

"Did it seriously never occur to you that you didn't need a Chosen One at all?" Sloane said.

"You act like others have not attempted to take him down," Nero said. "For every Chosen One we have had, at least ten ordinary men and women have died trying to kill him, and that does not, by the way, include all the thousands of people who have died in the Drains."

Esther's cheeks shone with tears.

"I kept it from you because it is alarming . . . and demoralizing," Nero said, quiet again. "Because I didn't want any of you to feel defeated before you even made an attempt. I knew that you, Sloane, in particular, were still fragile, incapable of accessing your magic reliably, and then you were taken by the Resurrectionist, and—"

"I," Sloane said, "am not fragile."

"I don't intend to insult you," Nero said. "But you suffered a unique trauma at the hands of your Dark One, and—"

"Shut *up.*" It wasn't Sloane who interrupted him this time, but Esther. She wiped her cheeks dry and tugged at the neck of her stiff blouse to draw attention to her siphon. "Or I will set you on fucking fire."

Nero showed his palms.

"Come on," Esther said to Sloane. "We have to tell Matt. Unless you have other lies to confess to?"

Sloane tried her best to look dignified as she hobbled toward the door, following Esther. When she reached the threshold, Nero spoke again.

"Don't forget," he said, and his voice was cold enough to make the back of her neck prickle. "All of you still need me to get home. And you need to kill the Resurrectionist if you want a home to go back to."

Sloane didn't turn; she just kept walking, unevenly, toward the elevator.

"I have returned with a gift," Matt announced from the doorway of Sloane's room. They had started calling it "the White Room," for obvious reasons. Matt's was "the Cabin," and Esther's was "the Church."

Sloane was sitting with her back against the headboard. Esther, wearing sweatpants, was on the floor, two fingers stuck in a jar of peanut butter. They had all taken to eating peanut butter—in sandwiches, on apples, spread over crackers—because the brand, Nutty Buddy, was the same on Earth and Genetrix, and so was the flavor. One of the only perfect matches they had found.

Matt held up a bottle of dark liquor. "Bourbon," he said. "Courtesy of Cyrielle."

Esther applauded.

"Was she apologizing for not telling us we're fucked?" Sloane said from the bed.

"She didn't know," Matt said. "She's only been working for Aelia for a year."

Sloane snorted.

"Do not scorn the one who got us bourbon," Matt said. "Just because you just got affirmed in Trusting No One."

"My worldview is the correct worldview," Sloane said, "and you expect me not to gloat?"

Matt laughed, and for a moment they were what they had been before. He unscrewed the cap of the bourbon and took a swig. As he swallowed, he passed the bottle to Esther. "I don't agree that we're fucked, though," Matt said.

"We're the fifth in line to fight the Resurrectionist," Esther said. "We're the only ones who don't really know how to use magic. One of us has already gotten kidnapped." She sat up and offered the bottle of bourbon to Sloane, who took it and sipped.

The bourbon tasted like vanilla and peanuts. Sloane winced and passed it back to Matt.

"We're fucked," Esther finished.

"That's the thing, though." Matt sat on the floor next to Esther, took a swig from the bottle, and passed it to Esther. "I think there's something to it, the whole history-repeating-itself thing."

Sloane raised an eyebrow.

"If history wants to repeat, that's fine with me," Matt said. "We *won* last time, remember?"

"Man's got a point," Esther said, pointing the bottle at him.

"I don't know," Sloane said. "I don't think we should fight at all."

"And just let the Resurrectionist destroy both of our universes?" Matt said.

"Nero lying about this means everything could be a lie. The universes might not be connected. The Resurrectionist might not be our enemy. The—"

"Not our enemy?" Matt was incredulous. "He kidnapped you. He's killed God knows how many people. He was controlling the Drain!"

"I know." Sloane leaned her forehead against her hand. "I know that, okay? I'm just saying—"

"We verified the connection between universes," Esther said, giving Sloane the bottle. "You found that article."

"One article doesn't prove it definitively," Sloane said. "And now we know Nero's a liar."

"And we know the Resurrectionist is a murderer," Matt said.

"I'm not saying we should go grab a beer with him or anything, just that we should be more thorough about confirming what Nero says!" She held the bottle out to him.

"Yeah. Okay." Matt grabbed it and drank.

A few hours later, the bourbon was almost gone, and Esther was splayed across the foot of the bed, fast asleep. Sloane had the bottle cradled in her lap, and Matt was on the floor, leaning against the wall. They had been quiet for a long time, but neither of them had left. Sloane didn't want to. She wanted to stay inside the quiet company for as long as she could.

"This sucks," Matt said, out of nowhere.

Sloane nodded.

"I don't know how to not be with you," he said. "Can't date anyone normal at home. Can't stop seeing you altogether."

"I mean, you *could,*" Sloane said.

He shook his head. "No. You and me and Esther and Ines . . . we're bound for life. It's like a marriage. Better or worse. Sickness and health . . ."

Sloane gripped the bourbon bottle tightly.

"You ever think we should just stay here?" Matt said. "Nobody knows we're Chosen here. Could go on a real date. Nobody staring. Nobody asking for an autograph."

"You wouldn't be able to get the best table just by winking," Sloane pointed out.

"Yeah." He sighed. "And probably they'd racially profile me. Win some, lose some."

Sloane stifled a laugh. It wasn't actually funny—none of this was—but the bourbon had made mirth bubble up inside her like carbonation, and everything seemed soft at the edges. She cleared her throat, trying to bring it all back into focus. "You'll figure out how to do this," she said. "We both will. We'll figure out how to be friends."

Matt sniffed. A tear ran down his cheek, and he wiped it away. "I know."

"I'm not okay," she said. "I know I seem like I am. I'm good as long as I keep moving, but when we're home—when I stop—" She made an explosion sound. "Pop goes the Sloanie."

"I guess that shouldn't be reassuring," he said. "But it is."

Sloane put the bottle on the nightstand and closed her eyes.

29

I T DIDN'T TAKE LONG for Matt to demand further proof of the connection between universes or for Aelia to agree to give it to him. She had to have heard about Sloane and Esther breaking into Nero's office, and she likely wanted to appease them—at least, that was Sloane's theory. So it was only two days later that Aelia, Cyrielle, Sloane, Matt, and Esther stood on the edge of the river, looking out over the water.

Two years after the fall of the Dark One, the five Chosen Ones had presided over the dyeing of the Chicago River on St. Patrick's Day. Esther had put on a green dress covered in sequins and a green wig to match it; she had looked like the queen of a parade. They had stood on the deck of a boat, the orange powder dye spraying behind them, turning the murky water electric, while a massive crowd cheered.

"There are places where the boundaries of our universes appear to be more permeable," Aelia said now. "We have been able to detect where a few of those places are. Water appears to be a commonality among them. This is one of them."

Sloane thought of the ballistic missile loosed from the USS *Tenebris* rocketing toward the deepest part of the ocean.

And of diving for the Needle, the flippers on her feet propelling her deeper than she ought to have gone.

And of the blast that had thrown her into the water when the

Dark One died, and the eerie glow of his cheek as he turned away from her.

Water, she thought. *Sure.*

"We do not have the power necessary to break through the barrier between our universes now," Aelia said. "Nothing will be able to pass through it. But our former Chosen One taught us that magic can be . . . observed. We can do a working to help one of you perceive the magical connections that exist. However, one of you must swim down to where the barrier is thinnest to witness what we have seen of the connections between universes. Which one of you is the strongest swimmer?"

Sloane felt everyone's eyes on her. She was, after all, the first one to have emerged from this same river and the one who had gotten her scuba-diving certification when training to retrieve the Needle. And the one who had spent summers at the community pool with Cameron, the two of them challenging each other to hold their breath longer, and longer, and longer . . .

"Me," Sloane said.

Aelia's mouth pinched like she was sucking on hard candy, but she nodded. Today she wore three clashing black-and-white patterns: striped billowing slacks; a houndstooth jacket with a long line of tiny buttons; a checkerboard cape with a high collar. She reminded Sloane of a circus performer.

"We can do a working on you so that you can breathe underwater for a short time," Aelia said. "If that's all right with you."

"Yeah," Sloane said. She bent over to untie her shoe. Her other leg was still wrapped in a siphon. "Sure."

As Aelia cast a working to keep Sloane warm in the cold water, Cyrielle produced a large handkerchief from one of her sleeves, shaking it out like a magician performing a trick. She placed it over Sloane's nose and mouth and tied it at the back of her head. Then Aelia brought all her fingertips together and let out a trill from her tooth implant, a note higher than she could have sung on her own. Sloane winced at the sound, but the kerchief inflated around her face like a balloon — her air supply.

Sloane shed her outer layer. Wearing just a shirt and her underwear, she walked to the edge of the river. There were goose bumps all over her legs. She stared into the dim water and saw no reflection.

"And now the working that will help you see the connections," Aelia said, her hand clasping Sloane's shoulder. Sloane felt the cold of the siphon's plates through the fabric of her shirt. Cyrielle clasped her other shoulder. The note from Aelia's implant was so low Sloane could hardly hear sound in it, only felt its vibration against the back of her neck. Cyrielle's joined in at a higher, dissonant pitch. Then both women's hands fell away.

Sloane turned around and saw—light. Strings of light enfolding Cyrielle, Matt, Esther, Aelia. Extending from their feet and into the ground, penetrating the cracks in the concrete sidewalk. Slants of light like the sun's rays passed over the buildings behind them. Light shone through the windows of the high-rises and wrapped around them like string around a yo-yo. The city was bright with magic, swollen with it.

"Go," Aelia said, and the light came out of her mouth like a waterfall. "Or you'll run out of air."

Sloane bent her knees and dove.

From beneath, the water was murky as a lake, but light from the world above followed her down. She kicked like a bullfrog, wishing she had her flippers. She could breathe, but the pressure against her ears and sinuses was oppressive.

A rope of magic stretched down from the surface of the water. She hadn't seen it above the river, but here it was, as thick as her arm. Sloane swam alongside it, each kick forcing her farther and farther down.

She had never felt so profoundly alone in her life—not just isolated or by herself, but truly *alone,* the only person in darkness that went on forever, with only the rope as company.

Even if she had not been able to see the rope, though, she would have known that something was wrong about this place. She felt the prickle of it in her fingers. The Chicago River was only twenty or so feet deep at its deepest, and she had already swum farther than that. Wherever she was now was not the bottom of the river in Genetrix.

And then she saw it: a flicker of light up ahead, at the end of the rope. A glint of gold. She kicked harder, swimming toward it, following the rope like a child chasing the end of a rainbow. Her head was in a vise of magic; tingles raced up her arms and down her legs. She felt like the river water was closing in on her, forming a black tunnel. The plants growing on the floor of the river brushed her bare knees.

The glint was a thread of silver—no, just something that looked like silver. The Needle.

Startled by the sight of it, she stopped swimming and drew herself upright. Her head hit something hard and grainy—a chunk of concrete. She put her palm against it and turned so it was beneath her. Just beyond the concrete was a twisted piece of metal. It took shape when she came closer—it was huge, broader across than her wingspan, and disappearing into the metal that surrounded it.

It was the top of a *P*.

It was one of the overlarge letters that had been on Trump Tower before the destructive magic that ended the Dark One's life had leveled the building. She had dived among this rubble that had sunk to the bottom of the river, searching for any sign of the Dark One's body. And now it was above her. Below her.

Sloane looked down—up—at the plants that were, impossibly, growing toward the rubble. There was debris hidden among the stems: soda cans, glass bottles, a warped hubcap, a fragment of metal with the Abraxas logo on it. That was Genetrix.

And below—above—her, the remnants of the tower they had destroyed while killing the Dark One.

Between them, afloat but somehow immovable, was the Needle.

As ever, Sloane was drawn by its magnetism, the tingling cold that washed over her body at the thought of it. She felt like she could have just swum over and pinched it between her fingers. It wanted her. She knew it. And she wanted it too. But when she reached for it, her hand *missed* it, like she had misjudged the distance. When she tried again, the same thing happened, her fingers glancing off to the right.

Odd.

She was about to try a third time when she saw something else. It was a pale, quick thing, like a fish without the glimmer of scales. As it turned, it took the shape of a man: hair floating away from his head, softened by the water; clothes dark; shoes with hard leather soles. Terror clutched at her chest.

The Dark One.

It was a memory. A hallucination. It had to be. She was just running out of air and it was messing with her mind. She needed to go back.

Instead, she swam forward, thrashing through the water with as much energy as she could muster, froglike, hands outstretched. She saw the gnarl of scars on the back of her right hand, where the Needle had been, and kicked harder, trying to catch the shoe. She saw the shadow ahead of her, and the glow of magic that surrounded it. Sloane screamed into the water, which tasted like weeds and mildew.

The shadow was shrinking, and the rubble had gone away, as had the Needle and the river plants. She swam harder, legs and arms burning—

And broke through the surface of the river, Esther's and Matt's faces right above her.

"I think—" She coughed, reaching for the hands they extended to her. She yanked the cloth down from her face, spat up some water, and began again. "I think the Dark One—*our* Dark One—is still alive."

"He can't be." Esther shook her head.

They were still on the riverbank. Aelia had dried Sloane off with a working, and she was now pulling her pants back on, her arms and legs trembling from exertion.

"We never found a body," Sloane said.

"You dove in the river," Esther said. "You found his button, part of his jacket—there was so much rubble—"

"We wanted him to be dead, so we convinced ourselves he was!" Sloane said.

"Then why didn't he come back to finish us off? It's not like we were so scary he had to run to another dimension to get away from us!" Esther's gestures were wide and frantic; she almost struck Matt in the face before he stepped away from her.

Neither he nor Aelia had spoken yet; they seemed content to watch as Sloane and Esther argued.

"I don't know," Sloane said. "Maybe whatever he was doing on Earth, he'd finished. Maybe he got tired of playing with us and wanted to find some new toys. I'm not a fucked-up supervillain; I don't know the logic!"

"But you know the logic of trippy underwater hallucinations?" Esther said. "You see him swimming away, and suddenly you're convinced he's alive, and we should just trust you on that?"

"When has my gut ever failed us when it comes to the Dark One?" Sloane demanded. "*I* said he would fall for our trap, and he did. *I* said I would be good bait, and I was. *I* said to let Albie come and fight with us, and he turned out to be the reason we won. And I was the only one who was so convinced the Dark One might not be dead that I fucking scuba-dived in the Chicago River—a *deeply* unpleasant experience, might I add—and now, yeah, I expect you to believe that my gut isn't wrong on this one! Is that really so insane?"

Esther stared at Sloane, her eyes full of tears. Sloane thought she might always remember Esther this way, her arms slack at her sides, her eyes shining, the moon glowing behind her, no matter what happened to them after this.

"Sloane," Matt said, and Sloane tensed in anticipation, though she wasn't sure why.

"Your gut never led us astray—*before*," Matt said. "But now it tells you all kinds of things. That you're still a captive of the Dark One in the middle of the night when you're at home in our bed. That you could trust that Mox guy, who probably sold you out to the Resurrectionist. That you needed to go visit Genetrix's Bert—"

"Fuck you," Sloane said in a low voice. "Don't you dare use a fucking night terror against me like that. You're just pissed because

my gut told me to dump you, because of course there must be something wrong with my head if I don't want to marry the goddamn
saintly Chosen—"

"God, Sloane, this is the fucking problem with you, you don't
know how to fight without drawing blood, and you never have!"

"Both of you, *stop*," Esther said, and she choked back a sob. "I can't
take it. *I need to get home.* Okay? I need to. My mom is dying. So why
don't you stop bickering like a bunch of children and tell me the fastest way to do that?"

Matt and Sloane stared at each other. His jaw shifted like he was
working on a particularly tough bite of meat. Sloane just felt tired.
She looked out over the river. She no longer remembered why she
was so convinced that the Dark One was still alive, that he had swum
through the barrier between universes instead of dying, only that she
was . . . and no one, not even Esther, believed her.

"Fight the Resurrectionist," Matt said. "We kill him, they send us
home. That's our best bet."

"Sloane?" Esther said.

Sloane felt the same *wrongness* she felt around the Needle, like all
her innards were in the wrong places, like the world had turned into
a nightmare and she didn't remember falling asleep.

"Fine," she said. "Sure. Let's do it."

But she wasn't sure if she'd said it because she meant it or if she just
wanted Esther to stop crying.

PART
THREE

EXCERPT FROM
The Manifestation of Impossible Wants:
A New Theory of Magic
by Arthur Solowell

What, then, is a desire? We may begin by stating what it is not. A desire is not a whim. It is not an idle wish concocted on a sunny afternoon. A desire is a profundity of want, a deep and abiding craving that cannot be denied. It is for this reason that it is impossible to force someone to perform an act of magic one does not truly wish to do. The magic requires desire, and a desire cannot be threatened or manipulated into being.

It may become clear to us, as we watch magic develop and change in our world, that certain people are not to be trusted with the wealth of power that magic offers. This is not because they are wicked, but because they are damaged beyond repair. They may proceed through the world as if their desires conform to those of the healthy and functional among us, but that may not be the case; when they do magic, their true selves will be laid bare before them and before us all.

In other words, magic is a mirror. It reflects us back to ourselves, and we may not always like what we see.

MEMORANDUM FOR THE RECORD

TO: Director, Central Intelligence Agency

FROM: Thomas Wong, Praetor of the Council of Cordus

SUBJECT: Project Delphi Prophecy

As requested, I have included the exact wording of the prophecy of ███████, code name Sibyl, made on 16 February 1999, verified by the Council of Cordus:

It will be the end of Genetrix, the unmaking of worlds.

Something stands between Genetrix and its twin. The Dark One will excise it, and the worlds will be crushed together, and that will be the end of all.

The Dark One of Genetrix will be hidden, but not secret, with a thirst that will never be slaked. Their Equal is the hope of Genetrix, born marred by magic and mastered by a power previously unknown to us.

Twice will Equals greet each other anew, and the fate of the worlds is in their hands.

Essentially, in order to cross into another universe, one must simplify one's understanding of what such an act entails. The magnitude of moving from one world to another is too much for the human brain, no matter how advanced, to handle; they will therefore not be able to summon the appropriate level of desire, as defined by Solowell in The Manifestation of Impossible Wants. However, if we simplify it so that anyone may understand it, we may be able to shuttle people of any intellectual capacity across universes.

The comparison that I have chosen is one of basic hospitality. A person's universe is her home. The permeable barrier between the universes is her front door. If a polite guest wishes to enter a house, he knocks on the front door, and the person within the house opens it to let him in. It is the same with universes: you must reach out with your magic to "knock," and someone dwelling in that universe must "open the door."

What makes this more complicated, of course, is that time behaves differently across universes. You may think you are knocking on a Wednesday at the reasonable hour of ten o'clock in the morning; however, in that universe, you may actually be knocking at the stroke of midnight or twenty years later, when the owner of the house is long dead.

30

A COLD WIND FOUND its way under the hood of Sloane's cloak, making her shiver. It was hours past sunset, and she stood at the border of Wacker Drive and the most recent Drain site, her last checkpoint before she got in position.

Even Esther had eventually come around to Matt's way of thinking. *You've been acting so strong since we got here,* Esther had said to her, quietly, the night of the incident. *Obviously your real feelings have to come out somewhere, right? It's your brain's way of telling you that you're repressing something.*

She had almost made Sloane believe it. Regardless of what else she had seen underwater, she had gone to a place where the universes touched. Earth and Genetrix were connected; Nero hadn't lied about that. Which meant they still had to help Genetrix to help Earth. And they had already brought down one maniacal mass murderer. They would use the same strategy to do it again.

That meant her job was to lure the Resurrectionist into the open. She would walk along Congress Parkway until it passed beneath the Old Main Post Office, where he and his army had their lair. She would have to go alone, but the Army of Flickering would follow her after she had made contact.

She had done this before. She had gone alone to the Irv Kupcinet Bridge to be bait for the Dark One on Earth. She knew too well the feeling of numbness that took over. If not for seeing the toes of her boots digging into the rubble, she might not have known that she was still on the ground. But she kept moving now, just as she had before.

She knew the path through the destruction of the Drain site. City officials had spent the last two months clearing it, but it was still a mess of broken bricks and cracked boards and bodies retrieved from basements. People of all walks of life picked their way through the wreckage, looking for the bodies of lost loved ones. Sloane wished that she could tell them not to bother. Their loved ones were likely in pieces; Drain victims almost always were.

The cloak she wore was one of Aelia's, heavy and dark. Flakes of snow from a late-spring cold front drifted through the light cast by emergency lamps, melting as soon as they touched the ground. Sloane's fingers were frozen even though they were clutching the folds of the cloak. She had insisted on wearing her own clothes beneath it—her Albie-funeral blacks, the ones she had worn when she first surfaced on Genetrix.

She reached the other end of the Drain site, her boots coated in dust. She walked a block west, then started to cross the same bridge she had hobbled over with a broken ankle, weeks ago.

Ever since then, she had been dreaming, not of the Dark One, but of the Resurrectionist. They weren't nightmares, though—just a playback of their brief conversation, over and over, the same thing every time. *You aren't being fair. You and your friends come to kill me and I'm not allowed to fight back?*

She had been tasked with studying the deaths of the other Chosen Ones summoned from other worlds. Despite Nero's promise to be more forthcoming, however, he and Aelia were still protective of the little information they had, dishing it out in small morsels. It was like having only a few pieces to a puzzle, and none of them fit together. All of them gave her questions that Nero and Aelia refused to answer.

Sloane didn't like it. Moreover, she didn't trust it.

This world, your world, they destroy themselves. All worlds do. They don't need me, the Resurrectionist had said. He hadn't seemed like the Dark One. Not a parallel version of him or the man himself.

Another piece she couldn't fit anywhere.

Sloane stopped in the middle of the bridge and looked out over the water. She didn't know what to think. She didn't know if the Resurrectionist was the Dark One under the siphons and the dramatic cloak or if the Resurrectionist was causing the Drains or how many Chosen Ones had died doing exactly what she was about to do.

So she needed to find out.

She started walking again.

Standing in the alley between the Old Main Post Office and the building next to it—the Chicago Central Carrier Annex; she had looked it up—Sloane found the window she had jumped out of when she'd escaped from the Resurrectionist. It didn't look high now, weeks later. But it was too high for her to climb without any assistance.

She wrapped a scarf around her face so only her eyes were uncovered and checked her hood to make sure it was secure. Her cloak looked too fine to belong to one of the Resurrectionist's tattered army, but there wasn't anything she could do about that. She rounded the edge of the building in search of an entrance.

Just off Harrison Street was a metal door with a push handle. The handle had a lock built into it—*Good,* she thought. *Not a deadbolt.* Sloane hunted along the ground for something to use as a hammer. She had to go back into the alley, but she finally found a large hunk of concrete so wide she could hardly get her hand around it. It would have to do.

Holding the concrete in both hands, she slammed it against the handle of the door. The door shuddered, and Sloane hit the handle again, and again, and again. Flecks of concrete broke off the hunk she held, and she gouged deep scratches into the metal door. Sloane kept hitting the handle until it broke off and dangled from the door by its inner mechanisms.

She forced the door open and walked into what appeared to be an old loading bay. Dilapidated equipment filled the space, all of it rusted and covered in a thick layer of dust. There were conveyor belts and chutes, rotten pallets and ladders, bins large enough to hold a grown man that rolled on busted wheels.

Sloane tried to affect the loping, shuffling gait she had seen from the undead man and woman who had first brought her here. She had gone in through the back, but the Resurrectionist's army might still be lurking somewhere nearby. She found the inner door of the loading bay and stepped into a worn hallway with a warped floor. Broken planks of wood had burst through the maroon carpet, and chunks of wall and ceiling were piled in her path. She stepped around them like she was playing hot lava with Cameron in their living room—everything that wasn't maroon carpet was lava.

As she walked, she tried to map out the building in her mind. She turned a corner and slipped into the emergency stairwell. So far, everything was quiet. She climbed two flights of stairs to get to the level where she had broken the window and jumped. Her ankle was still weak from that day, but the siphon had done its work, speeding the healing of her bones.

Soon she arrived at the threshold of the dilapidated office where she had found the mattress and siphon parts. The Resurrectionist's living space, or so it appeared. She was still confused by the floral sheets that covered the mattress. They seemed comically out of place.

She removed her heavy cloak. It would only get in her way, and she didn't need to hide who she was any longer. She took her tactical knife out of its sheath at her hip, crept into the space, and crouched beside one of the built-in desks, behind the cubicle wall.

Then she waited for the Resurrectionist to return.

Matt and Esther would be angry if they knew she was deviating from their plan. Maybe they would even hate her for it. But really, Sloane thought, they ought to have been suspicious when she agreed to be bait again. Besides, she wasn't necessarily abandoning the plan entirely; she was just . . . changing its timeline.

She waited.

Her heartbeat still hadn't slowed when she heard footsteps in the hallway. But no voices—he was alone. The door opened, and she heard his heavy breaths, the rustle of fabric around him. She tipped her head back just enough to see his hood over the low wall that surrounded the desk, and then she stood, stepped around the wall, and lunged—

She yanked his hood off with one hand and brought the knife up to his throat with the other, holding him by his hair—which was dark and long, for a man—and pressed the blade in just enough for him to feel how sharp it was.

"Hi there," she said.

She could feel the warmth of him, the life in him. She had known that he was human, but part of her had wondered if he was the same as his army, more dust than man. His breaths came fast through the siphon, crackling.

"Keep your hands still," she said. She held the knife above the siphon that covered his throat, but with her free hand, she reached down to undo the clasp of the siphon around his wrist. It was too strange, her skin brushing his as she felt for the release and tugged it; the siphon dropped, heavy, to the floor. She switched knife hands so she could do the same to his other wrist.

She was conscious of her breaths, which were just like his, fast and loud. Everything sounded muffled. He had almost killed Kyros in front of her with just a whistle. What else could he do before she could stop him? And here she stood with a tactical knife like an idiot.

"Should have known you'd come back." His voice came out tinny, warped by the siphon. "True hero and all. Your kind do tend to go on ill-advised suicide missions."

Sloane laughed harshly. "Your assumptions about my character are so off base, it's actually hilarious," she said. "I'm not here to kill you. If I were, I'd have slit your throat already. Because I'm also not here to die."

He held his hands out from his sides. They were big and pale, with oddly delicate knuckles. "Slitting my throat immediately would have been smarter," he said.

"As much as I wanted to, that would kind of defeat the purpose of my being here. I came for a trade," she said. "Truth for truth."

"Truth," he repeated. "I'm not even sure what that is anymore."

"Please, for the love of God, don't be one of those villains who waxes poetic about existentialist nonsense, because if you are, I really will have to cut you," she said. "How about we start with this: Who the hell are you?"

"You don't already know?"

When she didn't answer, he lifted his hands, slowly, up to his face. Sloane kept the press of her knife steady. He undid the latches of the siphon that covered his eyes and pulled it away. She saw his reflection in the windows across from them, but only faintly—just the paleness of him and his shape against the dark.

He was still as she moved around him, his hands up, palms facing forward. His wrists were scarred from siphons, the kind of marks worn into skin day after day, for years. His nose and mouth were still covered, but his eyes were dark and focused and familiar. She laughed.

"Mox," she said. "So I take it you didn't just *happen* upon me in the cultural center that day."

He undid the latches of his mouth siphon too, then wiped his chin of sweat. He set both siphons down on the desk beside him. He looked worse than he had the last time she'd seen him—wan, dark circles under his eyes, sweaty. Young.

"I gave you your truth," he said, and his voice was different than she remembered it from the cultural center or the Tankard, rougher. "Now give me mine."

Sloane saw something unsteady in him that she hadn't seen when she knew him only as Mox. A kind of agitation that would have been frightening if she had not known it so well herself. He was afraid, and for him—for both of them—fear was always anger and demand.

"No," she said. "I didn't ask you for your name. I asked you *who you are*. Are you the Dark One? In some kind of disguise?"

"The what?" Mox said, and his confusion didn't clear up anything. Sloane was trying to keep her breaths steady, but they kept coming out in little bursts. She didn't know. She didn't know if she was standing across from the Dark One or someone just as bad. A murderer, a psychopath, an evil sorcerer—she had no idea what Mox was.

"I had an enemy," she said. "I thought I killed him, but he came here instead. And I want to know—I need to know if you're him."

"If I tell you that I'm not," he said, "you won't believe me. And I'm not giving you anything else until you make good on our trade."

She had trusted her gut before. When she had just gone through puberty and her body had taken a new shape, she had known when there were eyes on her, when a man's kindness was a threat. When Katy McKinney had offered her a red cup of something at the one party she had gone to before leaving town, she had known not to drink it because there was spit in it. And at the end of the struggle with the Dark One, she had known to use the Dark One's interest in her against him.

I would know, she thought. *I would know if I was standing in front of the Dark One. I would feel it.*

"They're coming for you. Nero and my friends," she said. "I was supposed to lure you out to Congress Parkway. I came here instead."

His eyes widened. "Nero? He's with them? You're sure?"

"Um, yes?"

He grabbed the siphon he had set on the desk and pressed it roughly to his face, covering his nose and mouth. Then he bent over to pick up the wrist siphons Sloane had let fall to the floor.

"Hey! We are not done with this conversation!"

Mox looked up at her from where he was crouched, reattaching one of his wrist siphons. He whistled and waved a bare hand at her, and the knife crumbled in her hands like a snowball. The pieces scattered on the worn carpeting.

"Fuck!" Sloane snapped. "Really?"

"We can continue this discussion," he said, voice tinny again. "But I can't let Nero get anywhere near this building while I'm still in it."

"What?" She thought of Nero's workshop, packed with books, and of his floppy blond hair. He must be highly skilled with magic or he wouldn't have been able to orchestrate their summoning from another universe. But he didn't seem nearly as threatening as the Resurrectionist.

Mox stood and attached the eye siphons, transforming again into the creature he had been. "I will tell you," he said, offering her a metal-plated hand. "But you'll have to come with me."

And though Sloane knew it was madness to choose this man, this masked murderer who kept company with the dead, over Matt and Esther—over Nero and Aelia, even—she also knew that it was already decided and had been since she broke into this building.

She put her hand in his. If she died because of this, well, at least it was a death she chose.

31

Mox led her down the hall with the checkerboard-tile floor and the tall, boarded windows she had seen when she had first regained consciousness. It was as crowded with soldiers now as it had been then. They walked past a group of them crouched around a few scattered dice and a pair stitching each other's fingers back on with a needle and thread.

The woman with the hole in her jaw marched toward them. Her stringy hair was in two braids now, a girlish style that was at odds with her discolored skin. She stared at Sloane. "Sir," the woman said, "what—"

"She came to warn us," Mox interrupted. "We need to leave. Get everyone up and to the safe house."

The woman leaned in closer to Sloane, her teeth clicking together as she clenched her jaw. Sloane watched her tongue work behind them before she spoke in the same raspy, strained voice Sloane remembered. "Are you sure she's not setting a trap?"

"I don't believe she has that level of foresight," Mox replied.

"Fuck you," Sloane said. Over the woman's shoulder, she spotted the milky-eyed man who had carried her into the building over his shoulder. He was sitting with a few others, a siphon in pieces in his lap. He made a kissing face at her.

"I didn't mean *in general*," Mox told Sloane, sounding a little like the normal young man she had met in the cultural center even through the metallic warp of his siphon. "Sloane, this is Ziva, my lieutenant. Ziva, Sloane."

"We've met," Sloane said. "She chloroformed me."

"We thought you were some great magic-user," Ziva said, her upper lip curling in what might have been a sneer if her lips hadn't been taut and cracked, like dry earth. "If I'd known you were completely helpless, I wouldn't have bothered."

"Helpless?" Sloane laughed. "So how do you explain me escaping from right under your nose?"

"This building is about to be stormed by the Army of Flickering, but by all means, continue arguing like children," Mox snapped.

Ziva stood up straighter, then stepped away from Sloane and Mox. She stuck a whistle—attached to one of her fingers—between her lips and blew on it. Sloane brought a hand to her chest to steady herself when all the soldiers in the hallway got to their feet. It took some of them longer than others—Sloane watched a smaller woman slump against the wall and then shove herself up with both legs as a lever. When the woman turned, Sloane saw that she was holding an *arm,* one that had clearly once gone in her shoulder socket.

Ziva whistled again, bringing her hand up to her throat, where she wore a scratched siphon. Her voice came out twice as loud, though still raspy. "Emergency evac! To the safe house, and keep your eyes open. We're being pursued." Ziva looked over her shoulder at Sloane, and there was something odd in her expression. Something like hope and despair mixed together.

"Still can't use a siphon?" Mox said to Sloane. All around them, the soldiers of the Resurrectionist had picked up bags and were stuffing things—including, Sloane noticed, the woman's detached arm—into them.

"No," Sloane admitted.

"Then you're stuck with me at the front," he said. "Better keep up."

The army was forming a loose pack behind them. Someone pried the boards away from one of the doors, letting in a gust of fresh air. The blue geometric fixtures above Sloane's head swung back and forth in the wind. Mox loped toward the doors, his gait uneven but powerful, his cloak whipping around his shoulders. She felt the soldiers behind her creeping closer and ran to catch up with him.

She had left her own cloak behind, so the cold air cut right through her shirt, sending a shiver through her. She pulled her sleeves down over her hands.

Behind her, the Resurrectionist's army spilled into the street like a glass of water tipped over. They divided into smaller groups, silent except for the creaking of their bones and the shuffling of their feet. They disappeared down alleys and slipped between buildings, peeling away with every side street they passed, until it was just Mox, Sloane, and a trio of decrepit undead.

The streets were emptier here, south of downtown, and the buildings were farther apart. They passed a corner store lit up by pale fluorescents displaying a dozen brands of cigarettes—Rhabdos, Fairy Godmothers, and Fumus among them—and liters of soda in green, orange, and glittery blue. Behind the counter, a sallow-faced man gaped at them as they passed. Even shrouded in hoods and cloaks, as all the others were, they still made a strange sight: four hooded figures with siphon hands outstretched and one random woman making their way down the sidewalk.

A few cars passed, swerving away from them as if they were potholes, but their path was unobstructed until they reached Roosevelt Road. To the left was the train yard, the ground rippling with rails. And parked at the corner on the right was a police car. Though the vehicle's lights were off, Sloane saw two silhouettes in the front seats.

Mox stuck out a hand, and they all came to a halt. He let out a tweet, like a sparrow. Behind him, the undead soldiers stretched out their own siphon arms and bit down on whistles. In unison, all four magic-users made the same sound at the same pitch, high and light, a chorus of birdsong.

The police car lifted off the pavement and turned upside down. Sloane saw the officers inside it shifting, and then one thrust a hand against the glass, showing the unmistakable palm plate of a standard-issue siphon. Mox whistled again. The car righted itself and touched down on the street like it had never moved at all.

A chorus of dissonant sounds surrounded Sloane. She clapped her hands over her ears. The car's tires spun backward, sending it over the rails, through the barrier, and into the Chicago River.

Sloane stared at Mox. He began walking again, and the others followed him.

They traveled in silence over the water, then turned to walk along it. They passed gutters full of paper and half-crushed soda cans. Sloane kicked a rotting apple core out of her way. She was numb with terror and just as afraid of the Army of Flickering finding them as she was of the man who had just drowned two police officers.

Ahead of them, Sloane spotted dark figures. A shout rang out. There was a flash of fire, and in the orange light, Sloane saw the seal of the Army of Flickering on one man's jacket.

"Ziva!" Mox shouted, so loud the sound crackled in his mask. He ran.

The wall of fire cast by the Army of Flickering danced toward hunched shapes that Sloane recognized as Ziva, the lieutenant, and four other undead soldiers. Ziva and one of the other soldiers whistled, together, and ice formed at their feet, piling on itself until it had formed a knee-high barrier of icicles that reflected fractured moonlight.

Mox reached them, and he swept the soldiers off their feet with a low rumble. They landed hard on their knees on the street. Mox shouted instructions at Ziva that Sloane couldn't hear.

An arc of energy, almost like a bubble of air, swept toward him. It pushed him back, toward the river, and up, at least six feet in the air. Mox fell hard on his back, but as soon as he hit the ground, he thrust his arm up and let out a peal of percussive sound.

Chunks of pavement pulled away from the edges of the road and hurtled toward the soldiers. They threw up shimmering barriers of energy, and the rocks pummeled them but didn't break through.

Mox turned to Ziva and shouted, "Go!"

Ziva hesitated, and Mox whistled, sending a hiss of air toward her so intense, it blew the hood off her head. She ran, followed by the four undead soldiers under her command. Mox turned his attention back to the soldiers of the Army of Flickering, who had let down their barriers in the wake of the rock assault and were, together, raising water from the river. At the gesture of the lead woman, the water formed a massive orb the size of a car. It had no sooner taken shape than it enveloped Mox completely.

The orb warped and rotated almost as soon as it hit him, and then he was in the center of a cyclone, his hair clinging to his masked face and his soaked clothes whipping around his shoulders. The cyclone chewed up pavement as it charged at the soldiers, flinging rocks and water in equal measure at them.

As one of the soldiers cringed away from the onslaught, Sloane recognized her as Edda. Their eyes met just as Mox raised his hand again.

Sloane shouted, "Don't!"

Mox hesitated, and it cost him. Edda whistled, sharp and clean, and something silver shot through the air at him—a large fragment of metal that stabbed his side. His body hunched around it. He screamed through the siphon and, the next moment, let out a long, keening note. Day-bright light exploded from his hand.

Sloane threw an arm up over her eyes to shield them, but this was no momentary flash—she felt a continued heat against her forearm that meant the light was still burning. The Flickering soldiers were shouting at one another. A hand wrapped around her elbow.

"Keep your arm up," Mox said to her. "Let's go."

He steered her away from the Flickering soldiers, barked a command at the undead ones trailing them, and they ran.

Cordus Daily

THE BULLETIN BOARD: MEETING PLACE OF MAGICAL YOUTH

by Sarah Romanoff

CHICAGO, NOVEMBER 3: "If I have an idea for a working I can't do on my own," Elissa, seventeen, says as she staples a piece of paper to the bulletin board in Palmer Square Park, "I just put up a request for an assembly. You can specify ages, too, so I always do eighteen or under. We don't want any strange old men spoiling the fun."

Elissa's current assembly request? For a timed levitation. Her request is for five people, each with an object they would like to levitate, to meet in Palmer Square Park in two days' time, objects in hand. Together, they will set up a timed working for the next morning, at which point all their objects will levitate at once.

"Timed workings always require at least one other person, one to do the working and one to set the timer," Elissa says. "So they're the most common thing you see on here. Also glowing. People are *deeply* interested in making things glow these days."

For most of us, assemblies—the term for a group of magic-users con-

vening for a single working—were integral to our magical education. But in the past, assemblies were arranged by school staff, and they had to be supervised by a teacher. Now, students are taking their learning into their own hands, meeting freely and with young people from other schools, even other cities.

"I drove all the way to Indianapolis for one once," says Josh, sixteen, from Buffalo Grove, Illinois. "I told my mom it was for a concert. And I did go to a concert! But I also went to the group working. We built a rain cloud—some people did the illusion of a cloud, some did the water, one did lightning strikes, and one did thunder."

Some parents, naturally, are concerned. "What if they do something dangerous?" asks Ellen Higgins, founder of Parents of Teens Under Control (PoTUC), a community action group that seeks out unsupervised group workings and interrupts them. "They can't just run around doing magic without anybody knowing.

They could really hurt themselves! So we don't let that happen."

When I ask Elissa about PoTUC, she just rolls her eyes. "We have to use code in our messages now," she says. "I won't tell you what it is. But my next assembly is going to be supervised, so PoTUC can't spoil it."

32

B Y THE TIME the Sloane's vision cleared, they were inside the safe house, a large red-brick building perched on the river's edge. The space looked like it had once been elegant but had fallen into disrepair. The ceiling was wood-paneled, with skylights in a squared arch that let in the glow of the moon. As with the Old Main Post Office, the lower windows were boarded up, but judging by the position of the building on the river, she was sure that the view would have been of a stretch of skyline.

Crowded inside the space were the groups of the Resurrectionist's army that had arrived before them. Ziva wandered among them, distinguished by the braids swinging back and forth against her shoulders. When Mox walked in, he released Sloane's arm and hunched over the piece of metal buried in his side to give it a closer look.

"Don't go yanking that out," Sloane said. "Not until you can clean the wound and pack it."

Mox looked at her — or he seemed to, turning the mechanized siphon eyes in her direction for a moment. "Then it will have to wait," he said. "Stay here."

He loped across the dusty wood floor to Ziva's side. Sloane leaned against one of the wood pillars at the edge of the room and watched as he worked his way through the crowd of soldiers, clapping them on the shoulder or bending his ear to them. The woman who had carried her arm in a bag took it out when he came near her and showed it to him. Sloane was surprised when he knelt beside her and took something from his pocket—a leather packet about the size of his palm that, when opened, revealed a needle and some kind of thick thread.

Sloane watched with mixed revulsion and fascination as he began to stitch the arm back on. The woman held it in place as he did so, watching the skin split around the point of the needle, the string tugging through gently and then pulling taut. When he finished, he tied off the string and gestured over the sutures. Sloane assumed it was some kind of working, but she couldn't tell what it did. Regardless, the undead woman touched the side of Mox's head fondly and smiled.

Sloane had assumed that the Resurrectionist's undead army was in thrall to him, a mindless collection of zombie slaves. But it seemed clear now that they *knew* him. Perhaps they had even known him before they died.

It was a while before he returned to her, still with the metal embedded in his side, all his clothes damp from the Flickering soldiers' attempt to drown him.

"We have food and water stowed elsewhere," he said.

Sloane followed him out of the room. She knew she should be afraid to be alone with him—to be here at all. But it was too late to go back now. She had betrayed her friends. Edda had seen her with the Resurrectionist.

They went into a smaller room not far from the others, still in a state of disrepair—a crumbling half-wall separated it from a bathroom, and there were cobwebs in the exposed rafters of the ceiling—but swept clean and stocked neatly with cans of food and jugs of water. There was a pile of blankets in the corner, too, and a small table with two rickety chairs set up around it.

Mox stood before the table and started removing his siphons. The wrists came first, then mouth, eyes, and ear. Beneath them, his skin was sweat-slicked and pale.

"I'm not your nurse," Sloane said.

"Didn't ask you to be," Mox replied.

But she still picked up one of the water jugs and set it on the table in front of him, then searched the row of supplies for a first-aid kit.

When she found one, she dropped it next to the water jug, which she opened and gulped from greedily. Mox sat down in one of the chairs, heavily enough to make it creak, and reached for the little box with trembling fingers.

"Is that metal serrated?" she said, nodding to the fragment just above his hip.

"No, edge looks straight."

"Did it hit bone?"

Mox plucked a pair of scissors from the kit and cut from the hem of his shirt to the shard, then pulled the fabric away from the wound. It looked nasty, blood streaking his pale skin beneath the puncture, the tip of the blade — or whatever it was — sticking out behind him. But he had been lucky; it seemed to have gone through the meat of his hip, missing bone and organs both.

"Looks like you might be able to just pull it out," Sloane said.

Mox grunted in reply.

"I guess I could help," she said. "In exchange for some answers."

"Not sure where to begin," he said.

"How about you start with why you stalked me to the cultural center," she said. She was hesitant about stepping closer, but she forced herself to do it, then searched through the first-aid kit for antiseptic. She would have to sterilize the wound as best she could with the metal still in it, then pull it out and apply pressure to stanch the bleeding. She had done it before — Ines had gotten pierced with debris during a Drain once — but it felt different this time, in the quiet, with no battle raging around her.

"Ziva noticed something going on at the Camel. All the scurrying around. So I knew they had summoned another one. There's a . . . burst of energy when they do it." His face twitched a little. "If you're paying attention, you can feel it for miles in every direction. Like a . . . bubble of magic, popping. And I'd been waiting for it."

"You said that you 'knew they had summoned another one,'" she said. "Another *what*, exactly?" She poured water from the jug over the wound to clean off some of the blood, then doused the entry point and exit point of the wound in antiseptic. That would have to do.

Mox was unwrapping a square of gauze. "They bring warriors here from other places to fight me. You — your friends — are the fourth."

He offered her the gauze, and she took it and clamped it around the metal so she could get a firm — and clean — grip on it.

"Fourth," she said. "Nero said we were the fifth Chosen Ones they'd brought here."

"Chosen Ones?" Mox's brow furrowed.

"I'm going to pull now," she said. "Unless you'd like to do it magically?"

He snorted. "I would probably cut myself in half if I tried."

"Fair enough. Brace yourself."

Mox grabbed the edge of the table, and Sloane pinched the flat of the shard between thumb and forefinger on both hands. She took a deep breath and pulled as hard as she could. Mox screamed, stuffing his fist into his mouth to muffle the sound. The fragment moved, but only a little. Without delaying, she pulled again, and this time, the metal pulled free. She set it aside. Mox was trembling but trying to open another packet of gauze. She smacked his hands away and did it herself, then used the gauze to apply pressure to both sides of the wound.

"Yeah," she said, picking up where their conversation had left off. "Who did you think they were summoning? Random mercenaries? They've all been Chosen Ones — people who have defeated some kind of evil figure in their own worlds."

Mox's eyes were unfocused, likely from the pain, when he blinked up at her. "I didn't know," he said. "At first I tried to — talk to them. But they wouldn't stop." His face went blank. "So I killed them instead."

Fear prickled in Sloane's chest. But a moment later, Mox blinked, and his expression changed. It was almost like he had come back to the surface of his own mind.

"You could have hurt me in the cultural center," she said. "And then again in the Tankard. But you didn't."

"I didn't know how many of you there were or what I would be up against," Mox said. "I always wanted to know why they wanted me dead, these warriors from other worlds. Wanted to know what was in it for them."

"But isn't it obvious why they wanted you dead?" She swallowed hard. Maybe it wasn't wise to press him on this issue, but she had to. "The Drain. They wanted to stop the Drain."

"As I said before," he replied, looking up at her, "I suppose I should be flattered that you think I could cause that level of destruction by myself. But I can't."

"So the Drains—they aren't you."

Mox shook his head.

"Who controls them, then?"

"Nobody knows," he said. "But my theory is they're a natural phenomenon. A . . . byproduct, you might say. Of the connection between universes."

"No, they aren't. Here, take this." Sloane waited until his hand had replaced hers on the gauze, then fumbled with the contents of the first-aid kit, looking for a bandage. All she could find was a packet made of stiff plastic. "The Dark One—the evil figure in my world, the one we defeated—caused Drains all the time. They stopped once he was gone."

Mox's hand stilled hers. He took the packet from her and flicked it open. What fell from it was a long, flat siphon, like the one the doctor had attached to her broken ankle. It looked like a bracelet with wide, flat metal links. Plain, unpolished, but still elegant. Mox held it over his hip, removed the gauze he was using to stanch the bleeding, and placed the siphon over the entry and exit wounds both.

"It stops bleeding, deters infection, and speeds healing," he said, almost as if he were reciting something he had read in a textbook or an ad.

Sloane frowned at the strip of pale skin still visible over the waistband of his pants. "You can't be saying the Dark One didn't cause our Drains. He was present at every single one of them, and they stopped when he disappeared. What else could it have been?"

Mox frowned back at her. "I don't know everything that can be done with magic," he said. "Especially across universes. Dimensions. But I know what I can't do. And I know that I've never encountered anyone here as powerful as I am. Maybe your Dark One was." He shrugged. "Unlikely."

She snorted. "Not suffering from a lack of confidence, are you?"

"No," he replied, but he didn't sound boastful, only . . . sad. "Not when it comes to raw power, I'm not. But there are more important things — you know that. It's how you escaped." He smirked a little. "Very clever, by the way."

"Thanks," she said stiffly.

Mox stood, using the table to steady himself, and went to a small cabinet in the corner of the room. Inside it was a small stack of clothes — all dark colors, of course, because supposedly evil sorcerers who commanded armies of undead couldn't wander around in bright orange, after all. He took a shirt from the stack and limped into the bathroom behind the half-wall to change. "It's my turn," he said. "For a question."

Sloane sat in the other chair and started gathering the scraps of gauze and wrappers from her stint as nurse — exactly what she had told him she wouldn't be. Not a good precedent to set, she knew, but it was already done.

"You said — when you were trapped — that you didn't choose to come here," he said. She could only see the back of his head and one of his shoulders over the crumbling wall, but the flash of bare skin made her feel uneasy.

"You mean when you kidnapped me and held me against my will?" Sloane tilted her head. "Yeah. Before I got pulled into Genetrix, I was in the middle of a funeral, and the next thing I knew, I was almost drowning in the Chicago River."

"And — you weren't given a choice to return."

"No." Sloane almost sighed with relief when Mox came back into the room with a shirt on, his hair tied back in a low knot. "They told us that the fate of our world and the fate of Genetrix were intertwined. And that we would need to fight the Resurrectionist — I mean you — if we wanted to save them both."

Mox stared at her for a moment. His shoulders started to shake.

For a single, horrifying moment, Sloane thought he was sobbing —and then she saw he was laughing, holding one hand against the wound in his side.

"My God," Mox said, sounding almost giddy. "This is what I meant. What's more important than raw power? Elegant lies, that's what."

"So . . ." Sloane narrowed her eyes. "Earth's and Genetrix's fates *aren't* intertwined?"

Mox flapped a hand at her. "Not that part. The part about me. Fighting me. Killing me. As if you could. As if it would help anything at all."

"First of all, if I had decided to stab you in the jugular instead of having a conversation earlier, I would totally have been able to kill you," Sloane said. "Magic is great and all, but you're still just a sack of meat at the end of the day."

Mox spread his hands—big even without the siphons to add bulk to them—in acknowledgment.

"Second—what's the point of all this?" she said. "Why do they want you dead so badly they would take people from another dimension but won't go after you themselves?"

"Not *they—he,*" Mox said, now agitated. He paced away from her. "Nero."

"Nero," Sloane repeated. "Not that I doubt you, but he seems kind of . . . nonthreatening. Are you sure he's—"

"Am I *sure?*" Mox spun on his heel, and the pile of cans along the wall lifted from the floor all at once. They slammed into the ceiling, then flew in all directions. Sloane ducked as one rocketed toward her head; it hit the wall behind her and started leaking yellow juice.

Both of them were breathless, Sloane with fear, and Mox, she assumed from his wild-eyed stare, with anger.

"There's no need to have a fucking tantrum about it," she said. "All I've seen of Nero is that he's Aelia's lackey most of the time. Not exactly evil-mastermind material. Especially compared to a guy who just attacked an innocent can of green beans."

She picked the can up and slammed it on the table, the dented side facing him.

"Raw power," Mox said, "isn't everything."

"Clearly," she said, disguising the quiver in her hands by making fists.

"He doesn't just . . . do things," Mox said. He started pacing again. "He gets other people to do them for him. He's good at it. He's whoever you need him to be whenever you need him to be it. Until suddenly—he's not anymore. He brought you here—keeps bringing people here, over and over—to kill me. And if they fail, well, fine, it keeps everyone distracted from what he's doing. Either way, he wins."

Sloane cast a net in her memories of Nero, trying to catch a single instance of what Mox was describing. But the only time she had seen him deviate from his affable persona was after she and Esther had broken into his workshop. His voice had been so cold. But that wasn't enough.

"What is he doing," she said quietly, "that he wants to distract everyone from?"

Mox's pacing slowed. "I'm not sure, but my guess is a working. Something that will make him more powerful than I am. Than anyone is. Fill him with magic."

The words reminded her of the Dark One and how she had thought of him as no more than a mouth, devouring. That crafty as he was, the true horror of him was simple: Nothing, not magic, not pain, not power, would ever be enough. He ate just for the sake of eating. And there was no argument she could make to someone like that to get him to stop hurting Albie, to let them both go, to do anything other than what he wanted.

She stared at her boots.

Bare feet meant the past. Boots meant the present.

She crossed her arms. "Do you have any proof?"

Mox stopped pacing altogether and faced her.

"Surely you understand why I can't just *believe* you," she said. "There has to be something other than your word that I can rely on."

"I haven't killed you yet," he suggested.

"Lots of people haven't killed me yet," Sloane replied. "That doesn't mean you're telling the truth about Nero."

"Well," he said, "there's Sibyl."

"Sibyl?"

"The prophet. The one who made Genetrix's doomsday prophecy." He sat again, across from her. He was so different now than he had been when she knew him only as Mox. He had been charming and levelheaded then—no sign of the chaos beneath. She wondered how he had managed it, even for a few minutes at a time. He didn't seem capable of it now.

"She knows who I am," he said. "She knows who Nero is. And she can tell you how the end will come."

"Where is she?"

"A haven city. Where no magic can touch her. She hates it, the way it feels. Hates the way *I* feel too. But she'll bear it for an hour or two if I ask her to." He scratched the back of his neck, nails raking red lines into his pale skin. "St. Louis. Does your world have a St. Louis?"

Sloane nodded.

"I can take you," he said. "Tomorrow."

"Okay," she said. "But no . . . path of destruction, okay? No killing. We keep it quiet."

"I'll never apologize for defending my life," he said, his dark eyes finding hers with that focus that made Sloane feel like she was under a blowtorch.

"I'll never ask you to," she said.

He gave her a peculiar look, like he had never heard such a thing before.

The Mammoth Treasury of Unrealist Poetry, Volume 4

A Message to Haven Cities After the Installation of Magical Dampeners
by Fake and Bake

HAVEN CITIES
We fix you in our gaze of judgment
our gaze, a gaze
a walking stick
a steering wheel
WE FIX YOU IN OUR GAZE OF JUDGMENT
haven't you heard, haven't you
that it is illegal to swallow a person's magic
and burp up mediocrity?
you and your siphon dampener, your ball gag, your pacifier, your duct tape
    across the lips of your hostage citizens
WE FIX YOU
we cannot fix you
we fix ourselves
floating castles
paper fireflies
frozen flames
we make the impossible possible
and full of possibilities
DAMPEN US???
no, we dampen you

33

SLOANE WOKE the next morning with a start, then slid her hand underneath her pillow for the pair of scissors she had put there before falling asleep. She knew that scissors wouldn't do her any good against either ridiculously powerful sorcerers or walking corpses—as Mox had pointed out when he saw her take them—but she hated to be without tools.

Ziva was crouched at her bedside. Her bulging eyes swiveled to the scissors, and she let out a huff that might have been a laugh.

"A humdrum girl in a magical world," Ziva wheezed. "What are you going to do, trim my fingernails?"

"Underestimating my resourcefulness didn't work out so great for you last time," Sloane said. "Remember?"

Ziva sat back on her heels with another huff.

"The consul told me to give you these," she said, and she thrust a stack of clothes at Sloane. They looked like Mox's, which meant the pants would be long enough, at least. "And to tell you there's soap in his bathroom if you want to try to shower with a jug of water. Your train is set to leave in two hours."

"The consul?" Sloane said.

Ziva cocked her head. "Did you think we called him the Resurrectionist?"

"I thought maybe you called him by his name."

Ziva made a derisive noise, not through her nose but with the suck of her tongue against her teeth. In order to stand she had to move one of her legs with both hands and then shake out the other knee so it, too, straightened. Sloane wondered if the Resurrectionist's army had to oil their joints, like the Tin Man in *The Wizard of Oz*.

Sloane walked to Mox's room—and bathroom—with the clothes tucked under her arm. Last night she had carried a stack of blankets far away from the space where the army was housed to a corner near the stairwell, so she could make a quick exit if necessary. It had taken her a long time to fall asleep—not just because of the strange surroundings or the buzz of all that Mox had told her in the back of her mind, but also because of the guilt over abandoning Matt and Esther in the middle of a mission, without explanation. She had disappointed them in so many ways since they came to Genetrix. She wouldn't have blamed them if they never spoke to her again after this.

But the lure of the truth had been too strong. If reading the FOIA documents had convinced her of anything, it was that she had gone on too many missions without knowing everything there was to know. She had never made an informed choice in all her life. Bert had taken advantage of the eagerness of her young mind, and Nero and Aelia had intended to do the same.

But that wouldn't happen again.

Mox wasn't in his room when Sloane entered, for which she was grateful. She stripped down in the bathroom, a jug of water at her side, and cleaned up the best she could, shuddering from the cold the whole time. Mox's pants were hopelessly long on her, so she wore her own. She put on his shirt but rolled up the sleeves so they bunched around her elbows. She was braiding her hair when he came in, his hand in the beat-up green siphon he had been wearing when she first met him.

For a second, they just stared at each other, Sloane's fingers still tangled in her hair. Then she turned back to the mirror.

"I guess you don't have to worry you'll be recognized," she said.

"No," he said. "Only a few know my face. *Him* included."

That was how she might have talked about the Dark One. It was the way she had referred to him with Albie—as if the man were always in the room with them, never needing to be named.

"In Genetrix's doomsday prophecy," she said, "is it one person against another? One Chosen, one . . . destructive?"

"With Genetrix as the battleground," Mox said, sounding distant. "Two men colliding."

She nodded. "And you think Nero is one of them," she said. "Your Dark One."

"Is that what you called yours?"

She thought of him, his waxy face twisting with amusement as he told her to choose. Choose, between her and Albie, between one horror and another.

She swallowed, hard. "Yes."

"Then yes," Mox said. "That's what I think."

Sloane finished her braid and tied it off with the band she kept around her wrist. It was so tight that it tugged at her scalp when she moved her head.

"Here." Mox went to the little table where she had gulped down a cold can of soup the night before. He picked up his other wrist siphon. It was no finer than the one he wore, but it was more flexible, made of little black plates like the scales of a fish. He made a trilling sound, and all the plates stiffened, like he had sent an electric charge through them. He held it out to her.

"I know you can't use it," he said, "but in a city like this, you attract attention without one."

Sloane sighed and guided her left hand into the empty glove the plates made. As soon as her fingers were in place, the plates collapsed around her hand, draping over it like a piece of chain mail. Mox turned her hand over to tighten the wrist cuff. For a man with such big hands, there was an elegance to his fingers.

"Well," she said. "Let's go have a chat with a prophet, I guess."

They made their way to the train station on foot at first, walking along the river. Mox had an ease about him that confused her; he kept his hands in his jacket pockets, his head tilted back to take in the daylight. Sloane, however, felt hypervigilant. She twitched at every footstep or distant shout she heard.

Away from the Loop, the buildings looked even more like ones she recognized. They were made of the red brick that Chicago favored, rows of two- or three-flats with strips of grass and leafless trees between them. Every so often they passed something that was otherworldly to her: a house that was just an orb, turning slowly between two needle-like structures; a sculpture that looked like it was collapsing in on itself from one angle and rebuilding itself from another; a store façade that put art nouveau vines together with linear stickwork under a mansard roof, a visual mash-up that made Sloane cringe.

When they reached 31st Street, Mox hailed a taxi with a flash of light from his palm and a squeak from the whistle fastened behind his tooth. Sloane had seen other people wear whistles that way, silver glinting when they smiled and clicking when they ate. It was more convenient than sticking a whistle in your mouth whenever you wanted to do something, she assumed.

They were silent in the taxi, both listening to the radio playing from the dashboard.

"Stocks of Siphona Technica are at a record high this week, after hitting rock bottom last year when reports of misconduct—" The driver changed the station to one with instrumental music that sounded like deep-sea recordings of whales.

"So you don't really work at the Tankard, I take it?" she said.

"I do, actually," he said brightly. "Weekends and the occasional mid-week shift."

"How does that work with . . ." Sloane paused. "Your other job?"

"My other job is only demanding at certain times," Mox said. "And it doesn't pay very well."

The driver poked the radio dial again, and the news returned.

"Reports of a skirmish between the Resurrectionist and the Army of Flickering in Bridgeport last night have surfaced. There was only one casualty, a police officer by the name of Paul Tegen. He is survived by his wife and his two-year-old son." The driver changed the station again. Mox looked unconcerned, as if the mention of the Resurrectionist had no effect on him whatsoever.

They crossed the river and cruised down Canal Street, past a bright pink building that bulged on one side. It turned out to be a grocery store called Hey Presto! with a flying shopping cart as the logo.

The taxi stopped in front of Union Station, a wide, tan building with a row of Doric columns across the front. She remembered the Great Hall inside it, with its gridded skylight swelling up toward the heavens in a barrel curve. She had been there only once, as a child, taking the train from central Illinois to the city with Cameron and their mother.

She followed Mox in. It was difficult for her to keep up with him —a new experience for someone as tall as Sloane, but Mox's strides were long and purposeful. Once inside, though, he seemed lost in the chaos, twitching when people called out to each other or got too close to him. Sloane thought of the can of green beans slamming into the wall the night before. She dragged him toward the line to purchase tickets. "You've got cash, right?" she said. "Hand it over and stay here. I'll do the talking."

When she got back from the ticket counter, he was standing helplessly in the middle of the room, staring at her. She pushed a ticket at him, and together they walked to the right platform, with Sloane directing them. Mox seemed easily confused by signs and distracted by everything around them. She had to drag him along more than once before they made it to a bench where they could wait in the chill of spring, when no one else was outside. She wore the cloak he had worn the day before, the hem singed by magical fire, and he wore a jacket not unlike one she might have worn at home.

"You don't do a lot of traveling," she said to him once they were seated. Her words found a shape in the air, like smoke.

"I do magic," he said, and he chewed his thumbnail. "Never been good at the other stuff."

"Like . . . basic existence?"

To her surprise, he nodded. "I used to break all my mom's dishes. I'd be holding one and then—I don't know. I'd get distracted and— *crack*. Light bulbs too. Even forks and spoons, sometimes."

"What you told me about your parents and Arlington," Sloane said, "was that true?"

He nodded. "They put me on a plane to Chicago when I was . . . nine? Ten? I've only seen them a couple times since then." He ripped his thumb out of his mouth. "They think I'm dead now. It's better that way."

"They don't sound great," she said.

"Maybe they weren't." His thumb was bleeding at the cuticle. He had bitten down too hard. "Or maybe they just . . . weren't prepared to have a kid bursting at the seams with magic. It's still—" He shifted. "Too much. It's too much. Makes me—not settled. Not stable."

She put a hand on his arm. It was the only thing she could think to do. "I don't handle magic all that well either," she said, and she held up the hand that wore the siphon, letting the bright light of day reflect on its scales. "It's not that I've never done anything with it, you know. It's just unpredictable. And . . ." She shrugged. "I guess I don't like it."

"You don't like it?" He frowned at her. "But—"

The train was coming, the brakes squealing as it charged into the station. It was bulky and awkward-looking, with protruding lights on the front that blinked until it came to a stop. Mox and Sloane got up and walked along the platform to the last cars so they could avoid the crowd that had gathered around the first few.

Sloane climbed the narrow steps into a riot of color. The train's carpet was a garish pattern in yellow, blue, and pink, all triangles and circles and squiggly lines. But it wasn't a standard passenger train; it had compartments, each with two long bench seats facing each other. She ducked into one of them and settled in next to the window. Mox closed the compartment door behind them, whistled, then tugged on the door to test it. It didn't budge. He smiled.

"And you don't like magic," he said to her.

"If the only thing magic did was facilitate my curmudgeonly impulses, I would love it," she said. "Unfortunately it also has a tendency to rip people to shreds, so . . ."

Mox tipped his head in acknowledgment. He sat down across from her and draped one long arm across the back of the seat.

A few people tried the compartment door, but none of them made it through, so when the train pulled away from Union Station, Mox and Sloane were still alone. He was looking out the window, and she found herself looking at him. His face was an assemblage of opposites: stern nose and strong brow sitting over a vulnerable mouth, ears sticking out, childlike, through the tangle of hair, which had a few threads of gray she hadn't noticed before, despite his obvious youth.

"Feels like you're trying to take me apart," he said without looking away from the window.

"You're hard to figure out," she said.

He raised his eyebrows. "So are you."

"No, I'm not." Sloane shook her head. "You just haven't been to my world."

"Something tells me I wouldn't do well there."

"Are you doing well here?"

He laughed. "No, I guess not."

The train charged out of the city, following the path of the river southwest, Lake Michigan behind them. It was the same path Sloane had once taken to go to her childhood home. Her mother had told her to get her things out of the garage because she needed the space. For what, she hadn't said. So Sloane had packed up her stuff and Cameron's too and piled all the boxes in a U-Haul to drive back with her. She knew the big empty stretches that awaited them, cornfields crumpled by the chill of autumn, silos standing alone on the horizon. She didn't think Genetrix's rural Midwest would be any different than her own.

"Your soldiers will be all right in your absence?" she said.

"It's not the first time I've left them," he said. "The working that holds them to life will last a few days without me there to sustain it, so they won't fall apart." He paused. "Well, some of them might literally fall apart, but that's easily remedied."

Sloane cringed. "You were very — *tender* with that woman whose arm you stitched back on."

"Oh, Tera?" He shrugged. "Well, it's a delicate business, sewing someone's arm back on."

"I just didn't realize you had personal relationships with them."

"Ah." Mox had been calm, sitting back on the bench, his legs crossed at the ankle. But now he sat forward and started tapping his fingers together. "They're my friends."

She had to be careful. She wasn't sure what might make Mox's magic lash out, and they were on a moving train. "From . . . before?" she said.

"From before they were dead, yes," he said.

"How did you bring them back?" She wasn't sure that she wanted to hear the answer, really. Knowing it would make it hard not to try it herself with Albie or Cameron or Bert. Hard not to make them a barrier between her and the world.

"I wanted it," he replied, "more deeply than I have ever wanted anything."

"And that was enough?"

"That's just the part I can explain." His hands squeezed into fists. She reached out and covered them with her own. He flinched at her touch and stared at her, dark eyes wide.

"We don't have to talk about it," she said, sitting back.

But his hands were relaxing, his body uncurling. He was, she thought, a thousand things at once. A language she did not know.

"You said you were at a funeral when you were brought here," he said. "Whose was it?"

It had been a long time since she had thought about Albie. He crept into her mind, of course, when she wasn't vigilant. In unguarded moments before she fell asleep or when she woke up thinking about what she might tell him, only to realize she would not be telling him anything ever again. But she had not tried to think of him.

"Albie," she said, and the name was soft in her mouth. She added, "He was my best friend."

Mox nodded as if he knew, and perhaps he did know something about it. "Was it your Dark One who killed him?"

"No. Well, indirectly, maybe. He . . . killed himself." She hadn't said it out loud before — not like that, anyway. So plain, so bare. "We took down the Dark One ten years ago, but Albie never quite got past it. I guess I haven't either." She forced a laugh. "How do you get over that? The shit we saw. The shit we *did*." The knot of scars on the back of her hand was a constant reminder of that. "In some ways it's been easier, being here. Doing the same thing over again. I know how to do it, how to be *this*. But I never quite figured out how to be a regular person."

Mox smiled a little. "I know the feeling," he replied.

They lapsed into silence then, but there was no tension in it. Both of them just stared out the window, watching the passing buildings grow sparser and sparser.

34

Tᴇɴ ᴍɪɴᴜᴛᴇꜱ from the St. Louis station, Sloane felt something within her go quiet. It was as if loud music had been playing, and someone had cut the power. Mox gave her a knowing look.

"Haven city," he said. "They're not content to just outlaw magic within the city limits; they also have to dampen it. They would shut it down entirely if it were legal."

"They can do that?" she said.

"A siphon is just a machine that amplifies magical energy. It can also do the opposite." He offered her a grim smile. "Which is why it was so alarming to my parents when I had uncontrollable magic despite living in a haven city."

He really hadn't been exaggerating when he bragged about his raw power, Sloane thought. Her entire body felt heavy.

They exited the train and walked down a concrete tunnel that led to the Grand Hall. The building that housed it looked like a castle, with its stone walls and towers and pointed red roofs, but the hall itself looked like Chicago's Union Station, barrel-vaulted and spacious. There was no skylight, however, just green tile and decorative knots in the arches, with feminine figures holding lights featured here and there, offering their glow to the heavens. Red booths and chairs were arranged all around them, places for people to sit as they waited.

A security officer standing next to the doorway gestured for them
to go left, toward an area with metal lockers that was set off by velvet rope. Mox led the way to one of the lockers and unfastened his
siphon from his wrist and fingers. Sloane followed his example. He
placed the siphon lovingly inside the locker, and she nestled hers beside it.

They joined a line of people waiting to exit the roped-off area.
At the front were two security officers holding what looked like
metal paddles. They ran the paddles up and down people's bodies
and around whatever bags they carried, then waved them through.
Sloane raised an eyebrow at Mox.

"Siphon detectors," he said. "Can't have anyone smuggling in
magic, can they?"

"Guess not," Sloane said.

The line moved quickly, and Sloane made it past the paddles without a hitch. But the second the woman with the tight bun held her
detector up to Mox, he put up both hands and stepped back.

"I'm an Exception," he said.

The woman sighed. "ID card, please."

Mox had already taken a white card that looked like a standard
driver's license from his back pocket. The security officer held it up
to the light for a few seconds, then returned it to him.

"All right," she said. "You're good."

Mox strolled through the security checkpoint to Sloane's side and
led the way to the exit. She waited for him to explain, but it didn't
seem like he was going to, so once they were in the taxi line, she
poked him hard in the arm. "Exception?" she said.

He sighed and bent his head toward hers, almost like he was going
to kiss her. She lurched back, but he only pointed to his eye. He held
the lower lid down so she could see better.

Her cheeks warm, Sloane leaned in. His eyes were dark brown
with a hint of green near the iris. One of them was unremarkable,
but in the other, the iris appeared to be broken, as if the pupil were
spilling into it. His eye shifted minutely, and the misshapen pupil
glinted, iridescent as a fish scale.

"What . . ." she said.

"I don't know," he replied. "But it makes those machines go hay-wire."

He straightened and stepped out of the taxi line for the next available car, leaving Sloane standing there, strangely breathless.

Sibyl's house was a duplex with a chain-link fence and a set of kitschy wind chimes hanging next to the front door. A blue Toyota sat in her driveway, its bumper rusted. Mox walked up the porch steps, opened the screen door — which had several holes in it — and knocked.

When Sloane thought of a prophet, she imagined a man in robes warning of coming doom or maybe a fortuneteller in some smoky back room shuffling tarot cards. Sibyl was neither. She was small, middle-aged, wearing a green cardigan with a little star pinned near the collar. She had flung the door open in a panic — or a rage, it was hard to tell — and stuck her finger right in Mox's face.

"What have you brought with you?" she demanded. She looked over his shoulder at Sloane, standing at the bottom of her steps.

"I'll explain," Mox said, "but not out here, obviously."

"If you think I'm inviting *that* into my house," she said, jerking her head toward Sloane, "you've got another thing coming." She stuck her feet into a pair of slippers next to the door and stepped outside. "We'll go into the garage."

"Sib," Mox said.

"*Don't call me that!*" She looked around, wild-eyed, like a neighbor was going to pop out of a bush. "Good Lord, boy, have you forgotten where you are?"

She charged down the steps, giving Sloane a wide berth, and led them across her neat lawn to the garage. It smelled like mildew and gasoline, and it was packed with old furniture, sagging boxes, and rugs rolled up tight. For all that it looked like an assembly of junk, there was a kind of order to it, Sloane noticed. Sibyl wandered through the maze of possessions, turning on lamps, clearing chairs, plucking cobwebs from her hair.

"Sit!" she said, gesturing to the chairs. "You're both huge; it's intimidating to a little old lady like me."

"You're not an old lady," Mox said with unmistakable fondness. But he took one of the seats.

Sloane stayed where she was. "I'd rather not," she said. "It's pretty obvious you don't want me here."

"She doesn't mean anything by it," Mox said.

"Don't I?" Sibyl raised an eyebrow. "The magic coming off the two of you is going to choke me to death, even dampened. So what is she? Is she like you?"

"Dunno," Mox said. "Depends what you think I am, exactly."

"*Chosen,* obviously. You both stink of it," Sibyl replied, and Sloane felt like someone had dropped a stone directly into the center of her.

"Chosen?" Sloane looked at Mox. "You're—"

Splotches of red appeared on his cheeks and crept down to his throat.

"Now, now," Sibyl said. "Even the dark things of this world are Chosen. It's not a badge of honor. If anything, it's like a blinking arrow that says 'Kill me!'" She opened the refrigerator in the corner, took out a bottle of water, and fumbled with the cap, hands trembling. "In this case, though—Mox here is our fated savior, wrapped up in enough siphons to encase a city block in ice, and surrounded by dead bodies. Doesn't bode well for Genetrix."

Mox. Chosen. Sloane felt like a computer that had been fried by a power surge.

"Your faith in me always lifts my spirits," Mox said, with a bite to his words. "Sloane was Chosen, too, Sibyl. But in an alternate universe."

Sibyl looked Sloane over, then raised an eyebrow. "Interesting," she said. "Sit down, girl."

This time, Sloane did, finding a lawn chair near Mox and perching on the edge of it. She was wedged between a lawn statue of a cherub, worn by rain, and a cardboard box with *Charlie's Room* scribbled on it in permanent marker.

"On your other world, you fought a battle," Sibyl said, sinking down onto a fat tree stump. She set her water bottle down and sat slumped, her arms around her knees. She looked so small that way, the bones of her spine sticking out even through her cardigan. "It clings to you still."

Sibyl was looking down at Sloane's scarred right hand. Sloane resisted the urge to cover it up.

"That was not *your* battle," Sibyl said. "Not really."

Sloane's instinct was to argue. It had been her battle; of course it had. The Dark One had taken her brother from her. That she would fight him had been an inevitability not even worth discussing. But there was too much truth in what Sibyl had said for Sloane to deny it. It had been a battle worth fighting, but that didn't mean it was *Sloane's*. For ten years she had been jiggling her knee, waiting for something to make sense, for something new to happen. But until now, it had been too terrible to consider that there might be another fight in front of her and that it might be *hers* in a way the other had not.

"Why, exactly, have you come to see me?" Sibyl said.

"I was brought to Genetrix against my will by Aelia and Nero and . . . whoever else," Sloane said. "They told us the Resurrectionist was destroying our world along with Genetrix, and they wouldn't let us go home until we killed him for them. But Mox . . ." She frowned. "I just want to know what's real."

"What's real." Sibyl sighed and stood. "If we're going to talk about what's real, we'll need whiskey."

The first thing Sibyl did was put on a record: *Parsley, Sage, Rosemary and Thyme,* by Simon and Garfunkel. The plucking of the guitar was eerie in the dim living room, its furniture so old that the fabric on the seats was threadbare. The low pink sofa creaked when Mox sat on it; he looked like an adult perched on a child-size stool. The air had crackled around him when he walked into the room, and Sibyl had told him, sharply, to keep himself under control. It had no effect; Mox just scowled.

Sibyl went into the kitchen to pour whiskey, and as they waited for her to return, Sloane browsed her bookshelves. There were no books on them, just a vast collection of *National Geographic*s and knitting magazines. There were porcelain figurines, too, of ballet dancers and stretching cats and hot-air balloons. It was as if Sibyl had seen an encyclopedia entry about what belonged in a grandmother's house and had replicated it exactly, down to the doilies on the mahogany coffee table.

When the second song on the album started to play, Sloane snorted. "You really like to wrap yourself in clichés, don't you?" she said to Sibyl when the woman returned with three tumblers of whiskey.

Sibyl smiled. "The song discusses patterns repeating themselves," Sibyl said. "I thought you would both appreciate the sentiment."

Sloane sipped the whiskey, which was like swallowing a mouthful of smoke. Her eyes watered as she tried to stifle a cough. Sibyl, on the other hand, downed half her glass at once, then sat in the recliner next to the record player to watch the record spin.

"This is a gift I didn't choose and didn't want," Sibyl said after a while. "I was two years old when the *Tenebris* Incident occurred, and fourteen when I began to go into trances. They were frightening—I myself didn't remember them, but I was told I spoke in riddles, as if possessed. And people avoided me once my ramblings began to come true. No one wants to know their future, not really." She sipped the whiskey, and Sloane perched on the arm of the couch, where the pink fabric was torn and some of the stuffing was hanging out.

"It was an uncommon gift even among the magically adept—and even more uncommon was the large scale of my predictions. They pertained to world events. The outcomes of battles, natural disasters, the passage of laws. And eventually . . . the end of everything. I have a recording of it, actually." She stood and set the tumbler down on the table next to the record player. She lifted the needle from the record, then opened a nearby cabinet and searched through a large basket of cassette tapes. Sloane wasn't close enough to read the labels, but they were homemade, curling at the edges.

Sibyl found the right tape and took it to a little cassette player in a corner of the room, on a shelf next to the *National Geographic*s. There was a high whine as the tape rewound. Sloane drank more of her whiskey and tried not to look at Mox.

Sibyl pressed Play and stood before the cassette player like she was standing at an altar. The recording crackled and popped at first, then steadied, a voice taking shape.

"It will be," the voice said, low and strange, "the end of Genetrix. The unmaking of worlds. Something stands between Genetrix and its twin. The Dark One will excise it, and the worlds will be crushed together, and that will be the end of all."

Sloane's body jerked to attention. She thought of the thread of light she had seen connecting Genetrix to Earth, at the bottom of the Chicago River.

This world and its twin. The Needle.

The low croak went on. "The Dark One of Genetrix will be hidden, but not secret, with a thirst that will never be slaked." Sibyl, standing before her cassette player, was mouthing the words along with the recording. "Their Equal is the hope of Genetrix, born marred by magic and mastered by a power previously unknown to us."

Sloane watched Sibyl's fingers tapping her leg, as if the prophecy were a song and she was dancing to it. Perhaps it was—perhaps the light threads she had seen made music, like the strings of a violin or a guitar, and the music came to Sibyl in prophecies.

"Twice will Equals greet each other anew, and the fate of the worlds is in their hands."

Mox was staring at his hands, clasped between his knees so tightly his knuckles had gone white.

The Sibyl of the recording spoke the last line again but so quietly that Sloane could hardly hear it, and then the tape stopped.

"Your eye," Sloane said. "You're marred by magic."

Sibyl was still standing behind her, but she found herself speaking only to Mox.

Mox nodded. He seemed unsteady, like he might shake apart at any moment. "Nero was my teacher for a decade," Mox said, lower lip trembling slightly. "He betrayed me." His eyes were locked on Sloane's, the fault in his iris now imperceptible again without the light shining through it. "He murdered the army meant for the Chosen One, the first Army of Flickering. He blamed it on me. Twisted the prophecy against me."

The words scraped out of his throat, sending a chill down Sloane's spine. She thought of the Resurrectionist's long fingers working stiff thread through the soldier's detached arm and drawing it tight, of the desperate way he had screamed Ziva's name in the street near the safe house. If his raised soldiers were the army meant for the Chosen One, then of course he had known them before they died, had trusted them to stand with him against an evil he didn't comprehend.

Nero. The man with the unquenchable thirst.

They would meet on the battleground of Genetrix, and the fate of the world — the *worlds* — was in their hands.

The Magic of Cruelty
by Erica Perez

In his book *The Manifestation of Impossible Wants: A New Theory of Magic,* Arthur Solowell makes the bold claim that "desire cannot be threatened or manipulated into being." While I agree that simple threats do not produce reliable magical results, it is naive to suggest that coercion is never effective in influencing magic. Perhaps Mr. Solowell was fortunate enough to grow up in a community of moral adults who never exerted their influence against children, but I was not. I saw the way that cruel parents shaped my peers and, therefore, their desires.

And it came in all forms too. Sometimes a strict religious upbringing turned an open mind into a closed one that could perform only basic, practical workings. Sometimes utter neglect created a complete disregard for boundaries, pushing someone to involve other people in unethical workings. Pressure to succeed at the highest level turned friends away from creativity and imagination in their magic. Emotional abuse twisted a person's work to become more brutal, less finessed. One of my most talented friends lost the ability to do workings entirely and now lives in St. Louis, a haven city.

A desire is not a whim, as Solowell aptly states. But a desire is not immovable, unchangeable. The variable to consider is power. Who has power over the individual in question? Does anyone have too much power? Are any of those in power abusive spouses, family members, or friends? Is the individual particularly susceptible to manipulation, with a desire to please—or simply to avoid pain? Have they been isolated from their peers or the outside world? We must learn to recognize the signs. We cannot pretend this problem doesn't exist. The future of our children depends on it.

35

THERE WASN'T MUCH to say after that, so Sibyl invited Sloane and Mox to stay for dinner, likely to fill the silence. Sloane accepted because she didn't know what else to do. So they were all trapped together in the little house, orbiting each other in silence. Sibyl busied herself at the stove shoving lemon slices in the body cavity of a raw chicken, and Sloane knelt on the beige carpet near the cassette player, looking through the magazines. There were photographs of countries she had never heard of, their names and shapes and fates altered by the division between the universes. She saw rough-looking siphons on the hands of villagers in rural Romania and remote Siberia—an oddity still, the accompanying article said, but not unheard of in the younger generation.

"Mox said he doesn't think the Drains are controlled by anyone," she said, looking up from a photograph of a tractor on a small farm in Argentina. There was an island separating the kitchen from the living room. Sibyl stood behind it, chopping something. Onions, judging by the smell.

Mox had disappeared a few minutes before, enticed by Sibyl's offer of a shower and a change of clothes. Her husband had left plenty when he died, and they were still in her bedroom dresser. Sloane could hear the spray of water down the hall.

"It's important not to confuse causation with correlation," Sibyl said, scrutinizing the pepper grinder she held in both hands. Even though she was a widow, she was still wearing her wedding band. "However, we know that a Drain happens every time one of you shows up to kill him, so they do seem to be related."

"Wait . . . they do?" Sloane set the magazine down and got to her feet. "So you think they're maybe caused by . . . the presence of an outsider?"

"All I know is you're not supposed to be here," Sibyl said. "Maybe the Drains are like the world's allergic reaction to you." At Sloane's raised eyebrow, she scowled. "Well, I don't know, girl, I'm not a scientist."

Sloane leaned against the island. "What *did* you do for a career? Spitting out prophecy's probably not that lucrative, right?"

"It is not lucrative at all in a haven city," Sibyl said. "But magic grinds up against me like sandpaper, so I didn't have much of a choice, did I?" She shrugged. "I was a teacher. Retired now, obviously."

"Grinds up against you like sandpaper," Sloane repeated. "That's . . . odd."

"What does it feel like for you?" Sibyl asked.

"Like sticking my head in a vise," Sloane said. "Makes my hands go numb sometimes. I'm not wild about it myself, actually."

"Hm." Sibyl put on her oven mitts and picked up a heavy pot with the chicken in it. Sloane moved forward to open the oven door for her, and the chicken went in.

"He loves it," Sibyl said, nodding toward the hall bathroom where Mox was showering. "To him it looks like . . . beams of light or something. He plays magic like guitar strings. *Pluck*—your gravity's gone. *Pluck*—your house is on fire. Delightful."

Beams of light. It sounded like the working Aelia had done on Sloane before she had dived in the river. Maybe Aelia had learned it from Nero, who had learned it from Mox.

"Have you ever met Nero?" Sloane said.

"I have." Sibyl's eyes hardened. "He wears masks on top of masks, that man. Can't ever get a look at what's underneath." She set the kitchen timer, which was shaped like an egg. Painted on it was the phrase *Have an Egg-cellent breakfast!*

"You, girl," she said, leaning closer to Sloane, "have the grittiest of all magic. Fate's grabbed you hard and it's not letting go. So I want you to remember something." She closed her fingers around Sloane's arm tightly, her grip strong for a woman of her size. "The line between a Chosen One and his opposite is hair-fine, so don't get too cozy on one side of it."

The smell of onions was pungent enough to make Sloane's eyes sting. She tugged her arm free. "All I want is to go home," she said.

"That," Sibyl said, her eyes glittering, "is the fattest lie I've ever heard. You want *everything*. You're a bottomless pit. Makes me feel exhausted just thinking about you."

"You know, you're not such a peach yourself," Sloane snapped.

Mox called out from the bedroom, his low voice carrying easily across the house. "Sloane. Can I get a hand?" She remembered the blade stuck above his hip just the night before and left the kitchen. The hallway was painted the same milky pink as the living-room sofa, and it was covered with pictures—of Sibyl and her husband and children, Sloane assumed, from the way people were arranged, stiff and formal. It was hard to believe that this woman, with her aggressively normal house and family, could have spoken so many prophecies, including one about the end of the world. No wonder magic was so repellent to her. It was the opposite of the life she had built for herself, in all its rigidity.

Mox was standing in the bedroom wearing a pair of worn blue jeans and a gray T-shirt, which surprised her, since she hadn't seen either type of garment since she arrived on Genetrix. He stood braced against Sibyl's dresser, hands tight around the edge and his head down. His hair was straight when it was wet, and longer, almost brushing his shoulders. His feet were bare.

He was, she thought, very solid. Spare through his midsection, likely due to the difficulty of his life for the past ten years, living on cans of soup, but his long arms were sturdy enough to fill out T-shirt sleeves, and his shoulders were broad, like he was built for more muscle than he had. Maybe in another universe.

And he was also losing control; the pressure of the air around him was so different from that of the air in the hallway that Sloane's ears popped when she drew closer to him.

"Sorry," he said in a tight, small voice without looking at her. "But you calmed me down . . . on the train."

"Oh." Sloane tried to think of what she had done on the train. She'd touched his hands. The prospect of touching him right now was far more daunting. On the train, it had been instinct, but here . . . she would have to mean it.

Air pressed against her face the same way it had when she was a kid and biked to the top of Oak Street just so she could ride down again. Like she could take fistfuls of it.

Coward, she said to herself, and she put a hand on Mox's shoulder right where it joined with his neck. His wet hair tickled her knuckles. She leaned closer to him. "What is it?" she asked. He didn't answer. He was hyperventilating, she noted, judging by the shifting of his rib cage under his shirt. She put her hand on the back of his neck and squeezed lightly. His skin was hot to the touch. It had been a long time since she had touched someone who wasn't Matt in this way, vulnerable and presumptuous.

"Talking about him—all the memories," Mox said, and it sounded like his teeth were gritted, though he was still hidden behind a curtain of hair. "It's—"

"A lot?" Sloane supplied. "Well, let's just . . . sit for a second."

She pressed down gently, and as Mox went to his knees, she went with him. She sat with her back against the dresser, one of the drawer pulls digging into her spine. He knelt there, his arms shaking, still refusing to look at her.

"Me and my friend—the one who died," she said, and she felt that old, familiar terror rising up inside her. "We were taken captive by Earth's Dark One. It was only for a day." She dug her shoes into the carpet. Sibyl had raised an eyebrow when she walked into the house without removing them, but she hadn't said anything. "But the Dark One gave me a choice."

She felt a sensation like knives piercing her throat when she swallowed.

"He told me that one of us—me or Albie—would suffer, and I

would decide which one." *You or him?* She didn't close her eyes. If she had, she would have seen it, the Dark One's placid face as he waited for her answer in the doorway, leaning against the frame. "I didn't want to. But he said that if I didn't, it would happen to us both, and why should both of us endure that?"

Mox had straightened ever so slightly to look at her through his curtain of hair. It was curling as it dried.

"So in the end," Sloane said, forcing out the words that she had never, not even once, said out loud, "I chose him. I spared myself."

The horror was so close to the surface now. If she had wanted to, she could have released it, shuddered with it, screamed it into being. She was afraid to look at Mox, afraid to see the revulsion she was sure he felt. He had killed, but only to save himself; he had not done this, thrown a dear friend into the fire to keep himself from burning. No one Sloane knew had done that.

But she made herself look at him anyway, because she deserved it, deserved to know just how disgusting she was, how she had betrayed Albie and ruined him and set him on a path that would lead to his death—

But Mox was just looking at her.

The pressure in the air had diminished; Sloane no longer felt like she was chewing on every breath. "I know," she said, choking a little, "about the rage that takes over when you think about someone. About the rage that changes you."

Mox tucked his hair behind his ears with both hands. His face looked thinner this way, and pale. He was tired, and no wonder— he had lived for years just scraping by in abandoned buildings and warehouses with an army that fell to pieces every time it moved, and sometimes even when it didn't, and the burden of what had happened to them falling on his shoulders. He was as tired as she was.

He said, "There's a thought experiment—moral philosophy— called the trolley problem, have you heard of it?" She shook her head no. "Basically it says there's a trolley on a track, and if it goes one way, it will kill five people, but if you flip the switch, it will only kill one. And you're supposed to say whether you would flip the switch, whether you could bear to be directly responsible for a death even if you're sparing lives." He scowled. "I always hated it, *hated* it, and I used to tell my teacher that what I would do is take the person forcing me to make the choice and throw *him* on the tracks, because he's the one who really deserved it."

He smiled a little, forcing a crease into his cheek.

"Not really the point of the exercise," he said. He covered her hand, balanced on her kneecap, with his own. It made her feel small, but in a good way — in a way she never got to feel, being as tall as she was. "But the person who asks you to make that kind of choice, between you and a friend, between pain and guilt — *fuck* that person."

His hand tightened on hers. For a moment they just stared at each other, and she felt like the horror was farther away, that it had settled deeper inside her again.

They ate Sibyl's chicken in silence, all of them transparently relieved when Sloane took her last bite. Mox and Sloane busied themselves in the kitchen scooping potatoes into containers for the refrigerator, scrubbing plates and pots. Sibyl let them take over and went out to the back steps to smoke a cigarette — "My afternoon indulgence," she had called it, not that Mox or Sloane had said anything. Then she started up the engine of the old Toyota and drove them to the train station, wearing thick glasses with green tortoiseshell frames.

As they drove past the rows of low brick buildings and empty lots that patched the land between Sibyl's house and the station, Sloane marveled at how barren everything looked without the magic-influenced architecture that defined Chicago. She had gotten used to it, even in the short time she had been on Genetrix. The most interesting buildings in St. Louis were churches, which seemed to have gotten more plain in the absence of Unrealist or Bygoneist architects — flat, white buildings with sharp corners that reminded her of minimalist structures on Earth, but with glass-block windows arranged in the shape of crosses.

Sibyl gave Mox a hard look when they pulled up to the curb next to the station and said, "Keep your eyes open."

He leaned in and kissed her cheek, even though she looked just as stern and irritable as she had since they arrived. "Thanks."

Sloane got out without saying goodbye. She was distracted by a buzzing sensation on the surface of her skin, like a purring cat. They had to be closer to the limits of the magic-canceling siphon's power here. When Mox shut his door and the Toyota pulled away, she turned to him and asked, "How did you meet her, anyway? I never got to meet the prophet on Earth."

"I did a lot of poking around at the Camel," he said, tipping his head back to look at the sky. It was cloudy, the sun covered with a pale haze. "They could never keep me out of any room for long. Something's off—do you feel that?" He wiggled his fingers. "All bright and shiny for me. Magic's back."

"Why would they turn off the dampening?"

"I can think of only one reason," he said. "Because they know I can use magic whether the dampener is functional or not, and they want to be able to use it too."

"Well," Sloane said, "let's get our siphons before they find us, then."

Mox led the way to the row of lockers where they had stored the siphons. When he entered their combination and opened the door, it was with a sigh of relief. The siphons were there, side by side. He put the green one on his hand and flexed his fingers, then took the tooth attachment from its little pouch and stuck it in place over a canine. Sloane put on her siphon grudgingly, hating the coldness of it against her hand, and the weight, and the way it pinched her wrist.

Mox watched her fumbling with the clasp for a few seconds, then reached across her to take her wrist in his hands. He tucked a finger under the band to test its tightness, then pushed the clasp in place with a flick of his wrist. She felt heat where his fingertip had been against her skin. And she knew what that heat meant and where it might lead, if she let it, but it felt like another betrayal.

She shut the locker door and turned back to the Grand Hall. In Chicago, most of the people she saw wore the dramatic clothing that, she had learned, was a trademark of the magical elite. But in St. Louis, a haven city, there were no sweeping fabrics designed to display throat siphons or wrist siphons, no elaborate updos dotted with round gold clips that accentuated ear siphons, no modern mimicries of wizard garb. In fact, the fashion seemed to have gone in another direction, as a reaction: a woman in a collar so high it cradled her jaw rushed past them, tiny buttons drawing a line from throat to bellybutton; a man in a startlingly bright pink and orange shirt had fabric around his wrists and his upper arms, but between them was mesh showing bare skin, untouched by magical technology; a sullen-looking child wore a gray shift that looked like a monk's robe. The child eyed Sloane's wrist, then scowled at her. Sloane scowled back.

Then a quick movement caught her eye—someone darting behind a pillar. She reached behind her and slapped Mox's stomach a little too hard.

"Ouch," he said. "What—"

Sloane raised her siphon hand and pointed it at a Flickering soldier, approaching under the shadowed awning that framed the room.

Mox stiffened and turned too, facing the other direction, so they were almost back to back.

"Sloane."

She recognized the voice; it belonged to Edda, who had been with her and the others during the Drain. Edda stepped around the red faux-velvet furniture on Sloane's left, her hand up and gleaming black. A spark danced across her palm, her siphon ready to launch its working.

"Hey there," Sloane said, her gaze shifting from Edda to the other soldier, a small, spry woman with a crown of curly black hair. She wore a siphon over her eye, a half-mask of smooth chrome fitted to her eye socket and cheekbone. "You're kind of harshing the vibe of my St. Louis vacation, Edda."

"Sloane, he's used some kind of working on you," Edda said steadily. "Some kind of mind manipulation."

All the civilians around her had already ducked behind tables and chairs, huddled together in the corners, or fled out the doors. The little girl in the monk garb was crouched near Edda's feet, shivering.

"Nope," Sloane said. "Next theory."

"I don't have any other theories," Edda said.

"Here's one: you've been lied to," Sloane said. She was just delaying, scanning the room for emergency exits. There was a solid wall of lockers on her right, but beyond it, she remembered the red glow of the sign. If she could get Mox to blast the lockers out of the way, they could make a run for it.

"Not possible." Edda was shaking her head. Sloane leaned back slightly to feel the press of Mox's shoulder against hers.

"I mean," Sloane said, "it's always *possible* that you've been lied to." She was nudging Mox with her elbow, the one facing the lockers. Gently, she tapped the locker door with her knuckles.

"Lieutenant, she's—" The soldier in front of Sloane started to say something, but Mox slammed a hand against the locker bank and let out a sharp sound almost too high to process. There was a deafening crunch as the lockers crumpled like a ball of aluminum, and Sloane began climbing over them the second she could get a foothold. She grabbed Mox by the shirt so she wouldn't lose him. The lockers collapsed while she heaved herself over them, throwing her off balance. She stumbled and dropped to her knees on the tile.

The masked soldier was singing a pure, clear note, and Edda joined her in harmony. The combination of voices made a weight settle on Sloane's shoulders and *press,* so she couldn't help but fall forward on her elbows. She screamed into her teeth and tried to crawl, but the weight was only growing heavier, crushing her, squeezing the air from her lungs—

Mox's palm flattened on the ground, and the whistle in his mouth sounded guttural, as deep as a lion's roar. The ground shook beneath just him at first, then rippled out, shuddering under Sloane's body, then rattling the remains of the lockers, then jolting, violent, launching her up and slamming her back down onto the tile. Mox reached for her and hooked his free arm around hers as he changed the pitch, sliding it up, up—

A sharp *crack* sounded, and Mox screamed, his concentration broken by a metal rod slamming into his back. It seemed to have sprouted from Edda's palm. Mox collapsed onto the tile. The masked soldier was just a few strides away from Sloane. Sloane knew that if the woman got a hand on her, they were both lost, captives of Nero.

So she did the only thing she could think of: She raised her hand, and whistled at what she hoped was exactly 170 MHz, to perform the magical breath. She focused on what Sibyl had said to her before they left, that Sloane wanted *everything,* that she was a bottomless pit, a creature of craving that stank of magic. Fire charged through her, burning in every limb. Still she whistled. Air rushed past her, roaring, and beneath that deafening sound was fabric tearing, glass shattering, screaming.

She watched Edda topple, her heels going over her head. The masked soldier was thrown against a pillar behind her. The locker bank, now a heap of twisted metal, creaked on the supports that bolted it to the ground, about to fly loose.

Mox's arm, solid as a girder, wrapped around her waist. He dragged her to the emergency exit and shoved the door open with his shoulder. Only when she saw the orange light of sunset did Sloane let herself stop whistling, her throat raw despite how brief the sound had been. She leaned into him, certain that she would collapse, but not yet, not yet.

Mox ran out into traffic, making one car veer and the other screech as the driver slammed on the brakes. He let go of Sloane and ripped the car door open.

"Get out," he said through gritted teeth, holding up his siphon.

The driver was a teenage boy with a cluster of pimples on his chin. He stared at Mox, unblinking. Sloane was already getting in the passenger's side and sinking gratefully into the seat.

"Now!" Mox roared, and fire danced over his fingertips, curled around his wrist, and crept toward his elbow. The boy scrambled to unbuckle his seat belt, grabbed his backpack, and bolted from the car. Mox got in and put his foot on the accelerator. The car lurched forward, and he jerked the wheel, almost sending them onto the sidewalk.

"Do you know how to drive?" Sloane demanded.

"No," Mox replied tersely.

"Gas right, brakes left," Sloane said. "Slow down! They don't know we took this car yet. You're just making it more obvious." She was feeling woozy. She slammed her hand into the dashboard to wake herself up. "Shit," she said. "Get to a highway as quickly as you can, then find a place to stop. Somewhere shitty—a motel, or . . ." She blinked; everything was shifting like the air had turned to molasses. "I'm going to pass out now."

"Sloane!" was the last thing she heard before collapsing back into the seat.

36

Sloane woke to the jerk of the brakes. The car — which smelled powerfully of the teenage boy's deodorant layered on top of cigarette smoke — was lurching into a parking spot off a narrow road. Across a stretch of tangled grass was a sign that read MOTEL, with the L losing its luster by the second. It was exactly the kind of place Sloane would have chosen if she had been awake.

"Good job," she said, her voice sounding strained. She watched Mox fiddle with the gearshift for a second, then reached over and put the car in park for him.

"The highway almost killed us both," Mox said. "You're not allowed to pass out again."

"Sorry, was that inconvenient for you?"

Mox was smiling as he opened the car door. He climbed out stiffly, likely sore from the metal rod Edda had hit him with. Sloane followed him. She felt tired but no longer dizzy.

Mox passed her a handful of coins, and she went to the main office to get them a room while he searched out a vending machine. It wouldn't be safe to stay long with the car parked in plain sight, but they could get a few hours' rest before leaving. She waited outside until Mox showed up with two bottles of water and a pile of snacks cradled against his stomach, and together they walked along the row of rooms to the one on the end.

The room was dark, thanks to few windows and the wood paneling on the walls, ceiling, and floor that made her feel like she was inside her own coffin. The bed was wide, with a dip in the middle. Sloane grimaced, went to the bed, and ripped the floral coverlet off. She stuffed it in the corner. Mox raised an eyebrow at her. Beneath the coverlet were white sheets that looked reassuringly starched.

"What?" she said. "They never wash the comforter, it's disgusting. Don't walk around barefoot either. Oh! And the phone—don't touch the phone."

He laughed. "I live in a warehouse and sleep on a pile of old blankets, remember?"

"Right," she said. "Speaking of which. Why don't you just . . . leave Chicago? Leave the country entirely?"

Mox dumped the food in a pile on the little table in the corner and drew the curtains closed. A whistle had all the lights in the room aglow.

"Before I learned to raise the army," he said, opening one of the water bottles and taking a long drink from it, "I tried to leave. He followed me. And everyone I had spoken to—everyone who helped me—" He made a strangled noise and stopped talking.

"Oh." Sloane crossed the room and set a hand, lightly, between his shoulder blades. "Is your back all right?"

"Don't know," he said.

She knew the smart thing would be to pull away. To refuse to play nurse, as she had in the beginning—unsuccessfully. But she couldn't bear it. Her hands dropped to the hem of his shirt and she smoothed it up, exposing an expanse of pale skin, the bumps of his spine, the faint lines of his musculature. *Very solid,* she thought again.

"I should tell you—" he started, and then she saw it, the metal plates stark against his fair skin and climbing up his back. Their color was warm, something between copper and gold. It was a siphon.

Her cheeks were hot, and she was glad he couldn't see them. She tried to focus. Nero had told her something about spine siphons. That people didn't use them. She didn't remember why, but she didn't want to ask Mox to explain it—

"He placed it there. Nero," Mox said, his voice low. "It means that when I'm near him, he has control over my magic. And only he can remove it."

His skin was already discoloring where Edda's metal rod had struck him high across his shoulders. But it hadn't broken the skin. Sloane laid her hand on top of the siphon, the set of interlocking plates that imitated the shape and curvature of his vertebrae. They were flat, almost flush with his back, so they would be undetectable under clothing. The metal was warmed by his skin, and now hers.

"I was young. Barely more than a child," Mox went on. "It can't be placed without consent. But he told me it would help me—like a set of training wheels for my magic, to make it less overwhelming until I was ready for it—"

"I'm going to kill him," she said evenly, and she stepped back, letting his shirt fall.

Mox looked over his shoulder at her. Her entire body was hot now, and burning, like acid was eating away at her chest. For Mox, this was when magic would come and level the little motel room even if he didn't want it to. But Sloane had not felt this way in a long time, had always subsumed anger into some other emotion because the anger itself was too much to handle. She breathed in through her nose.

"I," she said, "*hate* him."

Mox hesitated, just for a moment, before touching her cheek. She found something stable in the cool lines of his fingers, the utter stillness in his eyes.

"I know," he said. "I know."

They stood there for what felt like a long time, his hands on her, their faces close together. At first, Sloane told herself she would just stay there until the rage receded again. But then she couldn't bear to move. His breath smelled like chocolate—he had probably eaten some on the way back from the vending machine. His cheek was rough with five o'clock shadow. She brought her hands up to his wrists, not moving him, just holding him there.

"Kiss me," she said in a low voice. "Now."

He obeyed, gentle hands turned strict, buried in her hair. She backed him up against a wall and pressed into him, their hips and stomachs and chests warm against each other. It felt like the burn and tingle of magic but without the destruction, just the warmth and the *intent*. But magic was there too — and no wonder; Mox was drowning in it, suffused with it. Electricity danced over his fingers, and it was bright against her eyelids. She stopped to watch the lights play over his knuckles and laughed.

"Sorry," he said with a small smile. He looked smug.

"No, you're not, you ass," she said, and she kissed him again.

She thought of Matt only briefly, when she realized she didn't know the choreography anymore, didn't know how it worked when you were kissing someone so much bigger than you were, someone who wasn't so careful of you, who had just watched you send a dry gale through a train station that bowled over grown men and knew that you had murder in your heart because he had it in his too. Mox's arm wrapped around her back, and he lifted her clear off the ground. She laughed as he dropped her on the mattress and stood back to take off his shirt and his shoes without a trace of self-consciousness.

Sloane felt like the air was pressing in on her from all sides, and she wasn't sure if it was magic or just how it felt when you were with someone and you had stopped pretending.

She pulled him to her, and there was so much that he wasn't — wasn't shy about touching her, wasn't delicate as he slid her pants down over her ankles and tossed them aside, wasn't apologetic as he traced a new path up her body, wasn't put out when she laughed and tugged his hair to offer a suggestion. And God, his hair, tangled around her fingers; his teeth, teasing at her fingertips as he removed the siphon from her hand; his eyes, fixed on hers with unwavering focus as they discovered how to move together.

Sloane wanted everything, and then she had it — fire and gale and laughter; rage and warmth and comprehension.

She had just enough presence of mind to notice when all the objects in the room — pad of paper, bottle of water, bags of pretzels,

grimy remote, ancient TV set, dusty soap wrapped in lavender paper
—jerked up into the air and slammed back down again. She wasn't
even sure if that had been his doing or her own.

When Sloane woke, it was dark outside, and Mox was asleep on his
stomach with his hands folded under his head. His hair was rumpled,
but one curl trailed over his forehead, making her grin.

The spine siphon caught her attention, and she leaned over Mox's
shifting shoulders to get a closer look. Its structure was essentially the
same as any other siphon, with a sturdier plate at the top of Mox's
spine that, she assumed, held all the mechanics of the thing, and the
line of plates trailing down to the middle of his back. She was sure
they served their own function—greater skin contact might provide
a power source—from thermal energy, perhaps? Or it gave the device added stability?

She couldn't tell how it stayed put. It wasn't screwed into Mox's
vertebrae, but it was so stable it might as well have been. If magic
held it there, then magic had to be able to remove it, but as both Mox
and Nero had said, it was only the particular magic of the one who
had placed it that could remove it. That meant that every person had
a unique magical signature or fingerprint—that each person related
to magic differently, irrespective of ability or capacity.

But she couldn't get away from the idea that it was just a machine.
Deprive it of power, interrupt whatever energy it required to run,
and theoretically you should be able to disable it. It was possible no
one on Genetrix had determined how because they were so focused
on magic they had forgotten how to be practical, like Nero with his
magically secured workshop door.

"You're staring," Mox said. His eyes were open, though he hadn't
moved. He looked at her through the veil of hair hanging over his
forehead.

"Just . . . thinking," she said. "About how to get that thing off
you."

"So, the central question of my life," he said. "That or how to kill
someone who can control you."

She draped a leg over his back and pulled herself tight to his side so their faces were right next to each other.

"I was just thinking . . . it's a machine," she said. "And you can change the purpose of a machine by altering the way it runs."

"What," he said, touching his forehead to hers, "do you mean?"

"I mean, right now this thing channels magic," she said. "Can you turn it into a haven-city siphon? Can you make it channel . . . anti-magic?"

"Then I wouldn't be able to do anything."

"Yeah, I know, but I'm not thinking of the spine siphon, actually." She tweaked his forehead curl. "I'm thinking of that giant siphon in the floor of the Hall of Summons. If we could get it to disable *all* the magic, we could just kill Nero with our bare hands."

Mox blinked at her a few times, then crushed his lips against hers, pressing her back into the mattress. She laughed into his mouth, and he moved down to kiss her throat.

"You . . ." he said. "*Brilliant.*"

"You're telling me it . . . ah"—he was good at that—"*literally* never occurred to you that . . . okay, never mind."

He rolled on top of her. He was heavy, but she liked the full embrace of the weight and the way the top of his feet pressed against the bottom of hers.

"I know siphons," he said. "I fix mine, I fix Ziva's. Everyone's. And they break, you know, make you incapable of doing anything."

She tucked his hair behind his ears and smiled. "So let's break one on purpose," she replied.

It was night when they drove back to the city, one of Sloane's favorite times to drive through the Illinois prairie. It was just the highway and the twinkle of lights on the horizon: the runways of regional airports, farms in towns so small they didn't appear on most maps, the glow of a McDonald's arch next to a fueling station. Some towns had integrated magic into their everyday lives, Mox said, but for the most part, the residents of areas around haven cities were slow to adopt it, with the exception of the younger generation.

"That you could end the world with it doesn't seem to occur to most people," he remarked, tapping his fingers on the window.

Sloane smiled. "Most people lack ambition."

Mox laughed at that and turned down the music. They had discovered a CD that Sloane recognized in the glove compartment: *Pet Sounds* by the Beach Boys. Mox had read through the names of some of the more recent albums, and not a single one was familiar to Sloane. Certainly not the band Unfathomable Cosmic Blackness, which had produced the first album made entirely by magic. If you sang the notes exactly as written in one of the songs, Mox said, you could make multicolored lights dance across your dashboard.

"I think I figured out your siphon problem," Mox said. He kept flicking magical breaths at her every so often, trying to get her to laugh. She had threatened to take away his tooth whistle more than once, not that it would have made much of a difference.

"Oh?"

"Yeah. They probably talked to you about intent, right?"

Sloane rolled her eyes in answer.

"Right. Well, intent is important, but the essence of a magical act is—"

"Desire." Sloane smirked. "I read that book."

Mox raised an eyebrow at her. "You've read *The Manifestation of Impossible Wants*? Do they have that in your dimension?"

"No, it was in my room when I got here," she said, "and I broke my ankle jumping out of your bedroom window. So I had a lot of free time."

"Sorry about that."

"Sorry for trying to kill you," she said. "I mean, I know you turned my weapon into a very fine powder, but—still."

"I admired the effort, actually," he said. "Not everyone would be so gutsy."

"Anyway," she said. "Desire, you say?"

"Right. Well—have you considered that maybe when you were trying to create a magical breath, you didn't *want* to create a magical breath? That the one thing you actually wanted was a destructive indoor hurricane that broke all the windows?"

Sloane opened her mouth to object—of course she had wanted to do what she was supposed to do with the magical breath. She had spent days so frustrated with the siphon she wanted to hammer it into fragments. But really, hadn't she found herself wondering why she cared about puffs of air and summoning elevators without touching buttons and flinging open doors when all those things were simple enough to do without magic? Hadn't she broken that skylight in the Hall of Summons by tapping into whatever it was that gnawed inside her, telling her to take more, more, more while she could get it?

"You may be onto something," she said.

"You can't force someone to want something," he said. "And knowing what you want—not just vaguely but really *specifically* what you want—is a big part of magic. You don't pick the act and then force the desire. You know the desire—the exact shade of it—and then choose the act accordingly."

"So that's why you learned that . . . lung-collapsing move?" she said with careful nonchalance. She was referring, of course, to the working he did when he killed people. The one that had almost killed Kyros.

"Yes," he said, sounding a little strained. "That particular method—collapsing lungs—was . . . a good match for me." He shook his head, not as if he was saying no but as if he was trying to shake the memory out of his mind. "It's . . . awful. I know, I—"

She reached across the center console and put her hand on his leg. He had started bouncing his knee, but he stilled it at her touch.

"I know my match too," she said quietly.

And she told him about the Dive.

They reached the city when the moon was high. Mox sent this car into the river just as he had the police car a few days ago. They walked into the safe house when the windshield was still visible above the water.

Austin Chronicle

NEW SPINE SIPHON LAW PASSED IN TEXAS

by Kiersten Reichs

AUSTIN, FEBRUARY 2: Texas governor Colin Hauser (R) announced legislation Wednesday to legalize spine siphons on a limited basis for the purposes of medical treatment.

The federal government outlawed spine siphons three years ago with the Ethical Siphon Use Act (ESUA). The passage of the act was not difficult or contentious at the time, but with the rise of haven cities, the issue has again come into question.

"We don't want spine siphons used casually—not by anyone. No one is disputing that here," Hauser said in an interview Wednesday afternoon with the *Washington Magical Monitor*. "But there are extreme cases in which they might be useful, and we want to allow for that, especially in haven cities like Arlington."

The "extreme cases" to which Hauser refers involve "uncontrollable, destructive magical power" that doesn't respond to intensive training or other treatments, including relocation to a haven city where a magical dampening siphon is in effect.

Some members of the community expressed relief. "My son went to school with a boy who couldn't control his magic despite teachers' best efforts to rein him in," said Mary Millay of Dallas, Texas, mother of two young children. "I was scared every day my son went to school that I'd get a call telling me he was set on fire or had floated away due to a gravity-reversal working or something. This makes schools safer for everyone."

But not everyone felt so positive about the new law. "This legislation disproportionately targets the elderly, mentally ill, and children," says Darcy Atwood, of the Magical Freedom Society. "It will empower bigoted people who hate magic in all its forms to suppress the magical gifts of the vulnerable—which is, of course, illegal. We don't even completely suppress magical abilities in haven cities because our government decided it fell under the category of 'cruel and unusual punishment,' so how in God's name is *this* okay?"

37

THE SAFE HOUSE was in chaos. Rows of Resurrectionist soldiers lay head to head on the wood floor, and in the space between them were dismembered hands and feet, arms and legs. One soldier was hunched over a fractured wooden beam that protruded from his belly, oozing something dark. At the far end of the room, Ziva was perched on a table holding a large sewing needle between two clumsy fingers as she tried to stitch a man's leg back on above the knee. As Sloane watched, she dropped the needle and swore.

Mox swore, too, charging down the aisle of body parts to Ziva's side. Sloane forced her eyes away from a jagged white bone protruding from an undead knee and ran after him.

"What happened?" he said, and she hadn't realized how controlled he had been during their journey back to Chicago until he was the Resurrectionist again, all chaos and fury. Ziva glared over Mox's shoulder at Sloane.

"*Her.*" Ziva abandoned the one-legged soldier and heaved herself to her feet with a grunt. "She happened. Her people came looking for her. *He* came looking for her."

"Nero was here?" Sloane said.

"He wasn't our primary concern, but yes, he fucking did. Skittered in right at the end like an insect after his minions had blown us to pieces," Ziva said. "He left something for you."

Her braid swung back and forth as she stomped away. Sloane noticed a gash in one of Ziva's shoulders and a dark patch of — whatever that undead body fluid was — as the lieutenant bent to pick up a bundle from the corner. She carried it over and dropped it at Sloane's feet.

Sloane tasted something sour and sharp, like the bite of carbonation. She crouched in front of the bundle. Everything within her screamed at her not to open it, but her fingers were already searching out the edge of the folded fabric and pulling it back.

Nero had brought her a pair of boots. Black and caked with dried mud and grass. One of them had black laces and the other had red, the ends frayed from where a dog had chewed through them. They were Sloane's boots from years ago.

The Dark One had taken them.

Sloane felt Albie's weight at her side, the burn in her shoulder from carrying him. His skin was slippery with blood, and he smelled like sweat.

She felt his whimpers against her ear, but the only thing she could hear was her heartbeat, even once they made it through the dew-damp grass to the road.

Something stung her foot, and when she looked to see what she had stepped on, she saw a piece of glass buried in her heel.

"Gotta go," Albie said, and it was like he was speaking underwater. She could only just make out the words.

Shoes meant the present. Bare feet meant the past. But now the present and the past were folding together. The Dark One was alive.

The Dark One was Nero.

"Sloane." Something warm against her cheek. "In. Hold. Out."

She recognized the pattern and followed it instinctively. Breathing in, holding, and releasing. Dr. Thomas had coached her in their sessions to keep her from hyperventilating. Counting breaths, counting holds, counting releases. Sequences of five.

She wasn't with Albie. Albie was dead. Her head knew it but also didn't know it. *I feel like I've got one foot in the past all the time,* she had told Matt once, and that was when he had grabbed the toe of her shoe and wiggled it. *In the past, you were barefoot,* he had said to her. *And in the present, look! You've got shoes on. So you know both feet are here.*

It was Mox's rough palm against her cheek and his voice, low and clear, that told her how to breathe. But she sat down, hard, and stuck her feet out in front of her anyway so she could stare at the matte suede of her new boots, the ones she had worn to Albie's funeral. Salt had stained the toes gray in an uneven line.

Bare feet meant the past. Shoes meant the present.

Mox took his hand away when he saw that she was no longer panicking, but he stayed crouched in front of her, his riot of tangled hair pulled back into a knot, so his ears stuck out like a little boy's.

"I take it those are your boots?" he said.

Sloane nodded. "The Dark One took them," she said, sounding strangled. Feeling strangled. "I never understood why he took my shoes."

"*Your* Dark One?" he said, even though there was only one answer to that question, only one Dark One to speak of.

She nodded.

"And Nero had them," Mox said.

"But how . . . *how* could Nero be him?" Sloane said. "They look so different—"

"There are ways to produce that effect by magic," Ziva said.

"So, then . . . the Dark One survived somehow. He's Nero." *I would know,* she had thought. *I would know if I was standing in front of the Dark One.* But she had stood in front of Nero half a dozen times. Dragging herself out of the river. Searching for answers in the library. Fumbling with the siphon. She had stood in his workshop with his voice surrounding her. She had—

"Oh my God." Sloane put her head in her hands and rocked back and forth.

The origami. The paper crane she had found in Nero's office with scribbles of color on the notebook paper. It hadn't just resembled Albie's; it had *been* Albie's. The Dark One had kept it, whether as some kind of sick trophy or some kind of foundation for magic, she didn't know.

She didn't know a goddamn thing.

———

He had been standing at her bedside when she woke. She had seized up at the sight of him, freezing somewhere between lying down and sitting up.

Hello, Sloane. Despite the friendly form of address, his voice had been cold and almost robotic. *Did you get some sleep?*

They had been careless, her and Albie, as they crept toward the enclave of Dark One supporters, just the two of them, off a country road in the night. They had been in Iowa, and the air had smelled sweet, like yellow grass baking in sunlight. For Sloane, the place had felt familiar: roadside gravel, prairie plants scratching her ankles, a big, star-dusted sky. And maybe that was the reason she had let her guard down a little. Or maybe there was nothing she could have done to prevent it. But they had taken her, taken Albie, swarmed them, knocked them out. When she woke, she had such a bad headache she could hardly open her eyes.

The Dark One's question had seemed ridiculous. What she had gotten hadn't been sleep. It had been unconsciousness.

He hadn't needed an answer. *I hope so, because you have a big decision to make today.* She had forced herself to her feet and noted the exits. Behind her, a window. Simple enough to break with a lamp or a bedpost. And behind the Dark One, a door, simple wood with a push-button lock. A hairpin would—

You wouldn't leave without your friend, would you? the Dark One had said. Could he read thoughts or could he just read *her*? Either option terrified her.

His face, though, was what terrified her most. It was like the face of a wax figure in that it resembled someone she had seen once in passing on the street or as a placeholder in a picture frame, but it had no identity of its own. His skin was smooth—too smooth—and his hair was a nondescript shade of brown that could almost have been blond. A face constructed, it seemed, to be forgettable—but by someone who didn't know what it was to look human.

I would like to know where your cache of magical objects is located, the Dark One had said. *In return, I will give you a profound gift. I will show you to yourself, Sloane. Such a rare treasure, to see yourself.*

To his credit, she supposed, he had done exactly as he promised.

"He's kept his identity a secret for a long time," Ziva croaked. "Why does he want you to know who he is now?"

Sloane stared at the boots, the red laces still knotted at the ends so the fraying wouldn't spread. She felt frozen even though Mox had led her to the storeroom and made her sip some water. The boots were lined up next to the door as if the warehouse were her grandmother's place. "I . . . I don't know," she said dully.

"Something's different now," Mox said. He had pulled the other chair over to sit right in front of her, so her right knee was wedged between his legs. "You left."

She found herself staring at him, at how he made the chair look child-size, his knees higher than his hips and his big hands hanging limp between them. *Hot praying mantis,* Esther had called him. "He has my friends," she said. "He knows I'll go back and try to help them if I find out he's dangerous."

"No." Mox shook his head. "You can't do that."

"Why would he care where you are?" Ziva said. "You can't do magic. You don't know anything he doesn't. What's so special about you?"

They were such obvious facts, Sloane couldn't even be offended. She shook her head. She didn't know. She had never known why the Dark One showed a particular interest in her; she had only known how to manipulate it.

She got to her feet, swaying a little. Everything was a little blurry in the aftermath of panic; she felt as unsteady as a boat adrift. But she checked her siphon where it clasped her wrist and looked for a clear path to the exit.

Mox's hands closed around her arms. He spoke right above her ear. "When a maniac all but summons you to him," Mox said, "you don't just *obey.*"

"My friends," Sloane said. "My—"

"I know." Mox sounded almost terse. He squeezed her arms, hard, one hand cold with the metal that encased it, the other warm and callused. "We'll go. But we won't go without a plan."

Ziva stomped over to them both and planted herself in front of Sloane so she couldn't have walked out of the safe house if she had wanted to. Ziva folded her arms over her chest and Sloane realized there was a plate of armor screwed right into her forearm, a gauntlet anchored to bone.

"I'm not allowing either of you to march like fools toward a man who, apparently, *both* of you have failed to kill on more than one occasion," Ziva said. "So get a firmer grip on yourself, Chosen One."

"Ziva," Mox said, chastising.

But Sloane only nodded. There was something bracing about Ziva's manner, like a slap to the face that brought her back to herself. She ran her hands through her hair and nodded again.

"Okay," she said, tugging herself free of Mox's grip. "Let's make a plan, then."

38

Sloane had never had to plan an operation like this without her friends before. Her mind was a maze of city streets and entry and exit points. Her talent was in observation, not in strategy. Not like Matt, who had an instinct for people and exactly how they could be pressed, or like Esther, who could think five moves ahead of her opponents, whoever they were. All together, they had not been great wielders of magic, but they had been like the fingers of a hand moving to make a fist.

And now she was just a single finger. *The middle one, probably,* Sloane thought with a kind of faint hysteria.

Mox and Sloane sat on the table in the safe house's ballroom that Ziva had been using to stitch up the soldier when they returned. Mox had finished the job himself, sewing deftly, like he was darning a sock. He asked the soldier about his luck with dice, a game he apparently played with the others in his platoon and often lost. They bet scraps, the soldier explained to Sloane when he saw her looking confused. Pretty bits of glass, old bottle caps, nuts and bolts they had found in the gutters. He gave her a piece of rounded blue glass that he had sanded into an oval.

"Can you sew?" Mox asked her, and Sloane looked out at the room of groaning, shuffling bodies and sighed.

"Yes," she said, and that was how she ended up with a sewing needle in hand, swallowing hard to keep herself from vomiting as she pinched a woman's dead skin together just above the elbow to sew a cut closed. Mox had gotten her a pair of gloves so she could keep her hands clean, but the dark fluid that seemed to serve as blood for the undead army got all over her gloved fingers and ran down the back of her hand. It stank like mold and mildew.

She tried not to think of the last needle she had held, the one she had used to blow a hole the size of a house into the Dome.

At least stitching up zombie soldiers was distracting. Her thoughts kept drifting back to the boots. Flakes of dried Earth mud falling onto a Genetrix floor. Nero wanted her to know what he was. Did that mean he was going to keep her friends alive until she got there, or did it mean he had already killed them? Some of the gray ooze splattered on her cheek after an enthusiastic stitch, and she wiped it off with the back of her wrist, trying not to grimace. The Dark One she knew wasn't erratic; whatever he had done, he had always thought it through.

Ziva and Mox spoke freely in front of the soldiers, with Mox explaining to Ziva Sloane's revelation about reversing the effects of the siphon fortis in the Hall of Summons. He didn't act as if the soldiers weren't there—every so often one of them weighed in on the conversation, and Mox was happy to engage. "Do you know how to do that to an ordinary siphon?" a woman propped up on her elbows to watch the stitching of her leg asked. "Because if you can't do it to a regular one, you probably won't be able to do it to that massive one."

"Good point," Ziva said. "We can't just barge in there and expect to figure it out on the fly."

"What do you suggest?" Mox said, talking around the needle between his teeth. He was holding it there while he checked his stitches. Sloane had moved on to yet another pungent gash. Her gloves smeared fluid on the undead man's shirtsleeve.

"Hey," the man grunted. "Just got this thing clean."

"Well," Sloane said, scowling, "it's my first time sewing rotten flesh back together, so you'll have to forgive me being a little clumsy about it."

"'S not *rotten,*" the man said. "'S *rotting.*"

Ziva's teeth whistled as she laughed. "Don't take offense, Pete. She's a little wound up right now."

Sloane gritted her teeth and tied off the last stitch. She didn't bother to keep it neat. *Pete*—what a ridiculous name for a zombie.

"Gotta stay loose," Pete said, and he wrenched his arm out of its socket so he could waggle it around a little.

Sloane bit back a laugh. "That doesn't hurt?" she said.

"Eh, not really," Pete said. "'S more like the memory of pain, if you know what I mean. That's how everything is for us—echoes."

Sloane glanced at Mox. He was acting like he hadn't heard.

"Ziva," Mox said. "What do you suggest we do?"

Sloane pulled a length of tough thread through the eye of the needle. How had she not known who Nero was from the first second she had laid eyes on him? His unassuming flop of hair, his passive smile, his submissive attitude toward Aelia—all constructed so that he could move unsuspected right under her nose. But what was the purpose of *that*? She cut the thread. Her hands were shaking again.

"What I suggest," Ziva said, "is that me and your nemesis-slash-lover over there—"

"Excuse me?"

"I'm dead; I'm not stupid. You two are . . ." Ziva flapped her hand at Sloane and Mox. "So I propose that she and I go on a little reconnaissance mission in order to document the innards of the siphon fortis."

"You and Sloane," Mox said. "Without me?"

"Well," Ziva said, her voice gentling—as much as it was possible for that raspy, bone-rattling voice to gentle. "Your spine—"

"Right." Mox scowled at his hands as he jerked the needle too hard, making the soldier in front of him jump. "Sorry, Fred."

Fred. Honestly, Sloane thought. "Do you know Nero's range?" she asked. She needed to focus. If Esther were here, she would snap her manicured fingers in front of Sloane's face. *Feel later, think now,* she would say, and Sloane did. "How close do you have to be before he can control your magic?"

"I haven't tested it much," Mox said, sighing. "A couple blocks is the closest I've come."

"Well, then, you can still help us get there," Sloane said. "I'm sure they're on high alert. We might need you. I'm still unpredictable with the siphon, and what if the blond cadaver's head falls off?"

"*Unpredictable*? I think the word you're looking for is *useless*. You are *useless* with the siphon," Ziva said. "But this raises another question: How are we even going to get in the Camel? It's not as if she and I can just walk in unnoticed."

"We could put some tape over that hole in your face," Sloane said.

"Careful, flesh-bag, or I'll give you one to match," Ziva retorted.

Mox coughed as if to disguise a laugh. He shook his head. "It would be better if we could go in from underneath, but—"

"Wait," Sloane said. When the Dark One had narrowed his range of attacks to the Midwest, Sloane had gobbled up as much information as she could about every major Midwestern city, especially Chicago. It meant she knew all the oddities of it, the secret passages and the back doors and . . . "Do you guys have the pedway here?"

"The what?"

"There are underground tunnels for pedestrians in the Loop, and one of them opens up under the Thompson Center—sorry, in this universe, it's the Camel," Sloane said. "They started building the pedway before our universes split, I'm pretty sure. We could pop up right in the middle of the building."

"Our universes . . . split?" Mox said.

"I mean, it seems like we were running right alongside each other —hence the term *parallel*. But then you guys developed big magic, and we didn't." Sloane shrugged. "I thought it was the *Tenebris* Incident that caused the split, but now I think it's because Genetrix's World War Two was fought primarily on water instead of air, so they focused on underwater surveillance, which is what *precipitated* the *Tenebris* Incident and . . . what?"

They were both giving her odd looks.

"Where," Ziva said to Mox, "did you find this fucking nerd?"

Sloane wolfed down two cans of soup for dinner, the first one luke-warm because she started spooning it into her mouth the second she

got the top off, and the second warmed over Mox's siphon as he whistled out a controlled flame. Both of them were quiet. Mox seemed almost glum as he twirled his spoon in a can of corn.

She wondered what he would be like when he didn't have to fight
for his life anymore. He had spent so long locked up with the remains
of his friends, separate from the world. Would he even know how to
go back to a regular life?

She hadn't fared very well at that herself. She had her friends
around, but she was still leaping across rooftops to avoid journalists
with questions, grimacing through public events, lying to her loved
ones, spending her nights in recurring nightmares and panic attacks.
And now Albie, who had anchored her, was gone. She had been able
to delay the grief somewhat because she wasn't even in the same dimension as his remains. But she wouldn't be able to delay it forever.

"What is it?" she asked Mox after he had twirled his spoon for the
twentieth time.

He glanced up at her. "It's stupid," he said, making it sound like a
warning.

"So?"

He smirked and set the can of corn down on the table. She was
sitting cross-legged on the floor of the storeroom on top of a folded
blanket. The wool was making her ankles itch.

"We're closer to taking him down than I've ever been before,"
Mox said. "And I should be eager to do it. But seeing the army like
that, I . . ." He shook his head. "I'll have no excuse to keep them
around once he's gone."

"No," Sloane said, "I guess not."

"And if they're gone," he said, digging a knuckle into an eye socket
as if to work at a headache, "then I'll be alone again."

And she would be leaving too if they succeeded, she thought.
Something neither of them was saying, because they had known each
other for only a few days, and it was ridiculous to get attached after
such a short time. Yet she had. It had been so long since anyone had
talked to her like she wasn't eighteen-year-old Sloane Andrews.

Still, it wasn't the impending loss of *her* that plagued him. She had
seen the way he looked at those oozing, marble-eyed people that

came forward to be mended. Heard the tenderness in his voice as he spoke to them. Noticed that he knew every single name, welcomed every comment. "They weren't just people you were supposed to command, were they?" she said. "You were close."

"Not to all of them, obviously," he said. "But to some. Ziva especially. You and I, we're fated to join this fight. But not her. It was her choice. She wanted to defend the world. I can't imagine taking on that kind of burden voluntarily." He smiled. "I seem to attract the chronically grumpy."

Sloane felt like she could see the person Mox had been before as he fidgeted with the cuff of his sleeve, picked at his cuticles, scratched an itch on his forearm. Always moving, and always elsewhere, watching the light of magic play across the room, maybe, or searching for the source of it inside him, the place where it started, the precise shades of his desires. He attracted people with a certain sharpness because he needed it—needed someone to give him a light smack and tell him to focus.

"She's the best friend I've ever had." Mox sighed. "You must think I'm fucking twisted, keeping a bunch of corpses around for company."

Knowing magic was about knowing yourself, she thought. If you could be honest with yourself, you could better predict what your magic could do. Only how was anyone supposed to know themselves that way? Almost thirty years in this body and she still had no idea where it was half the time or how it worked. If anything, it was becoming more of a mystery, not less.

"I mean," Sloane said, "I just had a panic attack because of a pair of boots, so I don't think I'll be winning any mental-health achievement awards anytime soon. But if I knew how to bring Albie back, or my brother, even for a moment, even a pale version of them . . ." She shrugged. "I would, I think."

"You would?"

She smiled. "You're not the only one who's been alone for too long."

"Yeah." He cocked his head. "Feeling better now, Sloane?"

She liked the way he said her name, heavy on the *Slow*. Like he was tasting every vowel before letting it out.

"Not really," she said. "I'm just trying to figure out how it was possible for me to stand right next to the Dark One without realizing it." She had thought that she would know him in any universe. That she could trust her heart to tell her what hearts knew. But her heart had never been that wise, had it? There were some things it just didn't seem to know. "But some pieces are fitting together now. Sibyl said she thought the Drains were a world's allergic reaction to the presence of someone who wasn't supposed to be there. We thought he caused them because he was there whenever they happened. But maybe they just happened whenever he was there—*he* was the wrongness in that universe, and the Drains were a way of Earth trying to right itself."

"But then he came here," Mox said, "and they started again."

"Did they? I mean, when did the first one happen?"

"After I was on the run. Everyone was saying I was planning something big, that I was dangerous, and then—" Mox paused, frowning. "And then he summoned the first challenger. The first Chosen One from another world, I guess."

"Which caused," Sloane said, "a Drain." She sat back with a satisfied smile.

"She was young, the first of them." Mox was lost again, his fingers chasing each other across his kneecap, hair falling over his face. "More deft than powerful, I'd say. Caught on to Genetrix magic so fast, it was like second nature, and she was clever with it, knew how to slide one working into another as easy as singing a song. It was her skill against my brutality, and . . ." He shrugged. "I feel trapped by it all," he said. "Stuck in it like mud."

"I wish I had some kind of answer for you," Sloane said softly. "But all the things I was good at were from before. Good at falling asleep fast and waking up faster, and running toward Drains instead of away, and making dark jokes afterward that made other people uncomfortable. If you're good at those things, how are you supposed to be good at going to work, getting married, popping out kids?

They're opposite lives." She shook her head. "Nobody ever prepared me for what came after. They just assumed I would never find out."

When she looked at Mox again, she was surprised to find that he was smiling a little.

"That's a false dilemma you've created, you know," he said. "It's not like you either hunt Dark Ones or get pregnant, nothing in between. There are many lives out there to live. Endless possibilities for you to sort through and discard."

She hadn't, of course, thought about it that way. She had asked him why he didn't run, leave the state, the country. And his enemy was still out there, hunting him. But hers—well, now she knew that he was still alive, but she hadn't before. She could have left Chicago, left Matt, left her entire life. Gone backpacking in Europe like a college graduate with wanderlust. Ate, prayed, and loved across India to find herself. Bought a bunch of land in Idaho and built her own log cabin. But she hadn't tried anything. Her only desire had been to be left alone.

No wonder she couldn't do magic reliably; deep down, she didn't even know what she really wanted. "You're right," she said. "But first, we have to survive this."

"True. But in order to do that, we'll need to get some sleep."

"We?" she said. "Who ever said *we* would sleep anywhere?"

His eyes danced a little. "No one," he said. "But, you know, we might die tomorrow."

"That's a good line." Her face broke into a smile. She couldn't help it.

"I'll take that as a yes."

TO: Aelia Haddox, Praetor of the Council of Cordus

FROM: Nero Dalche, Quaestor of the Council of Cordus

RE: Plan of Action for Dimension C

Dear Praetor,

Per our last discussion, I have verified that
Dimension C-1572, the third parallel universe we
have discovered that significantly overlaps with our
own, is a suitable candidate for our first Chosen
One summons. Said Chosen One has been identified as
Sergei Petrov, who outsmarted a dark force known as
the Black Cloud five years ago in that universe's
accounting of time.

Following the so-called rules of hospitality
governing travel between universes, I located a point
of vulnerability in Dimension C. We have previously
defined a point of vulnerability as an individual who
is susceptible to the influence of magical energy upon
their person, which is to say that when we knock,
he or she will open the door. Typically, a child
serves this purpose well, as children are not as
prone to questioning odd things as adults. However,
in this dimension, our point of vulnerability is
an adolescent girl with a suitably open mind and
childlike belief in the impossible.

Once I am able to travel to Dimension C, I will
locate an object significant to Sergei Petrov—that
is, an object that Petrov has personalized to a high
degree. I will carry this object back to Genetrix,
and we will then use this object to summon Petrov

specifically, since it is infused with his magical
energy.

As a reminder, without a significant object to guide
the working, the target is unlikely to respond to
the summons to move to another universe—the object
will work upon his mind such that when we speak our
invitation, the target will hear it in the voice of
a lost loved one, which he is more likely to trust.
If he accepts said invitation, even momentarily, he
will begin the process of entry. We, meanwhile, will
attempt to steady the time fluctuations inherent in
inter-universe travel so that Petrov doesn't arrive
in Genetrix at some point in the distant past or
future.

I will need a magical assembly of about ten skilled
magic-users, a group that must be cobbled together
from the Council of Cordus, for maximum secrecy.
The purpose of this memo is to brief you on my plan
of action as well as to request approval for the
assembly required for the summoning.

Let me know if you have questions or concerns.

Sincerely,

Nero Dalche

TOP SECRET

39

Sloane dreamed about the Drain. Matt, stepping too far, getting drawn into it as if tugged by an invisible thread. His body coming apart, arms popping out of their sockets, his heart bursting like a balloon. Esther, screaming, her cheeks stained with ash and the spray of blood. And Sloane rooted to the spot, her feet bare and then, a moment later, encased in concrete. *He* was there too—she felt him behind her, the same way she sometimes felt it when someone was staring at her.

She looked over her shoulder, and he was there, the Dark One, and he was Nero, face flipping back and forth between the one she remembered and the one she had seen on Genetrix, like the pages of a book caught in a breeze.

She woke with her hand in a fist in the blanket she and Mox slept on, her body shaking. Mox's arm tightened around her waist. He had fallen asleep with it there, heavy against her ribs, his fingers twitching as he dropped deeper into sleep. She turned over to look at him. He was awake, dark eyes alert.

"Okay?" he said.

"Yeah," she replied. "Just a dream. You?"

She realized, belatedly, that she hadn't woken up because of her dream but because of a loud crash. A cardboard box had gone flying across the room and hit a wall, sending individually wrapped bars of soap scattering in all directions.

"Same," he said, and he got up.

Well, Sloane thought, at least they had that in common.

The sun had just risen, and Sloane was already wound so tight, her head ached. She did everything she was supposed to: brushed her teeth (with Mox's borrowed toothbrush), splashed water on her face, got dressed, ate breakfast, put on the siphon, reviewed the map she had drawn the night before. She knew the way, and she even knew this feeling, that she might be walking to her own doom.

They met Ziva at the entrance to the safe house. She was shrouded in dark fabric, a siphon covering her mouth and hiding the hole in her jaw. When she saw Sloane, she reached into her pocket and took out the pair of scissors Sloane had kept under her pillow that first night with the army.

Something in Sloane cracked, and she laughed. Giggled, really, until some of the tension bled away.

Mox's eyes crinkled like he was smiling, but it was hard to tell— he wore a siphon over the lower part of his face, though a sleeker one than she had seen him don as the Resurrectionist. It was a seamless metal plate etched with feathers, like a flock of birds descending. It didn't warp his voice, as the other one had, and Sloane was glad. There was something warm and round about his natural voice, and she didn't want the Resurrectionist in her ear on this mission.

"I did a quick scan of the area," Ziva said. "There's no sign of the Army of Flickering anywhere. I think, since he intended to lure you with the boots, Sloane, that he's left us a clear path to the Camel."

"Well, that's a small mercy," Mox said. "Never thought I'd be happy to hear Nero's expecting us."

"He's expecting something he won't get," Sloane said. "I won't be going alone, and I won't be going to him. You figured out your distraction, Mox?"

Mox nodded. "Distraction's easy. But one big enough to pull most of the guards out of the Camel, well . . ." His eyes glinted. "That'll be a trick."

They walked a block down to the Thirty-Fifth Street bus stop.

An old woman waited there, her head wrapped in a floral shawl, a basket of pamphlets at her feet. Sloane was close enough to see the title: "The Lord: Genetrix's First Magic-User; How Magic Can Be Worship."

The bus pulled up a few minutes later. Sloane let the old woman climb the steps ahead of her, then paid all three of their fares at once so the bus driver wouldn't look too closely at Ziva. At Sloane's instruction, Mox had not dressed like the Resurrectionist but in the fashion she had seen some of the younger Genetrixae wearing, all ripped denim and heavy leather jackets and muted colors. Nothing that would cue any memories of the city's hooded, siphon-clad menace.

She led the way to the back of the bus and nestled against the window with Mox beside her. Ziva took the third seat, tugging her hood down over her eyes and slumping back like she was asleep. The cast of her skin was still unearthly if you looked at her closely, but they just had to hope no one would.

The bus lurched down 35th Street toward Comiskey Park—or whatever they were calling the place where the White Sox played on Earth. There, just beyond the stadium, they would get on the Red Line train going toward the Loop, where they could access the underground tunnels of the pedway. If Genetrix's Chicago *had* a pedway. Sloane was trusting her memory of Chicago history to guide them.

35th Street was wide and flat with low buildings on either side, most of them made of Chicago's favored red brick. It looked so much like it would have on Earth that Sloane felt, for snatches of time, like she was home. Then she would see a dingy sign in a shop window advertising cheap siphon repair or discount oscilloscopes or notice a bookstore boasting of selling all ten volumes of *Basic Practical Workings for the Average Siphon User* and she would remember where she was and that her mission wasn't complete. Had never been complete. She had yet to kill the Dark One.

Up ahead, in the distance, she could see a tall structure that had to be the stadium. She had been there twice in the past ten years, once incognito, with a White Sox cap shading her face, and a second time for the Crosstown Classic, sitting in the Sox owner's box with Matt. She had spent most of that game with other people's phones in her face, trying to smile for selfies.

When the bus drew closer to the stadium, though, Sloane frowned. The old Comiskey Park had been demolished on Earth in the early 1990s. It had been replaced by a bigger stadium with taupe outer walls and a towering upper deck. But on Genetrix, the face of the structure was still wide and white, with the words COMISKEY PARK in blue across the top. It was the original. She was sure of it.

"I can't believe it's still standing," she said quietly to Mox.

"They were going to rebuild it, but some Unrealist architects offered to use some of their techniques to support it and expand it . . . backward, or in reverse, or something," Mox said. "So they kept it."

Sloane grinned. She would have to revise her opinion of Unrealists. "Even though no one cares about baseball here?"

"Oh, it's not for baseball anymore," Mox said. "It's a track-and-field stadium."

"That's it. This obsession with ancient Greece and Rome has gone too far."

They cruised past the stadium. Beyond it was the interstate and the Red Line station's entrance on the 35th Street overpass. They used the back doors of the bus to exit there, getting out right by the awning of the train. She went to one of the machines to get passes for the three of them, leaving Ziva hunched by the curb, facing traffic, and Mox looking out over the interstate.

Behind the machine was a Genetrixae message board, a public corkboard with flyers pinned to it. Most of them were requests for partners in complex workings; any group larger than three was called an assembly. It was, evidently, how they transmitted information without the internet. Cyrielle had seemed confused that people would want to sit down and stare at a video rather than do something on their own. *Why be on the internet when you can set things on fire with your mind?* Matt had said with a shrug.

She hoped he was okay.

Hit with another wave of nervousness, Sloane waved Ziva and Mox over and handed them their passes. Together they went through the turnstiles and walked down the ramp to the Red Line platform. There were more people here than there had been on the bus—more people to notice Ziva and Mox, but also more people to ignore them, bury them in a crowd of people going to their jobs.

A group of women near the end of the platform wore loose, gauzy robes in all the colors of the rainbow that shimmered when they moved. One of them had her hair tied up in a scarf that was equally colorful. They were like caricatures of tarot readers, their bracelets jingling, eyes wide as they peered into the future. After meeting Sibyl —paranoid, magic-hating Sibyl—Sloane thought they looked ridiculous. Who wanted to see the future anyway?

But there were other nods to magic-users of the past among the people lined up on the platform. A teenager in a magician's top hat and white gloves—the rest of his clothes were more typical—stood next to a girl with a flower crown, like a nymph. A woman standing near them wore a large, elaborate amulet; her companion had a high, face-framing collar, like something out of *Snow White*.

"Everything's gotta be ironic now," Ziva said, her voice gritty from the siphon. "You don't see me wrapping my entire body in bandages or something."

"You could make a convincing Frankenstein," Sloane said. "Just stick real bolts in your skull."

Ziva narrowed her eyes at Sloane.

"I saw someone in a pointed hat the other day," Mox said, shaking his head, "casting runes on the sidewalk. Some guy tripped over one, almost fell flat on his face."

The light of the train caught Sloane's attention. It was approaching their stop. Sloane steered them away from the people in gauzy robes and toward one of the middle cars.

The train wasn't the sleek silver Sloane was used to; it was older, painted brown along the bottom and orange along the top. The sides were flat, the edges squared, like a shoebox. Inside, the seats were plush and arranged in forward-facing rows, but there was a small alcove in the back where the seats faced inward, separated from the rest of the car by a barrier. Sloane elbowed a man in red suspenders to get there first. The barrier would be useful for hiding Mox and Ziva.

Ziva sat in one of the seats, Mox across from her. Sloane stood so that she was blocking the aisle between them and looked out the windows as the train pulled away from the platform.

The train stopped at Cermak/Chinatown, and a woman in mint-green hospital scrubs got on, her bag tucked under her arm, along with a man in beat-up sneakers. Ahead, the tracks bent toward the lake and then plunged down, the train charging into a tunnel. All through the car, Sloane heard low, quick whistles as people did small workings like turning on reading lights or putting barriers around themselves, apparently to block out sound. It was like listening to pigeons roosting.

At the Jackson stop, Sloane gave Mox a meaningful look. The next station was theirs. The train squealed as it eased to a stop, and Mox and Ziva followed her out of the car, going past the minty-green nurse and Sneakers, who was trying a working, snapping his fingers and whistling. Whatever the working was, it didn't seem to be going well.

They climbed the steps to street level and fell into the rhythm of pedestrian traffic — the flipping of the Walk signal, the brushing of shoulders and elbows. Ziva kept her head down, pinching the back of Mox's sleeve so she wouldn't lose track of him. Sloane kept him in her peripheral vision, her hair hanging loose around her cheeks.

She paused, briefly, next to St. Peter's Church, a low stone building wedged between two glass giants. A massive crucifix was carved into its face, with Gothic windows behind it and wooden doors below. The familiarity of it steadied her. Of course, on Earth, she had never seen a man in front of it juggling balls of floating water, siphons on both wrists — but she would take what she could get.

It was another block to the Daley Center, the brown building she had recognized on her first venture into the city, Kyros at her side. On Earth, the entrance to the pedway was in the courtyard in front of it, so if it was going to be anywhere on Genetrix, it was there. She recognized the decorative grate, painted pale blue, from a distance. It marked the steps that descended underground. It was also where they would leave Mox, a block away from the Camel.

She stopped by the grate, a strange pressure against her chest as she looked up at him.

He reached up and undid the clasps holding his siphon to his face. He brushed a hand over his upper lip to get rid of the sweat that had collected there. Then he bent toward her to kiss her.

Even with stale breath and damp skin from the siphon's restriction, with the bustle of bodies around her and the nervousness that had destabilized her, she found herself tilting toward him on tiptoes and burying her bare hand in his hair.

"Don't fuck around," she said quietly as she pulled away. "We all get out of this alive."

He smiled at her and fastened the siphon over his face again. She turned to Ziva and jerked her head in the direction of the pedway entrance. Ziva pinched her sleeve right over her elbow and held on as Sloane led them down the steps.

40

THE PEDWAY SMELLED just like one of the underground el plat-
forms: musty, like an old garage, with a hint of stale urine. The
path they followed was lined with dark gray tile, cracking in some
places and broken in others. But here and there, there were stained-
glass windows set into the tile with a light behind them, as if they
were outside. Some were leaded-glass geometry; others were swirls
of color broken up into fragments or cyclones of interlocking circles
in monochrome or checkerboards of lead and gold leaf.

The pedway was confusing, and only Sloane's innate sense of direction kept her from getting lost. She had convinced Ziva, via a hard
stare, to link arms as they walked; Ziva's rotting hand was buried in
her sleeve. Her arm felt fragile, like a dry branch. Sloane forced herself not to hurry as they passed the stairway that led up to City Hall.
All they had to do was walk under Randolph Street and they would
be beneath the Camel.

She hadn't been sure how they would know when they were in the
right place, given the lack of clear signage, but that turned out not to
be a problem. Up ahead, between two grand columns over which the
words CORDUS CENTER FOR ADVANCED MAGICAL INNOVATION AND
LEARNING were painted in rich purple, was a shimmering veil. Sloane
glanced at Ziva.

"Well," Ziva said. "Here goes."

Sloane stepped through the veil, and a strong wind blew her hair back and pressed her clothes to her body. The siphon on her hand lit up like a lantern, and white light danced over the back of her right hand, where the Needle had once been. Across from her stood a soldier with the seal of Flickering on his chest.

Ziva's hood had blown back, revealing her grayish skin and bulging eyes. As soon as the wind stopped, Ziva hurried to cover her head again, exposing her peeling fingers and claw-sharp fingernails when her sleeves fell away from them. The soldier glanced in their direction, looked away, then looked back. Sloane steered Ziva away as quickly as she could without running. She didn't check to see if the soldier was following.

"Fucking Camel assholes," Sloane mumbled. "What kind of pervy excuse for staring at a woman's tits is that working, anyway?"

"Shows you all kinds of things, I'm sure," Ziva said. "Let's just hope that fellow thinks I have one hell of a skin condition."

They were away from the pavilion now and walking down a hallway of gray stone that matched the area surrounding the Hall of Summons, the one that always looked storm-dark, like it was raining outside. Sloane felt something tickling at the back of her neck, like the Needle was scratching her skin from the space between worlds.

She finally dared to look over her shoulder when they made it to the staircase. She didn't see the soldier behind them, but that didn't mean he hadn't noticed Ziva or that he hadn't gone for reinforcements. They climbed the stairs to the Camel lobby. Sloane turned away from the elevator bank and toward the hallway of stained glass that separated the area surrounding the Hall of Summons from the rest of the Camel. Green light danced over her body as they walked through it, the delicate fans aglow with daylight.

Just past the hallway, Sloane tugged Ziva into an alcove with a small stone bench in it. They were supposed to wait for Mox's distraction, which he had promised would be loud enough for them to hear even from within the building.

They were quiet as they waited—well, as quiet as they could be with Ziva's every breath rasping into her lungs and shuddering out of her mouth.

"Do you feel like yourself?" Sloane said.

Ziva narrowed an eye at her. The other eye seemed to be missing its lid entirely. "You're not thinking of bringing some friends back to life, are you?"

"No," Sloane said. "Well—it's sort of hard not to consider the possibility once you know it exists."

"Having considered it, then, you can now dismiss the idea."

"So you're not glad to be back. To be alive again."

Ziva looked her over. It was remarkable, Sloane thought, that someone so stiff and inhuman could look so wary.

"I have a thirst for justice," Ziva said, "that being back helps to satisfy. I don't remember much about—the time in between. But I don't get the impression that I was—settled. As you might suspect of a . . . murdered spirit."

"But," Sloane said.

"But." Ziva sighed. "But the longer I'm here, the more distinctly I feel that—my time is done, and every moment that I extend it is a violation of . . . something." She lifted her shoulders in an exaggerated shrug. "Besides—look at me. I'm a horror." She tapped her jaw where the siphon covered the hole that exposed her to the roots of her teeth. It was the first time Sloane had considered that maybe the same revulsion she had felt when she first looked at Ziva was what the woman herself felt when she looked in the mirror. No one wanted to wake up as a living dead thing.

"Have you ever talked to Mox about this?"

Ziva shook her head. "He needs me. I can't leave while he still does."

Sloane nodded, but she couldn't help but think that people didn't just spontaneously stop needing their friends.

A loud, deep sound startled Sloane into a yelp. Dust shook loose from the walls and fell all around them like snowflakes. Sloane heard distant shouts and footsteps through the walls.

One of Ziva's eyes rolled over to focus on Sloane. It was time.

They walked the path Sloane remembered, the one she had memorized as she followed Cyrielle to the Hall of Summons that first time, when she had shattered the skylight with her siphon and then collapsed. She led the way around pillars and beneath arches, through the grayish light of a coming storm. And then they reached the heavy doors of the Hall of Summons with the gold plaque that named the room and the year it was constructed, 1985.

Standing beside the doors was a security guard. Ziva whistled sharply through the siphon and sent him into the wall; his head smacked into the stone and he crumpled. She bent over him, poked her fingers between his lips, and took the whistle off his tooth. "You get the siphon," she said to Sloane.

Sloane felt dazed. She crouched by the guard—who was alive but obviously stunned—and unclipped the siphon from his wrist, thankful the mechanism was simple. She slid it from his fingers and tossed it into the Hall of Summons, where Ziva waited. Sloane followed her in, and Ziva closed the door behind her.

"I can set a temporary working to bar the doors," Ziva said. "But it will deteriorate within minutes. If we need more than that, I'll have to reset it, so don't let me forget."

Sloane nodded. She walked to the siphon in the floor, which was covered by a gold plate, six feet across. The tickle she had felt at the back of her neck below the Camel was now distinct pressure on both sides of her head, like someone was trying to crush her skull. There was no mistaking it anymore—the Needle was calling to her. The question was whether she wanted to answer.

Ziva was kneeling beside the siphon fortis. She had tried to lift the large metal cover with a whistle, but it didn't budge. Now she had hooked her fingers beneath it and was pushing against its weight. "It's resistant to magic," she said. "I think we have to move it by hand."

Sloane knelt beside her and braced herself against the lip of the cover. Even with both of them pushing against it, it hardly moved, and the edge bit into Sloane's palms.

She thought of marching into the Dome, of the way the Needle had sent the front door right through the roof and made it hover.

"Shit," Ziva said. She brought her hand down on the cover, hard. "Shit!"

"You used to live in this building, right?" Sloane said, feeling oddly detached. The Needle was another heartbeat in Sloane's chest, a presence at her shoulder. She felt it even now, a universe away from it. And the Needle was where she always turned when she was desperate.

"Why does that matter?" Ziva sat back on her heels.

"I might have a solution," Sloane said. "But it requires me getting to the river without going out the way we came in. Where does that door go?" She pointed to the other end of the room, where there was a rusted door. It looked small enough for a child to crawl through it, given the size of the hall.

The river was only one block north of the Camel. If she ran, she could get there and back in ten minutes.

"It's a back door," Ziva said. "No telling what's out there, but you could find your way to an emergency exit."

"Can you hold those doors?" Sloane said, gesturing to the entrance. "Just for a few minutes."

Ziva squinted one eye at her again and then nodded.

Sloane ran for the little rusted door. Just beyond it was an empty hallway, like the one they had walked through to get into the hall, but shabbier, dirt and debris clumping in the corners, the gray stone splitting in places or missing whole chunks. It looked like a utility hallway, the pipes in the ceiling exposed.

She took a right, on a whim, and searched for the glow of an emergency exit sign. Two women pulled apart when Sloane passed them, intruding on their stolen moment. She huffed out an apology, already out of breath.

At the end of the next hallway, there was a sign directing her toward a stairwell. She burst through the door, then peered around the bottom of the stairs to check for another door. There was one, but she didn't know where it would lead. The stairwell smelled like garbage, and she could hear footsteps above her, echoing.

She decided to take her chances. The door opened into an alley, where a line of dumpsters waited, stuffed to the brim with black garbage bags and flattened cardboard boxes. It led her to a street she didn't recognize, but she could see the gap between the buildings ahead of her that signified the river, and she ran toward it, almost colliding with a taxi in the crosswalk. The driver honked at her and screamed something out his window, but she was already running.

Once she was across Wacker and close to the river's edge, she slowed and climbed on top of the barrier that kept pedestrians from toppling into the water one story below. There was no time to find the stairs that led down to the river walk. Sloane's body was burning now, tingling, aching with the need to reunite with what she had once hated so much she had mutilated herself to get rid of it.

She threw one leg over the railing and then the other, her back against the barrier . . . and then jumped.

The cold water made her gasp, so she surfaced coughing, her clothes heavy and her hair plastered to her face. Once she was able to take a deep breath again, she dove, kicking like a frog.

This time, there was no magical light to guide her down to the membrane between the worlds, thinner here in Chicago than in other places—she believed that there was something special about this place, yes; she could feel the way the city had attracted her even from childhood, beautiful and strange and glittering in the sun. The darkness that surrounded her was absolute and directionless. She followed only the pull of gravity, as if she were holding a thread looped through its eye.

She kicked, at first measured and strong, then frantic, clawing at the water to get down faster and faster. Her lungs burned, but it was no different than the burning in her chest, in her head. It occurred to her that this sensation of being deep underwater—the fire inside her, the pressure against her head, the tingling in every limb—was what she had always associated with magic, and maybe this was why. Maybe all her life had not been motion forward but motion around this moment, like something circling a drain.

She needed air. Sloane remembered the siphon on her hand and started to hum, choosing a pitch that sounded roughly like her memory of Aelia trapping air behind the handkerchief the first time she dove and adjusting it higher. There was no question of her desires; she wanted to breathe. She envisioned a bubble around her head, like a cartoon of an astronaut, and the water around her face shifted like an ocean current. Then its weight pulled away from her mouth and nose, and when she exhaled next, she heard its rasp, as if she were aboveground.

My first magical breath, she thought, and laughed a little.

Above her was the rubble of the tower that made up the river bottom in Earth's Chicago, the *P* wedged between hunks of concrete and steel, and below her, the tangle of plants that grew from the river bottom in Genetrix's Chicago. She was in the space between the two worlds.

She had dropped the two pieces of the Needle in the river before Albie's funeral. She had known then that she would always be able to find the Needle if she needed to, that it spoke to her even when she ignored its voice. She stretched out her siphon hand and hummed, not thinking about the pitch, the frequency, the line that would show on the oscilloscope. She thought only about how the Needle had helped her when she needed it to break into the Dome and destroy the magical prototype, even when she had needed it to destroy the Dark One.

She needed it again.

She hovered in the channel between Earth and Genetrix without gravity pulling her in either direction. This was the closest she had ever come to feeling weightless. She thought of Albie's voice whispering in her ear to beckon her toward Genetrix, and she whispered into the pocket of air she had created around her head. "Come on . . ." she said. "Come on!"

Something in front of her glittered, despite the absence of light. Two slim fragments took shape in front of her; they were metallic in appearance, but not any metal ARIS scientists had been familiar with. Every part of her sang with relief. She reached for them.

The first brush against the Needle pieces shocked her and made her body go rigid. For a second she was afraid that they had pricked her again, buried themselves back in her hand, but then she saw them gleaming in her palm.

She had beckoned, and they had come. The phrase *the manifestation of impossible wants* had never made more sense to her. It was magic.

She pinched one half of the Needle between the fingers of her left hand and the other half with her right, keeping them in separate hands as she kicked up from the ground, swimming toward the surface.

The pocket of air around her face collapsed without warning as she swam away from the space between worlds, and she kicked harder. Her legs ached when she finally saw the light from the city above her, just a spark at first, a lit match in the dark, and then a glow. And then —air, and the river's edge. Sloane threw herself over it and collapsed to the concrete, gasping.

"*Slo.*" Esther's voice greeted her. She lifted her head. Esther stood with Matt, their hands raised—siphons cocked, as it were—aiming at Ziva, standing across from them.

Sloane coughed.

They were alive. They were safe.

Matt kept his siphon trained on Ziva, and Esther turned to point hers at Sloane.

"I can explain, obviously," Sloane said once she could breathe again.

"You better fucking start," Esther replied.

EXCERPT FROM

STORIES OF THE MULTIVERSE

by Rufus Egerton

Chicagoan, August 11, 1994

A man leaves his universe in search of adventure, and the unfiltered light of the sun through a torched atmosphere blinds him instantly.

A man leaves his universe in search of adventure, and he turns into a pile of ash because the heat of the parallel universe (at least three thousand degrees) causes his body to spontaneously combust.

A man leaves his universe in search of adventure, and he drowns in an ocean-covered planet. His body is devoured by opportunistic sea creatures.

A man leaves his universe in search of adventure, and he finds himself on a planet ravaged by nuclear war. He drinks contaminated water and dies.

A man leaves his universe in search of adventure, and he is murdered by cannibalistic post-apocalyptic scavengers for the meat of his flesh.

A man leaves his universe in search of adventure and he never finds his way back home.

41

"Nero is the dark one," Sloane said. It seemed like a decent enough place to start.

Esther and Matt didn't react at first. Sloane kept her body between them and Ziva, her arms held out from her sides. The river walk was empty, the sun only just setting. There was still time to get back to the Hall of Summons and document the internal mechanism of the siphon for Mox, still time to escape without Nero finding them. All she needed to do was convince her friends.

"Edda—who has a dislocated shoulder, by the way—said you were under some kind of . . . enchantment," Matt said. Guilt surged in Sloane at the sight of him, though she didn't want it to. There was no reason for it—she hadn't betrayed him, hadn't done anything she wouldn't have done again given the chance to go back—but she felt it anyway. His eyes had a sharpness to them that they wouldn't have had a few months ago.

But *that,* Sloane now recognized as an inevitability. Matt and Sloane had been living in a moment of held breath. The exhale had always been coming.

"And who told Edda that?" Sloane said. "Nero, obviously. Who, as I previously mentioned, *is the Dark One.*"

Esther was tilting her body so she could get a better look at Ziva.

Her hair was up in a high ponytail. "Is that a zombie? Is it in your thrall or something?"

Ziva cleared her throat, making a sound like a rock polisher. "It's rude to talk about someone like they aren't there, flesh-bag."

"Holy shit," Esther said, eyes wide. She was shiny—quite literally; silver thread woven in with the black fibers over cowl-necked jacket, polished chrome in the siphon over her throat, a silver line on each eyelid.

"How do we know you're not under the influence of something?" Matt said.

The pieces of the Needle made her hands, in fists at her sides, throb with energy. She still felt like she was underwater, and everything was close, right up against her.

Sloane didn't know what to say. If they believed the Resurrectionist had warped her, then they'd think everything she said could be the result of it. Nero had ensured that they wouldn't believe her. But she had to try.

"Last night, Nero sent me a message," Sloane said. "It was my boots. From . . ." She gave Matt a pleading look. "You know when. The Dark One is the only person on two planets who could possibly have had them. I don't know how he brought them here or why, and I don't know how he survived and jumped into another universe when we supposedly killed him, but that seems to be what happened." The doubt in Matt's eyes made her scowl. "You're the one who says that if you want to know who a person is, look at what they do," she said. "Nero helped kidnap us and then lied about it. But Mox—the Resurrectionist, I mean—didn't hurt me, even when he thought I was trying to kill him, and he took me to meet the prophet—"

"Wait," Esther said. "Hot Praying Mantis is the *Resurrectionist?*"

"Hot *what?*" Matt asked.

Esther flapped a dismissive hand at him. "Was he following you or something?"

"Not exactly," Sloane said. "Nero keeps summoning these Chosen Ones from other universes to fight him. He thought we were just more of the same."

"You *are*," Ziva pointed out.

"Wait," Matt said. "You said you met a prophet?"

Sloane nodded. "The one who made Genetrix's doomsday prophecy."

"While I know from experience that this is a *thrilling* tale," Ziva said, "we can't just stay here waiting for the Army of Flickering. I suggest your friends come with us to a safer location."

"Somewhere packed with the undead, you mean," Esther said. "Let me just turn over my brains right now, save you the effort."

"I don't give a shit who it's packed with as long as it's not a platoon of Flickering soldiers with siphons at the ready!" Ziva said.

"Ziva's right, we have to go," Sloane said. "We can go somewhere neutral." She gave Ziva a pointed look over her shoulder. "Public. Lots of exits."

"We can't go until we know what the hell is going on!" Esther said. Sloane hadn't noticed it before, but Esther looked tired again, despite all the powder and the shine. She remembered Esther telling her as they stared at Genetrix's rubble that she was afraid of her mother dying without her. And she believed Nero was the fastest way home.

But she had still gone to his workshop with Sloane to prove that he was lying to them.

"You can if you just . . . decide to trust me," Sloane said. "I know I don't deserve it, but I would never do anything to put you in danger. I hope you know that, at least."

Matt was already lowering his hand. "Yeah," he said quietly. "Okay."

"Actually," Ziva said, "we can't go until we have a look inside the siphon fortis in the Hall of Summons."

"Why?" Esther said.

"Sloane," Matt said. "Is that . . ."

Sloane had almost forgotten that she had a piece of the Needle in each palm. When she had lifted the security gate just outside the Dome, it had felt like breathing or blinking. But the Needle had been acid in her hands—a living, buzzing thing that had motives of its own. She could feel them still, muted in Genetrix, but distinct: the

Needle wanted to bury itself in her hand again. She pressed it back, tipping one of the pieces so it rolled to her fingertips.

"The Needle was on Earth," Matt said. "How did you get it here?"

"From the space between the universes." Sloane frowned down at the sharp sliver in her right hand.

She was about to go on when she noticed the tightening of Matt's jaw, Esther's hand going up to her throat, to the siphon she wore. She turned to see two men descending the terrace steps of the Genetrix River Theater, just beyond the small park where the four of them stood.

One of the men was Nero, his mask of mildness finally gone and in its place the cold, focused man Sloane had seen when she left his workshop. His hair was tousled, his cape flung over one shoulder, showing its rich navy lining. His gold Camel pin was askew, and his right arm was outstretched, his hand heavy on the back of the other man's neck.

The other man, of course, was Mox.

Mox no longer wore the siphon over his mouth and nose, and his eyes lacked their usual focus. Sweat dotted his hairline, and there was tension in the tendons of his neck, the rise of his shoulders. Nero lifted his hand from Mox's neck and whistled; a ripple went through the air that sent Mox stumbling toward Ziva.

"Consul?" Ziva said to him.

"Run," Mox replied, looking from Ziva to Sloane. He said it without hope.

"There will be no running," Nero said.

Now that Sloane was looking for the resemblance between Nero and the Dark One she had known, she saw it. Not in his face itself — which had likely been altered on Earth, unnatural as it had appeared — but in his bearing and posture, his shoulders thrown back and his chest out, his movements sharp and efficient. His voice, too, was the same, hard as flint, every word mechanical.

Nero whistled through the implant on his tooth, and an unnatural stiffness went through Mox's body, pulling his shoulders and head back. It reminded Sloane of the way the many-plated siphon had stiffened into a glove when she put it on, then relaxed once it was in position. As if Mox himself was being used as a siphon through the one attached to his spine.

All around them was the iridescent sheen of magical barriers, keeping intruders out—and keeping them from escaping, not that Sloane had been considering escape. She couldn't leave Mox to be Nero's magical puppet.

The Needle pieces hummed in her hands, reacting to Nero or Mox or perhaps both. She felt as she had once, growing up, when her fingertip slipped into the socket of a Christmas light as she clipped the strand to the tree—the energy traveling through her entire body, unpleasant but as benign as an electric shock could be.

"What's going on, Nero?" Matt said, stepping forward. His tone was one of forced calm, an act that Nero surely wouldn't believe.

Nero looked at Matt with only vague familiarity, as if he had seen him once but couldn't recall where. Sloane took advantage of his silence.

"Mox." Her tone was pleading, even though she hadn't meant it to be. Mox was bent over a little, clutching his side. "Are you hurt?"

"No. Just—uncomfortable."

"Mox?" Nero looked almost fondly at him. "Oh, I see. Micah Oliver Kent Shepherd. M-O-K-S. It suits you better than Chosen One."

Sloane spared a thought for the name Micah, best left behind, a name for a normal boy and not the man marred by magic who stood across from her, sweaty and hunched, unused to the draining of his power.

"Chosen One?" Matt said, wide-eyed, to Mox.

"The first," Mox replied, terse. "You—whichever one of you it is—would be the fifth."

"But . . . you killed the others?" Matt didn't sound accusatory, just confused. "Why?"

"I didn't know what they were," Mox said. "And I didn't want to die."

Matt gave Mox a sympathetic look with just a hint of condescension. Sloane felt the familiar, almost comforting urge to smack him.

Nero waved, humming. His voice was reedy, not rich like Mox's. A natural tenor. But the note was steady. Mox flinched again, and Matt screamed as his siphon crumpled into his hand, the metal plates crushed into his flesh. Blood ran down his fingers and dripped on the concrete. Esther's siphon, too, pulled taut around her throat, and she choked, clawing at the chain that held it in place at the back of her neck. She managed to break it, and the siphon clattered to the ground, out of her reach.

Ziva's mouth siphon was last; it wrenched free of her face, a chunk of rotting flesh coming away with it. The hole in her jaw was even larger now, showing more of her gritted teeth.

"Sloane," Nero said, "if you would please put the pieces of that Needle back together?"

He sounded almost . . . tired. The rich sunlight glowed through his fine hair, making it look like golden thread.

"No," Sloane replied automatically. She thought about hurling one of the two fragments into the river. But she wasn't sure she would be able to release it. That charge still hummed through both pieces, and though she couldn't say why, she felt certain that if she opened her fists and tried to tip the Needle's pieces out of her hands, they would stay put as if magnetized.

"You are needlessly defiant," Nero said to her, flicking a lock of hair away from his forehead. "I will not ask politely again."

"I don't have many rules to live by," Sloane said, "but 'When a murderous psychopath tells you to do something, don't do it' is absolutely one of them."

"Fine," Nero said, and he whistled, light and high as a finch song.

Mox drew up straight again, and Sloane could see the strain in his face, in his entire body.

Both pieces of Needle started wriggling in Sloane's hands, their sharp ends jabbing her as they fought to escape her grasp. She struggled to keep hold of them, but when one of them plunged deep into her fingertip, she yelled and shook out her hand, and suddenly the two pieces were hovering in the air in front of her face.

But she still felt them, burning, buzzing, stinging. Felt the acid of them in her veins. They wanted to be hers, not his. And all she had to do was *want* them.

Go on, then, she thought, and she turned her palms over, as if beckoning them.

There was a sharp and horrible pain in both of her hands as the two pieces burrowed into her, one half into each hand, into her index fingers, so her nails separated from her skin. The pieces worked their way down her hands, and she could see them moving, like worms wriggling beneath soft earth. With horror, she watched as the skin on the back of her scarred hand lifted away to accommodate the foreign but familiar object.

She had been the one to break the Needle, pushing every ounce of herself into the effort. But she knew it would mend without effort. It was eager to mend, just as it had been eager to bury itself in her flesh.

The piece of needle in her left hand was still moving, carving a line of agony down her arm and into the crook of her elbow. A bruise blossomed there as the Needle pierced a blood vessel. She bit her lip as it worked its way to her shoulder, sliced across her chest, then traveled down her arm, leaving another bruise, a twin to the first one. The pieces of the Needle united with a fierce glow, and a burning unlike anything Sloane had ever felt. She screamed, every inch of her skin now feeling raw.

Mox gaped at her, his cheeks pink with the effort of futile resistance. Sloane's blood dripped from the punctures of the Needle fragments. She let it flow, swallowing down bile.

"Now," Nero said, sounding frustrated, "I will have to cut it out of you."

He started toward her, and Sloane put up a hand to stop him. She didn't need to make a sound for the Needle to work. It expressed her purest desire, and what she craved in that moment was a second to think. A barrier formed between her and Nero, rippling as he touched it. He dug in with his own magic before focusing Mox's too. She could feel the difference between the two, one sharp and clever, the other rough and hot.

As repulsed as she was by the foreign body now lodged in the back of her hand again, Sloane also marveled at it a little, at the thought that such a small thing could be so powerful and so beyond her comprehension. It was like the sun—even at a great distance, filtered by atmosphere, its rays were strong enough to warm the Earth. All the most powerful things she knew were also destructive unless diluted in some way.

She stared at Nero—at the Dark One—through the barrier.

"Is this what it's always been about?" she said. "The Needle?"

She remembered that as the Dark One asked her about their weapons cache—right before forcing her to choose between herself and Albie—he had stared at her hand, at the scars there, with something like fascination. She had thought that he was fascinated by *her,* but as Ziva had said so plainly, there was nothing special about her, nothing powerful—except that the Needle was her weapon and no one else's.

"What is it that you want?" she said, and her voice sounded quiet, curious.

Nero's eyes focused on hers, and she heard a hum or a whistle, but she wasn't paying attention. She was somewhere else.

42

Nero grabbed the metal railing, water running down his knuckles. Waiting for him at the river's edge was Aelia, crouched, her red skirt tight around her knees. He held the pair of boots out with his other hand, and she took them from him, though she kept them away from her body as if disgusted by them.

"These, really?" Aelia said. "This was the object she poured herself into?"

"She is not sentimental, and she didn't keep a journal, unlike the last Chosen One." He hoisted himself up out of the water using the railing, then climbed over it, his limbs heavy from the swim between universes. "I needed something she had modified and kept close in order to summon her."

His clothes were waterlogged. Aelia set the boots down and performed the working to dry him off, flicking her fingers at his cloak.

"You can take that mask off now," Aelia said, cringing. "You look like a melting candle."

He unfastened the top button of his shirt and undid the clasp holding the siphon to his chest. The working didn't change his face, but it projected a different appearance to anyone who looked at him, even on Earth. Aelia had told him before that the projection didn't look precisely normal, which was perhaps even more desirable for his purposes. The people of Earth were vulnerable to even the most transparent of workings, given their denial of magic's existence.

He had amused himself by reading the latest theories: the Dark One was a government experiment gone awry; an alien invader pursuing world domination; a mad billionaire turned supervillain. The people of Earth, he had decided, read too many comic books.

He picked up the girl's boots, and together he and Aelia set out toward the terraces of trees along the river walk. It was before sunrise, and the city was as empty as it ever was. He heard a few cars rushing past on Wacker Drive, the homeless woman on the corner of LaSalle singing to herself, and the snap of Aelia's shoes. He had scolded her before for her ostentatious clothing and unsubtle footwear. It was important to remain discreet on these late-night missions or someone might notice them.

"Is it magic that she pours into the boots?" Aelia said. "I'm afraid I don't understand."

"That doesn't surprise me," he said. They began to climb the terraces, ducking under the pink blooms of crabapples and eastern redbuds. "And it is a kind of magic, if we think of magic as an energy of will. She has exerted her will over these boots, modifying them and repairing them, putting them on and removing them, just as the boy exerted his will over the paper crane." The origami had survived the journey from Earth to Genetrix in a plastic sandwich bag and was now perched on a windowsill in his workshop. "The emotional attachment to the object only strengthens the energy associated with it, which will empower me to summon them both here."

"And you don't know which one possesses the Needle."

"I believe it's the girl, but I prefer to be thorough."

"When will you go back?"

They had reached the street level. Nero paused and smiled at Aelia. "Don't tell me you are eager to be rid of me again?"

Aelia flinched a little, the corners of her mouth tugging down. "I merely want to prepare for my relocation if it's imminent."

"We are still several months away from the destruction of these universes, I assure you," Nero said. "I have secured your place in a new one; you have nothing to fear as long as you continue to help me."

Aelia gave a tight smile and led the way across the street, toward the Camel. As Nero passed the singing woman on the corner, he dropped a coin into the cup before her. There was no shame, he thought, in giving someone momentary relief, even if her universe was doomed to destruction.

It was Aelia's smile that was the last to disappear, staying steady as the Cheshire cat's as a new memory surfaced.

"You are not listening to me," he said.

They stood in his workshop, glowing orbs adrift around them. Nero was hunched over a notebook, scribbling a few stray thoughts before he forgot them. The electricity in the Camel had gone out, so the orbs provided the only light, lending an eerie glow to the new praetor's face.

"The collision is inevitable," he said slowly, as if he were speaking to someone who was quite stupid. He hadn't thought that Aelia was, but she had displayed a remarkable lack of comprehension in the conversation thus far. "I am holding the two worlds apart for now—with a substantial portion of my magic, I might add—but once I am dead, they will continue along the path they have been on since the Tenebris Incident connected them: toward destruction."

Lightning flashed in the windows, ominous. Thunder came soon after, like a drumroll.

"The Tenebris Incident?" she said. One of the orbs floated next to her ear, where she wore a gold-plated siphon that came to a point, a reflection of the ridiculous Genetrixae fashion trend of women dressing like elven princesses. Her gown was long and loose with billowing sleeves. "You never told me that was what forged this connection."

"What else could have accomplished such a thing?" He scowled at her. "The magical core of this planet shattered and sent fragments of Genetrix's magic into another universe and, due to the instability of time during universe-to-universe travel, back in time. Those shards became magical objects of legend on Earth—but there are so many false legends that it has been difficult to discern the true ones. That's why I must continue to go back and forth between universes. I am considering doing something more dramatic to draw out the truth more quickly. I am tired of stalling the inevitable."

"And there's nothing you can do, even with all your power, to sever this connection and save both worlds?"

"Even if I wanted to, which I do not, I am immortal, not all-powerful," he said. "And soon, circumstances permitting, I won't even be that."

"I'll never understand you." Aelia moved toward the windows, which were

rattling in their frames from the wind. Rain splattered across them, obscuring the view of the city beyond. "Many would kill to live forever; they would sacrifice their love, their children, every penny they own. And you spend all your time searching for the one who can end your life."

"Those who thirst for immortality have no comprehension of it." He walked to the drink cart that stood next to the doorway and poured whiskey into a clean tumbler. "For the first two hundred years, it is intoxicating, yes." The cut crystal of the tumbler caught the light of one of the orbs and sent it scattering across the floor. "But then everything becomes more and more meaningless. A life, a nation, an entire universe — their triumphs, their squabbles, their pathetic grasping at power, it is all the same, no matter where I go, no matter what I do." He sipped his whiskey, the spice of it stinging his throat. "I am tired."

Aelia glanced at him. She was not as afraid of him now as she had been when he first told her what he was and invited her to kill him. He had known she was the right one to tell because she actually tried to do it — tried half a dozen workings that had taken his breath, stopped his heart, and even attempted to sever his head. He had allowed it, though it was no more than he himself had tried. He had also tied weights to his ankles and jumped into the ocean; self-administered the venom of the most venomous snake on Earth, the inland taipan; and, in one universe, hurled himself into an active volcano. All the attempts — his and Aelia's — had failed, as his magic defended and preserved him.

Still, she sometimes betrayed fear. Like now, her eyebrows knit together, her expression haunted. "And this boy, you believe he will be able to do it?" she said.

"I have been in dozens of universes with dozens of Chosen Ones and warriors and magicians of renown," he said. "None have had the raw power of this boy. He may not have the skill or the focus, but I don't require him to. He is a blunt instrument only."

Aelia nodded. "But his desire to do so must be cultivated," she said distantly. "And desire cannot be forced."

Nero drained his glass. "Precisely what I need your help with."

The glow of an orb was what remained.

―――――

The door to the workshop shuddered as he flung it open with his siphon and then slammed it behind him. He was trembling. He cursed and shook out his hands. One would think that hundreds of years of life would eradicate this kind of weakness, but still it lingered.

He filled the air with whistles, one to lock the door behind him, one to set up a sound barrier around the circumference of the workshop, one to summon his notebook to the table before him, and the last to ready his pen to take down his dictation. He sank into a chair next to a stack of books and used his handkerchief to wipe his forehead of sweat. He tasted salt from his upper lip.

The pen stood upright, shivering in anticipation of his voice.

"It is done," he said. "The Army of Flickering is dead."

The pen began to move. He ran his hands down his legs to wipe the moisture from his palms.

"He will want to kill me now," he added, with some relief.

Sloane felt the hunger of the Dark One and, above all, the weariness. They felt both together.

He thought of Micah and his wry smile. Strange, he had always thought, that such an extraordinary child came from such ordinary parents. Nancy, host of a weekly knitting circle, last year's winner of the chili contest at the town fair. Phil, thinning on top, thickening on the bottom, manager of the local bank. They had eyed Nero's siphon uneasily when he shook their hands, and they hadn't fought him when he took their son away from them.

Micah didn't need a siphon to do magic. He hardly even needed intent. His desires simply manifested when provoked. He had lit his first bedroom in the Camel on fire. He had broken every single plate in the cafeteria at once. He had made flowers grow out of the stone floor in the Hall of Summons.

Now he sat on top of the siphon fortis in the Hall of Summons, looking small despite his early lankiness. It was the ears poking out of his hair, maybe, that made him look so young.

There was a cassette player in front of him, and Sibyl's voice, raspy and dry, played for the third time that morning: It will be the end of Genetrix, the unmaking of worlds.

"*What do you think?*" Nero asked him.

"'*Marred by magic,*'" Micah said. He tapped the corner of his left eye. "*Is that what this spot is? Magic?*"

"I believe so," Nero said, and though he despised sitting on floors, he sat across from Micah, just beside the siphon fortis. The cold from the stone seeped through his clothes, chilling him. "My theory is that the Tenebris Incident sent a few small pieces of magic flying, and one of them landed in your eye."

Said eye narrowed at him. "The Tenebris Incident was ages ago. I'm only eleven."

"Do you know what a wormhole is?" Nero said.

Micah shook his head.

"Let me explain it this way, then," Nero said. "A wormhole is like a tunnel. At one end of the tunnel, things can be moving very slow. At the other end, they are moving very fast. So if you go through the tunnel, you can get somewhere far in the future, but you can get there very quickly. Understand?"

It was how he had lived for hundreds of years, though his own Earth had been in the same century as Genetrix's when he was born. Time did not cooperate between worlds.

"So the magic exploded and went through a tunnel," Micah said, "and landed in my eye."

"I don't know. It's a theory."

"And that's why I have so much magic," Micah said. "Why my parents were so scared of me."

"Perhaps," Nero said. "And perhaps there is a way for you to keep it under control until you are ready for it. Would you like that?"

Micah nodded.

The poor child, Nero let himself think. *Teeming with magic, and not a single person in the world could understand it, not even Nero himself.*

"Let me tell you," Nero said, "about a particular kind of siphon that goes on your spine."

The spine, they thought.

———

Claudia tapped the vertebrae that stuck out from his shirt when he hunched over. Tap, tap, tap.

The fire was low. He had forgotten to add logs to it, and now the air was so cold, he could see his breath. It was difficult for him to remove himself from these preparations. He had been waiting so long for this night, the night when everything was finally ready. The objects of power in a wide circle in the courtyard, connected by a line of salt. He had gathered them over the past five years, following legends to dead ends, whispers to treasure.

The real treasure, though, ached in his chest. Only an x-ray had revealed it. The doctor had suspected a hole in his heart, and that was, in a sense, what he had found. But the hole had been plugged by something. A piece of shrapnel, he had pronounced it, but Nero had not been near any explosives. There was no immediate danger to his health, so Nero had gone on, short of breath and easily tired, with the fragment in place.

He straightened and pulled his suspender straps over his shoulders again. His sister, Claudia, stood behind him in a smart blouse with a bow in the middle, right above the dip between her collarbones. Her hair was parted on the side and curled at the bottom.

"You look pretty," he said to her.

"Don't I?" She stepped away and swayed her hips so he could see her long skirt shift back and forth. "I thought I'd dress up for your first day of eternal life."

He scowled at her. "You're dressed for the train and nothing else," he said.

She gave a small smile.

"And you're sure you want no part of it?" he said.

"I'll have an eternity in heaven," she said softly. "Though I am sad my brother won't be there to join me. You will still be here on Earth."

"I don't believe in heaven," he replied.

She nodded. "So you've said."

She leaned toward him and kissed his cheek. She smelled of floral perfume. When she pulled away, she still wore that small smile.

The fire crackled in their fireplace as the last of the kindling broke.

The feeling was fire.

When a birch log burned, the papery bark peeled away from the wood and turned to ash. That was what he felt was happening to his skin. Every layer of him—skin and sinew and bone—peeling apart and burning to cinders.

That was only the beginning. Later, in another universe, when he found the words for it, he would call it plunging headfirst into the sun. Hotter than lava, hotter than any heat he knew, and the sensation of twisting away from it, yanking one's hand off the stove or smacking the ember that had fallen on one's clothes, was there, but he couldn't move. He had become a cloud of dust, a loose association of particles, and he couldn't scream.

It took its own eternity. He had used the piece of something in his heart to dig deep into the earth without lifting a finger to form a connection with purest magic. He had not merely sampled it; he had drunk from it as through a straw, drawing in as much as he could bear, and then more. The connection, having formed, could not be broken—though he was desperate for it to.

Not until the pool had drained.

When he woke, seconds later, years later, he was alone, and everything that had been alive, every weed in every field, every flower on every tree, every insect that crawled and snake that slithered and bird that flew, and every single human being that had once walked the ground, was gone.

They had destroyed their world and would have to find another.

It is a strange thing, to bear the weight of a world. I never thought I would have so much in common with Atlas. For his mistake, for siding against the gods, he spent an eternity with the heavens on his shoulders — not the Earth, as the misconception goes — and for my mistake, for delving into the secrets of the universe, I must carry my wasted, dead planet around with me forever.

But it's not the flowers and the animals that haunt me most, or the trees and the wonders of the deep ocean, or the children whose faces I never saw and names I never knew. There are so many of those things that they fade into abstraction. Specificity, not scope, is what makes a thing meaningful.

And so, in the end, it is the woman down the street who gave me a slice of bread with butter on it every day on my way to school because she said I was too thin, and the alley cat who wove an infinity sign around my legs when I went outside to smoke, and our upstairs neighbor who taught me how to tie a secure knot — they are the ones who haunt me.

And, of course, it is my sister, Claudia.

Sometimes I hate the Resurrectionist for the magic he possesses, for knowing how to raise the dead. I have tried.

43

THE DARK ONE had tortured Albie with both brutality and delicacy; sometimes, paradoxically, with both at once. Sloane remembered an array of polished tools: wrench, knife, needle-nose pliers. They had looked like they were new, just purchased from the hardware store.

He had wanted something from her, and he had hurt Albie to get it. She had not given it to him.

The Dark One had seemed impressed.

"He wants to die," Sloane said, and she had almost said *we*— *We want to die*—because they had been so intertwined in his memories. A moment later she felt revulsion. Her stomach turned. She stumbled to the edge of the grass and vomited.

"What just happened?" Esther said. "What did you do to her?"

"I answered her question," Nero replied. "You need not concern yourself with how."

"If you wanted to die, you could have just said so," Matt said darkly. He was hunched over, in pain, his crushed hand cradled against his chest. "Any one of us . . . would be happy to oblige."

"No!" Sloane straightened. Her mouth tasted like acid. She wiped her lips with the back of her hand. "Genetrix and Earth are on a collision course. *He* is what's been holding them apart. Kill him, and we all die."

She struggled for breath. He had to die. But he couldn't die. But if they didn't kill him, as he wanted, he might stop holding Earth and Genetrix apart and move on to another universe, another set of victims. And then they would all die anyway.

There was no way out.

Sloane looked at Mox, bowed under the siphon, his hair hanging in his face. From the beginning, Nero had wanted to shape Mox's desire in order to shape his magic. Nero had formed him like a statue from clay.

And he had formed her too. Not over the course of years, but over the course of moments. Offering her the choice between herself and Albie. Walking into the trap she set on Irv Kupcinet Bridge. Beckoning her toward Genetrix with Albie's voice. But he had never had to change her desires, because what she wanted and what the Dark One wanted had always been the same.

"I didn't think it was possible," Nero said to her, "for you to soften toward me."

"I haven't," she replied.

She walked, slowly, toward him.

"Give Micah the Needle, Sloane, so he can do what he was made for," Nero said, and he didn't sound malicious; he sounded tired. "Or I will have to motivate you."

She knew his version of motivation. He had tortured Albie so that she would tell him where their weapons were — where the Needle was. He knew the softest parts of her, the most vulnerable parts. He knew that, above all else, she was lonely.

Mox was hunched over, his face streaked with tears and sweat. He had been used all his life, she thought. Sloane couldn't let him be used to end the world.

"Mox wasn't made for this," she said. "*I* was."

"Sloane, no!" Matt screamed, and it sounded like he was shouting into a strong wind. Perhaps he was, Sloane thought. Her hair whipped across her face, obscuring her vision for a moment as Esther lunged and grabbed the throat siphon that rested a few feet in front of her. She held it against her throat with one hand, stuck a whistle in her mouth with the other, and bit down hard. Before she could make a sound, Nero waved a hand at her, hurling her to the ground.

"Not everything must be lost, you know," Nero said to Sloane. "The energy that my death produces could be used to save something. Micah has a well of untarnished good within him, and he might *want* to save the world enough to preserve part of it. But you . . . you have only ever wanted destruction."

He was right, of course. Mox had said that magic was an expression of a person's deepest desires, which meant that when she eviscerated the crew during the Deep Dive mission, when she worked a gale instead of a magical breath in the Hall of Summons, when she blasted a crater into the side of the Dome, she had wanted it. She had never done a piece of magic that was not in service of ruining something. Somewhere inside her was a thing that wanted to take and take and take, until there was nothing left to give, just as Nero had done in his own universe, his thirst for power and magic not slaked until the well of magic under his Earth's crust was dry.

She lifted her hand, and Nero's body lifted high in the air. His cape snapped in the wind, pulled sideways over one shoulder, the pin up against his throat. The Needle sang inside her, sang her revenge. She dropped her hand, and Nero fell onto the pavement, his legs crumpling beneath him. Both broken, she assumed, from the snapping sound they'd made. She didn't care.

"Something stands between Genetrix and its twin. The Dark One," he said, and he laughed a little, grimacing with pain, "will excise it, and the worlds will be crushed together, and that will be the end of all."

"Yes," she said. "I'm told the line between a Dark One and a Chosen One is hair-fine."

A part of her did want destruction — but that wasn't all of her. She wanted other things too: justice and mercy, drinks with Albie, kisses with Matt, laughter with Esther. She wanted to wake early in the morning, when the light was pale and new, and run to the lake's edge. She wanted to sit in silence in the Modern Wing of the Art Institute and look at the Frank Lloyd Wright windows and think of Cameron. She wanted to teach Mox how to drive. She wanted to read the entire

Unrealist manifesto. She wanted to watch an olive dance in a cocktail shaker.

She would just have to hope that those wants outweighed the others.

Sloane raised the hand that contained the Needle and imagined herself deep in the ocean, a teenager, and, at that time, an expert on the legends of Koschei, the man who could not die, who had hidden his soul away in a needle. The pressure of the water was all around her, and so was the fire of magic, so painful it made her thrash against its hold. But beyond the pain was something else — a hunger pang. She had written in her journal that it was like wanting something so much you would die to get it. An acknowledgment of how deeply and how desperately she did not want to be empty anymore.

She imagined herself at the center of a Drain, her vision obscured by a wall of swirling debris. The dust marked the path of the air, tight around her shoulders, and flecks of rock, bits of flesh, fragments of bone, embraced her. Her hair whipped around her face, found its way into her mouth, and still her magic beckoned for more. More.

More.

She focused on Nero, her hand outstretched. It was the one with the Needle, the one with the web of scars from when she had turned animal, biting at her own flesh to free herself from a trap. And if desire was what fueled magic, then in this case, all she wanted was Nero's life, every minute of it. His eyes bulged, and he brought his hands up to his throat — or he would have if he hadn't at that moment risen into the air, held high above the river.

She was in the monument, the light of dead names glowing around her, and —

She was sitting with Albie at the bar, the line of empty shot glasses in front of them, and —

She was walking along the road barefoot, a piece of glass buried in her heel, and —

She was standing on Genetrix's river walk.

She wanted all the things the Dark One had taken. She screamed, the sound scraping out her insides, hollowing her out even further, and she filled herself with his life. The losses he had heaped up like chips at a casino. The magic he had hoarded from the worlds he had walked, possibly hundreds of them, so many he had forgotten their names.

She *devoured him*.

Nero's body ripped apart all at once, hovering eviscerated over the city, guts tumbling loose and dangling, heart still pulsing, attached to the threads of his blood vessels and veins. She saw a tangle of white nerves and the strict lines of his bones, and blood was everywhere, spattering. Perhaps he was screaming, and perhaps he wasn't, couldn't anymore, with his teeth pulled out of his skull and his tongue adrift on the wind.

And then she was on fire with magic, as she had been in Nero's memory, diving headfirst into the sun. Disassembling into a cloud of flesh and blood that could not scream. There was no exertion of will, just an extraction of *want,* as water crashed down from above, the thin membrane between the worlds breaking.

Water rushed over the river walk, flooding the terraces with their trees, swallowing the cars that drove on Wacker and the pedestrians on the bridge. Sloane rose, or perhaps she fell.

She fell down through the water again, up into the rubble of the tower they had destroyed, and slammed —

— *impossibly* —

— into the ground next to the Ten Years Monument, where they had sprinkled Albie's ashes.

┌─────┐
│ 44 │
└─────┘

S OMEWHERE NEARBY, a car alarm was going off. But it was muffled; Sloane felt like someone had packed her ears with dense
cotton. She brought a hand up to touch one, found a sticky — but
clear — ear canal.

There were more alarms now. A chorus, all bleating at different
intervals; a few security systems chanting about intruders, and sirens
coming from all directions. Sloane blinked up at the clouds. It seemed
strange that she should be looking up at clear sky, though she wasn't
sure what else she had expected to see.

She probed her head and neck with both hands for signs of injury
and then, finding none, sat up. One ear was ringing, and everything in
front of her tipped and spun. Which only made it look more unreal.

In one direction was the river and the Dark One monument that
stood beside it, a modest bronze block with a gap of an entrance.
And in the other was the undulating steel face of Genetrix's Warner
Tower, looming over the skyline. Across the street from her was half
of 300 North Wabash, a simple black structure of steel and glass. On
its eastern face, its innards were exposed, as if the building had been
sliced like a block of cheese. Sloane watched as half a couch, cut clean
through the center of a cushion, tipped back and plummeted twenty
stories to the pavement.

Sloane's mind had gone blank. Her body ached down to her fingernails. She tested her legs, found them shaky but mobile. *The others,* something whispered in her head. *Find the others.*

She crawled on all fours over the concrete for a moment, then lurched to her feet and stumbled toward the river. She felt like she was drunk. She saw a dark head surface and ran toward the bridge, where there was a set of stairs leading down to the water. In front of her, a boxy Genetrix taxi collided with a sleek BMW. The drivers both got out and started yelling at each other, one of them waving a siphon on his left hand that looked like a metal glove.

She sprinted down the steps and slid to her knees at the river's edge, where she had seen the man in the water. Mox spluttered, shoving his hair away from his face, and Sloane threw her arms around him, half plunging into the river, her hips flat against the concrete.

"Your ear is bleeding," he said.

"Perforated eardrum," she said.

He crushed his mouth against hers, graceless. She tasted river water and dust from the monument site and blood. He was alive.

She heard coughing and tore herself from Mox to see Esther a few yards away, braced on the edge of the river on her elbows, hacking up water. Sloane stumbled over and pulled Esther out of the water by her arms.

"Essy," she said. Esther coughed into Sloane's shoulder, clutched at her shirt. "Where's Matt?"

"I don't . . . I don't know," Esther said.

Over Esther's shoulder, Sloane saw Ziva dragging something out of the river. Water poured out of the hole in her jaw as she heaved Matt onto the shore. He coughed and rolled onto his side.

Esther said weakly, "The Dark One, is he . . ."

"Dead?" Sloane said. There were spots of his blood on her sleeve. "Yeah. He's dead."

They walked across the bridge in a pack. Sloane led the way, and Ziva and Mox loped behind. Matt was leaning on Esther for support, the pain from his crushed hand having finally hit him.

They passed people huddled next to the railing, looking confused. One of them was a teenager wearing ripped jeans and Converse sneakers; no siphon. Up ahead, Sloane spotted the Seventeenth Church of Christ, Scientist, a squat stone pod of a building that stood where Wacker split in two. The building that Sloane vaguely remembered being behind it, though, was gone, replaced by an Unrealist structure that peeled apart like a banana at the top, sending offices in all different directions, arching over the street.

They turned right on Wacker, ignoring the screams that were now coming from everywhere and the alarms that drowned them out.

"We have to find Ines," Esther said from behind her. "And my mom."

"The phones," Sloane said. "They probably won't work."

There were power lines in the street. Wires severed by buildings, by gas-burning streetlights.

"Then I'll drive to California," Esther said.

"First, find Ines," Sloane said. "You two can go together." She didn't add *if she's alive* because she refused to acknowledge the possibility that she wasn't. "Go to Mexico on the way back, if you can, maybe. And I'll . . ." She trailed off before she could say that she would look for her mother, because she suddenly felt sure there was no way her mother was still alive. Though *why* she was so convinced, she couldn't have said.

When she saw the Camel—not the Thompson Center—ahead of them, she almost fell to her knees with relief. They would need the collective magical knowledge the Camel offered if they were going to survive whatever was happening.

Her ears were ringing as they passed through the front doors of the Cordus Center and wove through the lobby, which was full of confused Genetrixae people yelling at one another over the din. A security alarm was going off, and it was hard to think of anything beyond the blaring. Soldiers from the Army of Flickering were here and there, shouting for everyone to calm down.

Esther and Sloane both watched, quiet. Sloane swallowed her rising hysteria. "What happened?" she said, her voice breaking. "Is this Earth or Genetrix?"

Esther looked around at the chaos in the Camel lobby. "A little of both, I think."

The first sign that Ines might be alive was that her apartment building was still standing.

It hadn't been a given. Esther, Matt, and Sloane had walked along the lakefront path to get here, leaving Mox and Ziva to locate the rest of the Resurrectionist's army, and they had turned on Wilson Avenue to walk through Uptown, where the peace of the waterfront had given way to madness. Some buildings were split down the middle, with half a living room exposed to the street or a bathroom sink hanging over the edge of a divided floor, about to tumble to the ground. They passed a kitchen floor that sagged over an alley, dropping tiles when the wind blew. A ladder was braced against the side of the three-flat, and a man was climbing into one of the windows of his second-floor apartment while his small daughter stood on the ground and shouted instructions. "The bear with the missing ear!" she cried out. Her eyes were full of tears. "Do you see him?"

Farther down the street, Sloane saw another one of those broken buildings, but with an arm and a leg hanging from one of the split floorboards of a third-story apartment. She tried not to look at it.

Across the street from Ines and Albie's building, where there had once been a dark pub, was a Genetrix park with a colorful statue standing in the middle of a small pond. Magical lights danced just under the surface of the water, unaffected by the collision of worlds.

"What is it?" Esther said. Sloane had been staring at the park for a long time.

"That shitty pub that gave Ines food poisoning is gone," Sloane said.

"You hated that place," Matt said, and not quite like he was reminding her; more like it was a revelation.

"Yeah." Sloane frowned.

"Ines," Esther said. "Remember?" She tugged Sloane by the elbow. "Come on, guys."

The buzzer was broken, so Sloane forced her way through the

front door—the lock had never been entirely secure—and climbed
the stairs to Ines and Albie's apartment. Now that they were here, she
couldn't bear the thought that Ines wasn't in the apartment. Esther
had to drag her up the last few steps. She pounded on the apartment
door. "Ines! Ines, it's Essy, open up!"

Sloane braced herself for silence. But she heard footsteps right
away, and Ines's low voice as she fumbled with the locks. "Oh my
God, oh my God," she was saying over and over again, wiggling the
door back and forth in its frame. The door opened, and Ines was
standing in front of them in her bare feet and a pair of drawstring
pajama bottoms, her eyes red and her hair tangled. She smelled like
weed and sweat and coffee.

"Where the fuck have you guys *been?*" Ines demanded.

They all fell together like a house of cards, just barely holding each
other upright.

45

THAT NIGHT, Sloane woke to a nightmare in which Albie's corpse climbed out of the river and shambled toward her. He croaked his condemnation for what she had done, for killing Nero, for destroying the better part of two worlds.

She woke breathless and shaking. A candle flickered in the center of the kitchen table. Esther sat with a bottle of water on one of the stools, staring into the flame.

"Esther," Sloane said, clutching a pillow to her chest. "I think . . . I think I figured something out."

Esther rested her cheek on top of the water bottle and looked at Sloane. Her eyes were soft with grief and tight with worry.

"Your mom's alive," Sloane said. She clutched the pillow harder, her heart pounding. "She must be, because I love her, and all the things that survived the collision, they're all the things I loved in both worlds." She choked. "My magic turned Nero's death into whatever this is, this fucking Frankenstein's monster world, so it's made up of all the things I wanted, and—"

Esther got up and walked over to the couch. She sat next to Sloane so their shoulders were touching.

"Some of the things I want," Sloane whispered. "Are . . . not good. No one should get to make their own world—"

"I know, Slo."

Sloane shoved her face into the pillow she held and tried not to scream.

Matt stepped out of Albie's room, where he had evidently been standing, hidden by shadow. He rustled in the kitchen cabinets for a few minutes while Sloane tried to get her grip on the pillow to loosen, then walked over to them, holding out a little yellow pill.

Sloane swallowed it.

The safe house was quiet. Someone had torn down most of the boards covering the windows, so sunlight filtered in through a layer of dust. Sloane passed the blankets wadded up by the door — her old bed — and the roomful of soldiers, sitting together on the floor, playing cards, repairing siphons, and, in the case of one group, drumming on old pots with their bony fingertips.

She went to the storeroom to look for Mox and found him sitting at the little table across from Ziva. Their hands were clasped, his big, warm palm all but encompassing her wasted knuckles.

"Sloane!" Mox said, and they jerked away from each other like they had been caught doing something embarrassing.

"Sorry, I can come back," Sloane said. She felt like she had interrupted something.

"No, stay," Ziva said. "I was just telling him about a conversation you and I had."

Over time, Sloane was sure, she would be able to tease out each thread of the knot of the past few days, but it was too soon for that. After taking the benzo, she had fallen into a heavy sleep on Ines's couch, then woken up, borrowed clean clothes, and, with Ines's help, hot-wired a car to drive across the city, but that was all she had managed so far.

What she had gathered, however, from conversations in front of the bodega down the street from Ines's place, was that no one had internet, cell service, or electricity. People in the Earth sections of the city had begun to poke their heads into the Genetrix parts out of curiosity and desperation, since the Genetrixae people had fared better in the wake of the disaster because their siphons were still functioning. But then the shopkeeper started ranting about sorcery, so that was the most she had learned about the state of the world around her.

"A conversation we had," Sloane repeated.

"About whether I was glad to be alive again," Ziva said. She worked her jaw up and down for a few seconds until it clicked. Sloane watched her tongue move behind her exposed teeth and wondered how, in just a few days, her disgust for Ziva's rotting body had all but disappeared.

"Ah," Sloane said.

"Z and I decided it's time for her to go," Mox said. He was staring at the table.

"Oh?" Sloane said. She didn't seem to be capable of speaking more than one syllable at a time.

Ziva nodded. "Nero is dead, which means the consul is out of danger and no longer needs us. I've spoken to the others, and they agree."

"I'll always need you," Mox said fiercely. "All of you."

"Mox," Ziva said, with as much gentleness as Sloane had ever heard in her rough, dry voice. She had also never heard Ziva use Mox's name. He was always "Consul" or "Sir."

Mox looked up at Ziva. She covered his hand with hers again. "You'll miss us," Ziva said. "Want us. But that's something else entirely."

Mox didn't respond, which was as good as agreement.

"Let's do this now, while Sloane is here," Ziva said, getting to her feet. "That way, I won't worry about you as much."

"Now?" Mox choked a little on the word.

"There is never a good time," Ziva said. "To let go, or to rest."

Ziva gave Sloane a crooked smile. Sloane returned it.

Together, they went to the main room where the rest of the army waited. When Mox entered, they all started clambering to their feet, some with more ease than others. The ones that were able-bodied helped the others up or held detached limbs the way a husband might hold his wife's purse.

Sloane would have had a hard time imagining Mox making a speech, and he didn't surprise her. He wandered through the ranks of the soldiers, greeting them by name, speaking quietly into their ears, putting his arms around them. As he made his way through the crowd, Sloane wondered if he would be able to do it, if the depth of his desire for friends would guide his magic away from it.

Sloane sat against the door frame and watched. The soldiers who had already said goodbye to Mox began saying goodbye to each other. Two of the women closest to Sloane laughed about an old joke, raspy, choking laughs that sounded like dying. One of the men sat down with his back against the wall and his severed foot in his lap, his hand tenderly wrapped around the ankle.

At last, Mox came to Ziva, who stood with her head high so her braid brushed the middle of her hunched spine. The sun was pale against her face, and bright, so it temporarily bleached away the green tint to her skin. Sloane tried to imagine what Ziva had looked like when she was alive, her cheeks full and pink, her shoulders broad, her eyes gleaming.

Mox held Ziva tightly, almost lifting her off the ground. Ziva's skeletal hand cradled the back of Mox's head as he spoke softly to her, too quietly for Sloane to hear, not that she was trying. All around them, the soldiers had gone quiet, sitting on the floor again in their small groups, around their decks of cards and makeshift drums and piles of colorful glass, the treasures of their wagers.

Finally, Mox pulled away enough to touch his forehead to Ziva's.

When she collapsed, he was ready to catch her. A tension Sloane had not truly felt went out of the room all at once, like a change in air pressure. The bodies of all the soldiers went brittle and dry, unmoving. Mox lowered Ziva to the floor, his hair hanging in his face.

Sloane stood and made her way to his side. For a while, she stayed silent, watching his shoulders shudder. But when he went still at last, she offered him her hand and led the way out of the safe house.

And when the building went up in flames, she stood by the river and watched it burn with him.

Ines sat in the driver's seat of an old Jeep Wrangler, swearing at the steering column. Mox sat beside her in the passenger seat, a toolbox on his lap, offering suggestions that only seemed to make Ines swear more. Sloane observed it all from the curb, where she was keeping watch—there was a lot of looting going on as well as a fair amount of violence, and she had a pipe wrench in hand, ready to defend her distracted friends if necessary.

The Jeep was parked on the street just outside Ines's apartment, which meant they were lucky to have gotten to it first. Most of the good cars had already been stolen, leaving only rust-buckets and mopeds behind.

"Hey." Matt stepped out of the apartment building carrying a few bottles of water in one hand. His other hand, the one that had been crushed by the siphon, was wrapped in a thick bandage. Cyrielle had found a Genetrix doctor for him that morning.

He offered the water bottles to Sloane, and she took one. "Thanks."

"Just got back from our place," he said. "Or, rather, the public Genetrixae park that is now in place of our place."

There was a hint of accusation in Matt's voice. Sloane stayed quiet. He looked exhausted, his eyes puffy and his shoulders slumped.

"If your whole theory is true," Matt said quietly, "then our apartment is gone because *you* wanted it to be gone."

"It's not what you're thinking," she said. "That's—a place I was dreading going back to. Because I knew it would be hard. That's all."

Matt nodded, but his jaw still looked tight.

"You can have this one if you're eager to leave," Sloane said, pointing to the Jeep. They were all setting off on their own road trips: Ines and Esther were driving to California to check on Esther's mother and then to Mexico to see Ines's family; Matt was going to New York to find his parents; and Mox and Sloane were heading to central Illinois to find out if Sloane's mom was still there or if her entire hometown had blinked out of existence. Sloane was terrified to find out, even though, deep down, she already knew it was gone.

The worlds had combined according to her every whim, every preference, and every petty fear. She felt naked in a way she had not known was possible. But she was almost feverishly grateful that Matt was still here, that even though her desires were revealing themselves to be murkier and smaller than she had expected, she still wanted him to be in her world.

"No, I'd rather find something that's not a gas-guzzler," Matt said. "It's a long drive to New York."

"You sure you want to go alone?"

Matt nodded. "I think I could use the thinking time, actually."

Their breakup felt real now that they were back on Earth — more or less — and Matt had met Mox and they were quite literally going in different directions. But it was worse now than it had been before. Whatever misconceptions Matt had had about Sloane's mushy insides were gone now. All he had to do was look around at all the things she had destroyed to see the truth.

A victory shout came from inside the Jeep Wrangler as the engine roared to life. Ines stuck her head out the window. "And a full tank of gas too!"

"Okay," Sloane said. "I guess I'll see you in a month." They had all agreed to meet at Ines's place then to take stock of things.

She wanted to tell Matt so much. That she was sorry she hadn't saved their apartment. That she hadn't moved on from him as easily as it seemed. That she wished she were better. But their intimate drama seemed insignificant compared to the chaos around them, the uncertain fates of their families. So she stayed quiet. She handed a bottle of water to Ines and hugged her goodbye while Mox piled their bags in the trunk.

Then she stood in front of Matt, unsure how to let him go.

He leaned in first, wrapping an arm around her and squeezing her tight. She had only just begun to return the gesture when he released her.

"Stay safe," he said.

"You too."

"You're going to have to learn how to drive," Sloane said as Mox folded himself into the passenger seat. She had tried to find a car big enough to accommodate him, but that had proved to be impossible. At least the Jeep could handle the unstable roads on the drive south.

Mox had found his wrist siphon in Nero's intact workshop in the Camel, and it was now on his hand. He had offered to find one for her, but Sloane knew she didn't need one. She had the Needle.

In the back seat were two bags, one packed with clothes, the other packed with food and other necessities. Sloane didn't generally approve of looting, but there was nothing left of her earthly possessions, and she couldn't access any of her money—not that money was terribly useful right now anyway, with two standard U.S. currencies floating around. Money was just a bunch of green paper if you didn't have a government or a sense of order.

Sloane started down Lake Shore Drive, which was mostly intact, having been similar in both universes. There were ridges and cracks where the different pavements had come together, but she had heard people talking about the road being drivable.

Sloane hadn't wanted to make this trip, but as Mox had said the night before: *Maybe you just have to know.* Someday, he might find that he had to know, too, about his own family.

Mox fumbled in one of the bags for something. When he was hunched over, Sloane looked at the bumps of his vertebrae. The spine siphon had come loose as Nero died, he had told her. It was at the bottom of the Chicago River.

He produced a CD from the bag. *Pet Sounds*.

Sloane smiled.

As the first song came on, Mox said, "I think I know why you really did it."

"Why I did what?"

"Killed Nero."

"Oh." Sloane glanced at him. "Why did I really do it?"

"Because he was going to force me to do it," Mox said. "You decided that if one of us was going to have to bear the burden of it, it would be you. So in the end . . . it wasn't revenge, or inevitability, or some other dark purpose. It was a kind of . . . small mercy."

"There was definitely revenge in it," she said.

"Yeah, of course," Mox said. He tilted his head back and closed his eyes. "But there was kindness in it too."

He reached across the gearshift and took her hand.

They drove along Lake Michigan, and the water glittered in the sun.

Acknowledgments

Thank you.

First, to three people I absolutely could not have written this book without: John Joseph Adams, for being unflappable, funny, and wise, and for helping me to shape this story from the start. (Even if I didn't use that one excellent zombie joke.) Joanna Volpe, for ten years of friendship and fearless advocacy (!!!) and for never doubting me, even when I doubted myself. Nelson Fitch, for many days of agonizing over world-building with me and reading early drafts and doing everything possible to facilitate my writing and mental health. It's just you and me, buddy.

At HMH: Jaime Levine, the other half of the dynamic duo that made this book work, for being so lovely to work with at every stage. And to everyone else at my HMH home, especially Ellen Archer, Bruce Nichols, Helen Atsma, Fariza Hawke, Lori Glazer, Taryn Roeder, Matt Schweitzer, Hannah Harlow, Becky Saikia-Wilson, Jill Lazer, Katie Kimmerer, Jenny Freilach, Tracy Roe, Diana Coe, Chloe Foster, Emily Snyder, Rita Cullen, Christopher Moisan, Jim Tierney, Ed Spade, Colleen Murphy, Candace Finn, and all the names I surely missed from Editorial, Managing Editorial, Publicity, Marketing, Sales, Finance, Legal, and Subrights—thank you for your tireless work for this book and beyond. And to my audio team at Audible, specifically Kristin Lang, Rena Ayer, and Dan Battaglia, the same goes to you!

At New Leaf Literary: Jordan Hill and Abigail Donoghue, whose patience with me never fails; bless you. Mia Roman and Veronica Grijalva, who are absolutely killing it with foreign rights. Hilary Pecheone and Meredith Barnes, for keeping an eye on all the things that would otherwise completely escape my mind. Pouya Shahbazian, for your continued enthusiasm for each new story and wisdom in all matters film. Everyone else at New Leaf, for doing such fine work day after day, year after year.

Rawles Lumumba, for your invaluable feedback. Katherine Tegen, for always cheering me on.

Courtney Summers, Somaiya Daud, Maurene Goo, and Sarah Enni, you were particularly helpful and generous and fucking hilarious while I was writing this book; I will always strive to be for you what you were for me this year. Amy Lukavics, Kaitlin Ward, Kate Hart, Michelle Krys, Kara Thomas, Laurie Devore, Diya Mishra, Aminah Mae Safi, Zan Romanoff, and Elissa Sussman, for your support in the world of writing and for showing me all the many weird and wonderful things of the internet. Margaret Stohl, for being my emotional soulmate even when things go bananas for a while. These are just a few of the writers who buoy me when I'm sinking — what wealth I have; thank you all.

My family — Barb, Frank, Ingrid, Karl, Frank IV, Candice, Beth, Roger, Tyler, Rachel, Trevor, Tera, Darby, Andrew, Billie, Fred, Chase, Sha, and my three nieces — for bearing with me as I disappear into work and for reminding me I am loved beyond what I make. My friends who are not writers, for the same.

My readers, for taking a chance on each new story.

Discussion Questions

1. In the world of *Chosen Ones,* magic has proliferated Earth, and has slowed the development of certain technologies we make liberal use of today. Why do you think that is? How would suddenly being able to do magic affect your use of things like a computer or smartphone?

2. Magic in *Chosen Ones* is defined as "the manifestation of impossible wants." People perform magic by producing sound—through hums, whistles, and song—but the real mechanism of magic is "wanting the impossible"—and not everyone is very good at it. What do you think separates the characters who are good at magic in this book from the ones who aren't? What characteristics do they possess? If you lived in this world, do you think you would be good at magic? Why or why not?

3. Sloane is not exactly a straightforward "hero" figure—she is prickly, angry, impulsive, and withdrawn from the people around her. Could we describe her as an "antiheroine" instead? Do you think it's harder for a female character to be an "antihero" than a male character? Are our expectations for female characters different?

4. Each of the book's Chosen Ones—Sloane, Matt, Albie, Esther, and Ines—react to their sudden celebrity in different ways: Esther starts a lifestyle brand, Matt takes on social justice work, Sloane withdraws from the world, etc. Who do you think handles the fame best or worst? How do you think you would react if you suddenly became world famous?

5. The Chosen Ones have been through a past trauma, Sloane and Albie in particular. How do you think trauma informs their characters in the present? Would they react differently to what happens in the book if they did not have those traumatic experiences? Do you think they would be less prepared and capable, or more? Is being a "chosen one"—like Buffy, Frodo, or Alice (of Wonderland)—inherently traumatic?

6. The book is told in two different ways: a straightforward narrative from Sloane's point of view and extratextual documents, such as government memos, newspaper articles, and transcripts. How did these documents affect your understanding of Sloane's story and of the world she lives in? Why do you think the author chose to give information this way instead of restricting the book to Sloane's perspective?

7. The book explores both "chosen one" and "dark one" figures—heroes and villains—with some people staying firmly as one or the other and others shifting over time. Which one do you think Sloane is? What about Mox?

8. Did your understanding of the Dark One change once his true identity was revealed and his personal history came to light? Do you think the reasoning behind his actions and the choices he made was firmly good or bad?

9. At the end of the story, Sloane begins to suspect that the world now magically reflects her preferences and biases, no matter how petty—and it horrifies her. If someone made a world based on your preferences and biases, what do you think would be in it? What *wouldn't* be in it? Would you want to live there?